PRAISE FOR BARI

"The author's ability to present two differ[ent] stories inside her own novel and keep all the voices distinct is so impressive. Highly recommended."

—*Historical Novels Review*

"Delightful! . . . very satisfying. Barbara Davis endings usually are!"

—*Midwest Book Review*

"Will resonate with readers who love a tale full of heart and soul."

—Camille Di Maio, bestselling author of *The Memory of Us* and *Come Fly with Me*

"Davis creates nuanced and well-developed characters . . . a carefully woven tale that the reader won't soon forget."

—Emily Cavanagh, author of *The Bloom Girls* and *This Bright Beauty*

"I've voraciously consumed all of Barbara Davis's books . . . Highly recommend."

—Terry Lynn Thomas, *USA Today* bestselling author of *The Silent Woman*

"A bighearted gem of a novel sure to delight true book lovers everywhere."

—Christine Nolfi, bestselling author of *A Heart Like Home*

"Davis may have reached a new height in her career."

—Barbara Conrey, bestselling author of *My Secret to Keep*

"I couldn't have loved it more!"

—Julianne MacLean, bestselling author of *Beyond the Moonlit Sea*

EVERY
PRECIOUS
AND
FRAGILE
THING

OTHER BOOKS BY BARBARA DAVIS

The Echo of Old Books

The Keeper of Happy Endings

The Last of the Moon Girls

When Never Comes

Love, Alice

Summer at Hideaway Key

The Wishing Tide

The Secrets She Carried

EVERY PRECIOUS AND FRAGILE THING

A NOVEL

BARBARA DAVIS

LAKE UNION
PUBLISHING

Published by Lake Union Publishing, Seattle

www.apub.com

Amazon, the Amazon logo, and Lake Union Publishing are trademarks of Amazon.com, Inc., or its affiliates.

ISBN-13: 9781662514470 (hardcover)
ISBN-13: 9781662514463 (paperback)
ISBN-13: 9781662514487 (digital)

Cover design by Eileen Carey
Cover image: ©Mitoria, ©KRIACHKO OLEKSII / Shutterstock;
©Millennium Images / Gallery Stock

Printed in the United States of America

First edition

To every mother who has taken the child of another into her heart, to love and cherish as her own. Thank you for gifting the world with your special brand of love.

Be with me always—take any form—drive me mad!—only do not leave me in this abyss, where I cannot find you!
—Emily Brontë, *Wuthering Heights*

PROLOGUE

I linger, nearly untethered. The sound of my breathing fills the room, heavier all the time, and further and further apart. It won't be long now. The room is dark, or nearly so, lit only by the sliver of sallow light bleeding in under the door. How clear everything looks suddenly, how sharply in focus. You sit nearby, folded into an uncomfortable chair, your gray dress rendering you nearly invisible in the gloom.

You're so very quiet, fingers moving rhythmically over the strand of shiny black beads in your lap. You're holding your breath, I realize, listening with your whole body, counting the seconds as the silence builds, ticking off the minutes, the breaths, the heartbeats. Waiting for one more breath. Praying it comes. Praying it doesn't. Praying for some kind of miracle. There won't be one, of course. There's just the waiting now. And the soul-wrenching questions about what we've done.

So much time has passed. Years of emptiness, of longing for what was lost. And yet the loss remains. Even now, when you're close enough to touch. We made so many promises. Feverish whispers and talk of forever. How young we were to believe in such things, how foolish. But we meant them when we made them, didn't we? Now, a lifetime later, they lie between us in this hushed, dark room—unkept.

Fault on both sides, we realize now. Though I was the one who began it—the one who should have known better. You were young and so new to love. You weren't ready for what came next, for the testing of what we felt—for the fallout. But I wanted you so badly, so blindly and completely, that I put you in an impossible position and then blamed you when you failed the very first test.

One word from you might have saved me, saved us, but you couldn't utter it. Your silence, your unwillingness to defend me, to choose me, was the first wound. Years later, when you turned up out of the blue, I wasn't prepared for your tears—or your judgment of the choices I'd made—and so I wounded you to even the score. An eye for an eye.

Still, here you are at the end of things, and we've made new promises. For the sake of what we once shared—what we'll always share. There's still so much to say, so many things I've neglected to tell you, in spite of all my carefully laid plans. But there's a new weightlessness now as I watch you in your chair, the peculiar sensation of having slipped my skin, of being gradually unshaped—of leaving.

You look up suddenly and reach out—as if to hold me here. You bend down then and kiss me—that other me, already cooling against the dingy hotel sheets. The absence of sensation as your lips touch mine is startling, and I feel a stab of grief, realizing I'll never know your touch again.

Once again, we're separated.

You stare at the hand beneath yours, the skin almost translucent, all knuckles and veins. It seems impossible that I could be gone—even to me. You lean closer to make sure, touching wrist and then throat. Yes, my love, it's finished. You've kept this part of your promise, and now you must keep the rest.

You let out a sound as you step away from the bed, a half-strangled sob that makes me long to comfort you. But there is no comfort for such a moment, only regret that it had to happen like this—and that you had to be a part of it. Forgive me. There was no one else.

You straighten your shoulders and look around the room, assuming an icy calm. We've talked through what happens next. There are things to tidy, items to gather, a call to be made from the pay phone on the corner. Go now, and see to them. And then begin again, fresh. There are precious things—fragile things, my love—that require your care.

ONE

MALLORY

June 13, 1999
Boston, Massachusetts

Mallory dug her passkey from her tote and slid it into the reader, waiting for the dull buzz and the shift of the lock before pushing inside. In the five years she'd worked at New Day, she couldn't remember ever being called in on a Sunday. It wasn't that she minded. Or that she'd had plans. She never had plans. Unless reorganizing her bookshelves or purging her bathroom cabinets counted as plans. Work was what she had—and all she needed.

She'd driven herself hard—and left behind a ton of baggage—to get through school and secure her position as a senior counselor at New Day Wellness Center. Helping kids was all she'd ever wanted to do, to help them discover their unique gifts and find their place in the world. It wasn't always a bed of roses; at times, it could be downright gut wrenching. But she'd seen lives reshaped, families healed, love resurrected from ash and despair, and the chance to play even the tiniest part in that made the hard stuff worth it.

Like many of her colleagues, she saw social work as a calling. *Sacred work*, her herb-peddling New Age–y mother would say, a gift from a benevolent Universe. Mallory had never agreed with Helen Ward on much—almost nothing, in fact—but she did agree with at least part of that. The work *did* feel sacred, life affirming, and powerful, yet enormously humbling. She had attended concerts, graduations, weddings, and christenings that, but for the intervention of a caring professional, might never have happened, and each time she'd come away feeling as though she'd been given a gift, a poignant reminder that for some, second chances *did* happen. If that wasn't sacred work, she didn't know what was.

Still, she couldn't fathom what might warrant a call on a Sunday. Jevet had been oddly cryptic on the phone, saying only that she needed to come in as soon as possible. Could it be news about the IVP proposal she'd submitted last week?

The thought left Mallory with a sinking feeling in the pit of her stomach. She'd been working on the project for months, crunching numbers and getting input from local businesses, and believed her Immersive Vocational Partnership program, matching kids with local businesses to give them actual work experience, could be a game changer for kids from under-resourced communities. Funding would be the biggest obstacle—because funding was *always* the biggest obstacle for new programs. Perhaps Jevet had called her in to explain that the proposal, though worthwhile, would almost certainly be dead on arrival with New Day's board of directors.

Mallory winced as the door clicked shut behind her. In the absence of coworkers, the office felt gloomy and stale, the air heavy with the mingled scents of coffee, Xerox toner, and the carpet freshener the cleaning crew used when they came in to tidy up.

As instructed, she went straight to Jevet's office. The door was open. She paused, knocking on the doorjamb to announce herself. To her surprise, she was greeted by two men in dark suits. They turned in unison, eyeing her expectantly. One was tall and lean with a head of salt-and-pepper hair, the other younger, blond, and ruddy-faced. Neither was smiling.

Before she could ask what was going on, Jevet pushed up out of her chair. She was wearing leggings and a ratty sweatshirt, her smooth ebony skin uncharacteristically free of makeup. "Mallory, these are Detectives Muldowney and Nance. They're here because . . ." She paused, flashing an awkward look at both men. "Mallory, Tina Allen was found dead last night behind an abandoned car lot on the south side."

Mallory sagged against the doorjamb, a wave of queasy heat washing through her as the words penetrated. It was Jevet's way, blunt and to the point. She didn't believe in sugarcoating anything, not that there was any way to sugarcoat such news.

"How . . ."

The taller of the two men stepped forward, pulling a pen and a small black notebook from his shirt pocket. "John Muldowney, ma'am. I'll be the lead detective on Tina's case. We know this comes as a shock, but we were hoping you'd be able to answer a few questions."

Mallory looked up at him, dazed. Finally, she managed a nod. "Yes, all right."

"I'll need your full name and title for the report."

"Mallory Christine Ward. I'm a senior case manager at New Day."

"And you were Tina Allen's caseworker?"

"Yes," she replied dully, the words *found dead* reverberating in her head. "Please. Before you go any further, can you at least tell me what happened?"

Muldowney's expression softened. "We received a call around midnight that a body had been discovered in the vacant lot behind the old South Side Motors building. A vagrant looking for a place to set up camp for the night tripped over something in the weeds. Our officers found the body a short time later. As it turns out, Tina's mother had already called us. She was concerned that Tina hadn't come home from work at the usual time. Our best guess is that Ms. Allen had been dead several hours when her body was discovered."

Mallory squeezed her eyes shut, attempting to stave off a fresh wave of dizziness. "How?" she asked weakly. "How did she die?"

"We don't have a definitive cause of death yet. There was no weapon found at the scene. But there was bruising on the throat and blunt-force trauma to the head. It appears she was sexually assaulted as well. We suspect there were multiple assailants."

Mallory opened her mouth, then closed it again, afraid she might be sick.

Suddenly, Jevet was beside her, rubbing her arm reassuringly. "Why do you think there was more than one assailant?" she asked Muldowney. "Were there witnesses?"

"I'm afraid we're not ready to share that information." He turned back to Mallory, pen hovering above his notepad. "Ms. Ward, Tina's mother tells us you've been counseling her daughter for about nine months and that the two of you had developed something of a bond. We're hoping you might be able to tell us a little bit about Tina's friends—or anyone she might have mentioned having problems with."

Mallory squeezed her eyes shut, fighting the urge to bolt for the restroom. Her palms were hot and slick, and there seemed to be a band of steel cinched about her chest.

"Ms. Ward?"

Mallory willed her eyes to open. Jevet was watching her closely, clearly worried about her emotional state. "Yes," she said, forcing herself to look at Muldowney. "I'm sorry. I just . . ."

"Do you need to sit? Or maybe a glass of water?"

"No, I'm . . . I'm fine. But I do think I'll sit."

Muldowney pulled out a chair and waited until she was seated before prompting her again. "Whenever you're ready."

"I don't know what to say. What do you want to know?"

"Just start at the beginning. Tina was obviously in some trouble when you met her. Tell us about that."

Mallory glanced at Jevet, uncertain how much she should say— *could* say.

Jevet responded with a subtle shake of the head. "Tell them whatever you can."

Mallory took a breath and closed her eyes, summoning the details of Tina Allen's first visit to New Day. A cropped T-shirt and skintight shorts. Stringy blond hair and a sharp, heart-shaped face. An elaborate Celtic cross inked on the inside of her left wrist. A beautiful, vulnerable girl with a chip on her shoulder.

Her story wasn't unique. Nor were her offenses. Skipping school, stealing money from her mother's purse, sneaking out at night to hang with a group of dodgy friends. Unsurprisingly, things had progressed to drugs and petty theft. Eventually, she'd run away, leaving her mother—a single parent with two jobs and no support system—with no choice but to call the police.

Officers found Tina four days later, high as a kite and in possession of several wallets that clearly weren't hers. It was her second arrest in eight months, and the juvenile court ordered her to enter a pretrial diversion program. Two weeks later, Tina and her mother had walked into New Day.

Mallory sat numbly as Detective Muldowney continued to scribble in his little black notebook. It couldn't be real. She'd seen Tina last week. They had talked about the raise she'd just gotten at the market where she worked as a cashier, the role she was thinking of auditioning for in the school musical.

And now she was dead.

The room seemed to tilt suddenly, spinning dizzily until Mallory thought she might slide off her chair. She gripped the edge of her seat with both hands, swallowing hard.

"Mallory." Jevet's voice seemed to come from far away, though she was standing right beside her, holding out a plastic cup. "Drink this."

Mallory accepted the cup, sipping the water mechanically. Gradually, the room righted itself and she pulled in a breath.

Muldowney cleared his throat, signaling that he'd caught up with his note-taking. "I'm sorry, Ms. Ward. I know this is difficult. Just a few more questions and we'll be out of your hair. Would you say you and Tina were friends?"

"My relationship with Tina was a professional one. I was her counselor."

"But she shared confidences with you."

"Yes, that was part of my work with her."

"So you'd know if there was anyone new she'd been hanging out with. Friends, boyfriends, that sort of thing."

"You think it was someone she knew?"

"We don't think anything at this point. That's where you come in."

Mallory shifted uncomfortably, not sure how much help she would be. "Friendship wasn't something that came easily for Tina. It was a big part of our sessions, the importance of forging strong relationships. We talked about her building a new social circle of friends—safe, *healthy* friends—and she was making progress, but she wasn't always keen to share names. If you have a minute, I could check my case notes to be sure."

"Thank you, yes. Any additional information would be appreciated."

A short time later, Mallory returned clutching a thick green folder. She laid it open on the desk, fumbling through the contents with unsteady hands. Eventually, she looked up, shaking her head at the detective. "I'm afraid there isn't much here in the way of names. As I said, she was careful about what she shared with me. Like most teenage girls, she was worried about how much might get back to her mother."

"I take it there was some friction there? Between Tina and her mother?"

"Some, yes, but that isn't unusual between mothers and daughters. And things between them had gotten so much better. You can't think Charlene Allen had anything to do with her daughter's death."

Muldowney held up a hand. "These are just routine questions, Ms. Ward. What about behavioral changes? Anything you can think of that might have contributed?"

Mallory cut her eyes up at Muldowney. Had she detected a subtle whiff of victim blaming? It happened with girls like Tina. Poor. Rough.

Street savvy, but not savvy enough. The unspoken belief that, by putting themselves in a high-risk situation, they basically had it coming.

"I don't know what that means, Detective," Mallory replied tersely. "What kind of thing contributes to a fifteen-year-old girl being raped and murdered?"

Muldowney's face remained passive. "I think you know what I'm asking, but I'll ask it more plainly if you like. Do you have reason to believe Tina was using drugs again? It doesn't mean she invited what happened to her, but if she was using again, it might shed some light on what she was doing behind an abandoned car lot at that hour."

Mallory sagged back in her chair. It was a perfectly valid question, just not one she was eager to contemplate. Grudgingly, she ran the mental tape of her last session with Tina. They'd talked about a poem she'd written for English class and gotten an A on. Tryouts for her school's upcoming production of *Bye Bye Birdie*. And someone—a friend she'd met at AA, whose name she hadn't mentioned—who'd offered to help her study to get her learner's permit. And there'd been no red flags of any kind during her last in-home visit. Nothing to indicate she might be at risk of relapsing. Quite the opposite, in fact.

"She was better," Mallory insisted, wondering as the words left her mouth whether it was Tina she was defending or herself. "She and her mother were working through their issues, her er grades were up, and she was attending AA meetings. She'd just earned her six-month badge."

There were more questions, many of them repeats carefully reworded by Detective Nance to sound like new questions. Mallory did her best to respond calmly and professionally, but her chest ached with the need to howl at the incomprehensible horror of it, to weep until she'd wept herself out. Only she couldn't. Not here. Not now. Not in front of Jevet.

By the time the detectives finally slid their notebooks and pens back into their pockets, Mallory was both numb and exhausted, but she happily volunteered to step down the hall to make the requested photocopies of Tina's case file.

They were wrapping up when she returned, thanking Jevet for her time, assuring her they'd be in touch should they have additional questions. Mallory handed Muldowney the copied pages, then realized guiltily that she hadn't thought to ask about Tina's mother.

"Charlene . . . Tina's mother. You've spoken to her?"

Muldowney nodded grimly. "She's the one who sent us here. She thought the girl might have been more forthcoming with you."

"Is she . . . How is she?"

"About how you'd imagine. You never get used to that part of the job, having to tell a mother her kid isn't coming home. You can't help thinking about how you'd feel if the tables were turned and the knock came to *your* door."

Mallory noted the discomfort behind the detective's cool facade and nodded grudgingly. "Will you let us know how the investigation is going?"

"I told Ms. Cook that I'd be in touch when we had more information, though that may not be for some time. In cases like these, we like to keep our cards close to the vest—to protect the integrity of the investigation. There may be information we choose to withhold from the public."

"We're not the public, we're—"

Muldowney shifted awkwardly and his eyes suddenly went soft. "Believe me, Ms. Ward, when I tell you I know how hard this is for you. My wife's a retired juvenile parole officer, and she's been exactly where you are now. I saw what she went through every time one of her kids went rogue, the absolute hell she'd put herself through. The waiting was god-awful. And then when the news was bad . . ." He paused, shifting again. "Well, I get it, is all. And I hate like hell that you're going through it. Or that anyone ever has to go through it."

"Thank you for that," Mallory said thickly. "I just need to know—"

"Thank you, Detective," Jevet said, neatly cutting Mallory off. "I'll wait to hear from you. We will, of course, be reviewing Tina's case internally, and coordinating with Child Protective Services." She paused, throwing Mallory a quelling glance. "Let me walk you out."

◆ ◆ ◆

Mallory was in her office, still clutching Tina's case file, when Jevet reappeared in the doorway. Mallory braced herself for what she knew was coming. Jevet had been a friend before becoming her boss and the lines between the two roles had always been a bit blurred, but Jevet had never been shy about donning the boss's cap when it was required—as she was clearly about to do.

"You okay?" Jevet asked quietly.

"Yes, I'm fine."

"Are you sure? Thirty minutes ago you were heading for a full-blown panic attack and you're still as white as a sheet."

"I was just . . . When you called me in, I thought it was about something else."

"I'm sorry. I didn't want to tell you over the phone. I was afraid you'd be upset and then get behind the wheel. You tend not to . . . Well, I wanted to be with you when you heard the news."

"I told you, I'm fine."

"I'm not sure you are. You got a little snippy with Detective Muldowney. That isn't like you."

"It sounded like he was—"

"He was doing his job," Jevet said, cutting her off. "And *our* job is to help him. The review committee will coordinate with the police and CPS, to verify that proper standards of care were being followed. It's standard procedure with all child fatalities, and we welcome it." She paused then, smoothing out her tone. "It's all we can do for Tina now."

"I *know* all of that. I just can't believe . . ." Mallory's throat tightened as she allowed herself to contemplate the possibility that Tina's fate might have been prevented—that *she* might have prevented it. "I keep going over our last session. Was there something . . . some sign I should have caught? I thought she was making real progress."

"She *was* making progress. But relapses happen, Mallory. You *know* that."

Mallory stiffened. Jevet hadn't said Jacob Ellis's name aloud, but there was no need to say it. They both knew what she'd been referring to.

A year ago, less than a month after his case had been assigned to her, fifteen-year-old Jacob Ellis had died of a heroin overdose, his body discovered in the restroom of a convenience store, the makeshift tourniquet still knotted around his arm. Jevet had been the one to break the news. Within forty-eight hours, Mallory had entered full-blown meltdown territory.

She'd always had a problem with death, with the fact that life could be snuffed out like a candle, abruptly and irrevocably. It was simply a part of life, her mother—an expert on the subject of death—had frequently explained, just another phase in the cycle of the human soul, sacred and necessary. But Jacob Ellis's death had felt anything but sacred. It had happened on *her* watch and she'd been woefully unprepared for the emotional storm that followed: crying jags, nightmares that went on for weeks, pained looks from coworkers who wondered if she was up to the grittier aspects of the job. Eventually, she'd pulled herself together, but not before Jevet had a long and heartfelt talk with her about her future at New Day. Something told her they were about to have another of those talks.

"Please don't look at me like that, Jevet. This isn't like last time."

"No, it's worse. Because this wasn't self-inflicted. Someone did this to her. It'll be in the papers and on the news. I'd be lying if I said I wasn't concerned about the fallout."

"With the press?"

"No," Jevet said gently. "I'm worried about the emotional toll this is going to have on *you*. And before you interrupt, remember, this is me. I know you, honey. You'll keep saying you're fine, but you won't be."

"I wondered how long it would take you to bring up Jacob."

"I didn't bring him up—*you* did."

Mallory rolled her eyes. "We both know what you meant by 'relapses happen.'"

"I meant exactly what I said. Relapses *do* happen. They happen all the time. But knowing that doesn't make it easier. I saw the look on your face when you heard the news, and I'd be lying if I said I wasn't concerned."

"You don't need to be. I'm fine."

"Are you?"

"Yes. Of course. I'm not some new graduate, fresh out of her cap and gown. It's just . . . Two cases in a year, and both of them mine. It's only natural to wonder if maybe . . ."

Jevet let out a soft sigh. "Mallory, Jacob died because of choices he made long before he came to New Day. And we have no idea why Tina is dead. We need to wait until the police put it all together—if they ever do. In the meantime, focus on your successes and all the good you do. You're great with these kids. You have a way of opening them up, reaching them on their level. That's a gift."

"But that isn't the whole job, is it?" Mallory said quietly. "We're supposed to keep them alive too."

Jevet's expression morphed into one of empathy. "These are troubled kids, honey. We have to be prepared for unfortunate outcomes, even tragic ones, because as sad as it is, we get some of them too late. We do what we can, but not all of them *want* help. Admitting that doesn't make us heartless. It makes us professionals."

"I *am* a professional," Mallory shot back. "And I love my work."

"You love *some* of it. You love the happy ending. We all do. But you're right, there's more to it than that. This job requires a level of emotional distance, of detachment. We can't let it get personal. Not because we don't care but because it can take a toll. You set yourself up for a hard fall, and when it comes, you find yourself questioning everything. If you're lucky, you learn from it and grow thicker skin. Not so thick that you don't feel anything, but enough to allow you to do the work effectively and objectively. If not . . ."

Mallory stared at her as the silence between them stretched. "If not . . . *what?*"

Jevet shook her head. "Nothing."

"No. What?"

"It's your death thing, Mallory, how it triggers you. First there was Jacob, and yes, things got ugly with his father, but that's going to happen. Cases are going to land in the news, and the public is going to look for someone to blame. But then there was Beth Griner. Suicide by DUI. You were so shaken you couldn't finish out the day. And she wasn't even your case. Now it's Tina, and I see you trying to cover the panic. I thought that with time you'd overcome it—or at least learn to manage it—but I worry that today's events will retrigger all those old issues. I feel you struggling, and that's okay. Especially with something this hard. But honey, I'd be a pretty lousy boss—and an even lousier friend—if I didn't bring it up. Maybe think about what you need right now, and about how we can help."

Mallory looked away, unsettled by the stark concern in Jevet's expression, and by the fact that the woman could read her so well. It irked her to be seen as weak. "I've had a whole hour to digest this. I don't know what I'm feeling yet."

"Fair enough. This is a tough job on a good day, and this is definitely *not* a good day, but there is a history, Mallory, and I can't ignore that. My job isn't just looking out for our kids, it's looking out for the people who work for me too, making sure they stay in a good place. I love your level of commitment, how hard you work and how much you care, but there are times—you *know* there are—when you're far from being in a good place, and they usually occur after days like this. It might be time to talk to someone. I could make you an appointment with Rhonda Hurley. She works with a lot of health-care professionals. She might be able to help you work through your issues."

Mallory lifted her chin. She knew Jevet had her best interests at heart. Jevet always had everyone's best interests at heart. It was who she was, as both a boss and a human, but the suggestion, however well meant, that she seek professional help felt like one of those punches that lands before you have time to brace yourself. The kind that steals your breath and knocks you to the canvas.

"You're serious? You think I need counseling?"

"You're human, honey, and you've just been hit with some pretty tough news. I think it might help to talk to someone."

Mallory let out a breath, forcing her shoulders to relax. "I know you're just looking out for me, and I appreciate it. I do. But I really am fine. It's Tina's mother I'm worried about. I need to call her, to tell her how sorry I am."

"I'm not sure that's a good idea. She needs time to process too, time to grieve."

"But she has no one. Her sister's in Arizona. I don't think they even speak. She needs a support system right now."

"Maybe. But it isn't going to be you. I'll have Margaret or Frank check on her in a day or two. But not now—and *not* you. Go home and unplug your phone, climb into a hot bath, and stay there until your fingers go pruney. Find an old movie. Maybe take something to help you sleep. And for god's sake, do *not* watch the news. And I mean it—no contact with Charlene Allen."

"All right," Mallory replied grudgingly, relieved that Jevet had finally turned toward the door. "But I really am fine."

Jevet waved as she stepped out into the hall. Mallory waited until she was out of sight to tuck the second set of photocopied case notes into her tote. She wasn't obsessing. She was just going to take them home and look them over, to make sure she hadn't missed anything.

TWO

MALLORY

Mallory had no idea how long she'd been asleep when she finally jolted awake, but the room was dark and much too warm.

She dimly remembered coming home, pawing through the drawer full of take-out menus before settling for the bottle of chardonnay at the back of the fridge—a gift from Margaret last month, marking her promotion to senior counselor. One glass had led to three, which explained the dull pain behind her left eye. She knew better than to drink on an empty stomach, but it had seemed like a good idea at the time. At some point, she'd crawled into bed, surrendering to a combination of alcohol, exhaustion, and tears.

Lightweight.

It was what Aiden used to call her—a million years ago. But she didn't want to think about Aiden now. She didn't want to think, period. Instead, she flipped on the light and reached for the remote. She needed a distraction, a cheesy rom-com or an old rerun of *Laverne & Shirley.*

She flipped past an infomercial for a grill of some kind, then a pair of talking heads debating the strength of the Red Sox's bullpen, but froze when she stumbled across a blonde with beauty pageant hair reporting from the police station steps. The breaking news chyron at the bottom of the screen read LOCAL GIRL MURDERED.

"Police are asking for your help tonight after the partially clad body of a young woman was discovered in the vacant lot behind South Side Motors early this morning. The victim has been identified as fifteen-year-old Tina Allen, a sophomore at Boston's Excel High School. The cause of death is currently being withheld and police tell us they have no persons of interest at this time. The victim's mother could not be reached for comment, but a neighbor and family friend who has asked not to be identified has confirmed that the victim had a history of drug use and associating with what she called 'a rough crowd.' This neighbor also shared that the victim had been undergoing court-ordered counseling at New Day Wellness in an effort to turn her life around. She expressed shock and sadness that Tina's life had been taken so brutally and hoped the girl's killer would be found and quickly brought to justice. Meanwhile, a community remains on high alert tonight, and local youth leaders are already speaking out about the recent escalation of drug-related crime on the city's south side."

The camera shifted to the left then, as the reporter turned to a bystander for comment. Mallory felt an icy prickle along the back of her neck as a familiar face suddenly filled the screen. Below, a new chyron appeared: GREG ELLIS, YOUTH PASTOR AND COMMUNITY ORGANIZER.

Jacob Ellis's father.

She hadn't laid eyes on the man in over a year, but the sight of him still made her skin crawl. He was wearing the same tattered jeans and black T-shirt, a signature uniform meant to lend him a whiff of biker-turned-preacher, and his lank, dark hair was still slicked back from his brow and tucked behind his ears.

Convinced that only Jesus could save his son from the clutches of addiction, Ellis had objected to the court-ordered counseling mandated after Jacob's third possession charge, railing against what he called state interference in a family matter. Ultimately, his protests had failed and Jacob was forced to choose between detention and a diversion program that required him to attend weekly counseling.

A month later, after only two sessions—the latter of which had ended abruptly after just fifteen minutes—Jacob Ellis overdosed and his father launched an all-out assault on New Day and the godless system he held responsible for the death of his son. He'd started his own non-profit soon after, a youth ministry purportedly focused on keeping kids off the street, and here he was, in all his self-righteous fervor, blaming pornographers and corrupt politicians for the demise of the American family.

"We've reached a crisis in this city," he began, with carefully pitched zeal. "While society chases the almighty dollar, its babies are being devoured. Day after day, innocent children—my own son among them—are dying in the streets. Questions need to be asked! Answers demanded!" Ellis paused then, looking directly at the camera. "Who's caring for this city's most vulnerable? The bureaucrats at social services? The quacks at New Day? Tina Allen is dead—the third death in a single year under their so-called care—and for all we know, there are more. Three souls lost to the evils of drugs and promiscuity. Innocents allowed to destroy themselves—for profit. Because establishments like New Day have the judges in their pockets. Judges who want to strip God and family from the lives of our most vulnerable. Our children! Well, we've seen what comes of that. A fifteen-year-old girl—a beautiful, beloved daughter of God—is dead, brutally murdered, and left in the dirt. New Day and its staff of do-gooders have fresh blood on their hands tonight. Maybe it's time to ask why. I'm certain Tina Allen's mother would like to know."

Mallory's hands shook as she reached for her cell and punched in Jevet's number.

"Yes, I'm watching," Jevet said in lieu of a greeting. "But why are you? I'm pretty sure I advised you to steer clear of the news."

"I can't believe it," Mallory blurted, ignoring Jevet's gentle scolding. "And that reporter, just standing there letting him rant like that. No facts, just grandstanding and vitriol. He's actually accusing us of bribing judges! The police don't even know what happened, but there he is, insinuating that it was our fault. And she's letting him. Why doesn't she at least ask him what proof he has?"

"Mallory, honey, I need you to take a breath."

Mallory pulled in a deep breath through her nose, forcing herself to calm down. Eventually, she felt her shoulders begin to relax. "He doesn't give a damn about Tina, Jevet. This is about needing someone to blame for his failings as a parent. He's throwing around words like 'drugs' and 'promiscuity' when he has zero proof that anything like that was even involved."

"He doesn't need to have proof. He just needs to say it and point. The media will do the rest. Then the public will take sides. We know how this works—and so does he. The prayer vigils will start, followed by calls for heads to roll. Guys like Ellis know exactly how to work it. They make God the victim, gin up plenty of outrage, then tell everyone who to blame while the press happily fans the flames."

"And what happens when the public finds out drugs *weren't* involved? That the whole thing was hyped by a guy with an axe to grind?"

"Oh, they'll never hear that part. By the time the facts come out, the headlines will be about something else, something sexier. Ellis knows that too. Unfortunately, the people who do what we do wind up tarnished in the public's eye. Trust declines. Funding suffers."

"What are we going to do?"

"*We* aren't going to do anything," Jevet said flatly. "*I* will handle this, along with the review committee and our legal counsel. We'll draft a statement referring the media to the allegations made by Mr. Ellis, and then we'll demand a retraction. In the meantime, we have no comment. Got me? Not one word. To anyone."

Legal counsel.

The words chilled Mallory. Ellis had filed a negligence suit after Jacob's death. In the end, CPS and the review committee had exonerated New Day, and Ellis's claim was found to lack merit, but it had raised enough eyebrows to dampen funding for a while. What if Charlene Allen pursued a similar claim? Valid or not, the exposure could be disastrous.

"Do you think there's actual legal exposure for New Day? Maybe I should call Charlene and extend our condolences. I'm sure—"

"Mallory."

Mallory fell silent. "Right. Got it. Not a word."

"Good. Now turn off the TV and get some sleep. I'll see you in the morning—if you're still coming in. You don't have to, you know. A few days off might be a good thing."

"No. I'll be there."

"All right. Have it your way."

The next morning, Mallory swallowed two ibuprofen, dragged on the first thing she grabbed from the closet, and set out for the six-block walk to the office. It had been an ugly night of patchy sleep and horrific dreams, and she desperately hoped the fresh air—and the tallest coffee she could find along the way—would help clear her head.

She had barely set off down the sidewalk when a man in an ill-fitting blazer and aviator sunglasses scurried up behind her. "Ms. Ward?" He paused just long enough to avoid a woman with a stroller, then picked up again. "Paul Gray from the *Boston Herald*. Would you care to make a statement with regard to the murder of Tina Allen?"

Mallory halted briefly, startled by his presence. There were a hundred things she wanted to say to him at that moment, starting with *How did you find out where I live?* But Jevet's warning was still fresh in her head and she set off again, eyes focused straight ahead.

Not one word. To anyone.

"We understand you were the caseworker for Jacob Ellis when he died last year of a heroin overdose. Now Tina Allen is dead, also under New Day's care, reportedly the third death in a year. What do you think that says about New Day? Should hard-earned tax dollars be used to fund an enterprise with such a questionable record?"

Mallory's throat burned with the need to lash out. He talked about Jacob's and Tina's deaths like they were statistics on a spreadsheet, numbers to be scored and compared. It was clear he'd been coached by Ellis.

But had Ellis told him everything? How he'd enabled his son's addiction by refusing to allow him to suffer the consequences of his actions? She doubted it. But she couldn't say that—or anything else. She'd promised Jevet. And so she kept walking.

Gray kept pace, rattling off question after question, each more egregious than the last. Eventually, she darted for the curb, where a well-timed taxi was dropping off a passenger. If the driver was surprised by the vehemence with which she slammed the cab door, he gave no sign, and she was finally able to exhale when he pulled away from the curb and out into the snarl of morning traffic.

Jevet clearly knew something was up the minute Mallory appeared in her office doorway. She closed the folder on her desk and looked up with narrowed eyes. "What's wrong?"

"A reporter. Waiting for me when I came out of my building. He wanted a statement. About Tina."

"And you said . . ."

"Nothing."

"Good girl. They want to put a face on it and we're not going to let them do that. As it is, I've been dodging calls all morning. And I got here at six."

"Why six?"

"I wanted to beat the reporters."

Mallory stared at her, horrified. "Were they here too?"

"No, but they will be, and I want our attorneys on it before they are. You look terrible."

Mallory was too exhausted to take offense. "Rough night."

"Yeah. Me too. You can go back home, you know. You don't have to be here if you're not ready. We can reschedule your sessions."

"I'm not leaving you to face all the noise by yourself."

Jevet flicked her eyes up at Mallory. "I seem to remember us agreeing last night that that's *exactly* what's going to happen. In fact, I've had all your office calls forwarded to me for the next few days. So seriously, if you want to take the day. Or several days . . ."

Mallory gaped at her. "You don't trust me to answer my own phone?"

"I don't trust *them*, Mallory. The reporters and the zealots. They're going to try to turn this into some kind of cause. I've seen it before, how big it can get before it dies down—and how hungry. The last thing we need right now is the press taking shots at you when you're already shook."

"I am not . . . *shook*," Mallory countered defensively. "I just need coffee." But even as she said the words, the rawness in her throat was there, along with the urge to fold in on herself and sob.

Jevet tilted her head thoughtfully. "I think it's going to take more than coffee, but if you insist on staying, there's a fresh pot in the break room. Just keep your head down, okay? And remember, not a word to anyone."

Mallory couldn't help feeling a little miffed that Jevet felt the need to warn her yet again. "I get that you're trying to protect New Day, but I hope you know I'd never say anything to jeopardize this place."

Jevet responded with a weary half smile. "Of course I know that, honey. But it isn't New Day I'm trying to protect. It's you."

THREE

HELEN

June 13, 1999
Little Harbor, Rhode Island

I wake in darkness, surrounded by the pulse of waves from the beach below, the curtains sighing in and out at the half-open window. I look at the clock and swallow a groan. Too many hours until dawn. Too many hours of empty quiet.

I close my eyes, willing myself back to sleep, but it's no good. The memories are awake too, tattered now after so much handling, imprinted on the backs of my lids like old photos.

It's been a while since I've had a night like this, when the past comes calling, waking me from a sound sleep. But it isn't only the past that's calling tonight. It's tomorrow too, tugging at my sleeve. I've felt it for days now, a weight in the air, a heaviness I can feel on my skin. It happens like that sometimes, like a sudden drop in barometric pressure, alerting me that a disturbance is brewing.

I drag on my robe, already knowing where I'll end up. Where I always end up when sleep eludes me. But tea first, I think.

Downstairs, the house is dark and thick with quiet. I work by moonlight, setting the kettle on the stove. I gather what I need—tea, honey, mug, and spoon—then wander into the dining room while the water heats, eyeing the treasures entrusted to me over the years. My legacy, as it were. Sterling silver teaspoons: Rita Gower, pancreatic cancer. Antique dueling pistols: Howard Franklin, liver failure. A display of impossibly delicate crystal bells: Janice Randall, congestive heart failure. To name a few.

Many would find such treasures macabre, but they give me a strange sense of purpose. Some are costly, others nearly worthless, but to their previous owners they were *all* priceless, which is why *I* have them now. I am their keeper—a custodian of precious and fragile things.

There's a fancy name for the work I do—*doula*—but I don't use it. It's a Greek word that means "female slave," which I most certainly am not. Not many understand my work. Thirty years ago I'd never heard the word, nor was there formal training as there is now. Back then, it was simply a vocation. Important work. Sacred work.

I think of myself as a kind of midwife, only in reverse. Instead of easing souls *into* the world, I help to ease them out. But not just any souls. My charges are alone in the world. There's no one to carry out their last wishes, no one to recall their sorrows and their joys—and no one to tend to their things when they're gone. That's where I come in.

Most people see death as the enemy. I suppose I did too, once. But life has forced me to see things differently, to question the notion of a vengeful God and death as the wages of sin. For me, death is just one leg in an infinite journey. None of us knows for sure what's out there, but hope makes the unbearable bearable, and so I've chosen hope.

The kettle begins to whistle and I return to the kitchen to finish up the tea, then climb the two flights to my studio. The space seems to welcome me as I step inside, the walls and floor awash in moonlight. I move to the easel near the window, studying my current work in progress—a sea washed gold by a slow-sinking sun, clouds tinged pink and orange in a deep cerulean sky. It's nearly finished now, painted for some tourist I'll never meet.

I tend to paint the same thing over and over, re-creating the small pocket of beach visible from my window or the deck below, but they're never *quite* the same. Because no two sunsets are ever the same. Each day is its own singular gift, precious and so easily taken. And so I paint them, again and again, capturing the subtle changes of light and color, tide and tone.

But I haven't come to paint tonight. I move to the small desk beneath the window, a battered thing with lots of drawers and cubbies. Lots of scars too. I like scarred things. They've lived interesting lives— hard lives—and managed to survive.

The chair creaks as I settle into it, another rescue from some secondhand shop or other, purchased before my fortunes turned and a well-heeled charge left me this house on the craggy shore of Rhode Island.

The Admiral, dear man. What a stink his generosity set off in this town. Whispers and sidelong glances from my neighbors. Endless days in probate court. Threatening letters from distant cousins who suddenly came out of the woodwork, prostrate with grief for the wealthy relation they never bothered to visit while he lay dying.

In the end, the Admiral's will was found to be valid, and the suddenly aggrieved cousins were sent packing. The rest of the estate—the house with its stunning harbor view and prize-winning rose garden, all its furnishings, and a rather substantial amount of cash—came to me, a self-proclaimed death midwife. Though to hear the good people of Little Harbor tell it, I'm a shameless grifter who managed to build a rather posh nest for herself, feathered with the spoils of the dying. None of it is true, of course. There are no warrants attached to my name, no posters bearing my photograph, no rewards offered for my capture. My crimes are known only to me.

In fact, the Admiral was quite clear about his reason for leaving me this place. He wanted to be sure his wife's heirloom roses, as well as her ashes, lovingly scattered among the blooms after her death, would be cared for when he was gone. And care for them I have, for more than fifteen years now.

There are those who believe the Admiral must have been daft to stipulate such a thing, and a part of me understands. The thought of leaving behind what's most precious to us is unbearable, and so we cling to our memories in whatever way we can. The Admiral to the ashes of his beloved Patricia. Me to my book of scribbled yesterdays. They're hard memories to be sure, but all I have left now. Or almost all. And tonight they're calling me.

I open the desk drawer. Moonlight spills into the space, silvering the things there. My old fountain pen. Bottles of ink in blue, green, and violet. The journal covered in scarred blue leather, pushed nearly to the back, concealed but not forgotten. The box is there too, satiny rosewood with an inlaid lid.

It's the box I'm after just now, filled with shut-up bits of my past— *our* past. I lift it out and place it on my knees. My hand hovers over the carved surface, inlaid with bits of blue-green abalone. It's been some time since I let myself look inside, but I'm keenly aware of its pull tonight, like a compass needle signaling the way home. True north, back to you.

Still, I'm unprepared for the rush of emotion that moves through me as I lift the lid. A mistake, I think immediately, recalling Pandora's box with its seven evils. Perhaps I've been foolish to keep it all these years. Perhaps I should shut it up again. I don't, though. Instead, I tilt the box to catch the moonlight. I'm careful not to touch any of it as I make my inventory, though I know its contents by heart. Photos. Sentimental bits of jewelry. Dog tags on a beaded chain. A Saint Christopher's medal. It's all there, of course. No one comes up here but me. Not that I'm ever alone here. The ghosts are always close, rattling their chains, reminding me of my sins.

Well, here I am. Do your worst.

I close the box and return it to the drawer, then reach for my mug of tea. It's gone cold, and I abandon it with a shrug. There was never going to be any sleep tonight. Instead, I turn on the lamp, take up my pen, and slide the journal from the drawer. I lay it open, scanning line upon line of slanted blue ink, words recorded in fits and starts over the years. It's all there, our story from beginning to end. Memories I thought to purge. But some memories are indelible, etched into flesh and bone and soul. Some memories are forever.

It's been so long, but those memories are beckoning now, tugging me back to those early days. But I don't think I can bear them tonight. Instead, I'll just scribble, as I used to, in the hope that my words will find you.

My hand feels rusty as it hovers above the page. I struggle to begin, awkward after so many years of silence, as if penning a letter to a stranger. But nothing could make us strangers—not even death. And so I force my hand to move.

◆ ◆ ◆

Dearest,
How strange to be writing that word again. It's what I used to call you when we were young, remember? In the notes we used to pass in school. And I was Mouse. No names, we decided. We were children then—or not much more—but wise enough to know we didn't fit in and needed to be careful. You learn it early when you're different. How to cloak yourself in sameness, how to hide in plain sight. Only sometimes you get too good at it—as I did.

You may wonder, after years of silence, why I would take up my pen again so suddenly. I hardly know, except that I'm restless tonight, and unwilling to return to my bed. Was it you who woke me? Your slender, spectral fingers I imagined on my cheek? At my age, I should be immune to such fancies, to ghost stories and lost loves calling from the grave. Perhaps it's all those novels I read as a girl, making me wish for things I can't have, choices I can't remake, love I can't reclaim. But sometimes, when the night drags on and the quiet grows heavy, it's easier to think of you nearby, only a touch away in the darkness.

Your face is always with me. Not as you looked at the end, but as you were the day we met, so perfectly made that it nearly broke my heart to look at you. And then one day, you kissed me and the sun suddenly came out from behind the clouds. How far we've come since those days when we foolishly believed in forever. We've both suffered our share of disillusion since then—and inflicted our share of wounds. I cast the first stone, as it were. I won't deny it. But you eventually paid me back in kind.

At times it seems a lifetime ago, at others, only yesterday. We hurt each other so terribly. Sometimes without meaning to, but not always. We were young and loved each other so fiercely. Too fiercely, perhaps. But for a time, we were happy, weren't we? Blissfully ignorant of the dangers of the real world. We made so many plans, you and I. We were going to be together forever, making art and music, traveling the world. In the end, we did none of those things. Life had other plans for us.

You'll think me sappy, mourning all our lost tomorrows. Or perhaps you won't. Perhaps you're truly gone, and have been all these years. Perhaps the whispers I sometimes hear on the wind, the fleeting whiff of scent I catch when I enter a room, are only wishful thinking, like the pain of a phantom limb. But no, I can't believe that. I won't. I prefer to think of you always nearby, haunting the rooms of this great big house.

Most of what's written in this book is about the past, so I suppose I should catch you up a little. I live by the sea now, in a house with a tower that feels like it's from a fairy tale. A gift from a lovely man who built it for his wife while she was alive. He's gone now too, almost sixteen years. I was with him when he died.

It's the work I do now—tending the dying. A form of atonement, I suppose. Day after day, death after death, I walk my charges to the grave, a witness to their lives and their leaving. It isn't a life I ever imagined for myself. But I have only myself to blame for that. Things might have played out differently had I been braver in those early days. Instead, I was a coward. And because I was, we lost each other—and the years we could have had. Instead, there was only time to say goodbye.

Do I regret how things ended? You know I do. Still, I did as you asked. Not because I was brave, but because I didn't know how to say no. Even at the end, on that terrible night. You simply gave me no choice. But there was a gift too, given that night, one for which I'll always be grateful. Our girl. Our Mallory, who will always tether me to you, dearest.

She lives in Boston now and is a social worker who helps teens who've gotten themselves off track find new paths. I'm so proud of her. But she wants little to do with me these days. It's been months since we last spoke and that conversation ended badly, as most of them do. I always seem to say the wrong thing. And now I'm afraid something's wrong. I've had one of my feelings again. The terrible certainty that something has happened or is about to happen. Perhaps it's about Mallory.

I'm sorry to be an alarmist. You know how I get when left too long to my own musings. I'll leave you now, and get back to my bed. Please forgive the ramblings of a lonely woman.

H—

FOUR

MALLORY

June 16, 1999
Boston, Massachusetts

Seventy-two hours after Tina Allen's death, the internal investigation into Tina's murder was underway and the media storm was in full swing. The papers were full of graphic headlines, hungry reporters continued to gather outside the office, and segments about the unsolved murder appeared in the A block of every local news broadcast.

It hardly helped that Boston PD had released almost nothing since the initial presser, leaving the media and the public to fill in the blanks for themselves. And of course, Gregory Ellis was there at every turn, fanning the flames with his *war against God* rhetoric and whipping the public into an answer-demanding frenzy.

New Day's public statement had done little to quell the runaway train, and even Jevet, stoic in the face of every storm, was beginning to show the strain. Worst of all, she insisted on playing mother hen, casting looks of concern in Mallory's direction whenever they happened to run into each other in the break room, stopping by her office at odd moments just to *check in.*

Mallory was determined to keep up a brave face and continued to push through a full schedule of counseling sessions, but it was getting harder and harder to maintain the illusion that everything was fine. Since Tina's death, she'd eaten little and slept even less. She was exhausted and acutely aware of the low-level panic that seemed to crouch in her chest, ready to swallow her the moment she let down her guard.

More than once, she'd caught herself zoning out, staring off into space until something—or some*one*—jerked her back to the present. More often than not, that someone was Jevet. She preferred not to think about what would happen if Jevet were to learn about the photocopies of Tina's case file she'd made for herself and smuggled out of the office, or how many hours she spent each night poring over them, searching for something—anything—she might have missed.

Jevet had already cautioned her about jumping to conclusions about what had or hadn't happened to Tina, advising her to allow the investigative process to take its course, particularly where blame was concerned. It was much too early for speculation. But a girl was *dead*. It had to be *someone's* fault, didn't it? Kids didn't just die. They fell through the cracks, got sucked into trouble while no one was looking. That part of Ellis's tirade, at least, was true. And if anyone had been in a position to know if Tina was heading for trouble, it should have been her social worker.

She'd gone past Charlene Allen's apartment building three times since Sunday, intending to walk up the four narrow flights and knock on the door. To do . . . what? Grieve? Console? Ask for forgiveness? She honestly had no idea. But each time she went, she remembered her promise to Jevet and went back home. And then this morning, Jevet had received a call from Detective Muldowney informing her that Charlene had gone to her sister's in Phoenix to ride out the storm. Apparently, Boston's media circus had proven too much for her.

Mallory was torn by the news. She was glad Charlene would have the support of family while she grieved for her daughter, but her absence meant there was no one to fill in the blanks, no one to absolve her.

She couldn't shake the feeling that she had failed as a professional, and because of that failure, a girl would never graduate high school, never fall in love, never marry and have a family of her own.

She'd lost count of how many times she'd mentally replayed their last session, dissecting their exchange word by word. Had something gotten past her radar? Something that might have saved Tina's life? The question ran on a continuous loop, particularly at night, when she closed her eyes and the apartment was quiet. The result was a fatigue so heavy it was sometimes hard to hold her head up.

Sagging back in her desk chair, she closed her eyes and breathed out to the count of ten. If she could just manage a moment of quiet, she'd be able to get through the stack of reports on her desk by day's end. But the abrupt jangling of a phone in a nearby office disabused her of that idea. She bit back a groan, plucked her empty mug from the desk, and marched down the hall. Caffeine would have to do.

Thankfully, the break room was empty. Unfortunately, so was the pot. She rinsed the carafe, replaced the used filter, then robotically scooped in fresh coffee and pressed the brew button. Her eyes drifted closed as she inhaled the heady aroma, then flew open again when she registered the unmistakable hiss and splatter of hot liquid. She'd forgotten to put the pot back on the burner.

By the time she made a dash to the sink and returned with the pot, there was coffee everywhere, puddled on the counter, dripping onto the floor, soaking the front of her trousers. She grabbed a handful of paper towels and attempted to stanch the flow, realizing too late that the coffee was still flowing. Smothering a curse, she jerked her scalded hand back, sending the empty pot crashing to the floor.

Jevet was the first to come running. "What in the world! It sounded . . ." Her words died as she surveyed the chaos. "Mallory, honey, you're kneeling in broken glass. For heaven's sake, get up before you slice yourself to pieces."

"It's okay," Mallory blurted, trying not to imagine the scene as it must look to Jevet. The puddled coffee and smashed pot, her on her knees in the middle of it all, frantically trying to mop up the mess. "I'll just sop up the puddle, then go get the broom."

Jevet squatted beside her, eyes sliding to the angry red blotch on the back of Mallory's hand. "You've burned yourself."

"I'm fine. It's fine. I'll just get the dustpan—"

Jevet caught her by the wrist, her fingers firm but gentle. "Sweetie. Stop."

Mallory went still as she met Jevet's gaze, her eyes suddenly swimming with tears. She tried to form a response but nothing would come. Instead, she sat blinking as her tears spilled over, flowing unchecked.

"I'll take care of it," Jevet told her quietly. "Right now we're going to look at that hand, and then you're either going to the ER or home."

Mallory mopped her eyes, sniffling. "I'm fine. I'm just a little tired."

"You're not fine, Mallory. You haven't been fine for days. Now let me have a look at that hand." Mallory reluctantly surrendered the hand. Jevet frowned as she surveyed the deep-red welt already rising across her knuckles. "Well, it's going to hurt like anything, but I don't think you need the ER. Unless you want to go?"

"No, it just stings a little."

"It's going to sting a *lot* soon." She pulled Mallory to the sink and flipped on the tap. "Just stand there and let the water run. I'm going to get a broom."

Moments later, Jevet returned and set about clearing up the mess. Mallory knew better than to protest when she was wearing her *because I'm the boss, that's why* face. She was going to make a big deal out of this, blow it all out of proportion. Though, in light of her current emotional state, *out of proportion* might not be a fair assessment. Either way, she definitely wasn't letting it go.

When the broken glass was sufficiently corralled, Jevet leaned the broom against the fridge door, turned off the tap, and handed Mallory a paper towel. "Go home. Take some aspirin for that hand. Fix yourself an adult beverage and order some takeout. Maybe book a meditation class or a massage."

Mallory stared at her. "A massage?"

"I think some extreme self-care is in order. And maybe a little downtime."

"Seriously. You don't need to worry about me, Jevet." Mallory bit her lip, stifling a grimace as the pain in her hand began to make itself felt. "I just need a good night's sleep and I'll be right as rain."

Adam Blanding, New Day's IT guy and all-around handyman, poked his head in the door. He ran his eyes around the room, taking in the remnants of the shattered pot, now in a tidy pile on the coffee-spattered vinyl. "Wow. What happened in here?"

"Just being my usual clumsy self," Mallory quipped weakly.

Jevet shot Adam a strained look. "Did you need something?"

"Your two o'clock interview is here."

"Put her in my office. I'll be there in a minute."

Mallory eyed Jevet as she washed her hands. It was the first she'd heard that they might be close to filling one of the three vacancies they'd been holding open due to budget constraints. "You're interviewing someone? I thought there was no money."

"I made it work," Jevet answered distractedly as she reached for a paper towel. "Go on now. Get gone."

Mallory managed a nod, knowing further protest would prove futile. "I'll see you tomorrow."

Jevet opened her mouth, then abruptly closed it again. "Promise me you'll get some rest."

Mallory went out of her way to be early the next morning, determined to prove to Jevet that yesterday's emotional lapse had been a one-off. She'd just settled at her desk when she spotted the pink sticky note stuck to her computer screen.

Mallory, come see me. J.

Suddenly she was grateful for the triple-shot macchiato she'd consumed on the way in. With any luck, Jevet wouldn't notice the shadows beneath her eyes and guess that she'd tossed her way through yet another sleepless night.

Jevet was shuffling through a stack of file folders. She looked up when Mallory tapped on the doorframe, an uncomfortable expression on her face. Mallory's stomach did a little flip, kicking up her already caffeine-fueled pulse. Had the detectives learned something? Or made an arrest?

"Sit down, Mallory."

Mallory sat obediently, braced for whatever was coming.

Jevet folded her hands on her blotter, shoulders squared. "I've made a decision and I need you to be okay with it."

"Okay."

"I'm putting you on leave."

Mallory stared at her. "Leave? Why?"

"I'm going to assume that's a rhetorical question."

"It's not. Why are you putting me on leave?"

"I want you to take the summer—"

The word registered like a small explosion. "The *summer*?"

"I'm worried about you, Mallory. About your state of mind. And let me stop you before you tell me you're fine. You're not. The very *last* thing you are is fine. I've seen this before. Not sleeping. Not eating. Dead stares. The constant self-doubt. You're burning. Slowly. But you're burning."

Mallory struggled to keep her voice even. "I know you're my friend, Jevet. And that you're just looking out for me, but—"

Jevet cut her off with a shake of the head. "I'm not saying this as your friend. I'm saying this as your supervisor. Yesterday, you went to pieces over a coffeepot. Except we both know it wasn't about the coffeepot." She paused, eyes flicking away briefly. "You need a break—a real one. I checked with HR. You have plenty of paid time, and I've already reassigned your cases."

Mallory stared at her, digesting the news. Her cases. Reassigned. "To who?"

"I have a new caseworker starting tomorrow."

"The two o'clock from yesterday was—" She broke off, blinking rapidly. "You already filled my position?"

"I filled one of *three* vacancies we've been dealing with since the start of the year. But I'm giving her your cases for now. I mean it, Mallory. I need you to step back and take a breath for me. You're right on the edge."

"I'm not." Except she *was*. On some level she'd known it for days. She'd begun to spiral, slowly but undeniably. And it was getting harder and harder to cover.

"This isn't a punishment, Mallory. In reviewing Tina's case notes, I haven't found a single thing I would have done differently, and I don't think the review committee will either. This is just a well-earned break. But it's nonnegotiable. And for your own good. I'd like you to give some thought to whether this is actually what you want to do with your life. Maybe there's another path. One that would allow you to utilize your skills without all the emotional trauma."

Mallory shook her head dismally. "You make it sound like *this* is the job. Being informed that a fifteen-year-old in your care was raped and murdered, then having some religious nut blame you on television."

"That *is* the job," Jevet replied evenly. "Sometimes that's *exactly* the job. And the fact that you don't understand that is why I'm worried. This is going to happen again. Maybe not quite so tragically, but something *like* this. And I need to know you'll be okay when it does, that you won't let it eat you alive. So, as of today, you're on extended leave, through August."

"That's ten weeks! What am I supposed to do for ten weeks?"

"Talk to someone. Maybe ask yourself the hard questions. But definitely be a little bit kind to yourself."

"Why? When I haven't missed a beat? Not a single session all week. Yes, Tina's death hit me hard, but I've been doing the job, Jevet. I just had the wind knocked out of me."

"It's more than that, Mal, and we both know it. This is what needs to happen right now."

Sound bites from the local news suddenly filled Mallory's head. Ellis had been ranting nonstop for the cameras and Jevet was about to pour gasoline on the flames of speculation.

"That slimy zealot is out there talking to anyone with a microphone, accusing me of negligence. Now I'm on administrative leave? How is that going to *look*?"

Jevet met Mallory's eyes without flinching. "It's going to look like you're upset over the death of a fifteen-year-old girl and taking time off to care for yourself. All of which happens to be true, by the way. The rest of it is my business."

Mallory sagged back into her chair. "I'll lose my mind, Jevet. This job is my life."

Jevet nodded solemnly. "I know. And maybe that's the problem. Maybe you're using it to hide behind. We've talked about the stuff with your mom, about her work and how it might play into the things you struggle with here. I know it's the last thing you want to hear right now, but maybe it's time to deal with all of that."

"And by *all of that* . . ."

Jevet pressed her lips tight, as if considering her next words carefully. "All right," she said finally. "If you're going to make me spell it out. I'm talking about your *death* thing. Where it comes from and the way you let it shut you down. You've got baggage to unpack, and not just with your mother. The way you left home, without a goodbye, with no closure after the way things ended with Aiden and the baby. I know you think you're past it, but you're still carrying it around, like a wound you think no one else can see. You use this job to anesthetize yourself from it. And it works, mostly. Until something happens to one of our kids and the wound starts to throb again. Like now."

Mallory eyed Jevet sullenly. "You think I'm cracking up?"

"I didn't say that. And I absolutely do *not*. But the first step in healing after any tragedy is to look our pain in the eye and accept the fact that it's a part of who we'll be going forward. Maybe this is an opportunity for you to do that, to go back and face all of that stuff. I'm talking about digging deep, letting yourself cry it all out, until it can't hurt you anymore. You've never done that work. And you need to. We all need to."

Mallory found herself wishing she hadn't been quite so forthcoming about why she'd left Little Harbor. "What happened in Little Harbor has nothing to do with my work, Jevet."

Jevet's expression softened as she let out a sigh. "Everything has to do with everything, honey. They teach us that freshman year. And if that's not enough, we see it every day, in every case that comes through these doors. You're no different. None of us is. Something's going on with you. You may not be ready to look at it yet, but it's there, bubbling beneath the surface. But it won't stay there forever. We can only bury our pain so long before it finds its way out. And in my experience, the longer we wait, the messier it gets."

Mallory sat stiffly, stung by Jevet's unguarded assessment. At times, the woman could be painfully blunt with her advice, and this was one of those times. "I can't tell if you're being my boss now or my friend."

"I'm being both."

"Okay, *friend*. What am I supposed to do to keep from climbing the walls all summer?"

"Take a trip," Jevet said evenly. "Learn to parasail. Meet a man. Or . . ." She paused, meeting Mallory's gaze squarely. "You could go home and tie up your loose ends. Forgive who you need to forgive. Get some closure. And some perspective."

Mallory rolled her eyes. "I think I'll opt for parasailing if it's all the same."

Jevet cracked the tiniest of smiles. "All right. That's your business. But this place is mine, and so is every person who works here, and I feel like this is what you need right now. Time away and a little breathing room before you dive back in. I mean it, I don't want to see or hear from you."

Mallory let out a huff. It was becoming painfully obvious that she wasn't going to win. "You switched back to boss, didn't you."

"Yes, ma'am."

FIVE

MALLORY

June 17, 1999

Mallory made another circuit around her living room, on the hunt for something that needed tidying. After a day of frenetic activity, she had rearranged her bookshelves, alphabetized her CDs, organized the bathroom cabinets, and purged the fridge. What she hadn't done was turn on the TV or venture out of the apartment and she was feeling more than a little restless.

Jevet hadn't just reassigned her cases to the new hire, she'd also embargoed her online files and temporarily disabled her work email, precluding any possibility of her working from home. But none of it prevented the endless loop of questions running through her head. Had Tina relapsed into old behaviors? Drugs? Alcohol? Sketchy companions? What had she been doing behind an abandoned car lot at that time of night—or *any* time of night, for that matter?

Six months sober wasn't very long, especially for a teen with a history of keeping bad company. Mallory knew only too well how quickly progress could unravel, how one wrong step could send someone like Tina careening off the cliff. Still, it was hard to believe. Her grades were up, she'd made new friends, and she had just gotten a raise at work. All hallmarks of real progress.

Mallory had been through her case notes more times than she could count, fearing she might have overlooked some glaring red flag and, through her negligence, been culpable. Even now, knowing it was pointless, she felt the urge to pore over it all again. As much as she hated to admit it, Jevet was right: she was down a rabbit hole and well on her way to obsessing. But what was she supposed to do with herself for the next ten weeks?

You could go home.

She sat with the idea a moment. Maybe some time at the beach, swimming and soaking up the sun, would be a good thing. She could accomplish the same thing at a hotel, someplace quaint and quiet. But how long could she afford to hole up in a seaside hotel? Even a cheap one? Certainly not the entire summer. Going home would cost her nothing—financially.

But there was a reason she'd been home only a handful of times in the last ten years. And why every one of those visits had ended in terse words and bruised feelings. Old resentments died hard, and there were plenty of resentments waiting for her in Little Harbor. Still, she could feel the pull of it—of home. A place she'd been happy once, if only briefly.

How long had it been since she and her mother had spoken? Six weeks? Eight? Her birthday in March, so more like twelve. And the call hadn't ended well. Yet for reasons she couldn't explain, she suddenly felt the need to pick up the phone and dial her mother's number, just to hear her voice. Not that Helen would be home at this time of day. She'd be at work now, dispensing some vile herbal concoction and doling out pearls of New Age wisdom.

Helen Ward was a death doula by trade, an herb-wielding Florence Nightingale who had dedicated her life to caring for terminally ill patients who opted out of traditional care. *Charges*, she called them, since she wasn't actually a licensed health-care professional.

If only she'd found time to lavish a little of that care on the young daughter she'd left at home day after day. The one who'd gotten herself up and off to school every morning, who had eaten dinner by herself most nights and was usually asleep by the time her mother returned home. But Helen's charges had always come first.

Growing up, she'd never gone without the essentials. Her mother always made sure she was warm and safe and fed. It was her presence that had been lacking, the mother-daughter bond other girls her age had enjoyed, the normalcy of a parent who baked cookies and made costumes for the school play. Instead, her mother's time had been consumed by an endless succession of dying strangers. As quickly as she lost one charge, another would appear, often out of the blue, like names on some great cosmic waiting list.

Never mind the lurid rumors that seemed to follow Helen from town to town. She'd never believed them. Not really. But they were problematic at school. Still, there *had* been moments, times when her mother's clear-eyed wisdom had been a balm, imparting strength and soothing her broken places, holding her together when her world was fraying apart. And wasn't her world fraying apart now?

Before Mallory could change her mind, she marched to her bedroom, dragged the unused Samsonite from the closet, and laid it open on the bed. She didn't have to stay the whole summer, just long enough for the media frenzy to die down. With any luck, she could convince Jevet to let her come back in a week or two.

She frowned as she scanned the tidy selection of suits hanging in her closet—black, navy, beige, all carefully organized by color. On the shelf above, a collection of equally sensible pumps were lined up like somber soldiers. Not a sundress or flip-flop in sight. Nothing that said *summer*. Nothing that said *fun*.

Her reflection stared back at her from the full-length mirror on the closet door. A faded T-shirt. Lumpy gray sweats. Auburn waves pulled up in a messy bun. Not the kind the models sported in magazines; the kind that said you couldn't be bothered. And her skin—the same pasty white as every other city-dwelling office worker in Boston.

But she hadn't always been so pale. Her skin had been bronze once, and glowing, thanks to hours spent on the beach or at the pool. What had happened to that woman? The one who lived in cutoffs and bikini tops all summer? Who'd earned a box full of swimming trophies by the time she left school? She didn't think she even *owned* a bathing suit now. But did she really want to be that other girl? The dewy-eyed dreamer who believed in happy endings? She absolutely did not. But the one in the mirror didn't work for her either.

For now, she'd pack whatever she could pull together and figure out the rest when she got there. There were still some things in her closet at home, and she could always hit Little Harbor's touristy downtown and grab enough to get her through a few weeks.

Thirty minutes later, she was packed—or as packed as she was going to be. She was about to close the suitcase when she spotted something sticking out of one of the elastic pockets in front. Her passport. The one she'd gotten for Fiji . . . for the honeymoon that never happened . . . for the wedding that never happened . . . because the baby never happened.

It was the real reason she'd moved to Boston. Not work. Not school. Aiden. The concert pianist and boy next door, who'd backed out of their engagement when her unplanned pregnancy ended in miscarriage. And now she was going back, though not to forgive him, as Jevet suggested. He wasn't there and hadn't been for a long time. She simply needed a change of scenery, a place to ride out the media storm.

Resolved, she shoved the passport into a dresser drawer and closed the suitcase, then picked up her cell, pulled up Jevet's number, and tapped out a quick message.

Sigh . . . Leaving for Little Harbor. I blame you. 😕

SIX

MALLORY

June 17, 1999
Little Harbor, Rhode Island

Mallory's stomach lurched uncomfortably as she spotted the bright-blue sign. It was new since her last visit, embellished with the silhouette of a sailboat against a setting sun, the words spelled out in loopy cursive meant to look like sailor's rope: WELCOME TO LITTLE HARBOR, R.I. CITY OF SUN & SAILS. POPULATION: 7,293.

What was she doing here?

Suddenly her mother's voice filled her head, telling her there were no coincidences, that the Universe always had a plan and we must go where she points. Was that what this was, then? Some great cosmic wrench thrown into the gears of her life as a way of forcing her back to Little Harbor? Her mother would say it was. But Helen was one of those hippie-dippie types who believed in signs and affirmations. None of that had ever rung true for Mallory.

She could turn around. There was still time. But all that waited for her in Boston was Gregory Ellis and a bloodthirsty press. And so she kept driving, making the turn onto Center Street, which ran through the heart of Little Harbor's historic downtown.

Little Harbor had been just another sleepy New England town when her mother moved them here fifteen years ago, a quaint village with shady parks, tree-lined streets, and slate-paved sidewalks. It was the kind of town Helen always chose when the time came for them to move on: low tech and slow moving, happily distanced from the rest of the world. But it had become increasingly trendy since then, morphing into an artsy community brimming with galleries, cafés, and smart little clubs. And judging by the number of tourists crowding the sidewalks, it was still thriving.

New shop signs mixed with older familiar ones. Inkwater Books had been there for as long as she could remember. So had Jewelry Creations and Seaside Gifts. But Saffron & Salt, the Gin Palace, and Decora Studio were all new.

Mallory released the breath she hadn't realized she'd been holding as she exited the small roundabout and left downtown behind. She'd been worried about running into the old crowd. She would of course, at some point, but she was nowhere near ready. Not yet.

She headed east for a few miles, then turned onto North Ocean Way. The houses lining the shore were large and impressive, built of traditional stone and shingle, with sloping green lawns in front and carefully tended dunes behind. Most had belonged to the same families for generations, but a few were owned by newcomers, outsiders like the infamous Helen Ward.

Mallory slowed as she approached her mother's house, a sprawling three-story edifice of weathered shingle and buff stone chimneys set back from the street. Built in 1928 as a wedding gift for the wife of Admiral Alexander Grant, the house looked like something out of a New England fairy tale, part castle, part beach house with a long, sweeping drive and a rounded stone turret overlooking the beach.

She'd been just shy of fifteen when they moved in, and painfully aware of the locals' disdain, the salacious whispers about how Helen Ward had come to own a house so clearly beyond her means. But no one had been more vocal with their opinions than Estelle Cavanaugh.

Mallory's eyes slid to the stately granite home next door, separated from her mother's by a thick hedge of hydrangea. The barrier had been installed a month after they moved in, a public and unambiguous snub. And there'd been a hundred more since. Some of them unforgivable. But those were thoughts for another day.

Dragging her attention back to her mother's house, she goosed the gas pedal, pulled to the top of the drive, and cut the engine. No sign of Helen's old Audi. Just as well. She could use some time alone before having to explain her abrupt appearance.

She lugged her suitcase up the walk, dug out her old house key, and slid it into the lock. The door groaned softly as she pushed into the foyer. She stood there a moment in the tomb-like silence, blinking against the gloom. The parlor drapes were drawn, but a sliver of sunlight found its way through the opening, illuminating a narrow shaft of light, gold and silver flecks roiling in slow motion.

Mallory closed her eyes, breathing against the wave of vertigo she inevitably experienced on entering her mother's house. The level of clutter was simply overwhelming. Curio cabinets brimming with once-cherished keepsakes, all vying for space, all needing care. Not her mother's things. Other people's things. Dead people's things. Behind every door, crowding every corner and flat surface, like a bizarre cross between a museum and a curiosity shop.

Overwhelmed, she made a beeline for the kitchen. She had skipped lunch and her head was beginning to throb. She checked the fridge, hoping for a stray can of Coke. Instead, she was greeted by a rainbow assortment of fruits and vegetables, goat cheese, kefir, and a pitcher of some sort of murky green juice.

She settled for an apple from the bowl on the counter, munching as she wandered to the sliding glass doors that led to the deck and the beach below. She lingered a moment, peering out at the stretch of blue-green sea. For the first time since leaving Boston, she felt her shoulders relax. Perhaps this spontaneous trip home wasn't quite as inexplicable as she'd thought. Perhaps some part of her had known she needed to be here.

Pulling back the slider, she stepped out onto the deck, filling her lungs with briny air, savoring the familiar taste of salt at the back of her throat. She could do this. She could be here.

"Mallory! What on earth!"

Mallory whirled around, stunned to find her mother at the far end of the deck, scrambling to right a mug filled with paintbrushes. After finally managing to corral them, she turned to face Mallory, a fist clutched to her chest.

"You scared me to death! What are you doing here?"

She wore loose linen trousers the color of unbleached flax and a blousy white smock liberally smeared with paint. Her hair was well past her shoulders now, the smooth blond waves threaded with strands of silver that caught the sunlight—new since Mallory's last visit nearly four years ago.

"Hello to you too," Mallory replied dryly. "Sorry to scare you. I didn't realize you were home. Your car isn't in the drive."

"I finally made space in the garage. What are you . . ." She paused, eyes suddenly narrowing. "What's wrong?"

Mallory looked away, avoiding Helen's keen gray gaze. She didn't know, then. Thank heaven for that, at least. She never imagined the day would come when she'd be grateful her mother refused to own a TV.

"Why does something have to be wrong, Mother? Can't I just come home for a visit?"

"You can. But you don't." Helen shielded her eyes from the sun, her maternal radar clearly pinging. "What's happened?"

Mallory took a bite of her apple, chewing to fill the empty seconds. She'd planned to have an explanation in place before coming face-to-face with her mother but hadn't quite gotten around to it. "I had vacation days I needed to take," she said finally, opting to keep it simple.

"And you decided to come *here*? Out of the blue?"

"I wanted to go somewhere quiet to decompress. Should I go?"

"No," Helen said with a sigh. "You shouldn't go. I'm just . . . astonished." Her eyes slid briefly to the house next door. "It's hard to imagine you thinking of this as a place to decompress. And showing up like this after months of silence. No call to say you're coming. You just appear on the deck and scare the life out of me."

"I thought I'd surprise you."

Helen responded with a snort. "Well then, mission accomplished."

"I did say I was sorry."

"Never mind. Have you had lunch?"

Mallory raised the half-eaten apple in reply.

"That isn't lunch. Come inside and we'll throw something together. Then you can tell me what's really going on."

Mallory sighed, tossing the remains of her apple over the railing for the birds. Things were already off to a rip-roaring start.

SEVEN

HELEN

My breath nearly stops when I see her at the railing, backlit by the afternoon sun—like the ghost of summers past. The seconds stretch, spooling briefly backward, and for one jarring beat I'm frozen, caught in a blur of disjointed memories. And then, like a freight train, time resumes, and the fact of her, so utterly unexpected, and yet not unexpected at all somehow, slams into me, reminding me to breathe.

"Mallory! What on earth?"

I fumble it, of course, managing to sound angry instead of what I am—stunned. I feel a bit dizzy as I right the mug of brushes I've just toppled and spin around to face her.

She regards me coolly, the old resentment already bristling. "Hello to you too."

I study her with a mother's eyes, drinking her in after more than four years' absence. Her face is as familiar as my own. Not because she resembles me—there's nothing of me in her—but because she's the embodiment of the person I loved with my whole soul. But that stony expression, the mulish inflexibility stamped on her features. That she did get from me.

Her eyes meet mine, sherry colored with a fringe of auburn lashes. There's a shadow there, fleetingly glimpsed before she drops her gaze. When I ask her what's happened, she says nothing. A lie. But why?

Her hair is pulled into a messy knot on top of her head and a few strands have escaped, softening the sharp planes of her cheeks and jaw—so familiar it almost hurts to look at her. I do, though, because something isn't quite right. She looks hollowed out, spent in a way that makes me uneasy. First, she appears out of nowhere, scaring me to death, and then she tells me she's come to decompress. She's always been a terrible liar.

I continue to press her. She munches her apple, stalling for time, then gets huffy and threatens to leave. That's when I realize I'm about to ruin everything. If I don't watch myself, she'll go away again. And I don't think I could bear that now that she's here.

"Never mind," I say, and ask if she's eaten.

In the kitchen, she chops veggies for a salad while I make the dressing. We're careful now, treating each other like very delicate pieces of porcelain. Still, I find myself humming as I work. It's good to have her home, even if I don't know why she's here.

She sets the table on the deck and I bring out the salad. We sit across from one another, napkins spread neatly in our laps. I pick up my fork, still trying to think of a topic that might be safe to broach—work, friends, love life—then realize I don't have a clue what's going on in my own daughter's life. Our sporadic phone calls are superficial by design. Health. Weather. Occasional news about someone here in town. Polite trivialities meant to tick off the boxes and avoid uncomfortable subjects.

It's always been this way between us, strained conversations and prickly silences punctuated by the occasional explosion. Perhaps if I'd been less immersed in my work, things might have been different. I tried to include her and hoped she would follow in my footsteps, but she never wanted any part of what I do. I suppose I can't blame her.

To this day, I'm not sure she's forgiven me for the time she wandered into Madelaine Hoffman's bedroom and found me leaning over the woman's lifeless form. I heard her gasp and turned to find her standing in the doorway, eyes wide with terror. I could see the wheels turning, all the ugly talk she'd heard about me suddenly seeming to make sense. I did my best to explain, but she was too young to understand—and too horrified. Things changed between us that day, like a door closing. Little by little she began to distance herself. And I was so busy that I let her. Years later, here we are, polite strangers, tiptoeing around one another as we eat our lunch. And me, at a loss as to how to bridge the gap.

I watch as she pushes her food around her plate, still racking my brain for something to say, something that will break the uncomfortable ice between us. My gaze slides to the house next door. There are things I need to tell her, things I should have told her weeks ago, but the last thing we need right now is to head in *that* direction.

"I tried to call you a few weeks ago," I say, keeping my tone neutral. She looks up at me, frowning. "Did you leave a message?"

"You know I hate those machines."

"Was anything wrong?"

I hesitate just a fraction of a second before answering. "No," I say finally. "I just thought we could . . . catch up. How is Jevet these days?"

Mallory's eyes flick up from her plate, startled, defensive. "Jevet?"

"She's still your boss, isn't she?"

"Yes. She's still my boss."

"And?"

"And she's fine." It's there again, the skittery sense of avoidance I'd glimpsed earlier. She reaches for her napkin, dabbing at her mouth, then abruptly changes the subject. "I was surprised to find you home in the middle of the day. I don't remember you ever getting home before nine or ten."

She's deflecting now, trying to turn the tables, but I refuse to take the bait. "I hired someone last month," I say casually. "To spell me when I need a break. That's why I'm home today. Maureen's filling in."

Mallory's brows twitch up. "Actual time off? That's quite a change for you."

"It's usually just a few hours here and there, but my current charge is . . . Well, let's just say she's challenging."

"Anyone I know?"

"I don't think so. Claudia Auerbach. End-stage cirrhosis. She hasn't quite reached the acceptance stage, and it's been . . . difficult."

"Ah," she responds absently, checking that contraption she carries around all the time—her *cell* phone. She frowns and lays it down. Apparently, whatever she's looking for isn't there.

We focus on our food for a time, allowing the thrum of the sea to fill up the silence. I steal a glance at her now and then but she keeps her head down. She's got that look again, that same brittle fragility she wore the summer everything went south.

"What are your plans while you're here?" I finally ask.

She shrugs. "I haven't really given it much thought. Spend some time on the beach, I guess. Read. Swim."

"Maybe see some of the old crowd?"

She reaches for her tea rather than answering.

"There's a regatta next week," I suggest. "You always loved to go up to the point and watch them set out, and I'm sure a lot of your friends from the Harbor Club will be there."

"They were his friends," she replies tersely. "Not mine."

His friends. Meaning *Aiden's* friends. So we're back to that again. "Sweetheart, that isn't true. You all always had so much fun together."

"It is true." For the first time since sitting down, she actually looks at me, her copper eyes smudged with shadows. "They were *his* friends, not mine. And then after . . . it was . . . awkward. No one knew what to say. So I got shut out."

After the miscarriage, she means. After the wedding was called off. After Aiden left for London. Ten years ago now, and she still can't bring herself to say his name. Even to me.

"I'm not sure that's fair," I say gently. "You sort of disappeared."

"I didn't disappear. I left for school."

"In the middle of the night, with nothing but a note stuck to the refrigerator door."

Her eyes flash hotly. "Would you rather I'd stuck around, pretending not to know what everyone was saying? Yes, of course you would. You've never cared what people say about you. But I'm not like you. I *do* care. So yes, I disappeared. It's called moving on."

It's called running away, I nearly say but don't. Instead, I reach across the table and cover her hand with mine. "Sweetheart, you disappeared long before you left town. As for moving on . . ."

She smothers a sigh and pulls her hand free. "Let's not do this now, okay? I know you're dying to rehash it, but can we just eat without getting into everything else?"

"I just thought—"

"I know what you thought. You never miss a chance to point out whose fault you think it was, but I told you the last time I was here— my ex is off-limits. That hasn't changed."

"I understand. But there's something—"

"*Off*-limits," she repeats sharply.

"All right. Though I'm not the one who brought him up. It's just that . . ."

"What?" she demands, brows lifted. "It's just . . . *what?*"

I stare at her, wondering how on earth to tell her, knowing I have to. Letting her find out on her own would be disastrous. But she's only just arrived. Can I not have her for a day—for one lunch—before she leaves again? Because she will. I see it as plainly as she's sitting across from me. She might be here but she's already got one foot out the door, ready to bolt the minute things get uncomfortable.

"Nothing," I say finally. "Never mind."

"No." She folds her arms, chin jutting. "My suitcase isn't even unpacked but apparently we're doing this, so let's get it over with. What were you going to say?"

"Just that I don't think you *have* moved on. If you had we'd be able to talk about it. But you won't even let me say his name, Mallory. That doesn't sound like someone who's moved on. It sounds like someone who *can't*."

"I left town, Mother. In fact, I left the state. The last time I checked, that is the literal definition of moving on."

"No. That's changing your address. It's not the same thing."

She huffs and tosses down her napkin. "What was I supposed to do? Stay here and pine until he decided to come home? He made his choice when he got on that plane."

I fold my napkin and lay it aside, weighing my next words carefully. "I don't deny that Aiden handled things badly. But after the miscarriage, you closed yourself off from everyone. Including Aiden. His mother was pulling the strings and you just let it happen. You let that awful woman win."

Mallory drops back in her chair, then cuts her eyes up at me. "Seriously? Is this what the whole summer's going to be like? All Aiden all the time? Because if it is I'll just go now."

I blink at her, so surprised I ignore the threat. "You're staying the whole summer?"

She looks away and shrugs. "I don't know. I didn't really plan for this."

"And by *this* . . ."

"Coming home. Coming *here*."

"I don't understand. Did you mean to go somewhere else but wound up here by mistake?"

She drops her gaze. "I just meant it was spur of the moment."

"And you don't know how long you're staying?"

"It's open ended. There's some stuff going on at work and I might need to get back."

Her answer feels evasive but I know better than to press for more. "Well, however long it lasts, I'm glad you're home. And maybe this is exactly where you're supposed to be right now."

She sighs as she pushes back her plate. "Please don't start with 'the universe has your back' stuff. I'm here. It's not part of some *plan*. I'm just . . . here."

And clearly not happy about it, I think but don't say. "All right. What do you intend to do with your *vacation*? Have some fun, I hope."

Mallory shrugs and looks away. There are shadows beneath her eyes, and a distant, unfocused look about her, as if she's gone several days without sleep. "I'm not sure I know how to have fun anymore. Work is what I do now."

"You look tired, sweetheart."

"I *am* tired," she replies distantly, then seems to mentally shake herself back to the present. The breeze stirs loose wisps of hair into her eyes. She pushes them away. "Things at work have been a little . . . rough."

I study her a moment, wishing I knew how to penetrate the wall she's erected. She's always been reluctant to share her life with me, but this feels different. She seems brittle, as if she's trying very hard to hold herself together. It hurts to see it, but it hurts even more to think she might be in trouble and doesn't feel she can let me in.

"Should I be worried about you?" I ask quietly.

The question seems to startle her. "No, of course not."

"Are you sure?"

"I'm sorry I snapped. I haven't been sleeping and I'm a little frayed around the edges."

I reach across the table, touching her hand again, thinking of all the things I long to say. Things I should have said years ago but was somehow always too busy to tell her. *You're the most precious thing in my life. There's nothing more important to me than your happiness. I'm here for whatever you need.*

"I'm happy you're here," I say instead, because this isn't the time for fixing all of that.

She nods, forcing something like a smile. "Yeah. Me too."

I wish with all my heart that I believed her.

EIGHT

MALLORY

Mallory stared at the hand-lettered Do Not Disturb sign she'd made in eighth grade, still dangling from the knob of her old bedroom door. She'd jumped at her mother's suggestion to leave her with the dishes and get settled in. After their inauspicious beginning, retreat to her room had seemed the wisest course. Now, as she turned the knob and stepped inside, she wasn't so sure.

She ran her eyes around the room, basically untouched since she'd bolted for Boston. Bare walls painted cool apple green, gauzy white curtains at the windows, a vintage iron bed covered in a pink floral spread, the framed photo of the father she never knew on the nightstand. The hero of her girlish imagination. And if she opened the bottom drawer, she would find the flat black case her mother had given her when she was eight, inscribed with the words *Purple Heart*.

He had died in the Vietnam War, Helen explained, his chopper shot down while trying to rescue several brothers-in-arms. She'd slept with the box under her pillow for weeks and taken it to school for show-and-tell three years in a row, proudly reading aloud the words engraved on the back: For Military Merit. William H. Ward.

She'd left both medal and photo behind when she moved to Boston, afraid something might happen to them in the dorm. Ten years later, they were exactly where she'd left them. It *all* was—like a carefully pre-served time capsule waiting to suck her back in. She thought it would be a relief to retreat to her own space, to find a little peace and escape Helen's unrelenting gaze. Instead, the past seemed to crouch in every corner.

Did she honestly think she'd last the whole summer? When she and her mother couldn't get through lunch without an argument? She'd made it six days once, four Christmases ago, but only because a freak nor'easter had forced her to extend her stay by three days. It had been a visit of chilly silence and careful avoidance, ending in a bitter battle of words, because that's what they did—they battled. And now, she was looking at the whole summer.

The less-than-cheerful prospect continued to niggle as Mallory unpacked her meager vacation wardrobe. When she finished, she carried the empty suitcase to the closet, then groped along the top shelf in the hope of finding an old pair of flip-flops. Instead, she came across a box she'd forgotten was there, containing 125 hand-embossed wedding invitations with matching foil-lined envelopes. She didn't need to look at them. She still knew the wording by heart.

You are cordially invited to celebrate the wedding of

Mallory Christine Ward & Aiden Michael Cavanaugh

Saturday, August 5, 1989

Harbor Club

at five o'clock in the evening

She'd been addressing them when it happened. Cramping at first, followed by pain in her back, low and dull, like a toothache. Then came the terrifying gush of warmth and she'd gone down like a sack of bricks.

Thirty minutes later, she was at the ER with a split lip and a plum-size egg on her forehead—no longer pregnant.

Aiden had rushed to her side at the hospital, pale and clearly shaken. He'd held her hand while she cried, murmuring over and over again how very sorry he was. But once she was home and the shock began to wear off, his reaction began to feel more like relief. A bullet dodged.

On some level she understood. He'd been at a pivotal point in his career, on the cusp of every reward and accolade he'd been working toward since childhood. Marriage had always been part of the plan, but they'd agreed to wait until they were through with school. Then she found out she was pregnant and the need to get down the aisle became more pressing. It hadn't taken long for Little Harbor's rumor mill—fueled in large part by Aiden's mother—to catch fire.

No wonder they announced the wedding so suddenly. Well, they'd have to, wouldn't they? With a baby on the way? Poor Aiden. To have gotten caught like that, and just when he was set to leave for that fancy competition. Clever like her mother, that girl, always on the lookout for an opportunity. Of course he'd do the right thing. But what a shame to throw your whole life away because of one tiny mistake.

A mistake.

That was what Estelle Cavanaugh and her country club friends thought of her baby. And apparently, what Aiden thought too, as she soon realized when he suggested that with things *back to normal*, they slow down a little. Not permanently. Just until they finished school and he had a handle on his future.

The decision had caught her completely off guard; it never occurred to her that he would call off the wedding after it had been announced, the invitations nearly ready to go out. But it was the *way* he'd opened the conversation that hurt the most.

My mother thinks . . .

While Mallory was mourning the loss of their unborn child, Estelle had been busy nudging her son toward fate's handily timed off-ramp, suggesting that with the need for haste no longer a factor, a little distance might be the wisest course of action. Aiden had agreed to travel to London, where he would spend several weeks working with an old teacher in preparation for the prestigious Leeds Piano Competition.

Six weeks later, when Aiden hadn't returned to Little Harbor as planned, Mallory read the tea leaves and packed her belongings into her car, availing herself of a full-ride scholarship to Boston College. Aiden had chosen to remain in Europe, where, according to her mother, who felt the need to keep tabs on her ex-future-son-in-law, he'd recently embarked on another sold-out tour and was currently being showered with all the acclaim he deserved. Not that Mallory begrudged him his success; he'd earned every accolade the music world had bestowed upon him. But she could do without hearing it every time she turned around. At least she wouldn't have to worry about running into him. She had enough on her plate without the prospect of a messy reunion. That his mother lived next door was bad enough.

Suddenly, the room felt small and stuffy, too crowded with all her yesterdays. Mallory crossed to the window and lifted the sash. Fresh air poured in, moist and elemental, stirring the curtains and ruffling her hair. Here, too, were memories, caught on the brine-soaked breeze. Clambakes as the sun went down, with s'mores for dessert. Lifeguarding at the community center for pocket money. Laughing into the wind as she and Aiden skimmed the waves in his small sloop, the *Blue Note*.

It stung to think of that girl now, the one whose world had revolved around the boy next door and believed that love meant happily-ever-after. What a fool she'd been. And yet, part of her missed those simple times when she still trusted life to deliver all her dreams.

Her eyes slid to the beach, the sea silver-bright in the afternoon sun. It had been her favorite escape as a teen, a way to cool off whenever she and her mother butted heads. The first plunge, bracing, like a slap. The buoyant cradle of the waves, lifting her up, carrying her away from shore—away from conflict.

On impulse, she opened the bottom dresser drawer, where a jumble of brightly colored swimsuits greeted her. She grabbed the first matching pieces she could find—navy and white stripes with a little gold anchor clasp in front. It had been her favorite back in the day, but now she bit her lip as she eyed the tiny two-piece resting with alarming ease in the palm of one hand. Once upon a time, she'd been comfortable parading around in something so skimpy, but she couldn't possibly wear it now. If she wanted to spend time in the water this summer, she'd need a new suit—preferably one that wouldn't make her feel like Lady Godiva. For now, she'd have to settle for a walk. For better or worse, it was time to get this vacation started.

Mallory left her shoes on the deck and picked her way down the narrow path that led to the beach. Patricia Grant's rose arbor was in full bloom, the riot of pink petals perfuming the air with the mingled scents of honey, tea, and clove. She filled her lungs with the heady fragrance, reminiscent of so many summers, and instantly felt the familiar loosening of her limbs.

The gate latch was rusty after years of disuse, but after a firm jiggle and a sharp nudge, it yielded with a dry groan. The sand was soft and welcoming on the soles of her feet, the breeze laced with the tang of salt and warm, wet sand. She paused to cuff her jeans, then turned south, sights set on the craggy finger of rock stretching out into the sea—the jetty. How long since she'd been out here? Five or six years at least.

It had been *their* place—hers and Aiden's. It started as a bonding thing, an opportunity to commiserate about the mothers who drove them crazy. She couldn't remember how it came about, but at some point, they'd started sneaking out to meet at night. Aiden would wait until his mother went to bed and then the signal would come—three quick pulses of light from his bedroom window.

She would slip down the deck stairs and meet him on the sand, then they'd stroll to the jetty and climb out to the end. Sitting shoulder to shoulder, they would lose track of time, talking about everything and nothing. And then suddenly it *wasn't* nothing. Suddenly they were sharing dreams and making plans. Like the moors for Catherine and Heathcliff, the jetty had become their escape—a world entire. They had each other, and needed nothing more.

Mallory shoved the thought away as she halted at the base of the rocks. She briefly considered climbing up but ultimately decided against it, opting instead to linger at the water's edge and let the incoming waves purl about her ankles. She'd forgotten how cold the water was in early summer, the sting of it sending prickles of gooseflesh up her legs.

Part of her longed to knife into the waves and strike out for the buoy at the end of the jetty, but she was in no shape for that kind of swim. Nor was she dressed for it. Besides, it was getting late. The sun was already beginning to slide and the air would turn chilly soon. Summer nights in New England could be surprisingly nippy, especially on the coast.

On the way back, she set a brisk pace, skirting clutches of plovers and pipers in search of a late lunch. Slivers of silvery killifish darted about her feet as the waves slid up onto the beach, then disappeared again as the water receded. She halted briefly to watch a lady crab skitter across the packed sand and scurry back into the sea. It still amazed her how much life there was on the beach if one slowed down long enough to see it.

The gate was in view now and Mallory was preparing to set off again when she felt the uneasy weight of eyes between her shoulder blades. Pivoting, she scanned the beach behind her, then the handful of houses lined up along the bluff of beach rose and seagrass. There was no one. But her pulse ticked up as her gaze settled on Estelle Cavanaugh's house. Had she imagined the fleeting glimpse of a face at the terrace doors?

She didn't imagine Estelle would be happy to learn she was back in Little Harbor, even if her son *was* safely out of reach. She had pegged Mallory as an enemy from day one. And day one had begun right here, nearly on this very spot, a handful of days before her fifteenth birthday. The day she met Aiden.

She'd been for a swim and was coming out of the water when she heard it—notes on the breeze, slow and deep, like the rumble of waves, ebbing, then rushing in again. She'd gone still, breath held as the sound soaked through her skin and into her blood. It had taken a moment to realize it was coming from the house next door. She turned toward the music, irresistibly drawn, and without meaning to, found herself following the sound up the bluff to a slate-paved terrace and an open set of French doors.

She'd lost all sense of time as she stood there, like Catherine Earnshaw in *Wuthering Heights*, peering dreamily into the Lintons' impeccably appointed drawing room. It was *him*—the boy all the girls at her new school were talking about. The dreamy piano prodigy who lived next door and had studied at Juilliard. Only he didn't *look* like a boy.

Even seated, she could see that he was tall. But there was something else too—something about the way he held himself, so quiet and utterly composed—that defied the word *boy*. There was no wasted movement in his playing. In fact, there was an eerie stillness about him, as if his core were vacant somehow, with every ounce of energy being channeled into the music. And then there were his hands, lithe and long fingered, moving over the keys with such a fluid tenderness that it was hard to tell where the boy ended and the instrument began.

The piece he played was unfamiliar, but something about it resonated, like an unquiet storm waiting to be unleashed. She wasn't sure how long she stood there listening, but suddenly his hands went still and he turned to look at her with eyes the blue of a cold winter sky.

"Hello."

The absence of music was so abrupt, the void so complete, that she felt momentarily off balance. "Hello."

"What are you doing?"

"Listening," she blurted, horrified to have been caught spying. "I was on the beach and I heard music. It was so beautiful . . . I'm sorry. I didn't mean to bother you. I live next door."

He smiled, flashing a pair of startling dimples. "I'm Aiden. Do you want to come in? I'll play you something if you like."

And just like that she was in love.

He was seventeen then, not quite a man but not a boy either. Until that moment, she hadn't realized it was possible for a man to be beautiful, but Aiden Cavanaugh *was* beautiful. He had the kind of face they patterned superheroes after, like Clark Kent or a young Bruce Wayne. Strong jawed and straight nosed, with hair that fell in a nearly black wave over the left side of his brow. Yes, she wanted to come in. She wanted it desperately. But she was dripping wet and wrapped in a towel.

"I'm wet," she replied sheepishly. "And my feet are all sandy."

"Use the mat. It'll be okay."

She pulled her towel tighter around her shoulders and did her best to scuff the sand off her feet, then tiptoed across the carpet, eventually coming to stand beside him at the bench. "I'm Mallory."

"Nice to meet you, Mallory."

"What was that song you were playing? I've never heard it."

"It doesn't have a name yet. I just finished writing it a few days ago."

Mallory blinked at him, incredulous. "You wrote it? Yourself? How long did it take you?"

"A couple weeks."

He said it like it was nothing, like people his age wrote songs every day. "It's beautiful. Like a story."

Aiden cocked a blue eye at her. "A story?"

Mallory's cheeks went hot. "I just meant it makes you feel things, the way a story does."

"Thanks." He shot her a grin and the dimples reappeared. "It's what music's supposed to do, make you feel things."

Mallory grinned back, absurdly pleased by his approval. "How long have you been playing?"

He rolled his eyes, absently tinkling a few notes. "I can't remember *not* playing. But I think I was around six when I started lessons, so about eleven years. Do you play?"

Since he was *six*? It seemed impossible. Yet he'd said it without batting an eye. "No. I don't play, but I love music." She dropped her gaze as the words left her mouth. She doubted the stuff she listened to would count as music to someone like Aiden. "I just listen to the stuff on the radio, though. Not real music, like you play."

"It's *all* real music," Aiden corrected. "Elton John. Madonna. Prince. All of it."

"Prince?"

"Why not? Just because 'When Doves Cry' wasn't written by some guy in a powdered wig doesn't mean it isn't *real*—or good. All that matters is that the songwriter has something to say and knows how to say it in a way that will make people listen. That's what *real* music does. It gets people to listen long enough for you to say what you have to say. It doesn't have to be some lofty thing played by a string quartet. It just has to reach people, to speak to them."

Mallory exhaled for what felt like the first time since stepping through the French doors. She'd never heard anyone speak so passionately about music. But he didn't sound the way she thought he would, like a guy who'd spent three years in Juilliard's Pre-College program. "But no one plays Prince at a recital. Or Madonna."

"No, but maybe they should. Modern artists have plenty to say." He grinned then and scooted over on the bench, nodding for her to sit beside him. "Listen."

He closed his eyes, playing from memory. Mallory smiled, instantly recognizing the opening bars of Elton John's iconic "Candle in the Wind."

"Tell me that isn't real music," he said warmly. "Or this." Without blinking, he transitioned to a new song. Mallory knew it instantly.

"'Maybe I'm Amazed,'" she blurted proudly. "By the Beatles."

"Close. It's by Paul McCartney, who *was* a Beatle. But this was actually from his first solo album. He wrote it for his wife. And then there's this one." He began to play again, a new song.

"Simon and Garfunkel. 'Bridge Over Troubled Water,'" Mallory said when he stopped playing and looked up. "I love that one. It's not new but they still play it a lot."

Aiden nodded approvingly, like a teacher whose young pupil had finally solved the equation. "Yes, they do. Because it's about something we can all identify with—having someone's back when they feel lost and alone. Listen."

He closed his eyes and picked up the song again, but this time he surprised her by adding the lyrics. His voice was beautiful, warm like honey but with a slightly raw edge underneath. Mallory sat perfectly still, her towel forgotten as the lyrics poured out of him, achingly tender to begin with, but eventually building to something so intense it nearly brought tears to her eyes.

There was an awkward stretch of silence when the song finally ended. Aiden opened his eyes slowly, as if waking from a dream. They stared at each other in the freshly resonant silence. The contents of the room, the furniture, the art on the walls, even the piano, all seemed to fall away as the seconds ticked past, until there was only the blue of his eyes, the sooty line of his lashes, the faint sheen of perspiration gathered on his upper lip.

She felt dizzy, confused by a connection that seemed to require no words. Was *this* love, then? This giddy lightning-bolt sensation in the pit of her stomach? She'd heard girls talk about it. She just never knew it happened so quickly—or so completely. Yes, she concluded in that tongue-tied instant, it must be love. What else *could* it be?

Aiden touched her arm, a smile tugging at the corners of his mouth. He seemed about to say something when he was suddenly preempted by the sound of a throat being cleared. Their heads swiveled in unison, gazes fastening on the woman standing in the doorway—a woman whose eyes were the same startling shade of blue as Aiden's.

Everything about Estelle Cavanaugh was clean and spare, like something from one of those hoity-toity magazines in the grocery store checkout lines. She was tall and lean, with the kind of figure that looked good in clothes, especially if those clothes were expensive—which hers clearly were. She wore a tailored cream suit with a scarf of peach silk, and her low-heeled pumps perfectly matched her handbag.

Mallory forced herself to meet the woman's gaze, aware that she was being studied in return. In her present state, she wasn't likely to fare well.

"Having a concert, are we?" Estelle's voice dripped with thinly veiled annoyance. "Or perhaps it's a beach party? I can't tell."

Aiden ignored his mother's sarcasm. "This is Mallory. She and her mother—"

"I know who she is," Estelle said curtly. "And who her mother is. What I don't understand is what she's doing here. You're supposed to be practicing, Aiden."

"I *was* practicing. Mallory heard me down on the beach and came up to see who was playing."

Estelle shifted frosty eyes to Mallory. "Is that what you were taught? That a young lady just invites herself?"

"*I* invited her," Aiden shot back before Mallory could reply. "We've been talking about music. About modern versus classical, and what qualifies as *real* music."

Estelle's nostrils flared as if she'd suddenly caught a whiff of something spoiled. "I see. And you felt the need to demonstrate?"

Mallory pushed to her feet, realizing too late that her towel had fallen to the floor, leaving her standing in nothing but her still damp and much too skimpy bathing suit. She bent to retrieve the towel, fumbling to cover herself. "I'm sorry. I didn't mean to cause a problem. I'll go."

Aiden touched her arm lightly. "You don't have to."

Estelle aimed a perfectly penciled brow at her son. "She does, actually." She turned, offering Mallory a stilted smile. "My son has a recital next week in Providence. It's important that he practice. And that he do so without interruption."

Mallory nodded, cheeks burning as she sidled toward the open doors. "Yes. Of course."

"Wait," Aiden blurted, half rising from the bench. "I'll walk you down."

Mallory shook her head. "No, I'm good."

All she had wanted at that moment was to slink home and never see Aiden Cavanaugh again. It was apparently what Aiden's mother had wanted too. The next day, a flatbed truck with the words EAST COAST LANDSCAPING painted on its doors had appeared, and by the end of the day, a thick hedge of hydrangea bushes ran nearly the entire length of the property, neatly cutting it off from its neighbor—and the not-quite-fifteen-year-old girl who'd had the temerity to fall in love with Estelle Cavanaugh's son.

Now, fifteen years later, Aiden was gone and the bushes formed a nearly impenetrable wall of riotous lavender blooms, testament to the current state of relations between the Wards and the Cavanaughs.

Ancient history, she told herself as she turned her back to the hedge and made one last sweep of the beach. Not a soul in sight. And yet, as she set off toward the gate, she couldn't shake the feeling that she was being watched.

NINE

ESTELLE

June 17, 1999
Little Harbor, Rhode Island

Estelle stepped back from the French doors, hoping she hadn't been spotted. Snooping on one's neighbors was one thing, being caught in the act quite another.

Resisting the urge to peer out again, she wandered to the dining room, past the china-laden sideboard to the small but well-stocked bar cart. Her hands shook as she poured a few fingers of Lagavulin from the Steuben decanter. Dr. Novak wouldn't approve, but at this point, she didn't see what difference it could make. She took a pull from the glass, welcoming the burn as it went down.

So, she was back—again. How long this time? And why now, for heaven's sake? Perhaps her mother was selling and she'd come home to help her pack. But no. That would be too much to hope for. Why would Helen Ward sell when she hadn't paid a cent for the place?

Poor man, the Admiral.

It was bad enough to have lost Patricia so suddenly. But then to wind up sick himself and fall prey to a scheming caretaker. And not even a nurse—a shady, self-professed herb healer with no actual credentials of any kind. It was too ghastly. A crime, *some* would say.

Estelle had paid a detective a king's ransom to rake through her new neighbor's past. Sadly, he hadn't come up with anything useful, but the woman had lived in six towns in ten years. What normal person needed to pick up and move that often—and with a young daughter in tow?

It didn't make sense. Helen Ward earned a modest living at best, yet according to Aiden, she'd managed to amass a tidy amount of plunder over the years. Antiques, artwork, jewelry, not to mention the bizarre collections said to occupy the third-floor rooms, all conveniently left to her by a string of dying patients who had no living relatives to kick up a fuss when family heirlooms started to disappear.

And the daughter. Mallory. Cut from the same cloth, though perhaps a trifle more subtle than her mother. Estelle drained the remaining contents of her glass, recalling the day she'd walked in to find the girl sitting beside Aiden at the piano, moony eyed and dripping all over her carpet. It had been obvious from day one that the girl would be trouble, though just how *much* trouble she hadn't quite foreseen. Luckily, fate had stepped in.

Luckily.

Even now, the word left a sour taste in her throat—Lagavulin tinged with the bitter tang of guilt. A grandchild. Or it *would* have been. A little boy, perhaps, with Aiden's eyes and his gift for music. If not for fate.

But fate *had* stepped in. And she'd given it a hand, hadn't she, afterward, in the breakup part of things? For Aiden's sake. At least that's how she'd justified it at the time. As a mother, it was her job to keep her son from making a mistake that could ruin his life. And that's what Mallory Ward would have been. A career-stifling, society-crippling anchor around her brilliant son's neck. Of course, he had refused to see it; he'd fancied himself in *love.* But *she* knew.

Her boy, her baby, her gifted prodigy of a son had been on the brink of disaster. She'd been determined that he not make the same mistake she did when she married his father—for *love*. Because she'd learned the hard way, as a starry-eyed girl of nineteen, that sometimes love wasn't enough. In fact, it almost never was. Not when the marital scales were so grossly unbalanced.

She'd done everything she could think of to keep Aiden focused on his future, gently reminding him that he couldn't afford distractions. Marriage would come later. When he'd finished school and solidified his place as one of the world's most acclaimed pianists. But with a *suitable* woman from his own social sphere, someone who could help him achieve all he was meant to, as *she* had done for his father.

A summer dalliance was one thing, but choosing the person with whom to share your life required the careful weighing of pros and cons. Aiden had been too young—and too smitten—to understand all of that, which was why she'd gone out of her way to ensure that there'd be no missteps. The plans were all set to get him safely away. To London for preparation, then on to the Leeds and a brilliant win. Then the silly girl had gone and gotten herself pregnant and Aiden had been ready to chuck the Leeds and march down the aisle, grinning the whole way. Of *course* she'd stepped in. Her son was on the verge of throwing away everything he'd worked for. Everything they'd *both* worked for.

It took a bit of doing to get him back in, a few strings pulled, a favor called in here and there, but she'd managed it. And the girl had made it remarkably easy, essentially giving up without a fight. How could she know her son would take it so hard?

Once again, Estelle's attention fell to the decanter of sixteen-year-old scotch, glowing deep amber in the afternoon light. Maybe one more splash before she went to lie down. To help her sleep. Her gaze lifted to the gilt-framed mirror above the bar. Wide-set blue eyes stared back at her, less blue now than they'd been a year ago. Tired eyes in a tired face.

For a woman in her fifties, she was remarkably well preserved, unblemished and, for the most part, unlined, with high cheekbones and a still-firm jawline. Most of the women in her circle had had work done over the years—and continued to have work done. Nips, tucks, peels, injections. *Preventative maintenance*, they jokingly called it, but she'd never been tempted. Perhaps because she'd been blessed with her mother's bone structure and youthful complexion.

The most beautiful girl in Little Harbor, they used to say—a million years ago, now. But fate—or karma—had caught up with her too, hadn't it, and left its mark? Maybe not so much that others would notice—yet. She was careful with her hair and makeup. But it was taking longer and longer these days. Heavier foundation. More tricks with blush and concealer. Like theater makeup. You created a blank canvas, then layered it on good and thick, until you were who you were supposed to be. Mustn't be sloppy or lazy. Mustn't slip out of character.

The hair was harder, thinning at an alarming rate now. And there was only so much one could do there. At some point, you simply had to surrender. But not yet. She refilled her glass with a heavy hand, then met her gaze again in the mirror.

No. Not yet.

TEN

HELEN

It's near dusk, the setting sun brushing the horizon with strokes of plum and pink and gold, a muted echo of the canvas on my easel. I've gotten fairly good over the years, enough to sell my work at several of the galleries downtown and in Newport. I no longer need the money—the Admiral took care of that—but painting has always been my escape, a kind of refuge when my daily work begins to wear me down.

I glance at the worktable littered with brushes, paint tubes, and brightly smudged rags—company of a sort. And the only kind I keep these days. Except now there's Mallory, home without warning after more than four years.

I feel a bit like Job—*for the thing which I greatly feared is come upon me.* It seems my premonition was correct. Something is definitely wrong. I don't know what. She refuses to say. Or to even admit there *is* something wrong. But this sudden appearance, coupled with the news that she plans to stay the summer, can only mean something's happened. She hasn't stayed more than a handful of days since she left home, and now, suddenly the *whole* summer. Unfortunate timing, some might say. But I've never been the type to believe in coincidence. Her showing up out of the blue this way means something. And not something good.

I watched her earlier from my studio window, disappearing down the beach in the direction of that damned jetty. I should have known it would be the first place she'd go. The place she spent so much time as a teenager. The place they'd spent so much time *together*. But it's the last place she needs to be right now, submersed in all those memories, mourning what she's lost.

I knocked on her bedroom door not long after I heard her come in but she didn't answer. I assumed she was still angry, ignoring me the way she used to after one of our blowups. Instead, when I cracked the door and peered in, I found her asleep, curled up on her side with her hands tucked under her chin—the way she used to sleep when she was little.

I crept to her bedside and stood looking down at her, remembering all the nights I'd come home late to find her already asleep, her clothes neatly laid out for school the next morning. I was tempted to touch her, to stroke the heavy copper waves spilling across her cheek, but I held back, afraid I might wake her. She looked so fragile lying there, so absolutely done in.

It hurt me to see it, to know she's struggling with something and doesn't feel she can share it with me. I missed so much when she was young, so many important moments when I should have been there but wasn't. I grieve those missed moments now, and the closeness we could have had if I had been a better mother. But maybe this unexpected summer together is a chance for a fresh start, an opportunity to atone and create *new* moments. If I can keep her here long enough.

The shadows have stretched from lavender to indigo now, but I'm loath to turn on the lights and chase away the dark. I prefer to savor the last of the day, to stave off tomorrow for as long as possible. And so I sit here in the gathering gloom, staring at a flattening sea, fretting about how I'll tell her—and what I can possibly say to make her stay once I have.

ELEVEN

MALLORY

June 18, 1999

The scent of the sea tickled Mallory awake. She blinked against the spill of light filtering through the curtains. Not the watery gray of city light, flat and concrete colored—this light was soft and sun drenched. And there was a breeze coming from somewhere, perfumed with salt and the distant tang of old bonfires.

For a moment, it felt as if she'd tumbled backward through time, back to the days when summer seemed endless and the future felt ripe with promise. She lay with her eyes closed, drifting in a warm blur of clambakes and sunsets, Bananarama on the boombox and limbs liberally slathered with Hawaiian Tropic. Then she remembered where she was.

Swallowing a groan, she forced her eyes open. From the nightstand, her father's framed face looked back, movie-star handsome in his uniform. If she looked hard enough, she could see herself in him. The broad brow and sharp chin, the long, straight nose. But there was no spark of memory when she looked at the photograph.

He was a familiar stranger whose history she knew only from her mother's stories. And yet, she'd grown up with an inexplicable sense of missing him. Perhaps because after so many tellings she knew his story by heart. How he and Helen had been introduced by friends at a concert. How Helen had reluctantly agreed to go with him to see *Wait Until Dark* a few days later. How William had plied her with flowers and terrible poetry until she finally broke down and agreed to see him a third time. How he'd proposed the day his draft letter arrived—so he'd have a reason to come home in one piece. How they found a justice of the peace in some tiny town in upstate New York, then spent three days in Niagara Falls before he shipped out. But William hadn't come home in one piece. He hadn't come home at all. And Helen had been left with a newborn to raise on her own.

Her mother never wanted to talk about the end of the story, about the day she received the telegram that he'd been killed, or the Purple Heart honoring his sacrifice. It was her way, to avoid uncomfortable things. Memories, confrontation, truths she'd rather not face. It was one of the rare things they had in common.

Her father's things were supposedly in a box somewhere, though she'd never seen them. Helen claimed not to know where they'd gotten to after so many moves, but Mallory thought it more likely that William's personal effects evoked painful memories for her mother and so she'd never pressed the matter. She had his photo; that was enough.

With coffee on her mind, Mallory kicked off the covers, dragged on yesterday's clothes, and padded out into the hall. The door to her mother's room stood open, revealing an unmade bed and a white cotton nightgown puddled on the carpet, both uncharacteristic. Helen had always been a stickler about clothes on the floor, and she never forgot to make her bed.

Mallory listened for signs of life as she made her way down to the kitchen—the clink of dishes, the sound of running water—but like so many mornings growing up, the house was quiet. Unsurprisingly, there was a note waiting for her on the refrigerator.

Mrs. Auerbach has taken a turn and Maureen can't get her settled. Sorry to desert on your first day home. Zucchini muffins in the bread box. Back as soon as I can.

Mallory tossed the note in the trash, then went to make coffee. Maybe it was better that they took each other in small doses at first. There was less chance of clashes that way, and she'd be under no obligation to pretend everything was fine.

When the coffee finished brewing, she carried her mug and a muffin out to the deck. The air was chilly but the sun was already warm. She stood at the railing, fingers curled around her mug, watching warily as a pair of gulls reversed course and made a skimming pass over the deck, clearly eyeing her muffin. She waved them off and turned her eyes to the beach.

No wonder her mother loved to paint out here when the weather was warm. It was like something from a postcard. But Mallory had struggled to feel at home here in the beginning. Not with the house itself, but with the town and its judgmental inhabitants.

Eyebrows might be raised at the inheritance of a silver tea service or pricy antique vase, but when a beachfront home worth seven figures entered the picture, people were bound to talk—and talk they had. Rumors had swirled about patients being manipulated into signing away their fortunes, of poisons that were undetectable to both the palate and police. And there were the nicknames—Angel of Death, Nurse Reaper, Lady Styx—snickered when her classmates thought she couldn't hear. And sometimes when they knew she could.

But her new classmates weren't the only ones trafficking in lurid tales, as she soon learned when she overheard her brassy-haired English teacher, Ms. Stack, cackling to a colleague that one day they'd find out the Ward woman was *a modern-day Giulia Tofana.*

Mallory had never heard the term but felt certain it hadn't been intended as a compliment. It had taken a trip to the library to discover that it wasn't a term but the name of a seventeenth-century Italian poisoner who'd been executed for murdering more than six hundred men with a concoction called Aqua Tofana—a lethal combination of lead, arsenic, and belladonna.

She'd never really entertained the possibility that the rumors might be true. Not seriously. But part of her understood why people might think something sketchy was going on. They'd seen it on TV, after all. On that program that aired on Sundays after football was over. Stories about nefarious caregivers, patient exploitation, and so-called mercy killings.

The talk had never bothered Helen, but it *had* bothered her. It had bothered a *lot* of people. And that was what Mallory had never quite forgiven—the cost of being Helen Ward's daughter. How much of Estelle's refusal to accept her as a future daughter-in-law had been about those rumors? Not that it mattered now. What was done was done. Still, she'd wondered.

As if conjured, Estelle Cavanaugh suddenly strolled out onto the terrace next door. Mallory stiffened viscerally at the sight of her. But something was different. She looked smaller now, diminished somehow in her silvery green wrap, her dark hair loose about her shoulders rather than pinned up in its usual chignon. Maybe it was just the way she was standing, bent slightly forward, as if braced against an invisible wind.

Mallory watched as she reached into the pocket of her robe, withdrawing what appeared to be a pack of cigarettes, extracted one, and put it to her lips. When had she started smoking? Certainly not yesterday, she decided as Estelle lit up, then tipped back her head to send a plume of smoke into the air. There was an almost palpable sense of relief in the gesture, a craving finally sated. There was also a noticeable change in her posture. She stood taller now, more in command. More like the woman Mallory remembered.

She was still staring when Estelle's head suddenly snapped in her direction. Mallory looked away, unprepared for a confrontation, even at this distance. Nothing had changed since that first day in her parlor. Even now, across the hydrangea hedge, she could feel the woman's disdain. As far as Estelle was concerned, she and her mother would always be interlopers, unworthy and unwelcome.

Mallory squared her shoulders and forced herself to meet the woman's gaze. Estelle held the look a moment, then took a final pull from her cigarette, flicked the remains over the railing, and disappeared into the house.

"Good morning to you too," Mallory grumbled as she grabbed her coffee and uneaten muffin and headed back inside.

In the kitchen, she tossed the remains of her muffin and was about to top off her mug when she spotted a loose tea sachet on the counter. Not a standard tea bag you'd get at the market, but one made of unbleached paper with a little drawstring for closure, the kind her mother used for her medicinal teas. She held it to her nose. Ginger and lemon balm—for nausea.

She'd picked up snippets of her mother's knowledge over the years and could identify many of the more common herbs by their scent. She could even remember what some of them were used for, but that was as far as it went. Helen had tried to teach her when she was a girl but she'd wanted no part of the strange remedies stashed in the apothecary cabinet beside the sink.

She opened it now, almost warily, intent on returning the sachet to its proper place. A cloud of mingled scents wafted out, tickling her memory. Sweet. Bitter. Mysterious.

Growing up, there'd been no Neosporin or baby aspirin in the medicine chest, no blue jar of Vicks VapoRub. There was only this cabinet filled with peculiar jars and packets. In the event of an earache or sore throat, her mother would simply whip up one of her concoctions, most of which had been surprisingly effective.

Mallory ran her eyes over the shelves: small round tins of homemade salves, all neatly labeled and arranged by category; amber vials of herbal tinctures and fragrant essential oils; canisters of carefully blended teas. Nothing sinister. Nothing dangerous.

No Aqua Tofana.

Regretting the thought, she dropped the tea bag into the appropriate canister and quickly closed the cabinet, vowing to steer clear of it for the remainder of her visit. The encounter with Estelle had shaken her, and she could feel herself slipping into a mood. The kind that could lead her down a rabbit hole if she wasn't careful.

Her eyes drifted to the ceiling as she felt the familiar tug of Tina's case notes, carefully tucked away in her tote upstairs. She'd basically committed them to memory at this point, and found nothing. There was also no point in calling Muldowney. He'd made it clear that he wouldn't be sharing much of anything. All she could do was wait. Not her strong suit, by any means.

What she needed was a good book to get lost in, like the ones her mother had introduced her to when she was a girl. Jane Austen and the Brontës, Dickens, Gaskell. She'd gotten through entire winters on books like theirs.

Perhaps they were still here somewhere, packed away in one of the upstairs rooms. But the thought of venturing into those cluttered rooms sent a frisson of cold up her spine. She still hadn't shaken the shock of her last impromptu expedition, when she'd wandered into one of the rooms and found sixteen pairs of eyes staring back at her. Were they still there, she wondered—Mrs. Columbo's Victorian dolls, with their glossy curls and empty blue gazes?

She had stared back at them from across the room, breath caught and pulse skittering, waiting for one of them to blink or turn its head. But it wasn't just the dolls. There were plenty of unsettling things in those upper rooms: revoltingly lifelike insects sealed in airtight glass boxes, tiny bird skulls, pale as eggshells, and perhaps most cringeworthy, a pair of lovingly preserved cats named Gillian and Frank.

She had asked once, when she was little, why anyone would collect such creepy things. Helen had gently explained that, like love, *creepy* was in the eye of the beholder, and that loving a thing was all that was necessary to make it precious. Mallory had nodded, pretending to understand, but even now, thinking about those upper rooms made the back of her neck prickle.

On second thought, maybe she'd just head downtown to the bookstore.

TWELVE

MALLORY

At midday, Little Harbor's historic downtown bustled with tourists hunting souvenirs or savoring ice cream from the local sweet shop. Mallory paused on the sidewalk to shift her shopping bags and restore the circulation in her fingers.

She'd gone into Sea & Sand looking for a swimsuit and had ended up with a mini summer wardrobe—and a sizable ding to her credit card balance. She wasn't sure what she'd do with most of it once she was back in Boston, but it felt good to splurge on things that weren't strictly practical.

She had finished rearranging her bags and was about to set off again when she heard a familiar female voice over the hum of tourist traffic.

"Mallory? Oh my goodness! Is that you?"

She turned to find Sloane Pritchett heading in her direction. Sloane was a member of the *old crowd*, as her mother liked to call the circle of friends she and Aiden had been part of. She was also the girlfriend of Aiden's best friend, Kenny, who played trumpet, jazz mostly, and was a huge Miles Davis fan. He and Aiden had played a few gigs together back in the day, at the After Hours Club, and she and Sloane were always there, parked at a table in front, like regular groupies.

They hadn't seen each other since the breakup. But then she hadn't seen any of the old crowd since the breakup. And now, here Sloane was, grinning as if it had been ten days rather than ten years.

"It *is* you! I don't believe it!" Before Mallory could react she found herself swept into an enthusiastic hug. "I had no idea you were back!"

"I'm not," Mallory blurted awkwardly. "Back, I mean. I'm just here for a visit. It was sort of a spur-of-the-moment thing."

"How fun! When did you get here and how long are you staying?"

"I just got in yesterday. As for how long, it's still up in the air."

"Well, I see you've already done some shopping. Rather a lot of shopping, in fact."

Mallory glanced sheepishly at the bags dangling from both hands. "I didn't have much choice. I packed all wrong."

Sloane tossed her head, laughing her wide-open laugh. "Welcome to the club. Kenny says I do it on purpose so I have an excuse to hit the stores."

"How *is* Kenny?"

Sloane's goofy grin said it all. "He's Kenny. How's . . . your mom? I haven't seen her around much but I've been crazy busy."

Mallory hadn't missed the tiny pause. Or the quick dart of Sloane's eyes toward her bare left hand. After so many years it was natural to be curious. "She's fine. You know, always working, but fine."

Sloane stole a look at her watch, then made a face. "Rats! I'd love to do lunch, but I have to meet with the florist and then the caterer. I had no idea planning a wedding was a full-time job." She produced a notebook bristling with multicolored Post-its from beneath her arm, waving it for emphasis. "There's no end to it. I have lists of lists I need to make, and I—" She broke off abruptly, nipping at her lower lip. "I'm sorry. I didn't think. I felt awful when you and Aiden . . ."

Mallory managed a smile. "Don't be. It was years ago, and we were just kids."

"So you're okay about . . . *everything*? I mean, *really* okay? Being back and . . . all?"

"I'm very okay," Mallory assured her, eager to change the subject. "So whose wedding are you planning?"

Sloane beamed suddenly. "Mine!"

"Oh." The answer took Mallory by surprise. "I just assumed you and Kenny tied the knot years ago."

"Well, you know Kenny. He's never cared about all that traditional stuff. Doesn't need a ring or a piece of paper to legitimize . . . yada, yada, yada. But I decided I *do* care. We were always going to do the kid thing and just skip the rings." She paused, shrugging. "What can I say? I *want* the ring. So I proposed. Down on one knee. The whole bit."

This time Mallory didn't need to force a smile. "I'm happy for you. You guys were always great together."

"Oh, say you'll come! It's next Saturday. At the Harbor Club. The whole crew will be there!"

Mallory suddenly felt like a deer in headlights. The last thing she wanted to do while in Little Harbor was attend a wedding. "Oh, no. It's sweet of you to ask, but I couldn't. Really. We'll do lunch, though, and catch up."

"Oh, please, Mallory. You have to be there. Everyone will be thrilled to see you. I'll pop an invitation in the mail as soon as I get home, so you have all the particulars. Oh my gosh. I've gotta run. The caterer will be furious if I'm late again. Wait 'til I tell Kenny you're coming!"

And with that, she was off, hurrying down the sidewalk with her notebook under her arm, leaving Mallory to wonder how she'd scored an invitation to a wedding she had no intention of attending. She'd invent an excuse and politely decline, then send a nice gift. She wouldn't be missed and she'd spare everyone the uncomfortable questions that would ensue.

After one more shift of her shopping bags, she crossed the street, bound for Inkwater Books. It had been one of her favorite haunts back in the day, especially when the weather turned cold and the beach wasn't a possibility. She and Aiden would huddle together at one of the café tables, sipping hot chocolate and poring over travel books, planning all the places they'd visit one day. Rome. Greece. Fiji. They'd never made it to any of them.

Mallory shook off the memories as she stepped into the bookstore. The aroma of freshly ground coffee instantly enveloped her, along with the mingled scents of paper, ink, and freshly waxed floors. The place had always had a delightfully shabby vibe, with cozy armchairs and high, wide windows overlooking the harbor. It felt strangely good to be back, and a relief to find it unchanged since her last visit.

She ignored the bestseller table with its glossy thrillers and murder mysteries and headed for the literature section toward the back. One by one, she scanned the spines lined up on the shelves, smiling whenever she came across a familiar title, as if spotting an old friend in a crowd of strangers. In the end, she settled on *Jane Eyre* and *Wuthering Heights*, two of her old favorites, and *Bleak House*, which she had somehow managed to miss over the years.

She paid for the books at the café register, then ordered a latte and a blueberry scone.

The café was humming, filled with weary afternoon shoppers in need of caffeination, but she was lucky enough to snag a table near the windows. After a few sips of her latte, she extracted the copy of *Wuthering Heights* from her bag and was comforted by a warm rush of nostalgia.

For as long as she could remember, her mother had kept a battered copy on her nightstand and had gifted Mallory with her own copy on her sixteenth birthday. She'd been instantly drawn to the doomed lovers, the way their souls seemed bound by some enduring, invisible thread—the way hers had seemed bound to Aiden's.

She was settled back in her chair and had just turned to the first page when she spotted a trio of middle-aged women at a nearby table, heads bent close. Their faces were vaguely familiar, though no names came to mind. Mallory peered around her book, watching covertly as they whispered over their paper cups, unaware that their conversation was loud enough to be overheard.

". . . ninety-nine percent sure," the woman closest to Mallory was saying. "I'd bet money on it."

"Is it really?" The woman to her right frowned over the bright-blue readers perched on the end of her nose. "It's been so long. I'm not sure."

Woman number three shook her head as she lifted her cup. "I don't think so. Too young."

"No, it's her. Look at the hair. She's obviously back. I wonder if Estelle knows."

In unison, all three women glanced in her direction. Mallory slumped down in her chair, cheeks flaming. *She* was the *her* in question—the one who was *back*. If there had been a way to make a graceful exit, she would gladly have taken it. As it was, she was caught, forced to listen while the old crows picked her bones over afternoon tea.

"Well, if she doesn't, she soon will," the woman in the blue glasses replied gravely. "She'll be right next door."

"Still, someone should call her, to make sure. It would be awful to be blindsided."

"And I suppose you're going to be the one to call?"

"I didn't say that."

"No, but I know you, Peggy. You never miss a chance to stir the pot."

"And you're the soul of discretion, are you? I seem to remember you being pretty interested when it was all happening. And you've certainly had plenty to say about the mother over the years. You just hated it when she moved into that house."

The mother.

"Yes, well, they're hardly our sort. But the daughter is *not* the mother. It was sad, wasn't it, the business with the baby? Though I do wonder about the timing. Still, it must have stung, being thrown over like that. My goodness, you don't think she's back to . . . No, I don't suppose so. Not after all this time. At any rate, I say we keep out of it. Who knows? She might not be here long enough to cause trouble. They might not even cross paths."

"You said it yourself. She'll be right next door. Of course they'll cross paths. And then what? The woman already has her hands full—and now *this*? I say, forewarned is forearmed."

"Well, I don't suppose there's any way to stop you. Anyway, I've got to head out. My new glasses should be ready, and then I need to get to the market."

"Me too. I've got a dinner tonight. The Pattersons with their awful boys. I wish they'd get a sitter. Who brings teenagers to a dinner?"

There was the skitter of chair legs, the shuffle of feet. Mallory waited a few minutes before coming out from behind her book. Her cheeks stung as she gathered her belongings and disposed of her half-eaten scone. She nearly tossed her latte too, but decided to grab a lid instead and take it with her. She stepped up to the counter, waving to catch the barista's eye.

The girl looked up as she handed off a pair of iced coffees. "Need something, hon?"

"Just a lid."

"Oh, sure thing." The barista handed her a lid, already moving on to the next customer in line. "What can we get started for you, sir?"

"Tall, iced, half-caff soy latte."

Mallory wasn't sure if it was the order itself or the voice of the man who'd placed it that made the hairs on the back of her neck stand up. She pivoted slowly, breath caught. And there he was, staring back at her with those sky-blue eyes—Aiden.

"You're back," he said simply, his voice devoid of anything like warmth.

He was still insanely attractive, with his angular face and impossibly broad shoulders, but ten years had wrought their share of changes. His hair was longer now, grazing his collar at the back, and there was a shadow of dark stubble covering the sharp, square line of his jaw. It was a completely new look for him, miles from the well-groomed concert-ready Aiden of her memory. It totally worked, though she suspected this new, slightly scruffy version was a temporary aberration rather than an actual image choice.

"I thought you were in Europe," she managed, realizing the silence had grown awkward.

"Not anymore."

Mallory nodded, feigning a coolness she was far from feeling. "I didn't know, though I hear congratulations are in order."

Aiden blinked at her. "Congratulations?"

"On being the toast of Europe. I'm glad you got what you wanted."

The words sounded false as they left her mouth, the counterfeit sentiment of a scorned woman. But she meant it. She *was* glad for him. She just hadn't planned to have to look him in the eye and say so.

Aiden shifted, thrusting his hands deep in his pockets. "Your mother didn't tell you?"

Mallory blinked at him. "Tell me what?"

"I thought maybe—" He stopped abruptly, shaking his head. "Nothing. Never mind. I just assumed she would have told you I was back."

It took a moment but his words eventually penetrated. "My mother *knew?*"

"Everyone knows. I've been back at my mother's for almost two months."

She'll be right next door. Of course they'll cross paths.

Suddenly, Mallory understood. The old crows hadn't been worried about her running into Estelle. It was Aiden they'd been talking about. They assumed she'd come back because *he* had.

"I didn't know you were here," she said flatly, needing to make it clear that her return to Little Harbor had nothing to do with him. "I came because . . . I just came."

"How long are you staying?"

"I don't know. Things are crazy at work. I could be called back anytime."

He nodded stiffly. "I heard you nabbed a really good job in Boston. Looks like you got what you wanted too."

Mallory stared at him. Did he actually believe that? That she'd gotten what she wanted? She bit her tongue, opting to steer the conversation to safer ground before she said something awkward. "I ran into Sloane this afternoon. She told me about the wedding. I'm happy for them."

"Are you going?"

"To the wedding?" She shook her head. "No. Sloane invited me, but I'll likely be gone by then. And speaking of gone—I need to get home. I'm expecting a call."

"Right. Sure. Well. Guess I'll see you around—or not."

Not, Mallory thought as she turned and made a beeline for the door. *Definitely . . . not.*

THIRTEEN

MALLORY

Mallory's hands were still shaking as she turned her key in the lock and pushed into the foyer, cheeks flaming with a combination of mortification and fury. At her mother. At Aiden. At Estelle's horrid friends in the café. But mostly at herself, for coming back here at all.

Next door. For two months. And her mother had never thought to give her a heads-up. Knowing full well they'd run into each other at some point—and that she'd be completely blindsided when they did. And what about Aiden? Had Estelle mentioned this morning's encounter on the terrace to him? She didn't think so. He'd seemed as surprised to see her as she was to see him. But suddenly, she understood what Sloane meant when she asked if she was *really okay with it*. The question hadn't been about whether she was okay with their broken engagement; it was about whether she was okay with Aiden being right next door.

Well, the answer was no. She wasn't okay with it.

An hour later, Mallory had made a sizable dent in the bottle of merlot she'd found in the pantry. Not her wine of choice, but it would do in a pinch—and this was *definitely* a pinch. She was sitting in the breakfast room, still gnawing on what to say to her mother, when she heard her come through the front door. She took another gulp of wine and waited.

"Hey there," Helen said wearily, dropping her keys and work tote on the kitchen counter. She looked exhausted, her pale hair coming loose from its scrunchie and hanging in limp strands about her face. She frowned as she spied the open wine bottle at Mallory's elbow. "A little early for that, isn't it?"

"How *could* you?"

Helen stared back, her face briefly blank. Finally, her shoulders slumped. There was no confusion in the look, nothing to suggest she didn't understand. "Mallory . . ."

"Don't. Whatever it is you were going to say—don't."

"I wanted to tell you."

"When?" Mallory shoved back her chair and stood, in no mood for excuses. "When did you want to tell me? Two months ago, when he came back to Little Harbor? Yesterday, when he came up at lunch? You knew and you never said a word!"

"I was . . . waiting for the right time."

"The right time would have been before I ran into him at the bookstore, don't you think?"

Helen closed her eyes, sighing heavily. "I didn't know you were going to town."

"Ever?"

"Well, of course, I knew you'd go at some point. I just didn't imagine you'd go today. I didn't know I'd be with Mrs. Auerbach all day. I thought I'd . . ." She shook her head helplessly. "I *was* going to tell you, Mallory. I almost told you yesterday, but I wanted to do it the right way."

"Right way for what? How hard is it to say 'Mallory, Aiden is back'?"

"There's more to it than that, Mallory. A lot more. But I wanted to let you settle in a little, to get used to being back before I told you."

"I got ambushed today!"

"I know. And I'm sorry. That isn't what I meant to happen. If you'll just sit down and let me talk to you—"

It was all Mallory could do not to clap her hands over her ears like a child. Nothing she could say now would erase that fist-to-the-gut moment in the café. That her mother thought there *was* told her just how big a mistake she'd made in coming back. "I don't want to talk. In fact, I was about to go up and start packing when I heard you come in."

Helen's face fell. "You're leaving?"

"Well, I can't stay here, can I? With Aiden right next door. And you knew that when I showed up, which is why you chose to say nothing."

Helen dropped into her regular chair, shaking her head slowly. "Twenty-seven hours. I think that's a new record. You usually manage two or three days before you find some reason to run back to Boston."

"I'm not running back to Boston. I wish I could, but I can't."

Helen's head came up slowly. "Why can't you go back to Boston?"

Mallory looked away, cursing her wine-loosened tongue. "I told you. I have vacation I have to take."

"No. That isn't it. What's happened?"

"You're changing the subject."

"So are you. Please tell me what's going on, Mallory."

"No. We're talking about *this* now. I want to know what you thought you were accomplishing by not telling me Aiden was back. Did it never occur to you to pick up the phone?"

"Only about a hundred times."

"Then why didn't you?"

"I did. I told you I got your machine. But I didn't know how to tell you . . . all of it. So I hung up."

There was an unmistakable whiff of gravity to her mother's response, as if there were still something she hadn't said—something worse. Was he engaged? Married? She tried to remember if he'd been wearing a ring, but he'd kept his hands in his pockets the whole time.

"You've never been shy about sharing news about Aiden," she said warily. "Why now? What's different?"

"Everything's different, sweetheart."

Mallory braced herself. "Is he . . . Is he getting married? Because if that's it you don't need to worry. I don't care what he does with his life. Any more than he cares what I do with mine. But you should have said something yesterday instead of letting me find out on my own. I could have avoided town. As it was, I had to listen to Estelle's friends clucking about how she already has enough on her plate without having to worry about me being back. As if I'd come back—"

"Mallory, for heaven's sake! Please just let me talk!"

Startled by this uncharacteristic outburst, Mallory fell silent.

"Aiden isn't getting married," Helen continued quietly. "He's given up his music."

"What?"

"He's stopped playing."

It wasn't possible. "What? Why?"

"He had an accident. An injury to his left hand. That's why he's back. He's had three surgeries, but there's nothing more they can do for him. It's up to him now."

The words seemed to swim in Mallory's head and she found herself regretting the second glass of merlot. She felt unsteady on her feet, vaguely queasy at the thought of Aiden's music—the thing he loved most, the thing he *was*—going silent.

"What does that mean—it's 'up to him'?"

"The last surgeon referred him to a physical therapist who specializes in this kind of thing—like sports medicine, but for musicians. She prescribed a regimen of exercises to help him regain his strength and dexterity, but after a few weeks, he stopped going. He says it's pointless. If he can't play at full capacity, he won't play at all. But he's not composing either. He's walked away from all of it."

Mallory reached for the back of the nearest chair, gripping it so tightly her knuckles went white. She thought of Aiden in the café, standing with his hands stuffed deep in his pockets. It was an unusual stance for him, but she'd chalked it up to the awkwardness of the moment. Now she realized it was something else. "How do you know all this?"

"Melinda Redding's cleaning woman is also Estelle Cavanaugh's cleaning woman. She hears things. She knows you and Aiden were engaged, so . . ."

"So she tells you," Mallory supplied. "What kind of things?"

"Apparently, Aiden and his mother have been having some real knock-down-drag-outs. He's demanding she get rid of the grand piano. She refuses, of course. Not that I blame her. Music was his life. It must break her heart to think of him giving it up."

"This is what they meant," Mallory said, piecing it together. "The woman at the café. When they said Estelle had her hands full, they were talking about Aiden abandoning his music."

Helen nodded sadly. "It's hard to watch someone you love coming apart at the seams. And even harder when the coming apart is self-inflicted."

"Self-inflicted? You said he had an accident."

"He did. But he's chosen the rest of it. The quitting, I mean. The doctors say there's no reason he can't get himself back where he was. Or at least close. It won't be easy, but it's doable. He's just decided not to try."

"But why would he do that? When he's finally achieved everything he ever wanted?"

Helen looked at her squarely. "Has he?"

Mallory felt a series of warning bells go off. "Don't."

"I just wonder . . ."

"We haven't seen or spoken to each other in ten years. Not so much as a phone call. Please don't drag me into this."

"I wasn't. But I can't help wondering . . . If there was someone in his life, someone he cared for, who cared for him, would he be willing to fight?"

"Maybe there is."

"He's moved back into his mother's house, Mallory. Alone."

"So have I. So what?"

"I just thought he could use a friend. Maybe you could too. I don't know what's going on in your life, but there's something, and you clearly don't want to talk to me about it. But Aiden knows you. And you know him. You could help each other."

"No," Mallory said, shaking her head. "I see where this is going and you can forget it. You're not going to use this to work me. Or Aiden. I've got enough on my plate right now without walking back through *that* door. And I'm sure Aiden has plenty of friends he can talk to."

"But you're the one he needs, Mallory. The one who knows him best."

"Were you not listening? It's been ten *years*. I don't know him at *all* anymore. Sometimes I wonder if I *ever* did. And I'm guessing Estelle would have something to say about me getting involved."

"She might try but he's past listening to her. The years have changed him, Mallory. He's not the Aiden you left."

"I didn't leave, *he* did. And why on earth would he care what *I* had to say?"

"Because he would." Helen was silent a moment, her eyes suddenly clouded with sadness. "For most of us, there's someone—one person—whose soul we know as well as our own. The one we're meant for. The one who's meant for *us*. We know it the minute we meet them. We feel it. A recognition we sense in our bones. And it never goes away . . ." She paused, blinking away a sudden shimmer of tears. "Even when *they* do."

Mallory felt herself soften. She'd heard it before, the pain that crept into her mother's voice on the rare occasions when she spoke about losing her husband. "I know how much you loved my father," she replied gently. "But our story isn't like yours. Aiden didn't die. He left."

Helen pressed her lips tight and was silent for a moment. "He was twenty-two years old when he left for London," she said at last. "Still a boy in many ways, and groomed from day one to live *one* kind of life, to do *one* thing—make music. And all of a sudden he found himself in a situation he never prepared for. Toss in a mother with plans of her own whispering in his ear. Of course he left. He was scared and confused, and being pulled in far too many directions."

Mallory lifted her chin. "I never pulled him."

"No, you didn't. But you should have. He needed you to fight for him, Mallory, to help him find himself. Maybe he still needs it."

It was true. Or at least partly true. She hadn't fought for him. But she shouldn't have had to. Not if he truly wanted to marry her. Instead, he'd packed his bags and gotten on a plane, making what he really wanted all too clear.

"I can't," Mallory said thickly. "I'm crushed by the thought of him giving up his music, but I can't get pulled back in. Nor, as I've already pointed out, would Estelle allow it."

"And as *I've* already pointed out, I doubt Estelle would have much say in the matter. Aiden has changed. He's grown up now, and . . . hardened."

"So am I."

Helen nodded grimly. "Yes, you are."

Mallory stifled a groan. They were talking in circles now, and getting nowhere. "Look, I know what you want to happen, Mother, but it isn't going to work. I even get you wanting to wait a little to tell me Aiden was back. Sort of. But seriously, you have to stop pushing him at me. I'm not his fiancée anymore. I'm not his anything."

"I just thought if anyone can figure out what's holding him back, it's you."

Mallory stepped away, her limbs impossibly heavy. She couldn't go another round over Aiden. She simply didn't have it in her. "I'm going up now."

"To pack?"

"To sleep."

Hope flickered in Helen's eyes. "So you're staying?"

"For now. Though not for the reason you hope."

"No," Helen shot back dryly. "It's because you have all those vacation days."

FOURTEEN

HELEN

I raise the window, letting the night air pour in, still thick with the afternoon's warmth. I'm back in my tower, alone with my thoughts, wondering how, in less than two days' time, I could have made such a mess of things. A foolish question, and one to which I already know the answer. The same way I've made a mess of most of my life—with another sin of omission.

My specialty.

I had hoped to find the right moment—knowing full well that there would *never* be a right moment. Not for that kind of news. And now she's angry with me. Rightly so, I suppose, given the way things played out, but as with most things, there are two sides to Aiden and Mallory's story. The one she clings to and the one I actually watched play out. She made mistakes—they both did—but it might be fixable, if she'd just get out of her own way.

Aiden needs her, though I doubt he knows it yet. And she needs him. Much more than she's willing to admit. I saw her face when I told her the news. It was as if I'd told her his heart had stopped beating. That's when I knew. After all these years, all the heartache and tears, she's never stopped loving him. I know how it feels to love like that, and to then lose that love. But she doesn't want to hear it from me.

That's what comes of missing so much of your daughter's life. You lose your place, your right to offer advice and deliver hard truths. And after all, what could I, a middle-aged woman who's lived most of her life alone, know about love or heartbreak?

I can't bear to think of her ending up like me. Alone. Or worse, with the wrong man. Perhaps if she knew my story, or at least the beginning of it. But I can't tell the beginning without telling the end, which is why I've never told her any of it. I haven't forgotten the promise I made, to tell her everything one day. Not the half-truths she believes now, but how it *really* was. What I did—and why. And I will tell her. One day. When things are better between us.

It hurts to recall those bitter days, the pain of mutual betrayal still shockingly raw. But there were happy times too, in the beginning, memories painstakingly recorded on nights when I couldn't sleep, penned to keep the loneliness at bay. Letters to a ghost. Pages and pages of them. They're beckoning now, my unanswered scribblings, but can I bear to turn back to those early pages and relive it all again? The making and unmaking of us?

I think perhaps I can. Or at least must.

◆ ◆ ◆

July 12, 1984

Dearest,

It's me—your Mouse. But I suppose you know that. Who else would be scribbling in this book at this silly hour? I'm anxious tonight, haunted by the fear that my memories of you will fade and I'll lose what little I have left of you. Perhaps if I write them all down, fill these pages with every detail I can remember, I'll rest easier. How long has it been since that first miraculous day? Seventeen years? No, eighteen. But in my mind, in my heart, it's yesterday.

It's a frigid day in January. They've closed school because it snowed all night and the plows couldn't keep up. I hate snow days. Not because I love school, but because I hate being cooped up all day. My mother is gone, to mass first, then to work at the rectory office, where she attempts to earn her way into heaven each day by answering the phone and managing the books.

I bundle myself up to my eyes, drag on my boots, and trek the six blocks to the library, a favorite escape and one of the few places my mother lets me go on my own. Most of the tables are full—other kids with nowhere to go—but no one I know. I'm glad. I don't want to talk to anyone. I just want to find a corner somewhere and read my battered copy of Jane Eyre.

I've already read it a dozen times and practically know it by heart, but it's one of my favorites, along with the rest of the Brontë sisters' works. And there's Austen and Gaskell and Alcott too, all on my favorites list. I love the language, strange new words that feel like confections on the tongue. And the characters: breathless heroines on the cusp of adventure, dark heroes with secret pasts. It's how I wish I was, adventurous, defiant. But I'm none of those things. Which is why I devour them, I suppose— despite my mother's thinly veiled disapproval—to escape my own stifling existence.

I find an empty table near the back where the science books are shelved and peel off my scarf and gloves, then extricate my book from my coat pocket. My cheeks are hot and stinging after the walk, my hands stiff with cold. I settle back in my chair and open the paperback. I've reached the part where Jane discovers Mr. Rochester's bedroom is on fire, so I'm too engrossed to look up when someone drops into the chair across from me.

I feel eyes on me as I continue to read. Curious eyes that linger and annoy. I keep my head down and continue reading until the fire is out and Rochester has bid Jane an emotionally fraught good night. I look up then, ready to give my interloper a cold stare—and there you are, all copper eyes and russet waves, with a mouth that's not quite smiling but wants to.

Suddenly, I can't breathe, and I have no idea why. I've never felt so completely dazed, unable to respond in any rational way. I finally manage a nod and you smile. You're holding a tired-looking copy of The Great Gatsby, which I've never been crazy about—Daisy is a ghastly woman—and I wonder if you're reading it because you want to or because it's required for English class. I should ask, but I can't make my mouth move.

We sit like that for a while, staring at each other across the table. You're older than me. A year. Maybe two. And tall. Even sitting down I can tell. Finally, you look down at your book again, and I pretend to look at mine. I'm so very aware of you. Of the way you sit forward in your chair, the way you slowly turn pages, smoothing each one so it lies flat, the way you smell, all fresh and clean and green. Like summer.

The thought is still in my head when you look up and catch me staring. You don't say anything, just reach into the pocket of your coat and pull out a fistful of Tootsie Rolls. You put them on the table, closer to me than to you. An offering. In return, I produce a pack of Red Vines and set it down beside the Tootsie Rolls. Two hours later, the candy's gone and you push back from the table, gathering our wrappers and stuffing them into your pocket.

"I have to go," you say, as if apologizing.

They're the first words you've spoken and I'm briefly off balance, partly because your voice is so low and unexpected, but also because I realize I don't want the afternoon to end.

My own voice feels rusty when I finally find it. "Okay. Thanks for the Tootsie Rolls."

"I'll be back tomorrow. Around the same time."

Your words go up a little at the end, like a question, and my stomach does a little somersault. It's all I can do not to break into a grin. "Yeah," I say, trying to sound offhand. "Maybe I'll see you."

The next day I bring Razzles. You bring root beer barrels. We talk finally, about books mostly. You like the classics almost as much as I do, but your taste runs to Hugo and Dumas, even some Hemingway, whose prose I find tedious. I vow to convert you to my way of thinking. We laugh and get shushed by the librarian, and promise to meet again the next day.

And so it begins. Our reading dates. At the library until the weather breaks, then outdoors when the days finally warm. We trade books at first, and discuss them after, then start reading them together. After school, we find a tree behind the stadium and take turns reading aloud, playing the various characters, until you're forced to admit the Brontës are, in fact, superior to Hemingway, though perhaps not to Dickens.

I've never had a friend like you, or thought it was possible to feel this way, like I've finally found the other half of myself—like I'm finally whole. I tell my mother none of this. Not even your name. She'll want to meet you, and I can't let that happen. Since my father died it's just her and me in a house full of rules and mistrust. Never any laughter. Never any joy. Because happiness is a sin. For her, almost everything is. And so I keep you a secret.

◆ ◆ ◆

We see each other nearly every day. We go to the same school. You're a year ahead of me though, sixteen to my fifteen, so we don't share any classes. Still, we manage to connect, writing long notes during classes and slipping them into each other's lockers throughout the day. We're quite aware of how silly we are, a pair of misfits always huddled over our books, but neither of us cares what the other kids whisper. At least you don't, and I've learned to pretend fairly well.

By summer we've even taken to calling each other "dearest," a silly homage to the books we both love. We tell each other our deepest secrets, our dreams, our heartbreaks, our very worst fears. Yours is that you'll never be a famous folk singer. Mine is that I'll lose you.

Thankfully, my mother's too busy with God to notice I'm gone way more than I used to be, or that my grades have begun to slip a little. For the first time in my life, I have something other than books to keep me company.

We've started going to your house after school. You live with your mother in a small rented house with a saggy porch and a tiny backyard with a tree and a tire swing. Your mom's usually home in the afternoons. Her name is Donna but she goes by Raven, because her grandmother was one-quarter Pequot. And because it sounds more artsy than her real name.

She makes jewelry and grows herbs to use in teas and salves. She lets us hang out with her and teaches us about what she calls earth medicine. She also teaches me to paint.

She says I'm good. No one's ever said I'm good at anything before. I see now why you're so wonderful. How could you not be with a mother like that?

It's hard going home after spending time with Raven. My mother isn't artsy, or free-spirited, or fun. Her world revolves around mass and confession, lighting candles and atoning for sins, though what sins she might have committed I can't imagine. She drags me to mass every week and forces me to go to confession. I never know what to say to the priest and find myself wondering if the things I confess are actually sins against God or just sins against my mother.

Before we leave, we light a candle for my father, who died when I was seven. A heart attack, according to my mother, but I overheard a neighbor once talking about how he had too much to drink one night and wrecked his car and that no one was surprised that there'd been a woman with him when it happened. When I asked my mother about it she slapped me and told me to never repeat the lie again. I tell you though the very next day, because I tell you everything. In return, you confess that your mother doesn't even know who your father was and that neither of you is the least bit ashamed of it because what other people think doesn't matter. All that matters is living your truth.

I wonder when you say it if you're trying to make a point. You can't understand why I haven't brought you home to meet my mother. You think I'm ashamed of you, of who you are and how you and your mother live. But it isn't that. My mother wouldn't understand us, the bond we've forged, the way you make me feel. I barely understand it myself.

Who knew one kiss could change everything?

We're on your back porch and you're singing me a song you've been working on. You're not very good but I don't care. I can't take my eyes off your face, the way your eyes shine when you sing, and something in my chest turns over. You notice suddenly and put down your guitar, leaving the song unfinished. Then you lean over and touch your lips to mine.

I've never been kissed before, but I realize suddenly that I've been waiting for this moment since that first day in the library when I looked up from my book and saw your face. But how can that be? How can you want something you don't know exists? I do, though—I want it so badly I feel like my skin is on fire—and it terrifies me.

All I can think as I pull away is that this is the sin my mother warned me about. The kind that damns you to hell. The kind that can never be forgiven. I'll have to tell Father Ryan on Saturday, say out loud in that dark tiny space that even though I stopped you I didn't want to, that secretly I wanted more, wanted everything*—even if I didn't know what* everything *was.*

"I'm so sorry," I whisper as I pull away. "I know that you . . . that we . . ." My voice falters and my eyes fill with tears. Pushing you away feels like a betrayal, a denial of everything I feel, but this leap from friendship to something else, something so new and completely irrevocable, terrifies me. "I'm . . . I can't."

"It's okay." You smile, your voice so gentle it makes my throat ache. Because you understand what I can't yet, that every book and note and shared afternoon has all been leading to this moment. And that inevitably, this moment will come again.

FIFTEEN

ESTELLE

June 19, 1999

Estelle fought to control the tremor in her right hand as she placed her coffee cup back in its saucer. Her head was splitting and the morning sun slanting through the blinds wasn't doing her any favors.

Across the table, Aiden sat watching her, his breakfast untouched as he waited for an answer to his question. He'd barely spoken to her after returning home yesterday, saying just enough to paint a picture of the moment he'd bumped into Mallory at the bookstore. He'd been positively livid—and clearly still was.

"How long?" he demanded again. "How long have you known she was back? And don't say you didn't know. I saw your face when I told you about the bookstore."

"The day before yesterday," Estelle said finally. "I saw her on the beach. Then again yesterday morning when I was out on the terrace."

"Two days. And you didn't think to tell me?"

Estelle curled her hands in her lap, unnerved by her son's brittle calmness. He was always angry these days, but this quiet, impermeable rage was worse somehow. "I wasn't sure . . ." She broke off, groping for something that might assuage his anger—and exonerate her. "I'd hoped it wouldn't be necessary."

"You hoped it wouldn't be *necessary*? To tell me my ex-fiancée was back in town and living right next door?"

"She isn't *living* next door, Aiden. She just pops up every now and then, for a visit. But she never stays more than a few days. I hoped—"

"I know exactly what you hoped," Aiden shot back. "That she'd leave before I knew she was here. That somehow, in this fishbowl of a town, we would avoid bumping into one another."

Estelle folded her napkin and laid it aside with a calm she wasn't close to feeling. Aiden continued to stare, suddenly so like his father that she found it difficult to hold his gaze. The same dark good looks, the same wave of dark hair sweeping across his forehead, the same broad, unsmiling mouth. They were *so* alike. Clever. Driven. Soft spoken. Until crossed.

"Yes," she replied finally. "That's exactly what I hoped. I didn't want you to be distracted. You need to focus on getting well, Aiden. Dr. Stillwell says—"

"I don't give a damn what Dr. Stillwell says. We're talking about *this* now. About Mallory, and why you think it's your place to decide what I should and shouldn't know."

"I *told* you why. I didn't think it would matter." She hated that she sounded so rattled, so guilty, but the truth was she was both. "What was the point of upsetting you, dredging it all up again, if she was going to be gone in a few days?"

Aiden shoved back his plate, sending his knife clattering to the floor. "You just can't stop meddling, can you? You always know what's best for your darling boy. Except I'm not a boy anymore and haven't been for a long time. I get to decide what's best for me. Not you—*me*."

His words landed like a series of small slaps, stinging and sharp. Estelle lifted her chin, forcing herself to meet his gaze. "And if I *had* told you? What then?"

"I don't know. But it was *my* choice to make. Do you know what it felt like to run into her like that? To see her and think for a moment that maybe she knew I was here and that's why she came back?" He paused, raking his good hand through his hair. "And then to realize she had no idea I was even here, let alone the rest of it? All I could do was stand there like an idiot with my hands in my pockets, listening to her congratulate me on my success. My *success!*"

His words sent little fractures through Estelle's heart. He did that now, kept his hands in his pockets, behind him, or under the table, as if his scars were something to be ashamed of. "I'm so sorry, Aiden."

"Are you?"

Estelle blinked at him, startled by the question. "Of course I am. How can you even ask?"

"Apart from your history with Mallory, you mean?"

All right, she supposed she had that coming. There *was* a history, and not a pretty one. But she really *had* meant well. Surely he knew that. "I've only ever wanted you to be happy, Aiden. To have the kind of life you deserved. You were both so young and from such different worlds. Neither of you knew what you wanted. Not really. You needed time to grow up, to find yourself. And look how things turned out for you. And for her."

"Yes," Aiden growled. "Look how things turned out."

"I only meant—"

"I know exactly what you meant. You wanted me to have the life *you* thought I deserved. What I wanted never mattered. And still doesn't, apparently."

Estelle chose to ignore this. After everything he'd been through, she couldn't blame him for lashing out. "I know you're hurting, Aiden, that what's happened has knocked you down, but you'll feel better once you're playing again. Dr. Stillwell says . . ."

"Stop! We've been over this. I'm done with Dr. Stillwell. Done with the sessions. Done with all of it."

There it was again, the finality that had been filling her with such dread of late, but plainer now than she'd ever heard it. She willed herself to stay calm, to exercise restraint. "All right. What will you do instead?"

"Live off my trust fund, presumably."

Estelle stiffened in spite of herself. "That's not funny, Aiden."

"I promise you, I am the last person to whom that needs to be made clear. But let's not pretend, Mother dear. My music was never about needing to make a living."

"No, it wasn't. But you have a gift, Aiden. The ability to create music that touches people's souls. Beautiful, astonishing music. From the time you were little, you've dedicated yourself to developing that gift, exploring and honing it. All the practice and preparation, proving yourself over and over again, reaching the pinnacle of your profession. And now you're willing to throw it all away because it's suddenly gotten hard."

Aiden surprised her by smiling, as if she'd actually said something amusing. "That's what you think is going on? I'm afraid of the work?"

Estelle's brows lifted. "Aren't you?"

"No. At least not the way you're thinking."

Something in his voice sent a fresh pang of alarm through her. "Then *what?*"

"I don't care," he said simply.

Estelle sighed. It was a little boy's answer, peevish and sullen. "What don't you care about?"

"All of it. Any of it. I just don't care. And it terrifies me—or would if I gave a damn. But I don't. None of it means anything."

Estelle felt her face grow pale. "Oh, Aiden . . ." It was all she could do not to reach for his hand, to clasp it tight and tell him everything would be all right, but she knew better than to try. For the first time since his return, she began to wonder if everything *would* be all right.

"Please don't feel sorry for me, Mother. God knows I've had a bellyful of that over the past year and a half. The pitying looks and well-meaning clichés. Everyone's so damn supportive. But none of it can fix what's wrong."

Estelle sat silently, digesting his words. She'd heard it before, the bitterness and the tamped-down anger. But this felt different. This felt like resignation and it felt . . . final. Only she couldn't let it be. Not after everything he'd accomplished. "You know," she said evenly, "I've read that it's not uncommon to suffer depression after an injury. Maybe it's time to think of this as more than just a physical condition, Aiden. Maybe it's time to talk to someone."

Aiden let out a sigh as he pushed to his feet. "As usual, you've managed to not hear a damn word I say. But you're not off the hook. Not by a long shot. I promised to help Kenny and Sloane with a few things for the wedding this morning, but count on us continuing this conversation when I get back."

Estelle bit hard on her lower lip as she watched him go, the ache at her right temple thumping in earnest now. He'd calm down, and then she'd try again to make him see sense. Perhaps it really was time to consult with a therapist, someone who specialized in post-injury trauma. She'd done some reading on the subject when Aiden first came home. About athletes mostly, who were reluctant to reengage, even after doctors pronounced them ready to return to play. Aiden was exhibiting many of the same signs. Insomnia. Defeatism. Anger.

So much anger.

He'd always been so calm and steady, so hard to rattle. It was a trait that had served him well as he worked to master difficult skills and techniques, the ability to stay on task. Now the least little thing seemed to send him over the edge. One minute, he was fine; the next, he had a face like thunder. It was seeing Mallory again, and so unexpectedly, that had him so agitated. Why had the girl chosen now to come back and stir up trouble?

It had been naive to hope Aiden wouldn't find out she was back. Little Harbor was just that—little. No one kept a secret for long. Or almost no one. She'd kept a few, though, over the years, hadn't she?

Her husband asking for a divorce, for instance, just before boarding a plane for an overseas business trip. They'd had a terrible fight. Seventeen years of grievances erupting like Vesuvius after a long sleep, reducing their marriage to a heap of rubble and hot ash.

The argument had gone on so long he'd nearly missed his flight. He'd made it, though. And she'd begun planning how to smooth things over when he returned, to bring him around like she always did. If she was good at anything, it was bringing people around to her way of thinking. And then the call came the day he was scheduled to come home, someone in George's office telling her to turn on the news. A private jet carrying seven passengers and a crew of three had gone down over the Atlantic. No survivors.

And then there was the woman he'd been carrying on with. No one knew about *her* either. At the time, even *she* hadn't known—until weeks later, when she was hunting for insurance papers and found the evidence in George's desk. Receipts. Photographs. Letters.

Anna.

Not an upgrade by any measurable standard. Not younger. Not more beautiful. Rather plain, as a matter of fact. She'd gone to see her, to demand the truth. She'd gotten it too: it had been going on for four years and they'd planned to marry as soon as George was free.

She never told a soul. Especially not Aiden. The humiliation would have been too much to bear. And nothing would have been served by tarnishing George's memory. Instead, she had squared her shoulders and played the grieving widow. That part hadn't been difficult. She *had* grieved for her husband, more than even she'd expected.

It was the rest of the charade she'd struggled with, the pretense that George had been a devoted husband and father when he'd actually been preparing to bolt for greener pastures. People still talked about him. What a pillar of the community he'd been. What a generous philanthropist he'd been. What a fine boy he'd raised. But it had been her. The children's hospital wing. The new library. The community center. All of it had been *her* doing.

Especially the fine son.

Aiden had always been hers. Her *project*, George had called him on more than one occasion. When it came to their son's musical abilities, he'd been astonishingly apathetic. Or perhaps *resentful* was a better word. But a gift like Aiden's required shepherding: interviewing teachers, researching schools, overseeing practices, and arranging recitals. George had always been too busy for such things. With his business at first, and then with Anna.

Circumstances had dictated that she be both mother and father to her son, and she had been, always guiding him with a firm and loving hand. And she wasn't through yet.

SIXTEEN

MALLORY

Mallory groaned as she turned on the tap and bent over the bathroom sink, kicking herself for ingesting a second—had there been a third?—glass of merlot last night. She knew better than to drink red; it always gave her one of those ice-pick headaches behind her right eye. She'd tried to sleep it off, burrowing back under the covers until nearly ten, but the ache was still there, accompanied by a low-level nausea that probably had as much to do with yesterday's revelations as with her choice of libation.

Aiden home. Aiden hurt. Aiden abandoning his music.

And her mother's suggestion that she might be able to help. Ludicrous. Which she would have known had she been in the café yesterday to see the look on Aiden's face. He'd been polite enough, but so stilted and awkward, as if he'd just bumped into the local undertaker.

Stifling a groan, Mallory studied her dripping face in the mirror, pale and newly sharp, her eyes smudged with shadows. Had she looked like this yesterday? Worn down and hollowed out? No wonder her mother kept asking what was wrong. She needed coffee. And maybe an early swim to get her blood pumping. But definitely coffee first.

But before she could hit the stairs, the sound of her cell phone going off sent her scurrying back to the bedroom. Her pulse ticked up when she saw the 617 area code. Boston.

"This is Mallory."

"It's John Muldowney. I'm sorry to bother you while you're on vacation."

"No, it's fine. I'm just visiting my mom. Has something happened?"

"Maybe. Any idea when you might be back in town?"

Mallory's pulse ticked up. "Why?"

"Early on in your case notes, you mention a boyfriend, a guy who went by the nickname Sticks, but we didn't find any mention of his actual name. We were hoping you might remember it—or anything else about him. Maybe where he lived or worked."

Mallory perched on the edge of the bed as she combed her memory. She knew who he meant—the guy Tina had been seeing when she was picked up by the police. "I never knew his real name. Tina said he went by Sticks because he hung out at the local pool halls, hustling games for beer."

"Sounds charming. What else?"

"Not much, really. He was older than she was—five years, maybe six—and trouble with a capital *T*. It's all in the notes. She started skipping school after she met him, sneaking out of the house in the middle of the night. She'd get grounded for breaking curfew, only to slip out again the next night, over and over, until she finally ran away."

"And wound up in Lowell, charged with possession of stolen credit cards."

"Yes," Mallory said quietly. But Tina wasn't that girl anymore. In fact, she had never been that girl. She'd just gotten tangled up with the wrong crowd. Muldowney needed to know that. "She didn't steal the cards. They were just in the pocket of the jacket she was wearing when the police found her. She made a full statement when they brought her in. It was Sticks's jacket. She couldn't give them his real name; she didn't know it. And the only address she knew was the apartment where they found her, and that belonged to someone else. He disappeared after they picked her up. As far as I know, she never saw him again. Do you think he was involved?"

"When we worked the neighborhood, a cabbie remembered seeing a male in his midtwenties hanging around the vacant lot a few days before Tina died. Tall, thin, with spiky hair and a tattoo of an eight ball on the back of his neck. The tattoo jumped right out at me. Did you ever see the guy?"

"No. Like I said, he disappeared when . . . Oh, wait. I *did* see a photo once. A Polaroid of them taken at a park somewhere. Tina made a big deal of cutting it up and throwing the pieces in my trash can—like a kind of ritual."

"I don't suppose the back of his neck was visible in the Polaroid?"

Mallory closed her eyes, trying to summon the image. It had been of the two of them. They were drinking beer and goofing for the camera. Sticks's arm had been loosely draped around Tina's shoulder, a cigarette clamped between his fingers.

"No. Sorry. They were both looking straight at the camera."

"Do you know if Charlene Allen ever met him?"

"I don't think so. I can't imagine Tina bringing him around to meet her mother."

"Right. Not exactly boyfriend material. Charlene did mention a new guy Tina had been seeing, though, named Bobby Markle. Know anything about him?"

Mallory frowned, rolling the name around in her head. "No," she replied finally. "Tina never mentioned him. Is he . . . What kind of guy is he?"

"A Boy Scout by comparison. And his alibi checks. Probably not our guy."

"So you think it was this . . . Sticks?" She cringed this time as the name left her mouth. It sounded like something from a Raymond Chandler film.

"I don't know, but it's certainly worth pursuing. Be easier if we had a name, though."

"What happens now? Will you arrest him?"

"At this point, we're just calling him a person of interest. We've got a whole list of questions for him but we need to find him first. And when we do, we'd like you to come back and take a look. If we can confirm that Tattoo Man and Sticks are one and the same, we can establish both a relationship and a motive. If he's not, we can at least rule him out."

"You mean a lineup?"

"Something like that."

Mallory felt a flutter of dread as she contemplated what all of this might mean. It was hardly an original story—spurned boyfriend seeks revenge. But Tina hadn't mentioned Sticks in months. Nor had she mentioned anyone named Bobby Markle. What else might Tina have been keeping to herself?

"Ms. Ward? Did I lose you?"

"No. Sorry. I'm still here. Should I head back to Boston? I'm near Newport now."

"Not yet. You're an hour and a half away at best. Until we actually find him, just sit tight and enjoy your time with your mom."

Mallory's head was spinning by the time she ended the call. As someone who dealt with troubled teens on a daily basis, she was no stranger to the juvenile justice system, but the cases she dealt with usually involved drugs, petty theft, or sexual abuse. She'd never been involved in a murder investigation.

At least they had a lead. And a promising one, it seemed. Not that she relished the thought of coming face-to-face with the man—or at least *one* of the men—who'd murdered Tina Allen. But she'd happily do it if it meant justice for Tina—and closure for her. Plus, she'd be leaving Little Harbor with a perfectly valid excuse in her pocket. She wasn't running away; she was returning to Boston to do her civic duty.

Downstairs, she was surprised to find her mother in the kitchen. She just assumed Helen would be with Mrs. Auerbach again, but there she was, sliding a batch of blueberry muffins into the oven. She glanced up as Mallory entered and reached for a towel to wipe her hands.

"Good morning," she said tentatively, then narrowed her eyes, peering more closely. "Not a good night, though, I can see. You're looking a bit green around the gills."

Mallory chose to ignore the remark, mostly because it was true. "I didn't expect to find you home. I figured you'd be with Mrs. Auerbach."

Helen shook her head grimly. "Poor Claudia. She made it so much harder than it had to be, but she transitioned unexpectedly this morning. Maureen called to let me know. At least her last night was an easy one."

"She left you something, presumably?" Mallory remarked dryly. "Heirloom shot glasses or her collection of ugly Christmas sweaters?"

"A photo album," Helen replied without missing a beat. "She was the child of Holocaust survivors. She wanted to make sure someone remembered her family when she was gone."

Mallory dropped her gaze, instantly ashamed. "Sorry. That was crappy of me."

Helen sighed as she pulled a mug from the cupboard and handed it to her. "Forget it. I suspect it was a rough night for us both. Have some coffee. The muffins will be done in a few minutes. I can make eggs too. And there's fresh grapefruit juice in the fridge."

"No, thanks. Don't go to any trouble. Coffee's fine."

Helen's lips pinched tight, her expression suddenly pained. "I said I was sorry, Mallory, and I am. I should have told you about Aiden."

"It isn't that," Mallory replied, spooning sugar into her mug. She should just come out with it, tell her mother something had come up and she needed to go back. But she didn't want it to be a thing—and it would be. And before it was all over, she'd have to tell her about Tina, and she still wasn't ready to do that.

"Then what?"

"I've just got a lot on my mind. I told you that when I got here."

"You did. But you never said *what* things. I'm worried about you, sweetheart. You look like death warmed over and you're as jumpy as a cat. And don't tell me it's about yesterday. You've been like this since you arrived. Did you get fired?"

Mallory stared at her, startled by the question. "Why would I get fired?"

"I have no idea, but something's going on, and until you tell me what, all I can do is guess. Are you in some kind of trouble?"

Mallory heaved a long, slow sigh. Her mother clearly wasn't going to let it go. "No, I didn't get fired. And no, I'm not in trouble. But I might have to go back to Boston."

Helen's face fell. "When?"

"I don't know. A day or two."

"When will you know?"

"I'm waiting for a call."

Helen nodded, making a valiant, if failed, attempt to disguise her disappointment. "Well, then, I guess I better enjoy you while I can. Will you let me make you breakfast? We can sit out on the deck and talk."

The mere mention of food made Mallory queasy. "I'm not really hungry. I was thinking of taking a swim."

"Please, Mallory. Just breakfast. You can swim after." She broke off, swallowing hard. "You're not even gone and I'm already missing you."

"All right. But just—" Before Mallory could finish, her cell phone went off. She pulled it from her pocket. Jevet's name and number lit up the screen. "Sorry," she said, handing her coffee mug back to Helen. "I need to take this."

"Of course. I'll start on breakfast."

Mallory hurried out onto the deck pulling the sliders closed behind her. "Hey, Jevet. I was about to call you. Detective Muldowney phoned to say they might need me to come back for a lineup, so I was thinking I'd just head back this afternoon, and maybe—"

"Good morning to you too," Jevet replied, effectively cutting her off. "And let me stop you right there. Yes, they're looking at a guy, but that's all it is at this point. There's no reason to come back yet. Especially now that the details have started to leak. Ellis's mob is camped out in front of the building with signs and bullhorns. They'll pounce the minute you show your face—which is why you're not *going* to show it until you have to. Muldowney will let us know when they find the guy—*if* they find him. Until then I need you to sit tight."

Mallory closed her eyes, afraid to ask. "What kinds of details?"

"Don't, honey. Don't go there."

"Have they released the tox results? Or at least told you?"

"Mallory . . ."

"They did. Tell me."

There was a beat of silence, the slightest hesitation. "They don't really want—"

"So there *were* drugs? I don't understand. I saw her the week before. How did I not—"

Jevet sighed wearily. "Baby girl, *this* is exactly why I put you on leave. I get that you care. We *all* care. But you have to stop punishing yourself. It isn't healthy."

"I can. I will. As soon as I know what happened."

"And if it turns out you *did* miss something?" Jevet prodded. "It happens. They know what we want to hear, so that's what they tell us. What if it turns out Tina was playing you the whole time? Will you really be able to let it go? Or are you always going to be carrying this around, waiting for the next time?"

Mallory swallowed and was quiet for a beat. "I don't know."

"That's what I'm afraid of," Jevet said quietly. "And I'm not trying to rub salt in the wound here, but this gig isn't for everyone. It's messy and it's sad. Sometimes it's tragic. For most of us, the good we do outweighs the bad we see, but that might not be true for you. There's no shame in admitting that—and changing course if that's what you need to do."

Mallory knew she shouldn't be stunned but somehow she was. "You honestly don't think I'm cut out for this, do you?"

"I didn't say that. And it isn't about what I think. Or what the review committee is going to think when all of this wraps up. It's about how and where you want to use your gifts. I'd hate to lose you—you're a caring professional with so much to offer—but the old adage about securing your own oxygen mask applies here. You can't help anyone until you help yourself. That's where we are now, at the help-yourself phase. I'm not trying to be harsh. I know how hard this has been for you, but it's hard for me too, watching you fall apart every time something like this happens."

"I didn't fall apart."

"Yeah, baby, you did. You just hadn't fallen *down* yet. But that part was coming too." Her voice had taken on that warm, deep maternal tone, the one that made it hard to interrupt. "I need you to listen to me. As your friend, as your supervisor, whatever works. I've seen this before and I know where it goes if you keep ignoring it, and I promise you, it's nowhere good. I think it might be time to explore some other options, and to be really honest with yourself about what's next for you. You're not going to do that if you're back here, up to your neck in it. Which is why I'm asking you to just stay put and take care of yourself."

"I'm going crazy, Jevet."

Jevet responded with one of her snorty laughs. "Take a breath, honey. It's been three whole days. Find something to fill your time. Maybe something that makes you feel useful."

"Useful how?"

"That's up to you. And now I've got to get off here and get some work done. I'm meeting with the board tomorrow and I have a ton to do to get ready. I just wanted to make sure you were in the loop about the pool player. Now, hang up the phone and go have some fun."

Mallory ended the call and slid her cell back into her pocket. For a moment she stood staring out at the beach, replaying Jevet's words. *For most of us, the good we do outweighs the bad we see, but that might not be true for you. There's no shame in admitting that.*

Was it true? Was everything she'd worked for about to slip through her fingers? It wasn't as if Jevet hadn't broached the subject of her on-the-job struggles before. It had actually come up several times. But until now it had never been suggested that she consider another line of work. And there *was* shame in that.

SEVENTEEN

MALLORY

In the kitchen, Helen was topping off two mugs with fresh coffee. She added sugar to one and handed it to Mallory. "Everything okay?"

Mallory accepted it with a nod of thanks. "Yeah. It was just Jevet."

"So . . . what's the verdict? When do you have to leave?"

"That's on hold for now."

Helen's face lit up. "Really? What happened?"

"Nothing. I just don't need to leave yet. Can I help with breakfast?"

Helen's brows puckered the tiniest bit, as if not quite convinced. "Everything's done. But you can bring the place mats and silverware out to the deck and set the table."

Mallory threw a look over her shoulder, in the direction of the Cavanaugh guesthouse.

"He's not there," Helen said quietly. "I saw him leaving when I went out for the paper. But even if he was . . ." She paused, frowning. "Are you sure everything's okay? You look a little funny."

"Just too much wine last night," Mallory replied, which wasn't a lie. "I'll get the stuff and set the table."

A short time later, they were seated opposite one another, the table spread with a full breakfast of eggs, fresh fruit, and blueberry muffins.

Helen spooned eggs onto both their plates, then passed the muffin basket to Mallory.

"So, tell me about work," she said, helping herself to a slice of melon. "The last time we talked you were working on some big project, a vocational program of some kind. What's happening with that?"

Mallory looked up from the muffin she'd been about to butter, both pleased and surprised that her mother recalled the conversation, though the chances of the project actually moving forward weren't particularly good. "Not much, I'm afraid. Jevet loved the idea, but getting it off the ground would require a huge outlay, so the chances of the board green-lighting it are slim."

"Oh, that's too bad. It was such a wonderful idea. Brilliant, actually." Helen resumed nibbling her melon, then looked up almost shyly. "I'm very proud of you, Mallory, for following your dream. The world needs more hearts like yours. I'm so glad you found your niche."

They were silent for a time. Mallory picked absently at her eggs, her mind continuing to circle around the word *niche*. She thought she'd found hers—her *right work*—but apparently, the verdict was still out. Or maybe it wasn't. Maybe it was already a fait accompli. All at once her throat went tight, her vision smearing with tears she hadn't realized were so close.

Helen put down her fork with a clatter. "Mallory? Honey? What is it?"

Mallory blinked frantically but the tears just came faster. *Dammit.* She shook her head, the broken-glass sensation in her throat making words impossible.

"Sweetheart . . . what's wrong?" Helen scraped her chair back from the table, preparing to rise.

"I'm okay," Mallory choked, waving a hand. "It's okay."

Helen sank back in her chair, eyes narrowed. "It is clearly *not* okay. Talk to me. Please."

Mallory blotted her eyes with her napkin, then cleared her throat. "I need to tell you something."

Helen squared her shoulders. "All right."

"Before, you asked if I'd been fired and I said no. But something happened. A girl . . . one of my cases . . . was murdered."

"Oh, Mallory . . ."

"She was fifteen. Tina. That was her name. Tina Allen. They found her body in a vacant lot behind an old car dealership. She'd been . . . assaulted. More than once, they think. They're still looking for whoever did it."

Helen's face had gone pale. "I'm so sorry, sweetheart. I can't imagine how hard it must have been to get that kind of news."

Mallory nodded. "I'd been working with her for about nine months. She got into some trouble. Alcohol. Drugs. A few scrapes with the law. But she was doing better. She was clean, as far as I knew, off the drugs and back in school. And then last Sunday Jevet called me into the office. When I got there, two detectives were waiting." Her voice broke and she looked away. "I never saw it coming."

"Of course you didn't. How could anyone see something like that coming?"

"But I *should* have seen it. That's the point. It's my job to see it."

"You're not in trouble, are you? At work, I mean. Jevet can't hold you responsible for what happened."

Mallory mopped her eyes again, this time using her sleeve. "Not trouble, exactly. There's a process that happens anytime there's a child fatality, a case review. Child Protective Services coordinates with the police to make sure all standards of care were being met. Jevet doesn't think that's going to be a problem, but the media's all over it, and apparently there are protests now. The public needs someone to blame, I guess, and they've got New Day in their crosshairs—and me, since I was Tina's caseworker."

"I don't understand. How can they blame you?"

"It's a long story, but there's a man—a community organizer, he calls himself—whose son died of a heroin overdose. Two weeks earlier, his case had been assigned to me. And just six weeks before that, another one of our cases—a sixteen-year-old girl—drove her car into a tree. There was no evidence of negligence on our part in either case, but three deaths in the space of a year could be made to look like a pattern. So Ellis has been all over the news, demanding that we be shut down, and the media's been only too happy to give him airtime."

Helen's expression sharpened to one of thinly veiled disgust. "And you wonder why I don't own a television. This man obviously has an axe to grind. No one in their right mind would blame a social worker for a murder."

Except people *were* blaming her—or at least blaming New Day—and for all she knew, they were justified. "What if they're right?"

Helen stared at her, her expression a mix of heartache and disbelief. "Mallory, honey, tell me you're not blaming yourself for what happened to that girl."

"They found drugs in her system," Mallory said thickly. "Jevet just told me. But I would have bet everything that she was clean. I should have seen it but I didn't. If I had . . . What if she's dead because of me? A beautiful girl who'll never grow up, never have the life she was supposed to have? How do I live with that?" The tears came in a flood then, sobs scalding her throat until her ribs ached with the effort to suppress them. "How does her mother live with it?"

"Oh, honey." Helen reached for her hand, squeezing tightly. "I'm sorry you're dealing with all of this. And that you felt you couldn't share it with me before now. I can't imagine how hard it is. But blaming yourself won't help. Sometimes things happen that we just can't control. Death is one of them."

Mallory wiped her face with the soggy remnants of her napkin. "Jevet said the same thing, that it's part of the job when you work with kids from under-resourced communities."

"Sadly, that's probably true. And while it doesn't change what happened, it should help you deal with some of what you're feeling. It'll be hard for a while but you'll get through this. You'll be okay."

Mallory shook her head. "I don't think I will. Jevet's starting to question my *emotional* fitness for the job."

Helen blinked at her. "What does that even mean?"

Mallory breathed in, long and slow, holding it a moment before letting it out. This was the part she'd been dreading, the admission she couldn't quite bear to make. "A few days after it happened, I sort of . . . melted down at work. I was in the break room making coffee and I dropped the pot. The next thing I knew, I was blubbering like a baby. That's why I'm here. I'm on leave. Not vacation. *Leave.* Because Jevet wants me to take some time to think about my future. She's afraid I might not be cut out for the kind of work we do. And the worst part is I am too."

"It's one case, Mallory. And an extreme one at that."

"But it isn't. One case, I mean. It's happened before. With Ellis's son and the girl who drove her car into the tree. I can't seem to help myself. I fixate until it consumes me. Jevet calls it my 'death thing.' It's become . . . problematic."

Helen lowered her gaze and sat staring at her folded hands, as if carefully formulating her response. Finally, she looked up, her eyes full of regret. "You've never been comfortable with death—with the *fact* of it. That's my fault. It couldn't have been easy growing up with a mother whose calling is helping people die." Her gaze drifted out over the water and her voice dropped a notch. "I hoped you'd eventually grow out of it, but you never did. It's remained a kind of phantom for you. Always in the house, always between us. I'm sorry for that."

Mallory closed her eyes, desperate to shut out the mental image of Tina, lying battered and half-dressed in a patch of trash-strewn weeds, but it was no good. She would always see her that way, and wonder what those last, terrible moments had been like. "It isn't the same, though, is it? Tina wasn't one of your charges. She wasn't dying—she was murdered. Brutally and senselessly."

Helen dragged her eyes back from the sea. "We're all dying, sweetheart. All of us. Every day. We get out of bed every morning and we do our work. We make our contributions—or at least try to—but when our time comes, young or old, rich or poor, we all die."

Mallory blinked at her, bewildered by the calm in her voice. "How do you do it?"

"Do what?"

"The people you take care of—how do you look them in the eye every day, knowing the end is just around the corner? That every day means they have one day less?"

"By helping them through it," Helen said quietly. "By helping them manage their pain and their fear—and by making sure they're not alone."

"A minute ago, you said it was your calling—helping people die. Do you actually believe that? That it's the work you were always meant to do?"

Helen's gaze flicked away again, and for a moment she seemed to be struggling with how to answer. "I do now," she said at last.

"But not always?"

"No, not always. I used to think there was other work I was meant to do."

Mallory sat up straighter, intrigued by Helen's response. "What kind of work?"

Helen licked her lips, once, twice, then looked squarely at Mallory. "I was going to be a nun."

Mallory stared at her, astonished. "Why have I never heard this?"

Helen shrugged. "I changed my mind."

"You were raised Catholic?"

"Very."

"What does that mean—*very?*"

"In my mother's house, it meant there was a painting of Jesus looking down over our kitchen table every night—the kind with tortured eyes and a bloody crown of thorns. It meant eating fish on Fridays and lighting candles for a dead father I barely remembered, being dragged to the confessional every week to confess my sins, even when I had no sins to confess, and being sent away to Immaculate Heart, an all-girls Catholic school three hours from home, where the nuns were charged with saving my wretched soul."

All of this was news to Mallory. Helen had never talked about her childhood and Mallory had never pressed her. "How old were you when you were sent away to school?"

"Almost seventeen. It was my last year of high school."

Mallory digested this with a frown. Senior year felt like an odd time to send a child away to school. "Why so late? Did something happen?"

Helen turned her face back to the sea and was silent for a long beat. "I met someone," she said finally, the words laced with grief. "Someone my mother didn't approve of. We became . . . close."

Mallory felt a pang of sympathy as she regarded her mother, so quiet, so sad. "I take it the someone wasn't my father?"

"No. It was someone else."

"Were you in love?"

"We both were."

"So your mother sent you away to keep the two of you apart."

"That was part of it, but not all. There was some . . . unpleasantness at my old school. A scandal, my mother called it. And it *was* back then. We were caught by one of the teachers—in the equipment room behind the gym."

Mallory kept her face carefully blank. There was no need to ask what they'd been caught doing. The image was clear enough. Instead, she waited for Helen to continue. Eventually she did, her voice low and thick with memory.

"My mother was livid. Suddenly the whole town was talking about her daughter and she was mortified. Immaculate Heart was how she dealt with it. A public rejection of what I'd done—and of me. I hated it at first, but I worked hard and eventually made a few friends. The thought of going home at the end of the year, of living under my mother's thumb again—of having my every move watched and judged—made me sick to my stomach."

"But you would have been eighteen by then. Or close to it. You could have done what you wanted, *married* who you wanted. She might have disapproved but she couldn't stop the two of you from being together."

Helen squeezed her eyes tight, as if the thought caused her physical pain. "There was never any chance of that."

"So you decided to become a *nun*?"

"It was a way to not go home when school ended. My mother didn't want me home any more than I wanted to be there. And I didn't have the resources to live on my own, so I asked Mother Agnes if I could stay."

"Didn't you want to get married, have children?"

"I never thought that kind of life was in the cards for me. And I suppose part of me thought it was what I deserved—penance for my sins."

"For the sin of loving someone?"

Helen looked at her coolly, her face etched with an uncharacteristic bitterness. "For the wages of sin is death," she quoted softly. "Especially for girls who don't follow the rules."

Mallory had never heard her talk this way, about a cruel and vengeful God. It was more than a little unsettling. "You don't actually believe that?"

"With my brain? No. But when you're fed a constant drip of hell and damnation, it's hard not to believe it's just a little bit true."

Mallory sat quietly, trying to process it all. She was beginning to understand why her mother never spoke about her past. "So what happened? Why didn't you take your vows?"

Some of the bitterness left Helen's face, but not all. "Once you learn a thing about yourself, you can't unlearn it. You can pretend not to see it but it's always there, reminding you that you're on the wrong path. But eventually, something—or someone—*forces* you to see it. And once you do . . ." She paused, shrugging. "You can't pretend anymore."

"So you left the . . . nunnery?"

"The order. Yes, I left."

"Was it hard? To get out, I mean?"

"Not the way I did it."

Mallory narrowed an eye at her. "Should I ask?"

"I'd prefer you didn't. It was a lifetime ago. Two lifetimes, actually. And none of it matters now."

The silence stretched as Mallory pondered the response, still struggling to connect the loose threads of her mother's past. It was more than she'd ever shared before, and for that Mallory felt a surprising and almost tender rush of gratitude. But her words had been carefully chosen, the story short on detail, leaving Mallory to wonder why she'd decided to share it now—and what she might have omitted.

"Why are you telling me all this *now*? Why not before?"

"You asked if I always knew what I was meant to do. It seemed relevant."

"I suppose it was. And thank you. I know it wasn't easy to share all of that, but I'm glad you did. You were brave to choose a different path."

Helen pursed her lips, shaking her head slowly. "I was anything but brave. A brave woman would have demanded to be allowed to live life the way she chose, instead of buckling under like I did. I was bitter for a long time, about the hand I'd been dealt, the life I could have had if things had been different. But it was my fault. I wasted so much time being someone I wasn't."

"But eventually you were happy again."

Helen managed something close to a smile. "Yes. For a little while, I was happy."

Mallory knew Helen had suffered her share of heartbreak when William Ward was killed, but it never occurred to her that there might have been someone *before* William. Someone she'd loved first—*lost* first. It was strange to think of her that way, a girl in love, grieving for broken dreams.

"Do you ever regret leaving the order?"

Helen shook her head. "No. I was trying to fit into a niche that wasn't mine—do work that wasn't mine—and some part of me always knew it."

"So . . . you lost your faith?"

"Not exactly. It was more like finding *myself*."

"In the work you do now?"

"Partly, but in other things too. When we're young, we think we know exactly where we're headed. We map it all out and then burrow in, telling ourselves it's best to stay safe. But sometimes life has something else planned. Something better."

"And it had something better planned for *you*?"

"Yes, it did." She was smiling in earnest now, her eyes suddenly shiny with unshed tears. "Something so much better I never even knew I wanted it."

"What?"

"You, Mallory."

Mallory hardly knew what to say. It was the kind of moment mothers and daughters shared in movies, the kind that brought a lump to the throat. "Thank you."

"I love you, sweetheart, and have since the moment I laid eyes on you. All I've ever wanted for you was love and happiness. Things are bumpy right now—Tina's death was a tragic thing—but you'll get past it. And once you do you'll find your place. Your *right* place. Maybe it's doing what you're doing now. Or maybe it's something else. Just stay open. It'll find you."

Mallory exhaled slowly as she sat with Helen's words. "You make it sound so simple."

"It is simple. We're the ones who make it complicated. We get so stuck in that we can't see what else might be out there for us. But it *is* out there. Waiting for us to find it. And you will, sweetheart. Though for what it's worth, I'm glad you're not going back yet. I don't like the idea of you walking back into that mess."

"I'm not going back *right away*," Mallory clarified. "But I will have to eventually. That's the rest of the story. Before I came down, I had a call from the detective heading up Tina's case. He thinks they might have a lead. An old boyfriend who apparently resurfaced. I've only ever seen a photo, but they're hoping I can ID him when they finally track him down."

A sharp V had formed between Helen's brows. "We're talking about a police lineup?"

"Yeah, I guess."

"And you're okay with that?"

"Yes, if it helps put even one of the bastards away. And maybe I'll finally know what happened—and if I could have prevented it."

Helen's expression softened. "Sweetheart, you're a social worker, not a psychic. There's no way you could have foreseen something so heinous. I understand you needing closure, but you were not responsible for her death."

Mallory nodded. As much as she appreciated her mother's words of comfort, there was a ton she was trying to process, and she needed to be alone to do it. "Thanks for talking to me, and for breakfast. Would you mind if I took a swim after we clean up? To clear my head."

"Of course I don't mind." Helen pushed back from the table and stood. "But leave all this. I'll clean up. Then there are a couple of errands I need to run, including the market, so you swim as long as you like." She began gathering the dishes, then paused, a fistful of silverware in one hand. "I've decided not to take on any new charges while you're here. I don't know how long you'll be home, but I want to enjoy every minute."

Mallory felt a fresh prickle of tears and blinked them away. For someone like Helen, who never went more than a few days between charges, it was an enormous gesture. "What if I'm here all summer? You'll be bored silly."

"Some time off will do me good. And I won't be bored if you're here. I've actually been thinking about slowing down for a while now."

Mallory watched as Helen began scraping and stacking the breakfast plates. At fifty-two, she was still beautiful, but the years were beginning to show. She was notably thinner, and the fine lines around her eyes and mouth had deepened since her last visit. But what if it wasn't just the years? What if it was something else?

"Are you all right?" she asked abruptly.

Helen looked up from the dishes, clearly puzzled. "Am I *all right*?"

"You're not sick or . . . anything?"

Helen's face softened. "No. I'm just a little tired."

A moment of awkward silence stretched between them, the quiet weighted with unsaid things. "I really am sorry," Mallory said finally. "About the stuff I said last night, I mean. I was rattled after the bookstore. First, those awful women staring and whispering, and then Aiden acting like I was some girl he'd dated once in high school. I wasn't prepared for any of it."

Helen waved the apology away. "Nor should you have been. I should have told you about Aiden the minute I knew." She paused, face suddenly hardening. "As for those women . . ."

Mallory lifted a brow. "What about them?"

Helen gave her head the tiniest of shakes, as if trying to dislodge an unwanted thought. "Nothing. Go take your swim."

EIGHTEEN

HELEN

I peer over my shoulder as I cut across the yard, then duck like a thief through a gap in the hydrangea hedge. I'm supposed to be off to the market, and I will be shortly, but I have an errand to run first. I've left Mallory to take her swim, giving her space after my unexpected revelation.

She was more than a little surprised to learn about my early vocation, though not as surprised as I expected her to be. Perhaps because I told her only half the story, and omitted the trickier bits of even that. The secrets of thirty years are difficult to process all at once. But I will tell her—eventually. A promise is a promise, after all. For now, it's enough that I've begun it—and that I mean to finish it when the time is right. But I'm on a different mission just now. I've come to broker a truce with an old enemy.

I see that the polished brass coach lights on either side of Estelle Cavanaugh's front door are still lit as I approach the porch and that this morning's edition of the *Newport Daily News* is still lying on the walk. Both things surprise me. Estelle is known for running a tight ship in all things, especially her home.

I pick up the paper, shaking the last of the morning dew from the clear plastic bag, then tuck it beneath my arm and mount the porch steps to ring the bell. She answers on the second ring, and for a moment I'm not sure which of us is more surprised. I can count on one hand the number of times I've rung the woman's doorbell, and none of them have occurred in the last ten years. But it's her appearance that surprises me most. She's still in her robe, a flimsy thing of pale-green silk, tied at the waist with a matching sash. I fight the urge to check my watch, knowing it's almost noon.

"What are you doing here?" she inquires coldly.

I hold out the newspaper, ignoring her tone. She stares at it a moment, then takes it from me. "You're delivering newspapers now?"

"I came to talk to you, Estelle."

"About what?"

"I think you know. May I come in?"

She squares her shoulders and lifts her chin, but the gesture falls flat. Finally, she nods.

I follow her into the parlor, all ivory upholstery and gleaming parquet, pausing briefly to eye Aiden's piano, angular and shiny black against the room's otherwise feminine decor. It pains me to see it, to know it's going unplayed. As it must surely pain Estelle.

"I was sorry to hear about Aiden's accident," I tell her gently. "And that he's struggling. How is he?"

"He's fine," she replies stiffly. "And you shouldn't listen to gossip."

I'm stunned by the irony of the remark. That she of all people, a woman who never hesitated to fan gossip about my daughter, should now deign to lecture me on the subject, is rich indeed. "I hardly think I need that lesson from you, Estelle."

She rolls her eyes with a weary sigh. "Say what you came to say and then please go. I'm . . . busy."

I look at her more closely. She looks tired and unwell, her skin unsettlingly sallow. Though perhaps that's due to the green silk robe she's wearing. For the first time, I notice the glass of what looks to be scotch on the coffee table. Last night's perhaps, but something tells me it isn't. "We should sit down."

She opens her mouth as if to protest, then appears to change her mind and wanders to the nearest chair. "Yes, all right."

I take a seat opposite her but say nothing, determined to wait as long as it takes for her to look me in the eye. Eventually, she does, clearly annoyed. She's used to being in control of every situation. But she won't be today. I clear my throat, determined not to flinch under her cool blue gaze. "As I'm sure you know, Mallory is back."

"I'm aware, yes."

"She isn't here because of Aiden. She didn't even know he was back."

Estelle's brows lift the tiniest measure. "Didn't she?"

"The last she heard he was in Austria. She didn't know about his injury either. Until yesterday. Are you aware that they ran into one another downtown?"

"Aiden mentioned it, yes."

"And?"

"And nothing. He was there. She was there. What is it you want me to say?"

"I don't want you to *say* anything, Estelle. I want you to listen." I put up my hand, silencing her before she can protest. "Mallory is working through some things of her own right now. Hard things. That's why she's here. Not to pick up where she left off with Aiden. She just needs some downtime."

She stares at me, icy cool on the surface, but wary behind the careful composure. "You're intimating something, Mrs. Ward, though I'm not sure what."

"Your son was engaged to my daughter, Estelle. And for sixteen weeks, she carried your grandchild. I think we can use first names. And I'm not *intimating* anything—I'm here to tell you to call off your posse."

"My what?"

"Your little clique. And please don't insult my intelligence by feigning ignorance. I know exactly who was behind the rumors all those years ago—and why they were started. My daughter was never going to be good enough for your son, so you set your vultures on her, and had them paint her as some kind of gold digger. And I need you to know that I won't stand for it again. Mallory isn't after the Cavanaugh fortune. She *never* was. She loved your son. And he loved her. And if you hadn't interfered, they would have worked it out."

Her eyes go wide, as if genuinely astonished. "Surely you don't blame me—"

"Of course I blame you!" It's the first time I've raised my voice, and I'm pleased that I've caught her off guard. I press my advantage. "Have you ever considered that everything Aiden's been facing—the surgeries, the recovery, the uncertainty about his future—would be easier to get through if he had someone to share it with, someone who loved him? That maybe he'd have a reason to fight if he weren't alone?"

"He isn't alone," Estelle counters, sullen now. "And *I* love him."

I flash her a look of annoyance but tamp down my frustration, opting for a more measured approach. "Let's not play games. This is too important. Your son has given up on his music. The thing he's worked his whole life for. Why do you suppose that is?"

She's shaken now, far paler than when I first arrived. "How do you know all of this? Who have you been talking to?"

The fact that she's even a little bit surprised stuns me. "Did you really think it was a secret?"

She's gone still suddenly, her delicate features frozen. "People are saying *I'm* to blame?"

I smother a sigh. Leave it to the woman to make this about her. "I didn't say that, Estelle. But you *are* the reason he and Mallory aren't together. I don't know if there's been anyone for him since, but there hasn't been for her, and I can't help wondering if her life would be easier right now if there was someone with whom she could share her burdens."

"Someone like my son, you mean?"

"It was only ever Aiden for Mallory. Since the first time she laid eyes on him. And I'm pretty sure it was that way for him too. Have you ever known that kind of love? What it can mean? What it has the power to do?"

She sags back in her chair, shoulders slumped. "What is it you want from me?"

She sounds so weary, so utterly overwhelmed. But at least she's listening. "I'm asking you to stay out of their way and simply let things take their course. And to call off your poisonous crows. It may be too late for love—it probably is—but if they decide they can at least be friends, I'm asking you to let that happen. To let them be there for one another."

Estelle pushes to her feet without answering, her slender figure strangely heavy as she moves to a nearby credenza to extract a pack of cigarettes and a lighter. She slides one out and puts it to her lips. Her hands shake noticeably as she struggles to light it.

"Do you mind if I smoke?" she asks belatedly.

"No, I don't mind."

I *do* mind, actually, but know better than to say so. It's her house. And I need her to consider what I've been saying. I watch as she takes a long pull, then closes her eyes, savoring the smoke as it fills her lungs. But as I look more closely, I note the sharpness of her face, the shadowy hollows beneath her cheeks, the prominence of her jawline. She's unwell, I realize, as she opens her eyes again. Perhaps gravely so.

I continue to peer at her through the scrim of smoke now encircling her, focusing on her pupils. The right is discernibly larger than the left. *Anisocoria.*

I'm not a doctor or even a nurse, but after thirty years of caring for the terminally ill, I've picked up a good deal of terminology—and what it means. Unequal pupil size is often a sign of neurological trauma or pathology, and when coupled with weight loss, unsteady gait, and shaking hands, it's a very bad sign indeed.

I feel my whole body soften with the realization, the anger draining out of me, replaced with an empathy so keen it surprises even me. She *knows.* And suddenly, I realize my face has given me away. She knows

I know. Tears pool in her eyes, briefly obscuring the telltale pupils. She grabs the edge of the credenza for support, all pretense gone.

"How bad?" I ask simply.

"Bad."

I'm surprised when she allows me to help her back to her chair. Such a proud woman. But I've learned that nothing humbles so well as being faced with one's own mortality. She doesn't resist when I take the cigarette from her hand and carry it to the kitchen, or when I return with a glass of water and a paper towel with which to blot her eyes.

"What is it?" I ask when I'm seated again and she's gotten a handle on her tears.

"Glioblastoma. Stage four. Aggressive and essentially inoperable."

I nod, careful to keep my face blank. I know pity will not be welcome. Perhaps mine least of all. But thanks to a fairly recent charge, I'm all too familiar with the diagnosis. A brain tumor with few treatment options and a very poor prognosis. Transition within twelve to eighteen months of diagnosis. Two years in rare cases.

"How long have you known?"

"I've been experiencing symptoms for almost a year: headaches, dizziness, blurred vision. Occasionally, some slurred speech. I finally went to see someone. She performed a biopsy. I got the results a few days before Aiden's accident."

Once again, I struggle to keep my face blank. "Are you pursuing treatment?"

She shrugs. "They started me on a combination of chemo and radiation, which *could* slow the progress, but I'm not sure I'm going to continue with it. It's hard to make it to the appointments and they make me so sick afterward. There's no way to carry on normally."

Carry on normally? A thought suddenly occurs—a terrible thought. "Does Aiden know?"

Her eyes sharpen. "No. And he isn't going to until I'm ready to tell him. His focus needs to be on getting back to his music—and *nothing* else."

"Is that why you're thinking about discontinuing the treatments? Because you're worried Aiden will find out?"

The barest of nods. "I can't see well enough to drive now, and even if I could make the appointments without him knowing, he's going to notice eventually. There's only so much a woman can do when her hair starts falling out." The tears begin again and she mops at them. "This is the last thing he needs right now. He should be focused on his recovery, on his music, not an invalid mother."

"Shouldn't Aiden be the one to decide that?"

"He's in no shape to decide anything right now. I need time to bring him around, to make him see what he's throwing away. And he *will* come around. I just need . . . time."

I disagree with everything in me. But if experience has taught me anything, it's that you can't talk a dying woman out of her mission—especially when that mission involves her child. Your only options are to offer to help or walk away, and I've never been very good at walking away when someone's in pain.

"There are things . . ." I pause, uncertain about what I'm about to offer. Perhaps I'm foolish to even consider it. But, no, it's never foolish to be kind. "I could help . . . if you want."

She looks up at me, not bothering to hide her amazement. "Help . . . *me*."

"Yes," I say gently, understanding her incredulity. It seems inconceivable that someone she's gone out of her way to hurt for so long would now be offering help. "I could drive you to your treatments, give you things—*natural* things—to help with the nausea and the headaches. I could even help with your hair and makeup, so you could . . . carry on normally. Not inevitably, of course, but for a while. Until you're ready."

Her face is blank, uncomprehending. "After everything . . . why would you help me?"

And there it is, the question I knew was coming. "Because it's what I do, Estelle."

"I thought you didn't believe in doctors."

"It isn't a matter of believing. I believe all medical approaches have value. But I tend to favor a more natural course of treatment. So do most of my charges. That doesn't mean I can't help those who choose a more traditional path. For me, that's what it's about. Having choices."

"You're like a one-stop shop for the terminally ill."

She sounds wary suddenly, and faintly petulant. She's entitled to that, I suppose, given the cards she's been dealt. "You'd be amazed at what I've learned over the years, but yes, mine is a fairly holistic approach. I care for the whole patient—mind, body, *and* spirit."

Somewhere in another room, a clock chimes softly. Estelle starts, then glances at her watch. "Aiden," she says, clearly alarmed. "I don't know how long he'll be gone. You have to go. I could never explain you being here."

I nod, pushing to my feet. "No, I don't suppose so." I weigh my next words as I move toward the foyer. It isn't my place, but they need to be said. "Shouldn't he know, though? For his sake, as well as yours? You don't have to be alone through this. He'd want to be there for you."

Her face hardens. "I suppose you plan to hold this over my head, as assurance that I—how did you put it—let things between Mallory and my son *take their course?*"

I flinch as her words land, both startled and annoyed. "It's your illness, Estelle. And Aiden is your son. How and when he learns the truth is your choice. Whether you decide to accept my help or not. I just hope he understands you keeping him in the dark."

I leave her then, stung that she could think so little of me after the offer I've just made. But that's what you get when you poke your hand into a beehive—stung. Still, I'll help her if she wants me to. And say nothing.

This secret isn't mine to tell.

NINETEEN

MALLORY

Mallory inhaled long and deep as she turned her face to the sun. Despite its strange beginnings, it had turned out to be a glorious day, the sky a hard bright blue, the air lemony soft, heavy with salt and sunshine. The water would be chilly—sea temps rarely hit seventy degrees on the New England coast, even in summer—but she didn't care. She was itching to get in and stretch her limbs.

Her breath caught as the water closed around her legs. She paused when it hit midthigh, cupping a few handfuls and splashing it over her arms and torso, reveling in the icy needle pricks against her skin. Then, bracing herself, she filled her lungs and pushed off, arcing cleanly into the chilly waves. A moment later, she surfaced with an audible gasp, sights set on the end of the jetty, her old benchmark, roughly double the length of a twenty-five-yard lap pool.

She struck out with long, smooth strokes, reminding herself to keep her head down, her elbows high and her body narrow, to focus on her finger and forearm positions during the catch, to pull all the way through and rotate her hips, and then relax through the recovery phase of each stroke. It felt good to be in the water again, familiar.

Eventually, muscle memory took over and she found herself settling into a smooth, gliding rhythm. But by the time she reached the halfway point she was already feeling winded, and the dull ache of fatigue had begun to creep through her limbs. She'd pushed herself too hard. She wasn't a kid anymore and she hadn't been in the water in years.

Shielding her eyes, she looked back at the shoreline, farther away somehow than it had been when she used to swim every day. She should head in and call it a day, but she wasn't ready to go back to the house yet. Instead, she rolled over on her back and closed her eyes, abandoning her body—and her thoughts—to the buoyancy of the sea.

The last twenty-four hours had been filled with surprises, beginning with the news that Aiden was back in Little Harbor and resolved to give up his music, and ending with the news that her organized-religion-eschewing New Age mother had once contemplated becoming a nun. And somewhere in the middle of all that, there'd been a call from her boss, during which it had been suggested that she consider another line of work.

But it was her mother's shocking revelations over breakfast that currently occupied center stage, reminding her just how little she really knew about the woman who had raised her. A nun, of all things. Or *almost* a nun. She had no idea her mother had been raised Catholic. But that was only a fraction of the whole. There had also been a scandal, followed by banishment to a school full of nuns. For a woman who had always been so grudging with her past, it was quite an admission. And yet there were still gaps in her story.

Who was he—this boy Helen had fallen so desperately in love with? Not William Ward but someone else entirely. Someone whose name, she couldn't help noting, her mother had carefully neglected to mention.

She wished now that she'd pressed for a name, though she felt certain her mother would have declined to answer. Might this nameless *someone* be the reason she rarely spoke of her dead husband? For years, she had attributed Helen's reluctance to speak about her father to grief. Now she couldn't help wondering if it was about something else, something she preferred no one know. What else might her mother have chosen to keep hidden all these years?

The question was eclipsed by the sudden shrill of gulls overhead. Mallory opened her eyes, startled to find the sky filled with a flurry of white wings. Rolling over, she found her feet, and peered in the direction of the commotion. She saw him then: Aiden, standing at the end of the jetty, hurling bits of bread into the wind as the gulls swooped and dove for the scraps.

He hadn't been there when she got in the water—she would have noticed the neon-yellow windbreaker—but he was there now, outlined against the bright blue sky, seemingly indifferent to her presence. Was it possible he hadn't seen her?

Without warning, a memory suddenly surfaced. Jagged letters scratched into the surface of one of the rocks near the end of the jetty. AIDEN LOVES MALLORY. He'd spent a week etching them into the stone with his father's old Swiss Army Knife, a surprise for her sixteenth birthday.

Were they still there, she wondered? Or had time and the tides worn them away, like all the dreams they'd dreamed? She still found it hard to believe that what they had could have been lost so quickly, swept away in the space of a single summer. It had, though, whether the words were still there or not. Still, she couldn't help wondering, as she watched him throw the last of his crumbs to the sky, if he'd looked for those words—and if he ever thought about those dreams.

An hour later, her mother still wasn't home. Mallory threw a load of laundry in to wash, then folded the paint-stained smocks Helen had left in the dryer and carried them upstairs to put away.

The door to Helen's room stood open, the room itself tidy and uncharacteristically free of the clutter that filled the rest of the house. A pencil-post bed, a small table and lamp, a chair near the window, and a bureau with a mirror and a small vase of peonies. It was a place to sleep and nothing more.

Mallory deposited the stack of neatly folded smocks at the foot of the bed, but as she turned to leave, her eyes caught on the framed butterfly collection hanging above the nightstand. It had been there as long as she could remember, a simple frame filled with papery blue-and-black wings, each fragile specimen painstakingly pinned in place. She leaned close, peering at the largest specimen positioned in the center, its proper name neatly displayed beneath: *Agrias beatifica lachaumei Prepona laertes.*

It still surprised her. Out of all the treasures her mother had accumulated over the years, it was only the butterflies she chose to display in her room. When she asked why, Helen had explained that in many parts of the world, butterflies symbolized transformation and rebirth, the evolution and re-creation of life. Coming from someone in her mother's line of work, it had seemed a fitting explanation. And now it seemed fitting in a new way.

For years, she had known Helen Ward as mother and healer, but there was another Helen now, one she hadn't known existed until today, who'd been ready to renounce home and family in favor of the veil. It was faintly unnerving to think that but for a sudden spiritual change of heart, she might never have been born. But maybe it explained the disconnect she'd often felt between them as a child, as if there'd been a mix-up at the hospital and she'd been sent home with the wrong woman.

Years later, she still felt a twinge of resentment for all the nights Helen had climbed to the third floor, remaining there until the wee hours, painting presumably, though there was no way to know for sure since she'd been prohibited from entering that hallowed space.

Mallory flicked her eyes toward the ceiling. Did she dare? Before she could change her mind, she headed for the stairs, only to find herself second-guessing the decision when she actually reached the studio door. She could count on one hand the number of times she'd been allowed inside, and those had been by invitation. Entering now, alone, would amount to trespassing. But it wasn't like she was going to root through anything. She just wanted to see it again, to feel what it was like to stand in her mother's sanctuary.

She took hold of the knob, turning it cautiously, like a naughty child snooping for Christmas presents. The oily scents of paint and turpentine greeted her as she pushed inside, along with an eerie sense of stillness. The windows were closed and sunlight slanted through the panes, creating a bright grid on the scarred oak floor.

Her eyes went to the unfinished canvas on the easel near the window. Another seascape, but this one had a moodier feel than most of her mother's pieces. The sea felt unquiet, deep indigo capped with swells of foamy white, and a bank of dark clouds hovered ominously on the horizon. Even the colors were different, muted with lots of lavender, slate, and teal. What had her mother been thinking when she painted those clouds?

The question stayed with her as she wandered away from the easel, picking her way through the studio's carefully ordered clutter. Surprisingly little had changed since the last time she was here. The old desk was still in front of the windows and the hulking repurposed credenza still took up most of the opposite wall, its cracked marble top littered with paint tubes, rags, and an array of brushes and spatulas. Leaning in one corner was a collection of old picture frames, most of them in abysmal shape, but Helen had always had a tender spot for broken things and was skilled at repair and refinishing, as evidenced by the nearby shoebox bulging with nails, screws, rolls of wire, and assorted tubes of glue.

Mallory stepped over the shoebox, eyes fixed on what appeared to be a large unframed canvas leaning against the wall behind an old ladder. It was draped in a paint-stained sheet, and so well hidden that she'd nearly missed it. One of her mother's less successful attempts, she suspected, abandoned to ignominy. For a moment she considered picking her way through the clutter to have a look, but something held her back. For whatever reason, her mother had chosen not to share it with the world. Perhaps she should respect that and leave it where it was.

Before she could decide, the muffled thud of the front door shuddered up through the floor, sending a surge of adrenaline prickling through Mallory's veins. She darted for the hallway, pulse skittering as she eased the door closed behind her. The surest way to shatter the tentative new bond that seemed to be forming between the two of them would be to get caught breaching the sanctity of her mother's studio.

Moments later, she found Helen in the kitchen, immersed in unpacking a canvas tote brimming with produce, apparently none the wiser. "I was beginning to wonder if you'd gotten lost."

"Oh!" Helen started at the sound of her voice, sending a pair of lemons skittering across the counter. She darted after them, catching one in each hand. "I didn't hear you come down."

"Did you get all your errands done?"

Helen turned back to her vegetables. "I . . . yes. Yes, I did."

Mallory watched as her mother continued to empty the tote, lining her purchases up on the counter. She seemed uneasy, almost jittery. "Is everything okay?"

"Sure," Helen said without looking up. "Why wouldn't it be?"

"I don't know. You seem a little distracted."

"Just trying to get this stuff put away so I can start supper. I thought I'd paint a little tonight, if you don't mind."

"No, I don't mind. I was just going to read. I picked up a copy of *Wuthering Heights* yesterday."

"That's nice," Helen replied absently, crossing to the fridge with an armload of zucchini.

Mallory was surprised by the lackluster response—and by what seemed a concerted effort to avoid her gaze. Or maybe it was just her own prickly conscience, reminding her that she'd very nearly been caught snooping where she didn't belong.

TWENTY

HELEN

Shadows stretch across the studio walls and floor, the light milky blue where it spills through the window. I stare out at the sea, silver smooth against the inky night sky. Perhaps I should paint nightscapes, I think dully, imagining the palette I might use—pewter, platinum, lapis, and indigo. I'm briefly tempted to pick up a brush and try my hand, but I haven't come to paint. I'm too tired for that—and too troubled.

It's company I seek tonight. Or at least the illusion of it. An ear, a shoulder, a heart that knows my own. And so I flip on the lamp to chase away the shadows, settle into my chair, pull out my book, and begin.

◆ ◆ ◆

Dearest,

Forgive me for disturbing you at this late hour. Are there hours where you are? Watches or clocks or hourglasses filled with sand? No, I don't suppose there are. There doesn't seem to be much point in marking time in eternity. At any rate, here I am. Exhausted but unable to sleep until I've shared what's on my heart. There's so much that I scarcely know where to begin.

Mallory has told me the truth at last. A heartbreaking thing. A young girl, one in her care, was killed, and she blames herself. I told her she couldn't hold herself responsible, but I fear the girl's death will always be on her conscience. I know all too well the damage that kind of guilt can do. The questions, always with you.

I wish I knew what to say to her. You would know, wouldn't you, my love? Of course you would. How I wish you could whisper the words into my ear so I could pass them along.

But one thing has come of all this. Today, at breakfast, I told her about being sent away to school, about trying to hide behind a nun's habit but eventually leaving the order, although not how I left—or why. That will come too, in time. But there's something else on my heart just now, a new secret I must keep.

Estelle—Aiden's mother—is dying. Aiden doesn't know. No one does. I've offered to help, to do what I can to ease her symptoms, but she doesn't want my help. We have a history, she and I, to do with Mallory and her son. I shouldn't want to help her but it's what I've been called to do, and so the offer has been made. Whether she'll take me up on it has yet to be seen. Either way, I'm honor-bound to keep her secret. And what will Mallory say when she finds out, because she will find out. And she isn't likely to be pleased when she does. In her eyes, helping Estelle would seem a betrayal.

I could feel her watching me all through dinner, sensing that I had something on my mind. You'd think I'd be better at keeping secrets. Heaven knows, I've had plenty of practice.

I should probably go down now, and try to sleep if I can. But the thought of lying awake for hours holds little appeal. Perhaps I'll read a bit first. Will you stay with me, dearest, while I do? Just a page or two, to help chase away the shadows, and remind me of those last sweet summer days—back before I broke your heart.

◆ ◆ ◆

August 7, 1984

Weeks after our first kiss, we've gone no further. But things between us have changed. There's a tension between us now, a strange new hunger that stirs whenever our hands happen to touch. I tell myself it will pass, like any fever, but you fill my dreams now. The memory of your lips opening against mine, the inexplicable storm of sensation that followed, visions of what might have come next if I hadn't pulled away.

Apart from what I needed to know about basic bodily functions, my mother has never spoken of such things. She says nice women don't. But there's plenty of talk at school. About back seats and parking lots, about going "all the way." I don't know what it all means. Not really. But the idea of it—whatever it is—holds a vague sense of terror.

You say you understand how it is for me. I've been brought up to believe certain things, by my mother, by the church, and it's my absolute right to believe them if they feel true for me. But do they? You say we don't have to be anything more than we are right now. We can simply remain friends if that's what I want. But is it what I want?

For a time, I convince myself it is. I tell myself this safe thing we have is enough, and for a time we go back to just being friends, two people who love books and are happy simply spending time together. Summer passes in a blur of empty days, spent at your house mostly, in the shade of the saggy back porch. I paint while you pluck at your guitar, scribbling down song lyrics no one but me will ever hear, and we talk about the places our art and music will take us. The sights we'll see and the fun we'll have. It all seems so real when we're together. So simple. So possible. And yet charmed somehow, like we're living in a fairy tale.

On my sixteenth birthday, your mother makes me a cake—lavender and lemon with real sprigs of lavender as decoration—and the three of us have a little picnic in the backyard. I close my eyes as I blow out the candles, wishing for time to stand still, for it to always be like this.

Later, when we're alone, we lie back in the grass, silent but touching, content to watch the clouds scud past. The air is heavy and sweet. I breathe in the mingled scents of grass and dirt and sunshine—of aliveness. Suddenly something catches my eye and I turn to see a butterfly hovering just inches above your face. Your eyes are open. You see it too, but don't seem surprised. I hold my breath as it lights on the bridge of your nose, its velvet wings, a vivid blue, slowly opening and closing, opening and closing.

After a few moments, it lifts away and we watch it flit off toward the herb garden. Then you sit up, grinning at me. "It happens all the time. Ever since I was little. Raven says the butterfly is my spirit animal and that they show up when some kind of change is coming."

A year ago I would have laughed at this, but now, knowing you, I have no doubt it's true. But the thought makes me anxious. "What do you think the change is?"

You shrug. "School starting up again maybe."

I wrinkle my nose, unhappy to be reminded. School means being separated again, with you a class ahead of me. What if this year you meet someone you like better? Someone prettier. Someone willing to be who you want? "I don't want it to be that," I say quietly.

You smile, understanding somehow. "Okay then, what do you want it to be?"

"I don't know. Something that lets us be together always."

You pluck a dandelion from the grass, its round fluffy head trembling as you hold it close to my lips. "Yes," you say quietly. "For summer to never end and to be together always. Let's wish for that instead."

I close my eyes and make the wish, then push out a breath. We watch as the bits of fluff catch on the breeze and I pray that somehow our wish will come true. Neither of us could know what was coming.

TWENTY-ONE

MALLORY

June 22, 1999
Newport, Rhode Island

Mallory reached for the glass of iced tea the waitress had just delivered, sipping slowly. It was a perfect day for lunch by the water, the sky a cloudless and brilliant blue, the sun glinting sharply off the harbor. She was glad she'd let her mother talk her into coming to Newport for lunch.

Still, she couldn't shake the uneasy feeling that something was wrong.

Helen had seemed more than a little unfocused over the last few days, staring into the distance, occasionally even losing the thread of their conversation. And yesterday, she'd seen her foraging in her apothecary cabinet, surreptitiously slipping a fistful of tea sachets into the pocket of her smock. Mallory peered across the table, studying her over the rim of her glass.

"Is everything okay?" she asked abruptly. "With you, I mean. You seem preoccupied lately, and I'm wondering if there's something you're not telling me. I know I asked before if you were sick but . . . you're not, are you?"

Helen fussed with her napkin a moment, carefully smoothing it in her lap. When she finally looked up, she wore a tight smile. "I'm not sick. I'm just . . . at loose ends, as they say. It's strange having nowhere to be. Sometimes it feels like I'm playing hooky."

Mallory nodded. She knew firsthand how hard it was to not be doing the one thing you did well, the thing that gave you your worth and sense of self. "I get that. I can't remember you ever going more than a week between charges. They always seemed to just appear. Someone would die and someone else would find you. Sometimes the same day. And now, here you are, with no one to look after."

Mallory waited, watching as her mother reached for a roll and began to butter it with great care. When she showed no sign of responding, Mallory added, "Please don't feel like you need to stay home and entertain me all summer. Seriously. That isn't why I came."

Helen set down her knife and looked up. "I want this time with you, sweetheart, though I did want to mention something I heard yesterday, something that might interest you."

Mallory eyed her warily. "Why do I have the feeling I'm not going to like this?"

"The community center is looking for a water safety instructor."

Mallory wasn't sure what she'd been expecting but it certainly wasn't that. "I have a job—in Boston."

"Of course you do. This would just be for the summer. And it's perfect. You'd be in the water every day, your favorite thing. And working with kids."

"A lifeguard? At my age?"

"You're thirty," Helen pointed out dryly. "Not approaching Medicare eligibility. And you used to love working at the center. They have a brand-new pool and offer all kinds of classes, so it wouldn't *just* be lifeguarding. You'd teach swim classes and basic water safety, do CPR instruction. You're still certified, aren't you?"

"Yes. But I can't see myself back there."

"I think it would be good for you. You can't sit around the house all summer. You'll be bored silly. And you don't want to be glued to my side every day. Just say you'll think about it."

"All right," Mallory responded grudgingly. "I'll think about it. But I meant what I said before. If someone turns up who . . . *needs* you, I'd understand."

Helen held her gaze a long moment, as if preparing to say something, but seemed to change her mind. She spread her napkin in her lap, then made a show of surveying the umbrella-lined deck and surrounding tables. "This is such a great place, isn't it? I can't remember the last time I ate lunch out."

"Yes, it's nice," Mallory agreed, fully aware that her mother had just changed the subject.

"When we're through, if you don't mind, I need to pop into Malik's and pick up a check for two paintings that sold last month. And then I thought we'd poke around in some of the shops."

Mallory blinked at her across the table. "Since when do you enjoy poking around shops?"

"I just thought it would be nice. You could look for a dress."

"A dress?"

"For Sloane and Kenny's wedding."

Mallory put down her glass. "How did you hear about that?"

"Don't look at me like that. I haven't been spying on you. I ran into Katy Sanders at the market yesterday. Her daughter is one of Sloane's bridesmaids. Apparently, Sloane mentioned running into you. I'm surprised you didn't tell me. I remember the two of you being pretty close back in the day."

"I forgot."

"Forgot? Or decided not to tell me?"

"It was the day I ran into Aiden at the bookstore. I had other things on my mind."

"You should go."

"No, I shouldn't. It's Sloane and Kenny's day. Me being there would just make it weird."

"I assume this is about Aiden?"

"It's about everyone. The whole town will be there, staring and whispering. Call me a killjoy, but that isn't exactly my idea of a good time."

"Do you really believe not showing up will keep them from whispering? Everyone knows you're back. Don't give them the satisfaction of staying away."

Mallory closed her eyes briefly. "He'll be there."

"Of course he will. He and Kenny have always been thick as thieves."

"I don't think I can do it. Be around him for all that time. And at a wedding . . ."

"I know. There'll be memories—hard ones—but it's time to come out of hiding, sweetheart. Think of it as a kind of . . . coming-out party. You can do this. You'll see. You're braver than you think."

"I don't want to be brave. I want to send a nice gift and stay home."

"I know. But you can't."

Mallory sank back in her chair, arms folded sulkily. Her mother was right about one thing. Whether she went or not, there would be talk.

The waitress appeared with their food and Mallory was relieved when the conversation shifted to safer topics. To Helen's credit, she managed to make it through her Caesar salad without bringing up either the job or the wedding again.

When the check arrived, Helen handed the waitress her credit card, then excused herself to visit the ladies' room. Mallory waited at the table, sipping the last of her iced tea and watching a sailboat skim across the horizon, its colorful gennaker bellied out in the breeze.

The sudden flash of memory caught her unaware, like a sharp blow to the solar plexus. The first time Aiden took her sailing, the exhilaration when the sail opened with a crack and a huff, how the wind caught them, hurtling them up and over the wave tops, drenching them in salt spray, his body braced against hers as he showed her how to steer. How was it possible to still feel him when he'd been gone so many years?

"I think we're all set," Helen chirped, reappearing with her tote tucked into the crook of her arm. "Ready to go?"

Mallory started, then quickly looked away.

"Mallory? Honey?"

Mallory finally blinked up at her. "Does it still hurt? Losing your first love?"

Helen seemed momentarily surprised by the question. She pressed her lips together, but eventually nodded. "Yes. It does."

"Oh." It wasn't the response she'd been hoping for. "I thought maybe with time . . ."

Helen dropped back into her chair, her tote clutched in her lap. "Love doesn't stop, sweetheart. Not when it's real. Infatuation, passion, those things burn themselves out in time. But when you find that soul-deep connection with someone, it's forever."

"So what do you do?"

"You keep loving them," Helen said simply. "Because there isn't anything else *to* do. And if you're very lucky, someone comes along to help fill the emptiness."

Mallory was silent as she digested the words. It was hard to imagine loving anyone but Aiden. But her mother had found William. Not her first love, but a man she'd been willing to make a life with, have a child with. And then she'd lost him too.

"I'm not sure I want there to be someone else."

"I know it feels like that, and you'll never love anyone the way you loved Aiden. Every love is different because every *person* is different— and they make *us* different when we're with them. I'm probably the last person who should be giving life advice, but I don't want you to end up like me. You need someone in your life."

Mallory shrugged. "I'm comfortable alone. And frankly, it's easier."

"Yes," Helen said, nodding. "Love *is* hard. But alone is harder."

"It was enough for you."

Helen let out a tiny sigh. "No, honey. It wasn't. It's just . . . what there was. But that's me. It doesn't have to be that way for you. You're not ready to love again, but you will be."

Mallory sighed, shaking her head. "And in the meantime?"

Helen pushed back her chair and stood abruptly. "In the meantime, you're going to find something amazing to wear to Sloane's wedding."

Mallory cocked an eye at her. "Not the wedding again. Please."

"Yes, the wedding. You and Aiden are going to run into each other again. It might as well be on your terms—preferably while wearing something drop-dead gorgeous."

"This isn't about rubbing Aiden's nose in anything."

"Of course it isn't. But the *truth*—if Aiden wasn't going to be there, would you go?"

Mallory considered this. She and Sloane had been good friends. It would be nice to be there when she and Kenny finally exchanged vows. "Yes, probably."

"Then why let him stop you? Ten years is long enough. It's time to let it go."

Glowering, Mallory pushed to her feet. "I'd rather be invisible, thank you very much."

"Sweetheart, you couldn't pull off invisible if you went in a croker sack. Now, let's go see what we can find."

TWENTY-TWO

MALLORY

June 26, 1999
Little Harbor, Rhode Island

Mallory scrutinized her reflection in the bedroom mirror, wondering how she'd gotten roped into attending Sloane and Kenny's wedding when she'd expressly said she wasn't going. She was happy for them, but the last thing she needed right now was to watch a couple on the brink of happily-ever-after stroll down the aisle. The contrast with her own life was simply too glaring.

At least the dress worked.

In a moment of weakness, or perhaps insanity, she had settled on a teal chiffon A-line with a halter neckline and swingy skirt. She'd been leery when her mother first held it up. It looked so small, so filmy—so different from the sensible suits hanging in her closet back home. But it fit her perfectly and the color worked well with her hair and eyes. Unfortunately, the neckline revealed more cleavage than she was comfortable with. Hopefully, the necklace her mother had gone to look for would help distract from so much bare skin.

Cursing the humidity, she fiddled with her hair, tucking it behind one ear, pulling it free, then tucking it back again. She'd planned to wear it up but had changed her mind. Leaving it loose would help her feel less exposed, less . . . visible. And that was what she wanted, wasn't it? Invisibility. Nothing to draw attention or invite questions, nothing to remind them of the girl who'd slunk out of town after a hastily broken engagement. But perhaps ten years was long enough and no one actually cared. She'd know soon enough.

She glanced at the clock on the nightstand—4:15. Where was her mother? The wedding was at 5:00. The last thing she wanted was to make an entrance. She checked her phone one last time, dropped it into the beaded evening bag the saleswoman had talked her into, and poked her head out into the hall. "Hey, where'd you disappear to?"

She waited a moment, but when she received no answer, she went to Helen's room. "Sorry, I need to get going. It's okay if you can't . . ."

Her words fell away when she saw that the room was empty, then the sound of footsteps overhead drew her eyes to the ceiling. What on earth was she doing up there?

On the third floor, Mallory found the studio door open. Helen stood at the desk holding a wooden box of some kind, her eyes—and apparently her thoughts—fixed somewhere beyond the window.

Mallory stepped into the doorway. "What are you doing up here? I thought—"

"Oh, good grief!" Helen dropped the box into the open desk drawer and pivoted to face her. "I swear I'm going to hang a bell around your neck. You keep scaring me to death."

Mallory ventured in another few steps, eyeing the open drawer. "Sorry. I didn't mean to. What are you doing? I thought you were getting me a necklace."

Helen took a small step back, sliding the drawer closed with one smooth motion of her hip, then fumbled in her pocket, eventually producing something shiny. It caught the light as she held it up, splashing the walls with slow-swirling prisms.

Mallory frowned at the necklace. "Was that in the desk?"

Helen laughed and flapped a hand. "You know how I am. Clutter, clutter, and no rhyme to any of it." She paused, glancing at her watch, then made a face. "Good grief, look at the time. We need to go down and get this on you."

She shooed Mallory back into the hall then, closing the door behind her before turning to head for the stairs. Mallory followed but found herself glancing back over her shoulder, recalling the almost furtive way her mother had closed the desk drawer. It had been such an odd moment, with a vaguely surreptitious feel. Or perhaps she'd just imagined it.

Back in Mallory's bedroom, Helen ordered her to hold up her hair while she fumbled with the pendant's tiny clasp. Mallory did as she was told, fidgeting and trying not to look at the clock on the nightstand.

"Ha! Finally!" Helen cried as the necklace dropped into place at the base of Mallory's throat.

Mallory let her hair fall back and straightened, studying her reflection in the dresser mirror. The stone caught the light, setting off flashes of warm blues and greens. "It's perfect."

Helen smiled at their twinned reflections. "I knew it would be. The opal picks up the color of the dress."

Mallory fingered the simple opal teardrop, slightly cool to the touch. "It does," she breathed, catching Helen's eyes in the glass. "But where did it come from? I've never seen it before."

Helen turned away, stooping to collect a discarded pair of shorts from the floor. "It was a gift from an old friend from forever ago."

Something about her voice, the slight fraying on the word *friend*, gave Mallory pause, and suddenly she knew. It was from *him*—the boy her mother had loved and lost. For a moment she was tempted to ask his name, but it was hardly the sort of conversation to begin before dashing out the door.

"Are you sure you want me to wear it?" she asked instead. "If it's sentimental . . ."

"Of course I want you to wear it. It's perfect with your dress." She straightened, meeting Mallory's eyes in the mirror. "You look so beautiful. Just like . . ." She broke off, tears suddenly swimming in her soft gray eyes. "Just like a princess."

Mallory smiled back, touched. Growing up, she'd never seen much of a likeness between herself and her mother. Perhaps because she never *wanted* to see it. Instead of Helen's pert nose and deep-set eyes, she'd inherited William's wide mouth and long, straight nose. But now, standing side by side, she saw Helen too, echoed in the way they both stood with their hands to their throats, their heads tilted at similar angles.

She touched Helen's shoulder, giving it a squeeze. "We've always been . . . messy. But these last few days, the talking and the sharing, have been good. Thank you."

Helen blinked damp eyes. "Silly girl, don't go getting all mushy on me. You've got somewhere to be. And you should already be gone. Oh, I almost forgot. I put a few tissues in your bag in case you get weepy."

Mallory made a face. "Do I really have to go?"

Helen scooped Mallory's evening bag off the dresser and pressed it into her hands. "You don't have to stay late but you need to make an appearance. That's how you shut them up. You walk in with your head held high, you grit your teeth, and you just keep smiling."

Mallory was surprised by the brittle edge that had crept into Helen's tone. "Is that what you used to do? Hold your head high and grit your teeth?"

"It's what I *still* do," Helen answered glibly.

The response wasn't what Mallory expected. "I'm sorry," she replied softly. "For not knowing it was like that for you, I mean. You never seemed to care."

"I didn't, mostly. But I knew it was hard on you. My mother raised me to feel ashamed about everything. I didn't want you growing up that way. So I faked it. I thought if you saw me being brave, you'd be brave too. All I managed to do was make it worse." She shook her head. "And look at me. I'm doing it again. Pushing you to go to this wedding when I know you don't want to. I was wrong to make you buy that dress, wrong to make you do this."

"No," Mallory said evenly. "You weren't wrong." And in that moment, she realized it was true. She *did* need to go, to hold her head up and grit her teeth. Not for the gossips—for herself. "In fact, you were absolutely right." She turned back, planting a quick kiss on her mother's cheek. "It's time to be brave—or to at least fake it."

TWENTY-THREE

MALLORY

It was a perfect day for an outdoor wedding, and Sloane had chosen a perfect venue. The Harbor Club was the most exclusive yacht club in town: magazine worthy, with its monied New England charm, impeccably manicured grounds, and five-star cuisine. It had been her choice too, once upon a time. But fate had stepped in and that, as they say, had been that. Now she was here attending someone *else's* wedding.

Her stomach clenched as she picked her way across the lawn, fighting to keep her heels from sinking into the grass. She was later than she wanted to be and most of the guests were already seated. On the whole, the crowd was a young one, thirtysomethings mostly, smart couples looking trendy and fresh in their smart summer clothes.

There was one face, however, that was surprisingly absent, though she was certain Aiden would turn up soon. And what about Estelle? Was she somewhere in the crowd, watching and sharpening her knives? *Hold your head up and grit your teeth,* Mallory reminded herself.

Rows of tulle-draped chairs had been set up with perfect precision, divided down the center by a spotless white runner. At the end of the aisle, a lavish arch of pink roses would eventually frame the bride and groom, and a small lectern equipped with a microphone awaited the officiant. To the left of the lectern stood a glossy baby grand, its bench empty for now. Mallory's heart tripped at the sight of it. Perhaps Aiden's injury wasn't as serious as Helen believed and he was going to play after all. For everyone's sake, she hoped so.

Some fifty yards off stood the two-story clubhouse—weathered shingles and clean white shutters with a matching pair of chimneys and a smooth slate terrace. Its French doors had been thrown open, each entrance festooned with swags of ivy and pink roses to welcome the newly married couple and their guests to the reception. It was all so beautiful—and knowing Sloane, it would go off without a hitch.

And then she could go home.

A tinkling of piano notes caught on the breeze, presumably a signal for the guests to take their seats. For a moment, Mallory's steps faltered. But the head bent over the piano was blond rather than dark. Not Aiden. She let out her breath, forcing her feet to move again, sights set on one of the empty rows near the back.

There were faces she recognized as she settled into her chair. Old school friends. Friends of Aiden's who had eventually become her friends too. She waved and nodded, returning smiles when they were offered. She was aware of the surreptitious glances, as well as several double takes as onlookers caught sight of her, but all in all not as awkward as she'd feared. Still no sign of Aiden, though. Or Estelle.

The music began in earnest—Pachelbel's Canon in D—and the beehive murmur of the guests abruptly died away. The officiant appeared, a stout woman with an iron-gray pixie cut and cat-eye glasses. On her heels was Kenny in a dove-gray morning coat, looking stiff and distinctly nervous. And there at Kenny's side stood Aiden.

Of course he was Kenny's best man. They'd been tight for as long as she'd known them, playing weekend gigs at local jazz clubs and even writing a few songs together. She was glad they were still friends, relieved that he hadn't completely cut himself off from that part of his life. Kenny had been Aiden's pick for best man as well. Now the roles had been reversed.

Poor Kenny. He looked petrified, pale and lightly sheened with sweat, his legs braced wide apart, as if he feared he might faint dead away when Sloane's chiffon-clad bridesmaids began marching toward him. And then, in an instant, he was transformed as the woman he loved stood poised to make her way down the aisle.

Had Aiden seen it too, that moment of raw emotion? And if so, what was going through his mind? Was he remembering? Mourning what might have been? Or had his injury and the loss of his music eclipsed those feelings?

Mercifully, her thoughts were cut short when the guests pushed to their feet, turning in unison to watch the bride's entrance. Mallory stood too, relieved. She didn't want to think about might-have-beens right now. Hers or Aiden's. Instead, she fixed her attention on Sloane, who looked both blissful and breathtaking as she floated toward Kenny in a sheath of ivory shantung.

The ceremony was largely traditional, standard vows followed by the exchange of rings. But just before the final pronouncement, the officiant paused to look out over the audience. "And now, the bride and groom would like to share a song with you, their friends, in celebration of their union. It's a song Kenny and Sloane feel perfectly expresses the love they feel for one another, called 'Only Ever You.'"

All heads turned toward the piano as the intro began, a few notes at first, slow and clean, with plenty of empty space between. But gradually the song built into something more complex, layered and bittersweet. The pianist leaned into the mic, eyes closed, and began to sing.

> It was only ever you
> The one who came and found me
> The one who somehow knew
> All I had inside me, all that I could do
> The only song for me
> That was ever really true
> Was only ever you, only ever you.

It was an outpouring of gratitude, but a confession too, about how it felt to be lost, and finally find yourself in someone else's eyes, to be seen, *truly* seen, perhaps for the first time. But there was a rawness beneath it all, an echo that seemed to connect with something deep in her chest, a current of loss woven through the descending minor chords. Surely Aiden heard it too? She shifted slightly to look at him and was startled to find his eyes on her, hard and inscrutable.

The rest of the song seemed to fall away as the moment stretched, and she found herself holding her breath, probing his expression for some clue to his thoughts. But he gave nothing away. After a moment she looked away and joined the other guests in applauding the bride and groom's first married kiss.

Sloane and Kenny made their way back down the aisle, arm in arm and all but floating now that it was over. Gradually, the guests began to disperse, wandering in small groups toward the clubhouse. Mallory breathed a sigh of relief. She'd made it through the ceremony relatively unscathed. Now all she had to do was put in a brief appearance at the reception and she could slip away.

She'd prefer to avoid the receiving line if at all possible. Conversations were inevitable, polite small talk about what she'd been up to since the last time they were together—she'd even rehearsed a few answers—but she was in no hurry to throw herself into the fray.

Stalling for time, she fished her phone from her handbag and checked her messages. There was nothing new, of course, nothing from Jevet or Detective Muldowney, but she kept scrolling anyway, pretending to be thoroughly engrossed. Finally, she wandered over to the bar that had been set up on the clubhouse terrace and ordered a glass of chardonnay.

The bartender had just delivered her wine when a disembodied voice boomed through the open doors. "Ladies and gentlemen, it's time for the first dance. May I introduce, for the very first time, Mr. and Mrs. Kenneth Long!"

A cacophony of cheers went up, drowning out the opening notes of Etta James's "At Last." Mallory squared her shoulders and pasted on a smile. It was as good a time as any to slip in undetected.

Stepping into the Harbor Club ballroom felt like stepping into a fairy tale, all pink roses, bright crystal, and starched white linen, the windows overlooking the water aglow with curtains of soft twinkle lights, like tiny man-made stars. On the dance floor, the happy couple swayed in unison, eyes locked, oblivious to onlookers. The sight sent a pang of envy through Mallory.

She remembered those moments. She and Aiden would be in some public place, a club or a party, surrounded by people and noise, and yet somehow it would all fall away, leaving them headily alone, oblivious to everything but each other.

Pivoting discreetly, she sought him in the crowd. He was seated at the bridal table chatting with Carla McFadden. She watched as he threw his head back, laughing at something Carla had said. She'd missed his laugh, the smoky timbre of it as it rolled up from his chest. But the lines around his mouth—a mouth she knew as well as her own—gave him away. It was a show, a mask he'd donned for the day—not unlike the one she was wearing.

"Mallory?"

Startled, Mallory turned to find Bridget Finely at her elbow, wearing a warm grin. She swallowed her surprise and reached for a smile. "Bridget. It's great to see you."

"I was hoping you'd be here. Sloane said you would." There was an awkward juggling of handbags and wineglasses, followed by an equally awkward hug. Bridget was decidedly pregnant. "God, it's been forever! How on earth are you?"

"Good," Mallory blurted too brightly. "I'm good. Really good."

"Well, you *look* amazing. That dress is absolutely scrumptious. When did you get back and what have you been doing with yourself all these years? You're in . . . Boston, isn't it?"

Mallory experienced a moment of panic. She hadn't stopped to think that Tina's death might have made it to the local news, or that her name might have been included in the coverage. Thankfully, Bridget showed no sign of making the connection.

"Yes. Boston. How about you? What have you been up to?"

Bridget ran a hand over her swollen belly. "Well, this will make three, so basically, changing diapers and picking up after two very messy boys. Three if you count Mark. I love it, though. Best job I've ever had. And you? Any little ones at home? Or a hubby lurking somewhere?"

"No. No kids. No hubby either."

"Oh god." Bridget suddenly looked mortified. "I wasn't thinking. I forgot. I'm so sorry."

"Don't be. I've just been focused on work. I'll get around to it one of these days."

Bridget was clearly relieved. Her face lit with a conspiratorial smile. "Is there someone special?"

Mallory took a quick sip of wine. "I'm . . . between someone specials at the moment."

"Well, then." Her eyes slid briefly to the bridal table. "Maybe there's a summer romance in your future."

Mallory feigned a chuckle. "I won't be here long enough for that."

"Don't be so sure. It can happen in the blink of an eye. It did for Mark and me. Speaking of Mark, I'd better get back. Where are you sitting?"

"Well, I haven't really—"

"Come sit with us. There's room at the table. Then we can really catch up."

Mallory followed her, resigned. She had to sit somewhere and she'd be less conspicuous if she wasn't sitting alone. They arrived at a table near the dance floor where two couples were seated across from a man with a face full of freckles and a thatch of ginger hair. Mark, presumably.

Introductions were made and the conversation flowed easily, most of it about preschools, nannies, and pediatricians. Mallory pretended to follow along as she nursed a second glass of chardonnay, but with little to add to the conversation, she found her eyes repeatedly combing the crowd for Aiden. She spotted him once on the dance floor, moving mechanically with Carla in his arms, then again later, conversing with an older couple she didn't recognize, and finally, alone at the bar, brooding over a glass of amber liquid.

Mark followed her gaze, nodding in Aiden's direction. "Shame about the accident. Such a talented guy. You know he wrote that song, right? The one the guy performed at the wedding. Wrote it just for today. Kenny wanted him to sing it too, but he wouldn't. Tough break. His whole life wrecked because of a freak accident. You two used to be an item, right? Way back when?"

Mallory dropped her gaze, flustered by the directness of the question. "We were, yes. Way back when."

Bridget shot her husband a pained look. "Time to dance," she told him tersely. She hauled him to his feet then, mouthing a silent *sorry* in Mallory's direction.

Mallory shook her head, waving off the apology. "Have fun. Sounds like it's time for the chicken dance. I'm going to find the ladies' room."

Mark groaned. "Not the chicken dance, Bridget, I'm begging you."

"That's what you get for putting your foot in your mouth."

He looked at her, baffled. "What did I say?"

Bridget rolled her eyes as she caught him by the hand. "Come with me. I'll explain it."

Mallory waited until Bridget and Mark were on the dance floor to slip away. She didn't need the ladies' room. She just needed some fresh air. She filled her lungs as she crossed the lawn, bound for a small garden she'd glimpsed earlier. Unfortunately, several guests had beaten her to it, men mostly, smoking and waving drinks about as they swapped stories.

Reversing course, she wandered out onto one of the small docks lining the harbor, her steps heavy on the weathered boards. The music faded as she put distance between herself and the clubhouse. She halted a few yards from the end and stood gazing out over the water, watching the sailboats bob gently at anchor, white sails furled, masts jutting sky-ward like barren winter trees.

The sun had begun to dip toward the horizon, streaking the sky with shades of violet and peach. It was her favorite time of day, when everything seemed to go still, and the light reluctantly relinquished its hold on the earth. She let the quiet wrap around her, soft and blue. She breathed it in, willing herself to go quiet too. But she couldn't quiet the song running through her head, the lyrics stuck on a relentless loop.

The only song for me that was ever really true . . . was only ever you.

Of course the song had struck such a chord with her. It was Aiden's song, his music, his lyrics, written expressly for Kenny and Sloane. But Mark said he'd declined to perform it. Not because he couldn't—there was nothing wrong with his voice—but because he'd chosen not to.

That it had been a choice made it worse somehow. The Aiden she knew would have never passed up a chance to sing at his best friend's wedding. But life had reshaped him into someone she no longer recognized—a stranger who only looked like the man she'd loved—and the pain of it winded her, like losing him all over again. But beneath the pain was something else, a truth some part of her needed to cling to. He wasn't *completely* gone. Not if he'd managed to write that song. The music was still in him. *His* music. Somewhere. Sealed up behind the wall he'd built since the accident.

She closed her eyes, letting the last of the sun warm her face, hoping with everything in her that it was true. When she opened them again, Aiden was there, his shadow stretching beside hers on the dock's sun-bleached boards.

"I didn't know you'd be here," he said quietly. "Today, I mean. When I asked, you said you'd probably be gone by now, and Kenny didn't mention that you'd RSVP'd. Maybe they thought I wouldn't show."

Suddenly she was angry. Not for anything that had happened in the past, but because he'd quit. On Kenny. On his music. On himself. She could see it in his eyes, hear it in his voice, a blank and chilling vacancy. She recognized it because she'd been there herself once, and knew firsthand how tempting it was to sink into self-pity. She also knew how hard it was to climb out.

"Would you have? If you knew I'd be here? Would you have stayed home to avoid seeing me?"

"I don't know. I might have."

His honesty stung. But hadn't she been prepared to stay home for the very same reason? "The song from the ceremony," she said evenly. "It was yours."

His eyes narrowed but he eventually nodded. "Kenny asked me to write something."

"He also asked you to sing it. Why didn't you?"

"He told you?"

"No. Bridget's husband. So why?"

"Let's not do this, okay?"

"Do what?"

"Pretend you don't know what happened."

"I'm not."

"Then why ask the question?"

"I asked why you didn't *sing*, Aiden, not why you didn't play. There's nothing wrong with your voice."

"That's over too," he said flatly. "It's *all* over."

Mallory took in his slightly awkward stance, the way he held his injured hand at his side, stiff and slightly away from his body, as if it were no longer a part of him, and felt her anger evaporate. They hadn't seen each other in a decade, hadn't spoken a word to one another—aside from the brief exchange in the café—and here she was, hectoring him. Once upon a time she might have had the right. But not anymore.

"I'm sorry," she said softly. "I didn't know when I saw you at Inkwater. If I had . . ." She let her words trail, because the truth was she had no idea what she would have said or done. "I can't imagine how hard it's been for you."

Aiden responded with a shrug. "I never know what to say to that kind of thing. I hear it all the time, how sorry everyone is, how sad that it had to happen to *me* of all people. They mean well, but I never know how to respond." Another shrug, heavier this time. "I make people feel awkward, guilty somehow, for having two good hands themselves."

"Are you . . . is there still a lot of pain?"

He lifted the hand, staring at it as if it belonged to someone else, flexing the fingers slowly, stiffly. Finally, he shook his head. "Not much. Or at least not often. It's mostly just stiffness."

"The therapy should help with that, though."

"Don't."

"I just—"

"Don't. Don't pretend it's going to be fine."

"But they say with time you might play as well as you did before."

"Who is 'they'?"

Mallory shifted her gaze, unsettled by his caustic tone. "It's just what I heard. That in time, if you kept up with the therapy—"

"I don't need pity, Mallory. Not from you."

"Why not from *me*?"

Aiden blew out a breath. "Why did you come back? Now? After all this time?"

Mallory lifted her chin, piqued by the question. And by the insinuation that she'd had no right to come back, that she was encroaching on *his* territory, *his* friends, *his* world. "I suppose I came back for the same reason you did—I grew up here."

"But why now?"

Mallory dropped her gaze. She wasn't discussing Tina with him. "I had vacation I needed to take."

"You could have taken a cruise."

"I could have, but I didn't."

"How long are you staying?"

Mallory stared at him, chilled by this cool version of the man she once knew. She'd known him so well once, every furrowed brow and flicker of a smile, but his face was closed to her now, shuttered against any and all intrusion. What remained was an icy-flat resentment, not just for her but for the world in general.

"Don't worry," she told him coolly. "I'll be gone soon and you can have Little Harbor all to yourself again."

"I didn't mean it that way. I just wondered—"

"Forget it." She held up a hand, then let it drop. "I need to get back. I'm expecting a call and I left my cell phone at the table."

She brushed past him then and headed back down the dock, giving him no chance to respond. But part of her was listening, half expecting, half hoping that he would come after her. He didn't, though, and she told herself she was glad. Coming had been a mistake—there was no doubt about that—but they'd had their awkward moment now. She could stop dreading their next meeting.

TWENTY-FOUR

HELEN

I take full advantage of Mallory's absence, slipping through the hydrangea hedge with my small paper bag. Aiden will have gone to the wedding too, so there will be time to talk.

I've gathered some items I think Estelle might need—ginger and licorice root tea for nausea, butterbur tincture for headache, valerian root and lavender oil for sleep—and have scribbled down instructions for each. I'm probably wasting my time, but my conscience won't let me rest until I've tried once more. If nothing else, I may change her mind about keeping Aiden in the dark.

She takes her time answering the bell, but eventually the door pulls back and she peers out warily. Her face hardens when she sees me. "What do you want?"

I hold up the bag. "I brought you a few things to help with your symptoms. Natural things."

"I don't need your . . . medicine."

It isn't true. I can see it even through the cracked door. Beneath the heavy makeup, her skin has a pasty, sallow look, and there isn't enough concealer in Little Harbor to hide the dark smudges beneath her eyes.

"Estelle, don't be stubborn. These things will help you feel better."

"Nothing will make me *feel* better, Helen. I'm dying."

"Yes. You are. But the tea will help with the nausea, and perhaps even the dizziness. The tincture will take the edge off the headaches. And there's lavender oil to help you sleep. By the look of you, you're not getting much."

Her eyes shift to the bag and for an instant, I see a flicker of interest—of hope. But she's too stubborn to admit she needs help. Least of all mine.

"Have you thought any more about talking to Aiden?" I ask.

"No."

"I wish you would, Estelle. He'd want—"

"I know what's best for my son."

"I think you believe that," I tell her gently, ignoring her snappish tone. "I think you've *always* believed that. But I think you're wrong."

Estelle blinks, the slightest of hesitations. "Is that so?"

I realize I must sound harsh, particularly to someone not used to having her authority questioned, but it's time someone told her the truth. "You've spent your life trying to protect him. You kept him from playing baseball because he might hurt his hands, from marrying my daughter because you don't think she's good enough for him. And now you want to protect him from the truth—that his mother's dying. But he's not a boy, Estelle. He's a grown man. He can handle the truth and he deserves to know."

"This is none of your business," she informs me coldly.

Except it *is* my business. Perhaps not in the familial sense—I'm only a neighbor, and barely that—but fate made it my business the moment it placed Estelle Cavanaugh in my path. "I'll leave the bag," I tell her evenly. "In case—"

The door slams shut before I can finish. I blink at the polished knocker a moment, at the fancy letter *C* engraved there. I consider leaving the bag on the doorstep, in the hope that curiosity will win out once I'm gone. But what if Aiden should find it? Questions would be asked and I'd be blamed for outing her. Best to walk away—for now.

I'm halfway down the steps when I hear the door open again, presumably for some final parting shot, or another warning not to tell Aiden what I know. I don't bother to turn around.

"I'm sorry, Helen."

The words hit me in the back, bringing me to a halt. I pivot slowly and find her in the open doorway. Her suit of royal-blue silk hangs a little too loosely on her angular frame. With or without my help, it won't be long before Aiden guesses the truth.

"I'm sorry," she says again and clears her throat. "You were kind to offer help, given our history. I shouldn't have been . . ."

"Rude?"

"Yes," she says tightly. "I shouldn't have been rude."

We stand looking at each other for a long moment. I don't know what to say to her. Or what comes next. But I have the odd sense that if I move the wrong way or say the wrong thing, she'll startle and bound away like a deer in the woods.

"Will you . . . come in?"

I hold out the bag and she surprises me by taking it. We sit in the parlor, facing one another. No refreshments are offered, a telling lapse for such a practiced hostess. But we're not friends and this isn't a social call. We go on that way for what feels like several minutes, eyeing each other like opponents before a boxing match. I've already said my piece and am determined to force her hand with my silence.

"Thank you," she says finally. "I'm not really sure why I asked you in. I think I just wanted to talk to someone who . . . someone I don't have to be careful with."

I consider this. The need to be careful is something I know a little bit about. The constant worry that you'll let something slip and expose your secrets to someone who couldn't possibly understand. But this is different. "There's an old saying," I tell her gently. "A burden shared is a burden halved. You don't *have* to keep this secret, Estelle."

"You mean tell Aiden."

"Yes."

"I can't. Not yet." Her hands clench the paper bag in her lap, her knuckles pale. "You say he's a grown man, that he doesn't need protecting, but he's in such a dark place right now, and so full of anger."

"At you?"

She sighs. "At everything. But yes, at me. I don't know what would happen if I dropped this on him too. He might crack."

"Or it might give him something to focus on," I suggest. "Something besides self-pity."

Her face hardens, but I see I've struck a nerve. "He's lost everything," she says tightly. "Or thinks he has. It wouldn't be fair. After everything else . . ."

I remain quiet when her voice trails away. I know where she's going. I also know she doesn't *want* to go there. But I'm going to make her if I can. It isn't about humbling her. It's about making her see clearly. It's time for that now. Time to say what needs to be said, to come clean about how and why it all went wrong. Not between us. She and I don't matter. But Aiden does. And so I sit there with my hands on my knees, and I wait.

"You said something yesterday," she resumes at last. "You said things might be easier for Aiden if he had someone in his life, that he might have a reason to fight if he wasn't alone. I was furious when you said it but I haven't been able to stop thinking about it."

"And?"

Her expression is suddenly guarded and for a moment I think she won't answer. Then she opens her mouth and surprises me. "Are you and Mallory close?"

The question feels abrupt, like an attempt at deflection, but there's genuine interest in her tone and something that feels like despair. And in that instant, despite our history and our many differences, I see that we're the same. We're both mothers, painfully aware of our mistakes, and terrified of losing our children.

"Not as close as I'd like, no," I answer uncomfortably. "She never understood my work, but then most don't. There was always talk, silly rumors, which made school difficult. And we moved a lot. There was never much money so I worked constantly. I still regret not being there for her like I should have."

Estelle shakes her head miserably. "And *I* was there constantly. Always hovering. Always knowing best. And now, when my son really needs me, I have no idea how to help him."

"Aren't we a pair?" I sigh, only half in jest.

Estelle manages a smile, though it doesn't reach her eyes. "Aren't we just."

"There's time yet, to make things right—for both of us."

A frown puckers Estelle's brow. "Less for me than for you."

"Perhaps. But none of us know how much time we have left. The important thing is to use what we do have wisely—and meaningfully."

Estelle's eyes suddenly swim with tears. "It feels as though I'm being punished."

"I know," I say quietly—because I *do*.

I've heard it a hundred times before, the shock of having received a death sentence. We never stop to consider that a death sentence comes as part of the package, pronounced on us the day we're born. The number of years may differ, but the end is never in doubt. Still, we rail when it comes—unless we learn to see it differently.

"It feels unfair right now," I say evenly. "When there's so much left to do. You feel cheated. But death isn't a punishment, Estelle. It's a part of life. You can't see it yet, it's too soon, but knowing we're nearing this part of our journey can actually be a gift, a chance to start again from where we are now, but better equipped this time. We're reminded to spend the time we have left on what's truly meaningful, to lay down the things we can't control—things we finally realize we've *never* controlled—and live in the moment. We start looking back instead of always ahead, and feel a profound sense of gratitude for all we've been given. The acceptance has to come first. Then comes the grace. And sometimes, even joy."

"This is what you do," Estelle says quietly. "This is how you talk to your patients."

"I prefer to call them charges, but yes, this is how I talk to them. In the beginning, when they're still grappling with what comes next."

"I'm afraid," she whispers, as a pair of tears track down her cheeks.

"Of course you are. But you don't have to be alone. And I don't mean Aiden."

"You?"

"Yes. Me."

She wipes at her eyes with the heels of both hands, leaving behind raccoon-eye smears of mascara. I say nothing. It doesn't matter. Or soon won't. Beauty—and the vanity that sometimes comes with it—is often confused with dignity. But that kind of beauty is never more than skin deep, while dignity is rooted in our humanity, in our very soul, a birthright we either cling to or surrender. I can help her with that work, but she must be the one to ask. I won't push in where I'm not wanted. I'm risking enough going behind Mallory's back.

"I still don't understand," she says. "Why would you take care of me? We're not friends."

"No, we're not."

"Then why?"

"Because this is the way it works. One charge transitions and another appears. I don't question it. I just do the work."

She blinks spiky lashes at me, sniffling. "So I'm . . . your *charge* now?"

"If you want to be, yes."

"Well, then." She blinks at me again. "What happens now? Are there forms to fill out?"

"No, there aren't any forms. First, we'll discuss your symptoms in more depth, and I'll take some notes so I can help you manage those. And then we'll talk about your goals."

"Goals?" she echoes dubiously. "For dying?"

"Yes, but one thing at a time. For now, we'll start with the bag."

She glances at the rumpled bag in her lap. "What's in it? Medicine?"

"Of a sort. They're herbal and very gentle, so they won't interfere with anything you're already taking. I've written all the instructions down, nothing very complicated. The tea bags are for nausea. You just steep them like any other tea. There are drops for the headaches—three to four of those right under your tongue. Rub the lavender oil on your wrists and temples at bedtime. Or naptime if you can manage it. Sleep is still the best medicine. There's also ginseng to help boost your energy, but try not to take it too late in the day. Would you like me to brew you some of the tea now?"

"Not just now, no."

"How are you feeling today?"

"Fair. The headache is there, but it's not as bad as it is some days. It makes sleeping difficult. Last night was a hard night, so I feel a little shaky."

"Have you eaten today?"

She shakes her head. "I don't have much appetite since I started the treatments. It's one of the reasons I'm thinking of stopping them."

I meet her gaze squarely and wait until I know she's paying attention. "I won't advise you on that. That decision is between you and your doctors. My job is to make you comfortable and help you keep up your strength. You need to eat. Small meals but fairly often. I can bring you something to help stimulate your appetite, but controlling the nausea might be all you need right now."

She peers into the bag, then frowns at me. "Is it safe to take all this at once?"

"You won't be taking it all at once. Read all the directions and call me if you have any questions. You have my number?"

She nods. "It's still in my address book."

It's the kind of conversation I'm used to having with my charges. Assessing where they're beginning each day. She's surprisingly compliant. But then, many of my charges are happy to place themselves in my hands once the decision has been made, relieved to relinquish control to someone else. It's the first step toward acceptance.

"All right." I stand then and check my watch. "I don't know how long Mallory will be gone. She has no idea about any of this and I'd like to keep it that way."

Estelle tips her chin, her old pride rearing its head. "She wouldn't approve?"

No, I think to myself, she most certainly would not, but I don't say so. Instead, I opt for something with less sting. "I promised I wouldn't take on any new charges while she was here so I'd be free to spend time with her. I don't think she'd be happy to know I've broken my promise after one week."

"No, I suppose not."

"I'll do my best to come by every morning, but it'll depend on what time Mallory is up."

"And when Aiden leaves," Estelle adds anxiously. "I've asked him to take over some of my commitments now that he's back. I was afraid of him having too much time on his hands. He's usually gone by seven thirty."

I nod, but can't help shaking my head at the thought of us sneaking around behind our children's backs, partners in crime. "Aren't we a pair?" I mumble again under my breath.

Estelle smiles sadly as I turn toward the door. "We are, indeed."

TWENTY-FIVE

HELEN

June 26, 1999

Dearest,

Yes, it's me again, scribbling another letter to nowhere. But you were always my safe place when my heart was heavy—and my heart is heavy again tonight. Or perhaps it's my conscience that's heavy.

Mallory came home a few hours ago. I thought the wedding would be a good thing for her, proof that it's possible for her and Aiden to coexist here, but the look on her face when she came through the door told me it may have done the opposite.

She wouldn't volunteer anything, so I tried to coax it out of her. Even then, all she would say is that Sloane looked beautiful, Kenny was the happiest man alive, and there was enough food to feed an army. There was no mention of Aiden, and I knew better than to ask. Her silence told me all I needed to know.

But it isn't only Mallory on my mind tonight. As the saying goes, the plot thickens. While Mallory was gone, I went to see Estelle, to offer my help again. And this time she accepted. I know I shouldn't have offered—not with our history—but how could I not? The woman is dying, dearest, and she's frightened.

You know what it's like to leave a child behind, the thing most precious to you in all the world. You've done it. And now so must Estelle. I cannot turn my back on her at such a moment, though everything in me says I should. The hardest part will be keeping the truth from Mallory. Again . . . secrets.

But this secret isn't mine to tell, only to keep, as I promised Estelle I would. Still, the truth will out, eventually. The ravages of Estelle's cancer will become apparent soon enough. It's the timing we hope to manage. There are only so many times a mother can be forgiven for keeping the truth from her child. This is doubly true for me with Mallory.

You've been coming up in conversation again. She's curious about the stranger in the photo beside her bed, the father she never knew, her hero. I've dribbled out bits of the past, small careful snippets—omitting the most damning, of course. She wonders where you fit into it all, the cause and the chronology. But I'm afraid to tell it. Afraid to let myself even remember it. I must, though, I know. And so I will return to our story, further along now, nearer the end.

◆ ◆ ◆

October 14, 1966

Autumn has arrived and the weather has turned cool, driving us indoors, back to school, but back to our beloved books too. There's that at least. It's your turn to choose what we read and since it's nearing Halloween, you choose

Mary Shelley's Frankenstein. I agree, but only because you never say no when it's my turn to choose the book. The truth is the story has always given me the creeps.

I've only known the movie version of the monster—a thing cobbled together from various cadavers then vivified with a jolt of electricity—but the celluloid creature from the old black and white movies bears little resemblance to the complex character I discover on the page and I suddenly understand why you love the story.

It isn't about a monster at all. It's a thinly veiled commentary about our capacity for cruelty when threatened by something we don't understand, about the role of empathy in a so-called civilized society, and finally—and perhaps most eloquently—about the need to be seen for who we are beneath our skins, who we are in the deepest corners of our souls.

The rejection and isolation Shelley's "monster" endured—punishment for the simple crime of being who and what he was—touches something unexpected in me and I find myself weeping as I read, dimly aware that I'm somehow like him, too different to fit in with the rest of the villagers, too closed off, too strange. But not from you, dearest. Never from you. With you, I fit perfectly. Not just as a friend but as whatever we're on the brink of becoming—because we are on the brink, you and I, and have been from that very first day in the library. I know it now, and know all at once that I want to be everything to you, give everything to you.

It's funny how loving someone brave and strong makes you believe you're brave and strong too. You live in their shadow, draw strength from their strength. And then one day, you're tested—and you suddenly learn the truth about

yourself. That's how it happens for me, how I learn who I am—and who I'm not.

It's one of those warm autumn days when the earth tricks you into believing summer has returned. The air is sweet and heavy, thick with the scents of hay and ripe apples. We're sitting shoulder to shoulder beneath our usual tree, taking turns reading aloud. But when my turn comes again I stay silent and touch your hand instead. I hold your gaze but can't find the words to say what I want.

You stare back at me and swallow convulsively. Somehow, without a word, you understand. Moments later, we're alone in the equipment room behind the gym, daring things we've never dared, whispering things we've never whispered. Words like love and forever and someday. And we mean them when we say them. Like all young lovers, we're silly enough to believe loving is enough.

Neither of us hears the door open, but sunlight suddenly floods the space. Coach Belcher steps inside, shocked to find me pinned against a metal cabinet, my clothes in disarray. A look of horror flashes across her horsey face, accompanied by an outraged yelp. She yanks you by the collar, screeching absurdly for you to "unhand" me.

My hands shake as I fumble with my blouse buttons. All I can think is that my mother will find out—and that no number of trips to the confessional will ever earn her forgiveness. Like Shelley's monster, I will be despised.

Coach Belcher stands with her fists on her hips, red-faced and glaring as she sums up the situation. And suddenly I see the scene as she must. Me, quaking and half-dressed, pinned against the cabinet. You, in clear control—the aggressor.

No! I want to tell her. No! You've got it wrong. But before I can correct her, she grabs hold of your wrist and jerks you toward the door.

"You," she barks, "will come with me to Principal Gordon's office. And you, Miss . . ." She lifts her chin at me, her eyes softer now, filled with sympathy I don't deserve. "Go to the restroom and put some water on your face. When you've pulled yourself together, go to the principal's office and stay there until we decide what's to be done. And don't think of making us come looking for you. This is a serious business."

Thirty minutes later, the grilling has begun, with you in one room and me in another. They think that if they separate us I'll be more comfortable speaking out against my attacker. What they don't understand is that without you at my side, I'm unable to speak at all. I just sit there, frozen, as they buffet me with question after question.

Eventually, they realize I'm not going to answer and they send me out into the waiting room, where I sit with my bookbag hugged to my chest, a makeshift shield. When my mother walks in, stiff-shouldered and white as chalk, I begin to cry. My mouth fills with saliva and for a moment, I think I'm going to be sick. I eye the door, wondering where to find the nearest restroom, but the look she levels at me pins me to my chair.

"Didn't I warn you?" she hisses, luminous with rage. "I knew you'd shame me one day. It was only a matter of time until you brought something like this on yourself— and me."

I open my mouth to protest but she silences me with a finger. I know that finger, a warning not to cross her if I don't want to feel the crack of her palm across my cheek. "Not a word from you. Do you understand?"

The door behind her opens and Principal Gordon appears. His round cheeks are an uncomfortable shade of pink as he looks me over. So is the shiny place on top of his head. He clears his throat, tugging uncomfortably on his tie. "Mrs. Doyle. Might I have a word? In the hall, if you please, so we can speak in . . . eh . . . private."

My mother throws me a look, a silent admonition to stay put, and they step out into the hall. I sit very still, my hands between my knees to keep them from shaking. There are four doors that open onto the waiting room, all closed. I wonder which one you're behind and if you're as scared as I am. But no, I think, you aren't scared at all. You're never scared of the truth.

I pretend to ignore the curious glances from the secretary seated behind the large desk near the door. Her fingers keep up their steady peck-peck on her typewriter, but I feel her eyes slide in my direction now and then, intrigued by this unexpected drama in her usually humdrum day. My stomach churns as I try to decipher snatches of the muffled conversation taking place in the hall. The words rise and fall, like the hum of bees, angry and muffled, but I can't pick out specific words. I have no clue what's being said. All I can do is pray for the earth to swallow me up, to spare me the ordeal I know is coming.

Instead, the door opens and Principal Gordon returns with my mother. If possible, she's paler than when she stepped out into the hall. I can only imagine what she's been told. She doesn't look at me, but she doesn't have to. The revulsion radiates from her in waves.

The principal opens the door to his office and gravely beckons us inside. My mother yanks me to my feet, then steers me toward the open door—to the room where I know you're waiting. I'm expecting your mother to be there too, but she isn't. You're sitting in a chair off to one side, like a witness in a courtroom. For one ridiculous moment, I tell myself it will be all right, that as long as I can see your face, everything will be all right. Then I look around the room, at the faces looking back at me, and I know nothing will ever be all right again.

On the other side of the room is Coach Belcher, standing with her arms crossed. My mother and I take our places beside her. You sit stiffly, with your hands resting on your knees, your jaw clenched tight. You don't look at me as I enter, though I desperately want you to.

"Coach Belcher," Principal Gordon says when he's seated behind his desk. "Will you please relate the situation as you encountered it in the equipment room?"

To my mother's horror, Coach Belcher recites her story in excruciating detail. Not as it truly happened, but as she imagines it to have happened, with me as the victim and you the predator. An awful quiet descends when she finishes, silence filled with judgment, awkward looks, and unasked questions. I'm crying again, shaking my head, but no one is looking at me. They're all staring at you, ready to believe the worst.

Finally, Principal Gordon clears his throat and turns to look at me. "Miss Doyle—I'd like to hear from you now. We've been told that you welcomed these advances. Is that true?"

I open my mouth, trying to find the words, but before I can get them out, my mother holds up that finger again, this time at Principal Gordon. "Mr. Gordon, I cannot allow you to address my sixteen-year-old daughter in such a frank and unseemly manner. I will ask the questions."

To my amazement, Mr. Gordon closes his mouth and sits back in his chair. She rounds on me then, the finger pointed like a weapon, aimed between my eyes. "Helen Marie Doyle, did you submit willingly to this . . . touching?"

Willingly. So willingly.

The words fill my throat, but my tongue won't move. All I can see is my mother's hand looming close to my face. I imagine the crack of it against my cheek, snapping my head back until my teeth clack together, and I'm suddenly mortified. Not by the situation we've found ourselves in, but by my complete paralysis in the face of my mother's anger. By my cowardice.

Infuriated by my silence, she seizes my arm, squeezing so tight her nails bite into my flesh. "Answer me, young lady, or I'll shake the answer out of you. Have you and this filthy—"

Principal Gordon clears his throat as he pushes to his feet, dropping his eyes pointedly to my arm, blanched white now where my mother's fingers encircle it. "Mrs. Doyle, you're upset. And I do understand. This is a rather . . . unpleasant situation to be faced with. But perhaps I should be the one to question your daughter."

She drops my arm like it's something soiled she's found on the street. Her eyes flash one last warning as she takes a step back.

"Young lady," Principal Gordon begins, followed by another awkward throat clearing. "These are very serious allegations, and we need to get to the bottom of them. If things didn't happen the way Coach Belcher has portrayed them you need to speak up. Do you understand? If you insist on remaining silent, we can only assume we have the facts as they occurred."

I stare at him, stare at them all, holding their collective breaths, waiting for me to implicate one or both of *us. Suddenly I can't breathe. A dry sob scorches up into my throat, choking off any words I might have found. I feel like I'm being torn in half. How can I allow you to bear the consequences alone when we're both guilty? But to admit such a thing in front of all these people, in front of her—it simply isn't possible. Instead, I gulp back another sob and shift my eyes to the floor.*

"There," my mother says, the word like an ice pick piercing the silence. "You have her answer. This has nothing to do with my daughter and everything to do with that . . . that . . ." She pauses, jerking her head around to look at you. "That . . . deviant!" She hisses the word with a shudder of revulsion, then turns to glare at Principal Gordon. "I trust you will take appropriate measures, sir, to protect the young people in your care. They deserve better than to be preyed upon in the halls of their own school, molested and subjected to wickedness."

"Yes, yes of course," Mr. Gordon says, nodding and rubbing his hands together. "Nothing like this has ever happened during my tenure at this school, Mrs. Doyle. And I can assure you that nothing like this will ever happen again. That being said, I'd like to keep this incident between us. No sense in upsetting the other parents. They're just teenagers, after all, and there was no real . . . eh . . . harm done. However, I'll leave it to you to decide if we should involve the police and make an official report."

At the word police, my gaze slides to the opposite side of the room. For the first time, I see fear flicker in your eyes. But there's something else as you look back at me—the realization that you've been betrayed, that you suddenly see me for the coward I am.

My mother's expression freezes. The threat of this becoming public has shaken her—as I'm absolutely certain

Principal Gordon meant it to. "No. That won't be neces-
sary," she says, her voice crisp and imperious. "So long as
expulsion is immediate. And permanent."

She grabs my arm again and jerks me to my feet. I
drop my bookbag, sending a handful of markers spilling
across the carpet. I bend down to collect them, but she
jerks me back up, already hauling me toward the door.
"Leave them!"

I manage to turn as I reach the doorway, to catch one
last glimpse of you before she drags me away. The sight
splits my heart open. You're so still, so stoic in your chair,
a condemned prisoner staring back with empty eyes.

◆ ◆ ◆

I lay my hand flat on the page and close my eyes, the mem-
ories lodged between my throat and my heart, burning still.
I would give anything to erase that day from these pages,
to take back my silence and stand up for you, as I should
have done. But would I, if given the chance to do it over?
Am I any braver now than I was on that awful day? Even
now, I can't be sure.

What I do know is that even after all the heartache,
all the broken promises and shattered commandments, I
wouldn't trade a moment of the joy I knew with you. But
our story doesn't end there. There are pages yet. Harder
still, though I could not have imagined them then. Such
things are always unimaginable—until they happen.

TWENTY-SIX

HELEN

October 14, 1966

My mother drags me out to the parking lot and nearly throws me into the front seat of the car. When I try to scramble back out again, to go back to the office and blurt out the truth, she catches me by the sleeve and warns me through clenched teeth not to try her. She yanks the car door shut and pulls away. We drive in silence for several blocks while she fumes behind the wheel. I brace myself. I know what's coming. And eventually, it does.

"How could you!" she finally hurls across the seat. She doesn't take her eyes off the road, but the words keep coming as she accelerates through a yellow light, the torrent finally unleashed. "What on earth were you thinking? To let yourself be alone with that . . . that fiend! And in a filthy equipment room, like some common little slut! Did it never occur to you what might happen? Have I not told you what would happen?"

She throws me a look, waiting for me to say something, but all I can do is choke back more tears. She huffs, frustrated by my silence, then starts in again.

"Didn't I warn you about the way you dress? Those tight blouses and the skirts that ride up when you cross your legs. There are consequences for girls who extend those kinds of invitations, as you've just found out. I'd like to say I'm shocked that this has happened, but I'm not. I knew you'd get yourself in trouble one day and end up shaming me—just like your father. Well, he found out too, about the wages of sin."

"You mean the cocktail waitress he was with the night he died?" I fling the words across the car at her with a bitter kind of glee, because I'm suddenly filled with loathing. For her coldness and her piety, her utter lack of anything resembling a human heart.

I don't see her hand leave the steering wheel, but it does, cracking like a bolt of lightning across my left cheek, filling my head with a bloom of hot white light. I'm not surprised. I knew what would happen when the words left my mouth. I'm also not sorry. In fact, I'm glad to see the splotches of outraged color staining her cheeks, glad to know I've wounded her. But part of me is sickened too, to find that she's ready to blame me for what she insists was an assault. Not the perpetrator of the supposed assault— me. Either way, I'm to blame.

I glare at her mutely from the passenger seat, running my tongue over the bloodied place along my lower lip. She's silent for a time, her knuckles blue-white on the wheel, eyes fixed straight ahead, but I can see the next round of rebukes forming, gathering like storm clouds on her brow. And finally, the storm breaks.

"I always knew you'd find some way to ruin yourself. But this . . . How could you? It'll be all over town by tomorrow. You and that . . . My god . . ." She breaks off, swallowing convulsively. "Do you have any idea how

mortifying it was to listen to that man tell me what you'd done? How you'd been found? You'll be a scandal now. Branded as God knows what. And I'll be blamed."

I'm sent to my room the minute we're home, where I'm to remain until my mother has decided what to do with me. There's an ominous sound to that, but part of me is relieved to be alone with my misery. I have no right to feel sorry for myself. Not when I've left you to face consequences for something that never happened. Damned by my silence, by my cowardice.

I have no hope of being forgiven—what I've done is unforgivable—but I pray that there's some way for me to atone. Though just how, I can't think. My mother has informed me that I won't be returning to school on Monday, which means there's no chance of slipping away to see you. Nor of sneaking out while she's at work since she's arranged for time off from the rectory.

It's like being in prison and she's the warden, constantly here, constantly watching. I'm only allowed out of my room for meals and to do the dishes. The phone is off-limits. So is TV. Except for my Bible and the copy of Introduction to the Devout Life I found beside my breakfast plate this morning, she's taken all my books. I have no idea what she's done with them, but I feel certain I'll never see them again.

When I get up the nerve to ask what they've done to you, she claims not to know. I don't believe her. It isn't like her to let something like that go. Expelling you would send a clear message that her daughter was a victim—even if she doesn't believe it herself—and is therefore blameless. It's about appearances for her, about her reputation as a good and godly woman.

I hear her on the phone sometimes. I crack the door when it rings and eavesdrop, in case it's you. It never is, but I keep hoping. Women from church call to commiserate. They've heard, of course. There are no secrets in this town. And certainly not one as juicy as the sixteen-year-old daughter of the rectory secretary being caught in flagrante delicto.

One afternoon I overhear your mother's name being tossed about. I can't make it all out, but the gist is that she can't afford to put you in a private school and has no idea what to do about your senior year, and wouldn't it be sad if she were to have to move away? Only my mother doesn't sound sad when she says it. She sounds gleeful, spiteful.

I feel sick to my stomach. All of this because of me—because I couldn't bring myself to tell the truth. But suddenly I'm determined to tell it. Before I can change my mind, I burst into my mother's room. "I wanted it," I blurt, not caring that she's still on the phone. "I was there because I wanted to be."

My mother mumbles an excuse and hangs up the phone, then stares at me, horrified.

I confess it all then, in as much detail as I can manage. How I welcomed it, invited it, reveled in it—because I love you. She sags onto the edge of her bed, appalled that I should say such things, let alone feel them. I don't care. In fact, I'm savagely glad to see her so shaken. I tell her I'm going to tell Principal Gordon the truth, going to tell everyone the truth, and nothing she can say or do will change my mind.

She pushes up off the bed, approaching me with an icy, almost eerie calm, her face luminous with rage. Self-preservation tells me to flee, but I can't back down now. I owe it to you to stand my ground. Just this once. Whatever the cost.

The flurry of slaps briefly blinds me, landing again and again, until my eyes are streaming and my cheeks feel like fire. She wants me to cry, to plead, to take it all back, but I won't. I can't. My silence only inflames her further. She continues to pummel me, hands flailing wildly now, like the wings of an angry bird, beating out her fury.

My ears begin to ring, the room to shift and spin. I'm on the brink of passing out when the blows finally slow and then stop. My mother stands panting, arms limp at her sides. There's no remorse in the look she gives me, nothing to indicate she feels a whit of regret for her brutality. Instead, she points to the door and orders me back to my room, advising me not to show my face again until I'm called for.

I wake the next morning with a hideous bruise along my left cheek. My mother seems not to notice when she comes to my room and orders me downstairs for breakfast. I'm too nauseated to eat the plate of scrambled eggs she sets in front of me and the orange juice stings the oozing split in my lip. I sit like stone while she butters her toast and sips her coffee. Finally, she puts down her knife and coolly informs me that she's made arrangements to send me away to school.

"Away . . . where?" I ask, almost too stunned to speak.

"Father Ryan recommended Immaculate Heart, an all-girls school that specializes in young ladies who have . . . made poor choices. He made a call and they've agreed to take you."

"Where is it?" I ask, panic rising.

She spoons more sugar into her coffee, stirring briskly.
"Pennsylvania. About a three-hour drive."

I'm dazed, then furious. "I won't go."

She lifts her cup and sips, unaffected by my protest.
"We'll leave the day after tomorrow. You won't need to
pack much. You'll wear a uniform most of the time."

"You can't do this!"

"It's done. You need to be taken in hand, delivered
from temptation while it's still possible. I don't know how
you could have strayed so far from the teachings of the
church, but I've obviously failed you. And I've failed God.
I have to live with that. But I refuse to let you sink any
further into sin."

"It isn't sin!" I fire back, my voice fraying with
unshed tears. "We love each other!"

"Enough!" she barks, standing so abruptly she nearly
upsets her chair. "You are never to say such a thing in my
presence again! Do you understand?" She pauses then,
gathering herself in. When she speaks again her voice is
more controlled, her eyes carefully averted from my face.
"Marital relations are intended for the purpose of pro-
creation, a sacrament between a man and a woman who
have taken vows before God. Anything else is a deviation
from God's will and therefore a sin. It's my job to keep
you from sin. I failed once. I won't fail again. Now go to
your room and start gathering your things. I'll bring up a
suitcase when I finish the dishes."

"Can I at least call—"

"You may not."

"Please. Just to say goodbye."

"I said no." To make her point she steps to the
kitchen phone, lifts the receiver from its cradle, and lays
it on the counter. "In case you were thinking of using the

extension in my room. While we're on the subject, there are a few other things you may as well know. The sisters at Immaculate Heart are aware of your . . . transgressions, and will be keeping a close eye on you. Your mail will be scrutinized and other than a weekly call with me, you will have no phone privileges. Should you break these rules—or any other rule—you will be isolated from the other students for the remainder of your tenure. It will be hard at first but you'll adjust in time, though until you do, I think it best that you spend your weekends and holidays at school rather than coming back to Cumberland."

I stare at her, too numb to argue. "You've thought of everything."

She sighs, annoyed by my misery. "You don't think so now, but eventually you'll thank me for this. You're young, swept up in this awful infatuation, but it isn't what God wants for you. In time you'll see that, and know I was right to send you away."

Two days later, I watch Cumberland recede as we pull onto the highway. Beside me, my mother is stony behind the wheel, determined to complete her mission and save my soul. But she's wrong. I'll never thank her for this. And I'll never forgive her.

TWENTY-SEVEN

MALLORY

June 27, 1999

Mallory felt lethargic and vaguely disoriented as she made her way downstairs, as if she were suffering from jet lag or the onset of flu. She'd slept in—again—which made three days this week. It was the sudden loss of routine wreaking havoc with her body clock. She'd even started losing track of what day it was. The truth was that with nothing to do and nowhere to be, she was beginning to drift, and it wasn't a good feeling.

At least the coffee was still hot. She filled a mug and wandered out through the open glass sliders. Helen had already set up her easel and was at work with her paints and brushes. It was still surprising to find her home. So often growing up it had just been Mallory in the morning, scarfing down a bowl of cornflakes before she left for school.

Helen turned at the sound of her footsteps. "Morning, sleepyhead." She put down her paintbrush, wiped her hands on the front of her smock, and reached for her own mug on the railing. "I looked in on you earlier but you were still asleep, so I thought I'd paint a little."

Mallory eyed the unfinished canvas on the easel. It was the one she'd seen when she snuck into her mother's studio, the one with the stormy sea and looming clouds. "It's different from most of your paint-ings, isn't it? More . . . subdued."

Helen's brows flicked up briefly, clearly surprised that she'd noticed. "It is. That's why I'm working on it. I'm trying to brighten it up a little."

"Why?"

"It feels a little dark. Not very tourist friendly."

"Maybe, but it feels authentic. The sun *doesn't* shine all the time. Storms come. Things get dark."

Helen glanced at the canvas, then at Mallory, frowning. "Do you want to tell me about the wedding? You didn't say much when you got home, but you seemed pretty wound up. What happened?"

Mallory smothered a groan. "Do we have to rehash it? I haven't even had my coffee."

"Not if you don't want to, but I'd appreciate the company if you want to sit for a bit. It's a gorgeous day."

Mallory settled into a nearby deck chair with her mug, watching as Helen used a series of light, deft strokes to add a shaft of watery sunlight to the canvas. The effect was both startling and subtle, transforming the entire feel of the piece from heaviness to hope. She had to admit, she was impressed.

Other than the handful of lessons Helen had attempted when she was little, she'd never really seen her mother paint. It was something she'd always done behind closed doors, a deeply personal outlet, jeal-ously guarded against intrusion. And now, she'd been invited to stick around. It felt like another shift in their relationship, a door purposely left open.

"He was there," Mallory said quietly. "He was Kenny's best man."

Helen turned but was silent, waiting for more.

"Everything was perfect. The ceremony was on the lawn down by the water. There was a huge arbor of pink roses and they had a white baby grand set up. Aiden wrote them a beautiful song but someone else performed it—at his own best friend's wedding. I get him not playing, but there's nothing wrong with his voice. He could have sung it but he wouldn't. He's given up. Not just playing. *All* of it."

"Honey, you knew all that. I told you."

"You did. But it's not the same as hearing *him* say it."

Helen abandoned her canvas and came to sit beside Mallory. "So you talked?"

"I went out for some air and he followed me."

"And?"

"And he felt like a stranger. He looks like Aiden, but he's someone else now. Someone I don't recognize. When I told him I was sorry, he said he didn't want my pity. All he cared about was why I was back and when I was leaving."

Helen held her eyes a moment, her mouth open slightly, as if about to say something. In the end, she turned to gaze at the sea. "He's drowning, Mallory. Or thinks he is. That's why he's given up. Because he's run out of fight. He needs a lifeline. Someone who believes in him, who knows him."

Someone like you. That's what her mother wanted to say but hadn't.

"No," Mallory said firmly. "I know what you're thinking and the answer is no. I'm not going to be Aiden's lifeline. And even if I *was* willing—which I'm not—he doesn't want my advice."

"Maybe. But you know how to talk to people when they're hurting. It's what you do."

"I'm a social worker, Mother. He doesn't need a social worker."

"Then be his friend. He certainly needs one of those right now."

Mallory shook her head, ready for the conversation to be over. "Look, I know what you want to happen between us. But this isn't a movie. The girl doesn't always get the guy. Sometimes the guy gets on a plane and moves to London."

"And sometimes he comes home again," Helen said softly. "And together they figure it out."

Mallory blew out a long breath. For a woman who'd loved two men and lost them both, her mother was annoyingly sanguine when it came to matters of the heart. "I'm sorry. I can't."

"Can't or won't?"

"Both."

Mallory looked away, turning her face to the breeze. The beach was waking up, the mingled scents of warming sand and the incoming tide calling up bittersweet memories. For an instant, the old ache resurfaced, the need for him, for what they'd been *together*. But then, almost as quickly, the wound of his leaving opened up, oozing and all too fresh. She couldn't go through that again. She'd barely survived it the last time.

"I don't need any more complications in my life right now. And Aiden *certainly* doesn't. We need to deal with our own messes in our own ways."

"What if what's coming turns out to be more than he can deal with?"

Mallory brought her head around sharply, aware of something new in her mother's tone, something shadowy and ominous. "What do you mean by 'what's coming'?"

Helen looked down at her hands, scraping at a smear of white paint on her palm. "Nothing. I didn't mean anything. But sometimes things are harder than we expect them to be and we need someone to help pick up the pieces once they've finished falling."

"And you think that someone is me."

"I do, yes."

"Well, I don't. And I'm sure Aiden would tell you the same thing." Pushing to her feet, she wandered to the railing. It was time to change the subject before they ended up arguing. "When we were at lunch the other day, you said the community center was looking for a water safety instructor. I've been giving it some thought and if they're still looking for someone, I think I'd like to apply. Do you know who I'd talk to?"

"No," Helen said, blinking in surprise. "But if you're serious, I'll find out. Why the change of heart?"

"I guess I'm like you—at loose ends. I'm not used to having whole days with nothing to do. I need something to focus on, a way to feel useful."

"I take it you haven't heard anything else from the detective?"

"No. Meanwhile, my future is . . . I can't even see my future."

"I'm so sorry, sweetheart. Things *will* work out, though. You'll see. But I do think staying busy is a good idea. I'll call the center right now and get the contact info. I'm sure they'll be thrilled to have you back. And the timing is perfect."

"Thank you," Mallory said, managing a smile. She wasn't sure how perfect it was, but the center was in need of a water safety instructor and she happened to be available.

TWENTY-EIGHT

MALLORY

June 29, 1999

Mallory experienced an unsettling fizz of nerves as she crossed the parking lot of the George R. Cavanaugh Community Center. Though ostensibly named for Aiden's father, the center had always been Estelle's baby, and there was no reason to think that had changed.

Estelle had been only too happy to leave the day-to-day running of the place to others, preferring to make her contributions in less visible ways, organizing fundraisers, heading up the board, and managing the center's budget to the nickel. And it was hard to argue with the results. On her watch, the center had enjoyed steady expansion, including a state-of-the-art sports complex, classrooms for an impressive list of after-school activities, and a generous scholarship program focused on under-resourced communities.

And yet, as Mallory approached the double glass doors, she found herself questioning the wisdom of what she was about to do. Like most of Little Harbor, she had happy memories of the center. It was where she'd fallen in love with competitive swimming, racking up so many laps after school that they'd offered her a summer lifeguard position. She had jumped at the chance then, but it was different now. Every member of the staff would know her history with the Cavanaughs.

Still, she registered a pleasant wave of déjà vu as she stepped into the spacious lobby. With its vaulted ceilings and heavy wood beams, it had always felt more like a ski lodge than a community center, a safe and welcoming place where kids of all ages could make friends and explore new interests.

At the front desk, she gave her name and was told Ms. Rhodes, the center's sports director, would be with her shortly. While she waited she wandered through the lobby, browsing the rack of brochures listing the center's various classes, the bulletin board pinned with newspaper clippings, job announcements, and sign-up sheets for after-school programs.

She smiled awkwardly when a pair of giggling tween girls spilled out of one of the activity rooms. They fell silent when they saw her, eyeing her curiously, then darted past her in the direction of the exit, leaving a chorus of giggles in their wake.

"Ms. Ward?" Mallory turned to find a woman in tennis whites heading in her direction. "I'm Deborah Rhodes. Just Debbie around here. Thanks for coming in." She tucked the clipboard she was carrying under her arm and extended a hand. She was fortyish and petite, with a broad smile and a crisp blond bob. "I can't tell you how glad I am that you called. We were just days from canceling half our summer sessions. And I see you're a legacy member as well."

"A what?"

"You were a member when you were a kid. A trophy winner too. It also says here that you worked summers as a lifeguard. And now you're back. How wonderful."

"Just for part of the summer. I'm here visiting my mother. I actually live in Boston."

"Well, we'll take you for as long as we can have you. Let me give you the tour while we chat. We'll start with the classrooms. We've added art, music, computer classes, and even after-school tutoring since your time here."

Mallory fell in beside her as they navigated a maze of door-lined corridors. Some of the rooms were empty, but most appeared to be in use. Now and then bursts of youthful laughter bled out into the corridors. A happy sound. The sound of kids having fun.

"We're horribly shorthanded this summer, especially on the sports side. Our tennis instructor is out until fall thanks to a nasty skiing accident. Another of our coaches just had surgery for a detached retina after catching a soccer ball in the face. And our regular water safety instructor is expecting twin girls any minute. We're all trying to cover, but it's been a struggle. I'm already coaching tennis, volleyball, and girls' soccer. If I had to somehow fit swimming in there too, I think I'd lose my mind."

"I can imagine. This place is amazing."

Debbie beamed like a pleased parent. "Thanks. We're pretty proud of it. Of course, none of it would be possible without Mrs. Cavanaugh's generosity. We're always looking for ways to expand. The community response has been overwhelming. Now all we have to do is keep up staff-wise."

They turned down a wide hallway lined with skid-proof black mats. Debbie pushed open a pair of heavy double doors, revealing an impressive indoor pool.

"This is where you'll be."

The familiar smell of chorine enveloped Mallory as she followed Debbie into the high- ceilinged auditorium. Her mouth dropped as she ran her eyes around the soaring space, with its bright-blue walls and long, narrow windows. The pool was enormous, equipped with red and white lane lines, starting blocks, and a pair of diving platforms at one end. "Wow. It certainly wasn't like this when I swam here as a kid."

"No. This pool is only a year old. It's a deepwater pool, set up for both long- and short-course events. We've expanded the competitive swimming leagues to include four age groups now and hope to add a bonified competitive training program in the next year or two. That's why we went ahead and installed the bleachers and scoreboards. There are also locker rooms on either side. Boys there. Girls here. We hope to use the old outdoor pool area for a mini water park but that's still in the planning phase."

Mallory was agog—an honest-to-goodness aquatic center right here in Little Harbor. "This is really impressive."

"We think so too," Debbie replied, beaming again. "So, what do you say? We already talked about the money and the hours on the phone, and now you've had the tour. The only thing left is for you to say yes. *Please*, say yes. I'll beg if necessary."

Mallory found herself grinning. "All right—yes."

"Hallelujah!" Debbie hooked her arm through Mallory's and steered her back through the doors and down the hall. She halted when they reached an intersection of corridors. "I hate to run but I'm due out on the courts in ten minutes and I need to scarf down a PowerBar first. Can you come in tomorrow? Not to start. Just to do your paperwork, assign you a locker, and make you a badge. Then we'll go over the session schedules and you can meet the rest of the staff. Say, elevenish?"

"I'll be here."

"Great. I'm off, then, but feel free to hang out and explore if you feel like it."

Mallory watched as Debbie retreated, hoping she hadn't just made a huge mistake. She was supposed to be evaluating her career prospects. Instead, she'd signed up to teach water safety. At least she could tell Jevet she'd found a way to be useful.

She had just turned to head back to the lobby when she caught the halting plink of piano notes. Reversing course, she followed the sound down the nearest hallway, eventually stopping in front of one of the activity rooms. The door was closed, but the notes bled through along with a muffled voice counting steadily in an attempt to impose a sense of time on the awkward rendition of what she now recognized as Beethoven's "Für Elise."

Mallory smothered a grin as the song came to a halting and somewhat ignominious end. When Debbie mentioned music classes she assumed they were talking about "Frère Jacques" or "You Are My Sunshine," not Beethoven. Clearly, Estelle had had a hand in choosing the curriculum.

The thought was cut short when the door suddenly opened and a girl with honey-colored braids—presumably the budding virtuoso—burst out into the hall and nearly smacked into her. She halted abruptly, clearly startled to find a grown-up in her path. "Sorry," she lisped, wrestling a Hello Kitty backpack onto one shoulder before scurrying away.

Mallory checked her watch as the squelch of the girl's sneakers faded. If she left now, she could make it downtown before the shops closed. If she was going to spend the summer playing lifeguard, she'd need to pick up an appropriate swimsuit and a few pairs of warm-ups.

She hadn't taken a step when the classroom door swung open again and she found herself face-to-face with Aiden. He blinked at her, appearing every bit as uncomfortable as she felt.

"Mallory."

"I didn't realize . . ." Her words trailed as she struggled to make sense of his presence. "Was that . . . Are you teaching piano here?"

His jaw tightened. "Not by choice. I got roped into covering for the guy who used to do it. He's decided to open a flower shop with his wife, apparently, so I got volunteered until they can find someone else."

Her eyes slid briefly to his injured hand. "And then what?"

Aiden flicked his eyes away and shoved the hand into his pocket. "And then nothing. I'm going to be a man of leisure. I might bungle it at first, but eventually I'll get the hang of it."

Stop it! The words rushed up into Mallory's throat like bile. She swallowed them down again. There was no point. He'd made up his mind to throw in the towel and nothing she said was going to change it. But she wasn't going to watch him do it. She'd call Debbie in the morning and tell her something had come up.

"I take it you're here about the water safety instructor opening."

She blinked at him, surprised that he'd put two and two together so quickly. Or had he? The more she thought about it, the more she realized this had her mother's fingerprints all over it. "I was considering it but I don't think it's going to work." She turned away then and headed down the corridor, eager to be away from him.

Aiden's footsteps echoed behind her. "Mallory, wait."

"I'm in a hurry." She threw the words over her shoulder, increasing her pace when she reached the lobby and caught sight of the glass doors.

"Mallory. Stop. We can't keep having these hit-and-run conversations. We need to talk."

She halted, wheeling around to face him. "It's been ten years, Aiden. If there was anything to say we would have said it by now."

"Then we should be able to coexist for a few months, don't you think? The center's in a jam and you're a perfect fit. Don't let our history get in the way of helping out."

He sounded so reasonable, so infuriatingly grown-up. But she didn't want to be reasonable. She wanted to be angry, to *stay* angry. "Did my mother put you up to this?"

"Your mother?"

"She didn't know you were volunteering here?"

"I don't see how she would. It's my second day, and I'm only here because *my* mother guilted me into it. So unless our mothers have taken to chatting over the back fence . . ."

"So this—me being here and just bumping into you—is a *coincidence?*"

"Not completely, no." Aiden's gaze wavered briefly. "It was me. I wasn't sure how long you'd be here but I asked Debbie to make sure your mother knew about the position. Helen just did what I hoped she would and passed the information to you."

Mallory sat with this news a moment. It was a relief to know her mother hadn't been involved, but she was more than a little surprised that Aiden would consider her a suitable candidate. "Why didn't you mention any of this at the wedding?"

"I was afraid that if you knew I was behind it you'd say no, and I didn't want you to."

"Aiden—"

"No. Don't say no, Mallory. We've got staff dropping like flies. And it's not like we'd be working together. We'll barely see each other. Please don't make us cancel swim classes."

"Now who's doing the guilting? Your mother taught you well."

Aiden laid a hand over his heart, as if gravely wounded. "Call me silly, but something tells me you didn't mean that as a compliment."

"I didn't."

"But you'll take the position?"

"Yes. All right. For as long as I'm here."

He shot her a smile then, that boyish smile that made the dimple in his right cheek pop, and for a moment she caught a glimpse of the old Aiden—the one she'd fallen in love with more than a decade ago. He could still turn on the charm when it suited him, still tug at places she'd thought long shut up. She'd need to be careful.

TWENTY-NINE

ESTELLE

July 3, 1999

Estelle lay still against her pillows, exhausted after a night of violent nausea. The sun glinting off the sea lit the room with strange angles of light that made her head hurt. She squeezed her eyes shut, longing to return to the depths of oblivion, but her stomach was awake now, roiling and hot, her throat raw after hours of merciless retching. Thank god Aiden was staying in the guesthouse, well out of earshot.

Her eyes opened and she suddenly went still. Between the ringing in her ears and the thumping in her head, she wasn't sure if she'd actually heard the doorbell or just imagined it. Then it came again, two quick, impatient pulses. Was she expecting someone? The housekeeper, perhaps? She couldn't remember. Whoever it was wasn't going away.

Groaning, she threw back the covers and pushed herself out of the bed. Her limbs felt gelatinous as she fumbled with her robe, then stumbled clumsily into her slippers and headed for the stairs. The dizziness was worse this morning. *Was* it still morning? She had no idea. She'd stopped wearing her watch, afraid Aiden might notice it flopping loosely on her wrist.

Another ring. Damn it. Was that three now? Four?

Wobbly but determined, she navigated the dining room, then the parlor, using bits of furniture to steady herself along the way. Her legs felt untrustworthy, disconnected somehow from the rest of her, and the furniture's solidity was reassuring. She paused as she reached the foyer, startled by her own reflection in the entryway mirror. The exertion of getting down the stairs had left her face sheened with perspiration, and her hair hung limp about her face. But even more disturbing were the dried spatters of yellow-green bile down the front of her nightgown.

Pull yourself together, Estelle. You can't fall apart yet. Not yet.

Gathering her robe close to her throat, she patted hopelessly at her hair and pulled back the door a little. If it was the housekeeper she would send her away. Or the pest-control man. No. Not today. She couldn't pretend to be fine today. She'd get rid of them, then crawl back in bed.

"Yes, how—" The words died the moment she saw Helen. *Thank god.*

"Are you all right?" Helen demanded, her brow creased furiously. "I've been ringing the bell for five minutes."

Estelle wasn't sure whether to be annoyed or relieved. But at least with Helen, she didn't have to pretend. And if she was being honest, some tiny part of her was glad to see this strange woman with her pale hair and paint-stained nails.

"I'm fine. I just . . . had a bad night."

"You're not fine. Look at you. Have you been throwing up? I was afraid you might after the chemo appointment. I brought you something that should help. Something stronger."

"I just need to sleep."

"And you will if you take this." Helen pulled an amber vial from the pocket of her smock. "I made it up this morning. It'll calm the nausea and help you sleep. Real sleep, not just naps between trips to the toilet. Have you eaten anything?"

Estelle groaned. "Not since lunch yesterday."

Helen clucked disapprovingly. "All right, then, that's the first order of business."

"I can't eat anything." She was clutching the doorknob now, her knees threatening to fold. "Please. Just leave the bottle and let me go back to bed."

But Helen wasn't budging. "The sooner you realize I know what I'm talking about, the easier this is going to be. Now let me in."

Estelle let go of the knob and stepped out of the doorway. She was simply too exhausted to argue. She said nothing as Helen pushed past her and headed for the kitchen. By the time she managed to catch up, Helen had already extracted butter and eggs from the refrigerator and located a bowl and a frying pan.

"Scrambled eggs and dry toast for now. And tea. Just sit and I'll bring it."

"I don't want any eggs."

"No, but you're going to eat them."

She was banging around in the drawers now, looking for something. Finally, she found the silverware and produced a teaspoon. Out came the amber vial from her smock pocket as she approached the table. She unscrewed the cap, filled the spoon with brownish-green liquid, and held it out.

"Two of these. Can you manage?"

Estelle drew away, eyeing the spoon warily. "What's in it?"

"If I told you, you wouldn't take it. But it's nothing that will hurt you."

"How do I know that?"

"Oh, good grief," Helen said, rolling her eyes. "If I wanted you dead I'd just let nature take its course, wouldn't I?"

Once again, Estelle was caught off guard by Helen's blunt response. And then suddenly, inexplicably, the absurdity of it hit her and she nearly grinned. "Yes, I suppose you would."

Helen waved the spoon coaxingly. "Go on. Take it. Or do you want me to do it?"

Estelle took the spoon with a huff. "I'll do it myself."

"I should warn you, it's awful-tasting stuff."

Estelle made a face as the tonic coated her tongue. It was thick and tasted like the ground, like dirt and leaves with something bitter at the finish. She shuddered as it went down, then gasped. "My god, it's vile!"

Helen reclaimed the spoon and poured out another dose. "One more. If it comes back up, we'll try again later."

"Comes back up?" Estelle's eyes went wide. "I thought this was supposed to *stop* that."

"It will. But you have to keep it down first. Sometimes it takes a few tries." Her face softened then. "Trust me."

Resigned, Estelle took the refilled spoon, closed her eyes, and swallowed. For a moment she thought she might have to bolt for the sink, but gradually the wave of nausea began to ease and she settled back in her chair.

Helen was busy at the counter, cracking eggs into a bowl. She'd found the bread too and had already dropped a slice into the toaster. It was as if she'd done this a hundred times before.

Suddenly, it struck Estelle that Helen *had* in fact done this hundreds of times over the years, in who knew how many kitchens. The realization brought an unexpected pang of guilt as she recalled all the times she'd hinted—even claimed outright—that there was something nefarious about Helen Ward's chosen line of work.

"Is this all . . . part of the service? For your charges, I mean?"

Helen pushed down the toast, then poured the eggs into the pan. "Every case is different, but mostly, yes."

"For the Admiral?"

"Yes."

"He was a good man. So kind and so generous."

Helen looked up from the egg pan, meeting Estelle's gaze squarely. "Generous to a *fault*, some might say."

Estelle looked away, keenly aware of the point being made. There'd been plenty of talk about the Admiral's decision to leave his house to Helen. Talk she herself had started. "I was friends with his wife," Estelle said quietly.

"Patricia. Yes, he told me. You were in the garden club together, I think."

Estelle smiled sadly. "I was always so jealous of her roses. She had the touch, you know. I never did."

"The roses are why he left me the house," Helen said, giving the eggs a final stir before snapping off the burner. "He wanted to make sure they'd be looked after when he was gone." She scooped the eggs onto a plate and, after adding the slice of dry toast, carried the plate to the table along with a fork. "They're both out there now. Their ashes, I mean. Scattered in the garden."

Estelle stared blankly at the plate. The Admiral and Patricia, together in her rose garden. Yes, of course they were. How very like him to forgo the hero's funeral due him at Arlington in order to spend eternity with his beloved—and to ensure the continued care of her roses, the thing she'd cherished most in the world.

"I didn't know," Estelle said softly. "Well, I knew about her ashes—I was there when he scattered them—but I didn't know his were there too."

"He was afraid someone would buy the house and pull out the roses, so he left them to me. The house just happened to come along with them."

"I'm sorry."

"For what?"

Estelle met Helen's eyes, holding them. "You *know* what."

Helen nodded, the barest of acknowledgments, signaling that the matter was closed. "How's the nausea?"

Estelle closed her eyes a moment, assessing. "It's . . . better," she said finally, with some surprise. "Not gone completely but definitely better than when I woke up."

"Good. Eat as much as you can. Then we'll get you back to bed. You're going to feel a whole lot better after you get some sleep."

Estelle picked up the slice of toast and nibbled at one corner, watching as Helen filled the sink with soapy water and submerged the egg pan. How had they gotten here? After all the gossip, all the nastiness, how on *earth* had they gotten *here*, with Helen Ward cooking her eggs and cleaning up her kitchen?

Was it pity? The word—or anything remotely approaching it—chafed. She didn't want *anyone's* pity, Helen Ward's least of all. Perhaps because she deserved it least. She still couldn't fathom why a woman she'd never shown an ounce of decency would show her such kindness.

"I don't think I've said thank you," Estelle blurted. "For . . . all of this. I've never been very good with thank-yous."

Helen turned off the tap and fixed Estelle with a bland expression. "Perhaps this would be a good time to learn."

"I'm afraid time isn't something I have much of."

"Well, then, you'd best get on with it, hadn't you?"

Estelle studied Helen between minuscule forkfuls of egg, watching as she wiped and tidied. She kept expecting to see some thinly veiled show of glee—*at long last, the mean lady next door is receiving her just deserts*—but it wasn't there. She had misjudged Helen Ward. Badly, it would seem. The woman could be brutally direct, but there wasn't a malicious bone in her body. And perhaps she was right. Perhaps it was time she got on with it.

"Are you through?" Helen asked when she'd finished wiping down the stove.

Estelle glanced at her plate. She'd eaten only a few bites of the eggs and only half the toast but it was more than she'd expected to get down. "Yes. I think so."

Helen collected her plate, carrying it to the sink, then returned to hand Estelle a glass of water. "Dehydration is the enemy."

"I'm not much of a water drinker."

"You need to drink. You'll feel better. And when you feel better, you'll look better. Aiden will be home in a few hours. I assume you'd prefer he not see you like this."

Estelle looked down at her spattered nightgown and shook her head. "No."

"Well, then, let's get you cleaned up and back to bed."

Estelle pushed obediently to her feet. Part of her had wanted to protest, to insist that she was perfectly capable of taking care of herself, but the other part, the part that was exhausted and afraid, was forced to admit that it was a relief to have someone to lean on.

Maintaining a brave face for Aiden was getting harder and harder. Not that he was around much these days. And now that he was filling in at the community center, he'd be around even less, giving her some much-needed privacy as she learned to navigate the progression of her illness. And hopefully, time to get him pointed in the right direction.

She hadn't realized Mallory would be working at the center until Aiden mentioned it last night, or that he'd been the one to put her name forward for the job. Might he be thinking about rekindling their romance? A month ago, the idea would have horrified her, but now everything had changed. She had to change too.

THIRTY

HELEN

The ivory carpet muffles our steps as we make our way down the hall. Estelle leads the way, leaving me to follow in the wake of her resentment. It's hard for her, and it's going to get harder. She's used to being in charge, to giving orders rather than taking them. But she'll need to learn to surrender, to relinquish control, to trust. It won't come easily for her.

This is the business of dying well. The sorting out of what's worth the fight and what's not. The peeling off of old resentments. The laying down of arms. It's a time of reckoning, of balancing our books and paying those we owe. But when done well, with clear eyes and an open heart, we learn to cherish those last precious days, and perhaps even to be grateful. We realize at long last that life in this world is finite, and with our wicks beginning to burn low, we cast about for other sources of light. For memory and meaning. For love stripped of need or wound. Pure, perfected, peaceful. This is transition. Not a fight, but an easing, an embrace of the eternal, of who and what we will be on the other side. Complete.

Estelle stops at the door to her room and turns to look at me with uncertain eyes. I nod in answer to her unasked question. *Yes, I mean to go in with you.* Modesty, too, must eventually be relinquished. She might as well start getting used to the idea.

The room is like something from a magazine—hues of cream and blue with gilded mirrors and billowy silk curtains. I take in the antique chest of drawers, the dressing table glittering with French perfumes, knowing the grandeur will soon be eclipsed by the trappings of a sickroom.

Estelle is pale again after her trip up the stairs, and faintly green. "Do you need the bathroom? Or to sit a moment?" I point to the enormous four-poster bed with its brocade spread and tussle of untidy sheets—the bed of someone who has spent an uneasy night.

She shakes her head. "I'm fine."

She isn't, but there's no point in arguing. She'll learn to listen to her body—and to me. "Tell me where to find a fresh nightgown."

She stares at me, as if startled by the question.

I point to the spatters of vomit. "You need to change."

She nods. "Top drawer. Right side."

"What time do you expect Aiden home?"

"I'm not sure. Four maybe. But he'll go straight to the guesthouse. That's where he's been staying since he came home."

There's a catch in her voice I'm not meant to notice. "I'm sorry," I say, opening a drawer and pulling out a gown of peach-colored silk. "It must be hard, watching him pull away from everything he's worked for."

She nods as she takes the gown. "I don't know what else to do. He doesn't want to hear anything I have to say. Do you suppose . . ."

Her voice trails and her face goes slack, her eyes suddenly unfocused. The syrup is taking effect, making her drowsy. Good. Sleep is what she needs now. "Go on," I prod gently. "Go wash your face and I'll tidy the bed."

She looks better when she returns in her fresh nightgown, her cheeks pink from scrubbing, her hair gathered in a loose ponytail. I pull down the covers and nod at the bed. "Climb in."

"But if Aiden . . ."

"I'll set the alarm for three. You'll feel better when you wake up, but don't overdo it. A hot bath might be a good thing if you can manage it. If you still feel unsteady and Aiden's around, tell him you have a migraine and you're resting for the remainder of the day."

She nods, her eyes heavy as she relaxes against the pillows.

I reach into my pocket, withdrawing the bottle of syrup and a teaspoon and show them to her. "Two teaspoons before bed," I tell her, before secreting them away in the nightstand. "I'll be back tomorrow morning."

"You're . . . going?"

She sounds like a child, sleepy but anxious about being left alone. "I'll be right next door if you need anything. Just pick up the phone and I'll come."

Estelle closes her eyes and breathes out a sigh. She'll be out before I reach the bottom of the stairs. I'm almost to the door when I hear her say softly, "Thank you, Helen, for being . . . so kind." It's not until her voice cracks that I realize she's weeping. "I've made such a mess of . . . everything. And now there's no time."

"Don't do this now, Estelle. Not when you're in this shape. Focus on getting some rest. There'll be time for regrets tomorrow."

Her blue eyes, so like her son's, are awash with tears. "You don't understand. It's all ruined. *I* ruined it."

It's the syrup, I remind myself, coupled with grinding fatigue. But at the bottom of those tears is genuine regret, raw in all its sudden newness. Recriminations are often part of the end-of-life journey, but it feels different somehow in this woman I've disliked for so long. Almost familiar. She's like me, I realize with a tiny jolt—a woman with regrets.

I ease down beside her and touch her hand, willing her to calm. "Nothing is ruined," I say gently. "There's time. Whatever it is. There's still time."

"I've made so many mistakes," she mumbles brokenly.

I shake my head and sigh. "Haven't we all."

Her lids flutter open. "You?"

"Of course, me."

"I thought you were a *saint* or something."

I'm almost amused by her use of the word. I've been called many things over the years, but *saint* was never among them. "I'm flesh and blood, just like you, Estelle, a veritable font of mistakes."

Her eyes close and her breathing goes heavy, but there's the hint of a smile on her lips. "Aren't we a pair?" she whispers, the familiar words becoming a kind of joke between us.

"We are indeed," I whisper back, but she's already asleep.

I smooth her covers and for a moment, I stare down at her. Even sick, even exhausted, she's still a beautiful woman. Perhaps more so now. It's a strange thing, counterintuitive, but illness has softened her, made her vulnerable—more human. Suddenly, I find myself imagining the girl she might have been. Shimmering and generous and warm. The image startles me. That's the thing about seeing people stripped of their pride—it humanizes them in ways we're often not prepared for. We suddenly see our sameness, our connection, our ties. And once seen, they can never be *unseen*.

THIRTY-ONE

HELEN

July 5, 1999

Dearest,

I hadn't planned to write tonight. I meant to be asleep by now. But here I am, awake at all hours. Keeping secrets is heavy work, but heavier still when the truth isn't yours to tell.

I spent the morning with Estelle and it's left me uneasy. I've believed from the start that keeping the truth from Aiden is a mistake, and yet I've agreed to help her do just that—to deceive him. I have no experience with this end of things, navigating grieving loved ones. My charges are generally alone in the world. Concealment never enters into it.

She's resumed her treatments for the time being, in the hope of gaining a month or two. It's a hard way to go, but if time is what she needs to make her peace, I'll do what I can to help her find it, though I shudder when I think about the fallout of her deception, about the depth of it and what form it might take. To my trained eyes, her illness is plain, but if she's careful Aiden might not notice for a while—she can be a superb actress when she needs to be—but eventually, the truth will become evident and I'll be caught in the middle.

And yet, I can't help seeing a pattern in all of it, like a messy knot waiting to be unraveled. Am I a monster to wonder if behind all the tragedy, there might be some larger purpose? Some good that might come? For years, I've clung to the belief that the things that come into our lives—even the hard things—are actually meant to point us toward our highest good. For Mallory's sake, and Aiden's too, I pray it's true. And I suppose I wonder if there might be a nudge in it for me as well. A reminder that time is short and there are still confessions to be made.

My sins over the years have been many. Against my mother. Against my faith. And against you, my dearest. As the Confiteor says . . .

In what I have done.

And in what I have failed to do.

Through my fault.

Through my most grievous fault.

Once upon a time, I thought to take those sins to the grave. With both of us gone, who would know? But I would know, dearest. And the knowing would leave a bruise on my heart. And so, here I am at this ungodly hour, wondering how to go about it.

How does one utter such things out loud and hope to still be loved at the end of it? There is no way to prepare for this kind of confession, no Bible verse, no prayer. There is only the remembering, clear-eyed and unflinching—back to the beginning of our ending. But can I bear it? Can you, dearest? Would it mean letting go? An end at last to all this silly scribbling? Because I don't think I could bear that. My pen is my way of keeping you close, an inky tether across the ether, to wherever you are.

But it occurs suddenly that I'm being selfish in writing to you this way, holding you here where you'd rather not be. Perhaps you wish to be free of me. And why shouldn't you? Our time was over long before that final parting. You'd had another life, another someone. I merely came back to tie up loose ends, and perhaps to repay a debt. And it was paid in full, heaven help me. Our business concluded. Our accounts marked paid.

Except for one item. Except for our girl. She deserves to know how we began—and how we ended. Who you were—and who I wasn't.

◆ ◆ ◆

June 8, 1968

I am to leave Immaculate Heart at last. Looking back, it wasn't as bad as I imagined it would be. I made a few friends and there were lots of books. And plenty of time to read them since I never left the place, even when the dorms would empty out for the holidays. On Sundays I would receive my weekly call from my mother. It was always brief and cool, and I was relieved when it ended. I didn't miss her, or home. But I did—and do—miss you, dearest. I wonder how you are—and where you are. Do you ever think of me? And if so, is it with love or loathing?

Sometimes when I read, I hear your voice in my head, as if you're right here with me, reading aloud as you used to. I take comfort in these letters, long, newsy things filled with tender words you'll never read. They're not real letters, just scribblings in a journal I keep hidden beneath my mattress, away from prying eyes. It's silly, I know, but it helps me pretend you're with me, to imagine I'm not truly as alone as I sometimes feel.

I'm told you and your mother have moved away. Hard news but not unexpected. Still, something in me has died knowing you're not there anymore, and as my time at Immaculate Heart winds to a close I find I'm dreading the return to Cumberland. There's nothing there for me now. No love. No future. And so I've settled on a life of service.

There. I've written it at last. A commitment of sorts. And not an imprudent one, however brash it may appear. A convent seems the perfect place to retreat from the world, and even my mother can't find fault with the choice. I'm to become what's called an inquirer and begin my period of discernment. It's a long road with many hurdles to navigate but I'm in no hurry and Sister Eugenia has been advising me through it all.

It seems a lot for a girl of eighteen to give up, the possibility of a husband and family, but it's no real hardship. I've known for some time that such things weren't meant for me. But ghosts are devious things, dearest. You think you've laid them to rest, and suddenly they leap out at you from the darkness. You hear a thing, a casual scrap of news, and the questions begin to take root, shaking your faith to its core.

I heard your mother might be living in Baltimore. And so it begins. The need to be certain before I take the last step, to know once and for all that there's no chance for us. I lie to Sister Eugenia. I tell her my mother is ill and I need to go home, but I go looking for you instead. I take the bus to Baltimore first and find your mother in the phone book. She tells me you're living near Philadelphia. Sometimes I wish she had told me the rest of it. It would have spared us both a good deal of heartache. She didn't, though. I suspect she knew we had . . . unfinished business.

I can scarcely breathe as you pull back the door and find me on the stoop. Your face goes white, your jaw slack, as if you've come face-to-face with a ghost. Time grinds to a halt as we stand there, drinking in all that has changed—and all that hasn't.

Your face is exactly as I remember—the sharp angles and broad, full mouth, the copper-gold eyes that made my breath catch the first time they locked with mine, the small sickle-shaped scar above your left brow. For years, they've lived in my memory, frozen in time. Now, suddenly, they're real, warm and alive.

You step back, inviting me in without a word. We touch hands first, fingers twining shyly, desperately. Our eyes lock next, unspoken words sparking between us in the hallway's semi-gloom. And then you say my name, whisper it hoarsely and harshly. We fall together, mouths clashing, familiar and fevered. The joy of the moment nearly blinds me and in that instant I'm reborn. I'm no longer a novice bound for the veil. I'm the girl who sat across from you at the library, reading a battered copy of Jane Eyre, back again and still wildly in love, yours for the taking if you want me.

And you do want me. I feel it in the dizzying way you kiss me, cling to me, wind your fingers through my hair. But then, abruptly, you pull away. My face is wet with joyful tears, my heart near bursting. But your eyes are dry.

I should know instantly that something's wrong, but I'm too big a fool to notice the hardness that's crept into your expression. I reach for you but you shake your head and take a step back, hand raised to hold me at bay.

"We can't," you say quietly. "I can't."

"Can't . . . what?" I ask stupidly.

"This. Us. I can't do it."

I stare at you, confused. A moment ago, your mouth was on mine and now you spurn me. Not that I don't deserve to be spurned—I do. But somehow I believed that all would be forgiven. I see now that I was wrong.

"Please," I say, my throat thick with tears. "I know what I did was unforgivable. To let you take the blame when we both . . ." I break off, dashing away a fresh round of tears. "I've tortured myself every minute of every day, wondering how I would make it up to you if I ever got the chance. And maybe I can't, but if you'll let me, I swear I'll spend the rest of my life—"

"No," you say, taking another step back. "Listen to me."

Your voice is so calm, so steely and flat that it sets off a panic in my chest. "Please," I choke. "I love you. I've always loved you."

You wait a beat, until you're sure you have my full attention. "I'm married, Helen."

You hold up your hand, showing me the plain gold band on your ring finger. I stare at it, reeling. Married. I can't quite grasp it. We made so many plans, you and I. Things we'd do, places we'd go. Together. Yet here you stand, telling me you've taken vows with someone else.

"Married," I repeat numbly.

"Yes."

Your answer slices into me, so matter-of-fact, so unflinching. I blink futilely, sending a fresh river of tears down my cheeks. "For how long?"

"Two weeks."

This makes it worse somehow, the thought that I might have stopped you if I'd only come sooner. But it's probably not true. How could it be? If I ever had a claim to your fidelity, I lost it the day I failed to stand up for you. And yet, foolishly, some childish part of me has imagined you chaste and pining, waiting for me to come find you. It never occurred to me that you could belong to anyone else—that you could be happy with anyone else.

But you are and I should be glad for you.

I'm not, though. I'm shattered. And more bitter than I have any right to be. You belong to me. There has never been any question about that. Just as there has never been any question that I belong to you. So why? Why have you done this thing? The question continues to burn as I look at you, searing me raw, until it finally tumbles out of my mouth, a choked and desperate whisper.

"Why would you do it?"

Your face hardens. "Why does anyone get married?"

I flinch at the chill in your voice, shocked to realize you're glad to have hurt me. For the first time, I see the pain in your eyes, the toll my betrayal has taken on you— because you let me see it.

"Did you think I'd still be waiting? Two years and not a word. No explanation. No remorse. That was your choice, not mine. Just like the day in Mr. Gordon's office was a choice."

A terrible thought suddenly occurs. "Did you do this . . . to punish me?"

You laugh then, a brittle sound that rings off the paneled walls of your living room. "Is that what you think? That I've been carrying a torch all this time, plotting revenge with a loveless marriage on the off chance that you'd show up one day. I wanted a life. I deserve a life. And now I have one. It isn't with you, but that was your choice. You did what you had to do that day. I get that.

Sort of. In the end, we all do what we have to. And now it's my turn."

"But this is all wrong!" I protest, horrified by the matching sofa and chairs, the little doilies on the coffee table, the cut-glass bowl filled with pale-blue crystal mints. "This was never the life you wanted!"

"It's the life I want now." Your voice frays suddenly and you turn away. For a moment I think you might be crying, but when you turn back your face is strangely blank. "I don't know why you came today, but there's no point now."

I stare at you, astonished. "Why do you think I came? I wanted to make things right between us. To tell you I'm sorry and that I never stopped loving you."

You nod. Barely. "And now you've told me."

I'm stunned by the finality of your tone, by your icy calm. "So that's it? We're . . . finished?"

"We've been finished for a long time. You should know that better than anyone."

"I didn't know where you were!"

"Maybe. But I knew where you were. Your mother told me."

"When? How?"

"I went back to Cumberland, to your mother's house. She slammed the door in my face at first, but I refused to go away until she told me where you were. So she did. She told me you had taken vows or whatever it is girls do when they become nuns, that you'd given your life to God, as penance—for me. Because you realized you'd ruined yourself for anyone decent."

"That isn't true!"

"She lied?" you say dryly. "You're not . . . a nun?"

I look away, the lump in my throat almost too big to breathe. "It didn't happen the way she said. School was almost over and I couldn't bear the thought of going back to Cumberland, so I asked if I could stay. If I had known where you were . . . But none of that matters now. They'll let me leave. I'll just tell Sister Eugenia—"

"So it's true," you say, cutting me off. "I've lost you twice. The first time to your mother, the second to God."

"But you haven't lost me. I'm here! We can be together now."

You shake your head and the finality of it chills me. "No, we can't. We've made our choices. And now we have to live with them."

"Please. There has to be a way—"

You close your eyes briefly, as if steadying yourself. "There isn't. Now please go. You shouldn't be here."

And just like that, it's over. I walk all the way back to the bus station. I stupidly let the taxi go when I arrived. It never occurred to me that our time together would be so short, or that my exit would be so painfully abrupt. But then, so much never occurred to me.

THIRTY-TWO

MALLORY

July 17, 1999

Mallory slung her duffel up onto her shoulder and headed for the lobby, hoping to catch Debbie before she left for the night. The summer B swim classes were filling up faster than anticipated, and she'd been pondering ways they could manage the overflow without turning kids away, and this afternoon, while collecting abandoned towels in the girls' shower, it had occurred to her that staggering in a few evening classes might solve the problem.

It wasn't like she had anywhere else to be. After nearly a month of silence, she'd finally yielded to temptation and checked in with Muldowney. Apparently, there were no new leads on the elusive Sticks, making an imminent return to Boston unlikely.

She also hadn't heard from Jevet since their last conversation. Not that she was surprised. She was being given *space*, which she supposed she should be grateful for. As head of New Day, Jevet could have forced the issue, either pushing her to decide on the spot or firing her outright. Instead, she'd been given the summer to decide her own future—unless the review committee's investigation decided it *for* her. Thankfully, Jevet didn't seem to think that likely, which would leave the ball in Mallory's court. She wasn't sure what that would ultimately mean, but for now, she was glad to have the center to fill her time.

She rarely saw Aiden. She'd been carefully avoiding the classroom areas and suspected he'd been doing the same with the pool. If their mutual avoidance was obvious, no one mentioned it, though she suspected most of the staff knew their story. She was aware of their eyes darting in her direction now and then, when Aiden would walk into the break room or they happened to pass in the hall. It was getting easier, she told herself. Perhaps one day they'd be able to sit in the same room without her stomach tying itself in knots. For now, she'd just keep taking it one day at a time.

She was glad to see Debbie's office light still on when she came around the corner. She wouldn't stay long, just long enough to let her know she'd be fine with working a couple of nights a week if that helped.

"Hey," she said, poking her head in. "I'm glad I caught you. I was thinking . . . oh . . ."

Aiden glanced up from Debbie's desk, a sheaf of papers in his hand. "Sorry. Deb left about twenty minutes ago. Her daughter had a dance recital."

"Thanks. I just had . . . Never mind, I'll find her tomorrow."

"I wasn't rifling through her desk or anything," Aiden said with a lopsided grin. "She left some purchase orders for me to look over and I was just finishing up."

Mallory nodded, though she wasn't sure why he felt the need to explain himself. "Right. Well. Good night."

"Have a drink with me."

She had already turned to go, determined to beat a hasty retreat, but turned to look back at him. "What?"

"A drink," he repeated, pushing to his feet. "Have a drink with me."

"No." The one-word reply sounded faintly panicked, as if he'd just asked her to help him rob a bank. She cleared her throat, willing herself to speak calmly. "My mother and I have plans and I'm already late."

"Just one drink," Aiden pressed. "It's time we had that conversation, don't you think?"

"I don't, as a matter of fact. As far as I'm concerned, we don't ever need to have it."

"What if I said I miss you?"

The words curled around her like smoke, intoxicating and much too familiar. "Don't, Aiden." *Please.*

"Not like a date. Just . . . friends."

"I've been in the pool all day. I'm not dressed to go anywhere."

"Please," he said, pinning her with those sea-blue eyes. "For old times' sake."

That wasn't fair. He wasn't playing fair. "All right. One drink."

"The After Hours Club? Marcus will be thrilled to see you."

"No. Not the After Hours Club. Somewhere else."

Aiden nodded. "Fair enough. There's a new wine bar across the street called Cork. Great wine list and a nice tapas menu."

"Just a drink," she reminded firmly. This wasn't turning into dinner. Or anything else.

Aiden was waiting in the lobby when she arrived. He smiled when he spotted her, but there was relief in the expression too, and she realized some part of him had expected her not to show.

A slender redhead in a tuxedo shirt and a long black skirt appeared carrying a pair of menus. She smiled at Aiden, fluttering absurdly long lashes. "We have your table ready, Mr. Cavanaugh."

Aiden nodded, seemingly oblivious to her blatant flirtation. "Thank you."

They were shown to a dimly lit table with a pair of cozy leather club chairs and a small votive flickering in the center. The hostess left the menus, promising that their server would be with them shortly, then stepped away, leaving an uncomfortable silence in her wake.

Almost immediately, a young man with sun-streaked blond hair and a name badge identifying him as Todd appeared to take their order. Mallory glanced helplessly at the menu, then at Aiden. "Sorry, I need a minute. You go ahead."

"I'll have a glass of the Caymus cab. The nine ounce."

"Excellent choice." The server looked back at Mallory. "And for you?"

"I'll, uh . . . I'll have the Rutherford Estate Fume Blanc. But the six ounce, please."

"Very good. Any food for either of you?"

"No, thank you," Mallory answered quickly. "Just the wine."

The silence rushed in again with Todd's absence, overlaid with the haunting strains of Chris Isaak's "Wicked Game."

"You used to love this song," Aiden said to fill the quiet.

"It always made me cry."

"I remember."

Mallory lowered her gaze. She didn't want him to remember. Any more than *she* wanted to. She ran her eyes around the room, sprinkled with couples and work colleagues enjoying food and conversation at the end of a long day. None of the old crowd, thankfully.

"So, what should we talk about?" Aiden asked, as if they were merely catching up after one of them had taken a job out of state.

Mallory shifted in her chair, uncomfortable with his close regard. "It's your meeting."

"Is that what this is? A meeting?"

Todd reappeared with their wine, saving Mallory the trouble of a reply. When he was gone again, Aiden raised his cabernet with a pasted-on smile. "To old friends."

Mallory sipped her wine without returning the salute. Finally, she met his gaze. "Tell me about the accident."

"No."

"Will you at least show me your hand?"

"Is that why you agreed to come? So you could get a look at my scars?"

Mallory stared at him, stung. "I didn't deserve that."

Aiden blew out a long breath. "No, you didn't. I'm sorry." His eyes slid to his lap, to the hand he kept carefully out of sight. "It makes people uncomfortable. Especially the people who knew me before. The Aiden they knew played the piano. But that Aiden's gone and they don't know the guy who took his place."

"Do you?"

"Do I what?"

"Know the guy who took the old Aiden's place?"

"Don't analyze me, Mallory. That isn't why I asked you to come."

"I know. I just couldn't help noticing . . . Why do you hide your hand?"

A tic had begun in his jaw. "You're doing it again—trying to be my shrink."

Mallory settled back in her chair. That wasn't what she was doing. At least not consciously. In fact, she'd pushed back hard against her mother's suggestion that she get involved. So what *was* she doing? Not trying to get back to that place when they'd told each other everything—when they'd *been* each other's everything—because she absolutely did not want that. But it hurt to see him in pain, and he clearly was, even if he chose to mask it with hostility. If she could help him see it, acknowledge it, it might open a door.

"You said we were friends," she said quietly. "And friends tell each other things. Tell me what happened, Aiden."

She watched as he took another pull from his glass. For a moment, she thought he would refuse, but finally he met her gaze.

"I was in Brussels, at a party with friends. It was the last night of the tour and some of the guys were pretty lit. We were sitting around, razzing each other. I was next to an open window with my beer beside me on the sill. Out of nowhere, the sky opened up and the rain started coming down. It was blowing in from everywhere, soaking everything.

Everybody was yelling, running around shutting windows. I was reaching to take my beer off the sill when someone—I still don't know who—slammed the window shut . . . with my hand still in it. It was one of those two-hundred-year-old sash jobs. Heavy."

His eyes closed briefly and he shifted in his chair. "I could feel the bones crack one at a time, feel the glass from the beer bottle slice into my palm and then out the other side. It happened so fast, and the pain was so blinding, that for a minute I thought I'd been struck by lightning. When I saw my hand and realized what had happened, I keeled over cold. I came to in the ambulance, with my hand wrapped in a blood-soaked towel. I knew what it meant. The instant I saw it, all flattened and bloody with the hunk of glass lodged between my metatarsals, I knew it was over."

Mallory felt hot suddenly, and faintly queasy. Not in response to the physical description of the injury but to the gut punch he must have suffered on realizing the extent of the damage.

"I'm sorry, Aiden. Truly. I can't pretend to know what it's like to lose the thing that makes you *you*. You've been through a lot. I get that. But maybe you need to deal with the emotional wounds before the physical ones can heal."

"They *have* healed—or at least what the doctors consider healed." He surprised her by producing his left hand and laying it flat on the table. "Two broken metatarsals, three dislocations, two fractured phalanges. Moderate to extensive damage to both flexor and extensor tendons. Pretty, isn't it?"

Mallory forced herself not to look away. It was what he wanted, to silence her with discomfort. And actually, it wasn't as bad as she'd envisioned. His fingers, once so beautiful, so powerful, were marred by scars now, and the distal joints of the first three fingers appeared strangely waxy, but the hand was whole and supple, with no sign of contracture.

"Did the doctors tell you that you couldn't play, or did *you* decide?"

"It's *my* hand."

"But what did *they* say, Aiden? The experts."

"They said I was lucky."

Mallory blinked at him. "Lucky?"

"Apparently, it wasn't as bad as it could have been. They said it could take years to get me back to anything like concert shape, but if I continued to work with the specialist, my long-term prognosis was decent. Somehow I doubt the surgeon would have been as sanguine if it had been *his* hand that got mangled."

"But there's a chance you could play like you used to if you do the work?"

He nodded grudgingly. "Eventually. Maybe."

"So do the *work*, Aiden."

He stared down into his wineglass, his expression suddenly shuttered. "You have no idea what that means, how long it could take, what it would look like."

She was used to getting pushback from her counseling clients. Fear, resistance, or just plain stubbornness in the face of uncomfortable territory. Patience was the key, along with a staunch unwillingness to accept excuses. "Your music is who you are. You can't just give up because it's hard. It's *always* been hard."

"That isn't it."

"Then what is it?"

He was quiet for a time, contemplating his splayed fingers. Finally, he looked up, meeting her gaze with eyes that were unsettlingly empty. "I don't care anymore, Mallory. About the music. I haven't for a long time now. Since way before the accident."

The admission struck like a fist out of the dark. It couldn't be true. Not after all the work, all the sacrifice. "How is that possible? When it's what you built your whole life around?"

He shrugged, smiling bitterly. "I have a theory, actually. I've been doing a little self-analysis and there's a pretty good chance that I did this to myself. I mean, of all the parts of me that I could have injured—my *hand*? It gave me the perfect out. I never really wanted that life, the concerts, the awards, the acclaim, so I found a way, subconsciously, to extricate myself."

Mallory stared at him, stunned. Did he actually believe he'd sabotaged his own career? Or was he simply trying to convince himself that he felt no regret over the loss, like a child who breaks a longed-for toy, then sullenly claims he never wanted it?

"Accidents happen, Aiden. You can't blame yourself. And what you're saying doesn't make sense. That life was the *only* thing you wanted. In fact, you wanted it so badly you got on a plane and didn't come back."

He stiffened, eyeing her coolly. "What was I supposed to come back for? You were gone. But while we're on the subject, why are you back—out of the blue, after ten years?"

Something about the way he was looking at her, his eyes holding hers for a beat longer than was necessary, made her want to grab her purse and bolt for the exit. He'd always been able to see through her, to know when she was keeping something from him. And now he was waiting for her to say something—to *confess* something. Because that's how it had worked between them, once upon a time. No secrets. But that was over. She didn't owe him her secrets now. Any more than he owed her his.

"There's no *deal*," she said evenly. "I just felt like spending some time with my mother."

He surprised her by flashing one of his crooked smiles. "Because the two of you have always been so close?"

She'd forgotten how good he was at this part, getting around her with his boyish charm, exploiting the cracks in her armor. But it *was* good to see him smile. Maybe they *could* do this. Maybe they could leave the past behind and simply be friends.

"Things change," she said quietly.

"Do they?"

Something had shifted in his eyes, a flicker of something warm and familiar—and just the tiniest bit uncomfortable. Before Mallory could respond, Todd appeared, puncturing the tension with his easy smile and beachy good looks. "Another round for you folks?"

Aiden drained the last of his cab and surrendered the empty glass. "Please. And we'll do an order of the crab empanadas." He turned back to Mallory as Todd retreated. "Sorry. I know we said just drinks, but I'm starving. I'm guessing you are too after skipping lunch."

"How do you know I skipped lunch?"

"Because I looked for you."

"At lunch? Why?"

"Because I'm always looking for you. All day. Every day. Around every corner."

Warning bells suddenly went off. "Aiden—"

"Why did you come back, Mallory? The *real* reason."

There was an urgency to his voice now that made Mallory's belly tighten. The last thing she needed was him getting the wrong idea about why she was in Little Harbor. "My boss thought I was burning out, so she made me take a leave of absence."

Aiden inhaled deeply, holding the breath a moment before releasing it. "So . . . not because of me. Not because I was home."

"I didn't know. I told you that. If I had . . ."

"You wouldn't have come?" he supplied coolly.

"I didn't say that."

"Would you have? If you *had* known?"

Mallory looked away, her throat suddenly dry. "Let's not do this, Aiden. Let's not drag it all up again."

He was silent a moment, blue eyes clouded and dark. "Maybe I *need* to drag it all up again," he said finally. "Maybe that's exactly what I need. Because I still don't know what happened, Mallory. I don't understand how we just . . . ended."

Mallory shot him an imploring look over the rim of her glass. "Why does any of it matter now?"

"It matters because you're here. Ten years later, we're *both* here. And I need you to tell me why you left. And why, after everything we were, everything we planned, you thought I didn't deserve the courtesy of a goodbye."

Mallory lifted her chin, struggling to keep her emotions in check. If he was determined to have this conversation, then they'd have it.

"We said our goodbyes when you left for London. I didn't see the point in saying them again. You made a choice. So I made one too." She paused, forcing herself to hold his gaze. "Your mother was right, Aiden. Everyone was. I *was* holding you back. When you decided to go to London, I realized it. And so did you—eventually. That's why you stayed. You deserved the chance to chase your dream, to have the life you'd always wanted. And I deserved . . ." She waved a hand, leaving the rest unsaid. "Never mind. It isn't important. But please don't pretend you didn't want any of it, Aiden. I was here."

"You know, you act like you're the only one all this happened to, but I was here too. I was twenty-two years old and scared blind. Everything was happening so fast. All the work I'd put in, everything I was supposed to accomplish, all of it was suddenly on hold. But we were going to make it work. The three of us." He looked up finally, his face raw with anguish. "And then . . ."

"Yes. Then," Mallory said softly. "And just like that you were free to get on with your life."

"*You* were the life I wanted, Mallory—*us*. But after the baby . . . you shut me out." He broke off, silent for a time, a swirl of dark emotion roiling beneath his stony exterior. "I didn't know what to do. The window to enter the Leeds was closing, and missing it meant waiting another three years. I needed to figure out what I was doing with my life, but when I tried to talk to you, to ask you what you wanted, you shut yourself up and wouldn't talk to me. You acted like what happened was my fault."

Mallory swallowed hard, the memory still so raw it seared her throat. "Because I saw your face, Aiden. In the hospital, when the doctor told us there wasn't going to be a baby—I saw your face. I saw the relief."

"That isn't true." His response was immediate and emphatic, but his gaze wavered in the tiniest of tells.

"It *is*, Aiden. It's true. You never said so, but I saw it. And when you called off the wedding, I knew it for sure. Do you know how that felt? What it looked like? With one half of your mother's crowd whispering that I'd gotten pregnant on purpose and the other half convinced I'd never been pregnant at all? People in this town already thought I was a scheming little gold digger and you . . ." She paused, closing her eyes against the fresh tide of memory. "You poured gasoline on the fire and then got on a plane. So please don't tell me *I* was the life you wanted. You *chose* the life you wanted and it wasn't here."

"That's what you believed? All these years? That I was . . . *glad*?"

Mallory's eyes prickled with the threat of tears. She blinked them away, but they came again. "I'm sorry." She reached for her purse and pushed to her feet. "I told you we shouldn't do this."

"Mallory, wait."

She pivoted sharply, looking for the exit. Suddenly Todd was there blocking her path, a tray of food balanced on one arm. Only a deft step to her left kept her from barreling into him. "I'm sorry," she mumbled. "I have to . . . I'm sorry."

And she was. She was sorry she'd let down her guard. Sorry she'd come at all.

THIRTY-THREE

MALLORY

It was well past eight by the time Mallory got home. She'd barely shed her duffel and shoes when she heard Helen call out from the kitchen.

"There you are. I was about to give up on you. I started dinner without you."

Mallory followed the mingled aromas of garlic and tomatoes to the kitchen. Helen looked up from the stove, giving her daughter a quick once-over. "Everything okay? I thought we were cooking tonight."

"I know. I'm sorry. I got . . . hung up."

"Just as long as you're okay. I was starting to worry. You must be starving."

"Not really. But it smells delicious."

Helen put down her spoon, turning her full attention on Mallory. "What's wrong? You've been crying."

"Aiden asked me to meet him for a drink after work. And before you get excited, it wasn't that kind of drink."

"What kind was it?"

"He said he wanted to talk."

"And *did* you?"

"I told him I wasn't interested in dragging up the past and he agreed, but then he brought it all up anyway. So I got up and left."

"Oh, honey."

Mallory stepped away, busying herself with closing the various spice bottles lined up on the counter. The last thing she needed right now was a lecture. "It wasn't my fault. I was doing what you said, trying to get him to open up. But when I asked him how the accident happened, he gave me this crazy story about how he subconsciously *caused* it to happen."

Helen stared at her, clearly appalled. "Why on earth . . . why would he do that?"

"Because he never wanted that life—or so he claims now."

"How awful," Helen whispered, shaking her head. "Could it be true, do you think?"

Mallory closed her eyes, wishing she could shut out the image of Aiden's hand, crushed and bleeding. The idea that he had somehow willed something so horrific to happen seemed ludicrous, but she knew what it felt like to suffer an incomprehensible loss, to have your future erased in the blink of an eye. She also understood the need to make sense of tragedy—and how it could sometimes take you to a very dark place.

"I think he's trying to convince himself it is," Mallory replied. "He claims he stopped caring about his music before the accident even happened, but I think it's just a way of coping. He's pretending he never wanted the acclaim and the adoring crowds because it's gone now, but the truth is they were *all* he wanted."

Helen pursed her lips thoughtfully. "I wouldn't say *all*."

"He wanted them enough to call off our wedding in order to chase them."

"I'm not sure that's fair," Helen said, returning the lid to the pot of sauce and turning down the flame. "He was young, Mallory, and in way over his head. He was born with an extraordinary gift, and for most of his life that was his *whole* life—his music. He didn't know how to do the rest of it but he was trying. Then you lost the baby and you just checked out on him. On everything, really. That's why he left. Because there was nothing anchoring him here when Estelle started pushing him to go."

"He was perfectly happy to let her pull the strings," Mallory said dryly. "And she ended up getting exactly what she wanted—us apart."

Helen's expression shuttered abruptly. "Something tells me she'd do things differently if she had it to do over again."

Mallory blinked at her. "What?"

"I just meant people change. Now that she's had time to think about it, she probably regrets what she did."

Mallory shot her a look of annoyance. "You know, I get you taking up for Aiden. Sort of. But now you're defending Estelle?"

"I'm not defending her," Helen said evenly. "I'm just saying she's a mother whose child is in pain, and I suspect she knows some of that pain can be laid at her door. Motherhood doesn't come with a set of instructions. Sometimes, the box arrives damaged and some of the pieces are missing. But you own it now, this job you weren't ready for, and so you muddle through. You make mistakes, sometimes horrible ones, and there's nothing to do but live with them."

Helen fell silent then, as if startled by her burst of candor. Mallory couldn't help but wonder, as she watched her mother fill a pot with water and put it on to boil, if her soliloquy on the subject of maternal regret had only to do with Estelle.

"What about you?" she asked quietly. "Do *you* have regrets?"

Helen measured salt out into her palm and dropped it into the pot without looking up. "I don't think there's a mother living who doesn't— except maybe my own. She was never sorry for anything."

"Is she . . ."

"She died," Helen said, anticipating the rest of the question. "You were still tiny, three or four at most. I called when I heard she was sick. I offered to look after her, but she told me not to come. She never forgave me for shaming her."

Mallory was briefly silent as she digested this. It seemed odd that a woman whose work centered around death and dying hadn't been at her own mother's bedside at the end. "Do you ever regret it? Not . . . making your peace with her?"

"No," Helen answered flatly. "I regret that she was the way she was, but I don't regret staying away. I didn't even go to the funeral. I couldn't pretend to mourn her any more than she could pretend to love me. I reminded her of things she was ashamed of, her weaknesses and her passions, which made loving me impossible."

"I'm sorry," Mallory said thickly. "I wish I had known all this sooner. But I'm glad we're talking about it now. It helps me . . . understand things."

Helen nodded, smiling sadly. "If I could give you one piece of advice, Mallory, one thing to remember always, it's to never allow silence to come between you and someone you love."

"And by *someone*, you mean Aiden."

Helen nodded. "But not just him. Life hands us all our share of regrets. Don't live with the ones you don't have to. Mend your fences while you can—as *soon* as you can. If someone needs you, be there, whatever it costs. Because you might not get another chance."

Once again, Mallory found herself filled with a vague sense of disquiet. All this talk of regret and mending fences had a heavy, foreboding feel to it. "Is there something you haven't told me? Because if there is, I wish you'd just come out with it."

Helen looked up from her pot, still stirring absently. "I'm sorry. I'm just feeling . . . nostalgic. But no more gloomy talk, I promise. Now pull out the colander and go set the table. You need to eat something."

Mallory was relieved when Helen excused herself after dinner to go up and finish framing a painting she'd promised to deliver in the morning. It was late, and she'd wanted nothing more than to fall into bed and slide into oblivion.

But now, perched on her bedroom sill, she stared up at the velvet sky, too restless to sleep. It was a warm night and the air pushing through the screen felt heavy and damp, ripe with the metallic tang of coming rain. In the distance, lightning chased across the sky, silvering the edges of the clouds. She listened for thunder but heard none. Too far away. But it made her feel antsy and unable to settle.

From her place at the window, she could see the lights of the Cavanaugh house, bright smudges against the dark. How many nights had she perched on this very sill, waiting for the signal from Aiden's room? There'd been a comfort in knowing he was close by. She would imagine him studying or practicing—sometimes, when the wind was right, the notes would carry on the breeze and she would close her eyes, envisioning him bent over the keys, hair falling over his forehead as he labored over some difficult piece.

And at some point those three quick pulses of light would come and she would slip down the deck stairs and out to the beach. It was just walks at first, their hands touching now and then in the dark. Later, when they'd grown more comfortable, they would scramble out onto the jetty and perch on the rocks. She would bring snacks, sometimes a thermos of cocoa to share, and they would sit side by side, shoulders touching, and count the stars.

They never seemed to run out of things to talk about. Until they did one night and the silence, so thick and sweet and strange, had turned to clumsy kisses. They'd been her *first* kisses, though not Aiden's. More than two years her senior, he'd already had his share of girlfriends. The daughters of his mother's friends mostly, girls from his own social circle.

She had loved him from the first moment she saw him, quietly and desperately, but she'd never let herself hope that one day he might return those feelings. They came from such different worlds and had envisioned such different futures for themselves. When it finally happened, it had seemed too good to be true—and it was. Ultimately, they'd gone in different directions, only to find themselves back where they started. Except everything had changed. *They* had changed.

The muffled scuff of footsteps suddenly intruded on her thoughts. She saw nothing as she squinted through the darkness, but a moment later the floodlight in front of the guesthouse switched on, illuminating the small stone courtyard. And there he was, silhouetted against the door, fumbling with his keys.

He paused briefly, allowing his gaze to drift up toward her window. Mallory sucked in her breath and went still, grateful that she hadn't bothered to switch on the lamp. A moment later he was gone and the courtyard was plunged back into darkness.

Relieved, she settled back against the window frame, watching as various lights switched on in the guesthouse, imagining him moving through rooms she knew as well as her own, rooms they had shared—if only briefly—during that last summer. She closed her eyes, the memories like tiny cuts along already raw nerves. She was about to turn away when she saw the bedroom light flick on . . . and then off again.

Once. Twice. Three times.

She could feel the pulse of it beneath her skin, in her chest, her belly, and for a moment she couldn't breathe. She knew what he wanted, to pick up their conversation where they'd left it at the bar—where *she'd* left it. But she couldn't. If she'd learned anything tonight, it was that she wasn't ready for a postmortem of their breakup.

The light pulsed again.

Once. Twice. Three times.

She closed her eyes, swallowing the hot ache of tears. *I can't, Aiden. I just can't.*

THIRTY-FOUR

MALLORY

July 18, 1999

Mallory woke to a dull gray sky. The storm hovering offshore last night had moved in at some point, leaving the beach wet and dreary. She was fine with it, actually. A gloomy day suited her mood, and since it was Sunday she had the whole day to do as she pleased. She could do with a bit of downtime after breakfast, maybe a little Brontë, followed by a long, lazy nap.

In the kitchen, she found Helen mixing something in a large spatterware bowl. She glanced up, smiling. "You're certainly looking better than you did last night."

"I slept," Mallory said, reaching for a mug and the full pot of coffee. "What are you making?"

"Pancakes—with chocolate chips. I remembered how much you loved them when you were little and I thought you could do with a little pampering. We used to make them together. Do you remember?"

Gradually, the memory surfaced, the two of them in aprons on one of her mother's rare days off, the tiny kitchen of whatever apartment they happened to be living in at the time filled with the heady aromas of melted butter and bittersweet chocolate. She hadn't thought of those mornings in years, but she remembered them now and found herself smiling. No matter what happened to be going on between them, they always managed to come together in the kitchen.

"We did, didn't we. I'd forgotten."

"You'd always end up with flour in your hair."

"And I'd sneak chocolate chips from the measuring cup when you weren't looking."

"You mean when you *thought* I wasn't looking," Helen shot back. "I always measured accordingly."

Mallory feigned a pout. "And there I was, thinking I'd gotten away with something." On impulse, she snatched a handful of chocolate chips from the bag on the counter, giggling as she dodged Helen's playful slaps. "All right, all right. You caught me. Do you need help?"

"You can warm the syrup if you want. There's a brand-new bottle in the pantry."

Mallory was passing the window on her way to the pantry when she caught a flash of color out on the jetty. Aiden in his yellow windbreaker, sitting with his arms propped on his knees, his shoulders turned so that only his profile was visible.

For a horrible moment, she imagined him sitting there all night, waiting for her to come out. But no, the tide would have come in during the night, soaking the rocks. Still, he was there now, alone in the place that had once been theirs, and the sight tugged at something deep in her chest.

"He's been out there since I came down," Helen said, noting the direction of her gaze. "Just staring out to sea." She was spooning pancake batter onto the griddle now, careful to distribute the chocolate chips evenly. "Maybe you could take him some coffee. He's bound to be cold sitting out there on those rocks."

Mallory sighed and turned away from the window. "He isn't homeless, Mother. If he's cold he can go inside. And I'm sure he has his own coffee."

"All right. It was just a thought. How about pouring me some instead? I have a mug here somewhere."

Mallory had just located the mug in question and passed it to Helen when her cell went off. Her pulse did a little gallop when she noticed the 617 area code. "Hello?"

"It's John Muldowney, Ms. Ward. I'm sorry to call on a Sunday. I tried to get hold of Ms. Cook but had to leave a message. There's been a development in Tina's case and I thought you'd like to know. We received a tip yesterday via the hotline."

Her heart was thumping in earnest now. "What kind of tip?"

"The kind you hope for and almost never get. A guy claiming he overheard a kid bragging that he and a couple of his buddies drugged some girl and took her for a ride. He said . . ." Muldowney paused. "Sorry. I didn't think. Do you need a minute?"

"No, it's fine. What else did he say?"

"Long story short, he knew where the kid lived. And here's where luck comes into it. Turns out the kid—his name is Kevin Barnes—has been letting Sticks crash on his couch. Kevin and his brother Brian were both with Sticks the night Tina died. We grabbed Kevin first, right where our tipster said he'd be, stocking shelves at Costco. It didn't take much to get him to spill it all."

Mallory's legs turned to water. "He confessed?"

"To sexual assault, but not to strangling Tina. He and his brother both fingered Sticks for the murder. Apparently, he talked them into coming along for the ride. We've got both of them in custody."

"Both?" Mallory repeated. "But not all three?"

"Sticks is dead."

Dead. The word was slow to penetrate, but when it did, Mallory had to grab the edge of the counter to steady herself. "How?"

"Jackass tried to climb out a fourth-story window when we knocked on his door with a warrant, hit the pavement face-first. We got our ID, though. His name was Michael Barker. Quite a rap sheet too. Ultimately, the bastard got exactly what he deserved."

"But why did they do it?"

"I'm not sure there's ever really a *why* that makes sense. But from what we've cobbled together, he'd been pestering Tina to get back together. When she told him to take a hike, he recruited the two guys to help him grab her after work. He told them he just wanted to talk to her, to scare her into ditching her new boyfriend. She was walking home from work when they pulled up, dragged her into the car, and took off. Apparently, they gave her a Snapple laced with ketamine."

Mallory wasn't sure whether to be livid or relieved. She knew about ketamine—the so-called date rape drug. It rendered a victim incapable of fighting back. "So the drugs they found . . . she didn't take them willingly."

"No. It took her a while to realize they'd given her something, but once she did, she panicked and started to struggle. Unfortunately, it was too late and the ketamine kicked in. After they . . ." He paused, clearing his throat delicately. "When she came to, she started wailing for help. Sticks apparently panicked and tried to shut her up—and eventually, he did."

Mallory fought a wave of nausea as she tried to wrap her head around it all.

"Ms. Ward? Did I lose you?"

"No, I'm . . . I'm just processing."

"I know. It's tough stuff. Maybe it would have been easier coming from your boss, but I know how personal this is for you, and all I could think about was my wife, sitting by the phone, waiting for news. So I decided to call. The media's going to have it any minute now and I didn't want you to hear it that way."

"Thank you. Have you spoken to Tina's mother?"

"She was my first call. It was a hard conversation, but at least she'll have some closure knowing her daughter will eventually receive justice."

He thanked her then, for her help with the case, and for the work she did keeping kids out of trouble. She appreciated the kindness but felt strangely numb as she ended the call. She had expected to feel a sense of relief at the news that she hadn't missed some behavioral cue that might have saved Tina's life. But she didn't feel relieved. She just felt empty.

At some point, Helen had abandoned her pancakes and come to stand next to her. She laid a hand on Mallory's arm now, eyes wide. "What is it? Is it over?"

Mallory nodded. "They caught them. Well, two of them, anyway. There was a third—an ex-boyfriend—but he's dead." The tears came all at once, nearly choking her. "It wasn't my fault."

"Oh, honey, of course it wasn't."

Mallory managed another nod, but there was no *of course* about it. The truth was it could have been—and *might* be the next time. Because as Jevet had pointed out, there *would* be a next time. There was a reason they used to use the term *at-risk youth* to describe girls like Tina. The accepted terminology may have morphed over the years, but the facts hadn't.

Mallory stared out at the beach, her feet propped up on the railing, her coffee long since cold. Helen had left nearly an hour ago, headed downtown to drop off her painting, and the house had been too quiet to remain inside with only the disparate ticking of the late Mr. McInerny's antique clock collection for company.

She'd taken a walk up the beach, to the jetty and back, still trying to process the grisly details of Tina's death. She would always have questions about what happened that night, but at least she knew she hadn't failed as Tina's social worker. It wasn't her fault. But that didn't change the fact that Tina was dead. That Charlene had lost her daughter. That a beautiful girl who had turned her life around, who was learning to drive and planning to try out for a spot in the school play, whose future had finally begun to brighten, would never have a chance to leave her mark on the world. Those things would always be true—and they would *always* haunt her.

Mallory started almost guiltily when her cell phone went off. She picked it up, already knowing it would be Jevet. They'd been playing phone tag all morning. "Hey. I was just about to try you again. Muldowney called to tell me about Sticks and give me a heads-up about the press conference. He said he left you a message."

"Yeah, I got it. The presser just ended. You okay?"

"As okay as I can be. My god, Jevet, three guys and a Snapple spiked with ketamine. She never had a chance."

"No, she didn't. But you were right. She hadn't relapsed. She was the victim of a crime. Not random—she knew her killer—but it wasn't something you or anyone could have seen coming. It doesn't make her death any less horrific but knowing that must be some relief."

"It is, I guess. I don't suppose Ellis has issued an apology."

"He was 'unavailable for comment,'" Jevet replied snarkily. "Not that I expected him to step up and admit he was wrong."

"I'm just relieved that it's over—for me, at least. But it'll never be over for Charlene Allen."

"I'm afraid not," Jevet said gloomily. "But knowing her daughter will get justice is something. How are things at the beach?"

"Good, I guess, though I've been so busy I don't get out there much. I took a job at the community center."

"You what?"

"It's just for the summer, teaching swimming and water safety. I wasn't sure at first, but it's been kind of great. It's nice working with kids who just want to have fun, and the staff is amazing." She paused, then added, "Aiden's back."

"From Europe?"

"He's back at his mom's. In the guesthouse."

"You forgot to tell me that part?"

"I didn't know until I got here. And I didn't want you making it a thing. He's back because he injured his hand."

"Oh no. Is it bad?"

"Pretty bad, yeah. But his doctors say with therapy his chances for a full recovery are good. The only problem is he quit therapy. He's actually working at the center."

"With you?"

"No. Not with me. He's teaching music."

"Wow. That's gotta be weird, seeing him every day. So . . . how is it?"

Mallory let out a sigh. "Awkward."

"Mm-hmmm."

"Not like *that*," Mallory shot back. "He's angry, and probably a little scared, if he'd let himself admit it. He says he doesn't want to play anymore, but I think it's just denial."

"Sounds like the two of you are at least talking. Maybe you can help him work through it."

Mallory squirmed uncomfortably as she recalled the warmth that had crept into Aiden's tone last night. "I think it's better that we keep our distance. He's not in a good place right now and I don't want him getting confused about why I'm here."

"Or you either," Jevet added pointedly.

That too, Mallory thought. She'd nearly forgotten how it felt to be near him, to feel herself being pulled into his orbit.

"Would it be so bad?" Jevet asked. "The two of you finally working through some things? Might do you *both* some good."

"The only thing Aiden needs to be working through right now is whatever's keeping him from getting back to his music."

"And what about *you* and what you're there to work through? I'm not pushing. I'm just wondering where you are with everything now that we have some clarity around what happened to Tina. I'm expecting the committee to wrap up their review in fairly short order."

Mallory winced at the heavy-handed segue, though she would have been shocked if Jevet *hadn't* raised the question. Sadly, she wasn't any closer to an answer than she'd been before Muldowney's call. It was a relief to know she hadn't been responsible for Tina's death, but it was about more than culpability. Could she guarantee that no one else in her care would come to harm? No. No one could. No matter how dedicated. No matter how careful. Was it possible to become immune to such atrocities? Was that something she even *wanted*?

"I'm still working through it," she answered honestly. "If that's okay. I think I need a little more time."

"Then take it. You deserve to find your right path—whatever it is. And remember, there's no shame in deciding to make a change. When you know, you'll know."

Mallory felt a sinking feeling, as if the ground were slowly being pulled out from under her. Even now, with the review nearly complete, Jevet was continuing to nudge her toward the exit, making it easier for her to walk away if that was what she decided to do. She meant to be kind, generous, but the truth was it left her feeling uncomfortably unmoored. "Thank you for understanding."

"No problem. For now, just be good to yourself and— Oh my Lord! I just looked at my watch. I need to get off here. My niece turns five today and my sister will disown me if I'm not there to see her blow out her candles. Look, just keep me posted. Whatever happens, you know I'll always be here for you, right?"

"I will. And I do."

Whatever happens.

The words seemed to reverberate as Mallory ended the call. A few weeks ago, she would have had no problem telling Jevet she was perfectly fine and ready to resume work with a full caseload. But today, when given the chance to do just that, she'd balked.

Was it possible some part of her was beginning to realize Jevet was right? Was she truly not cut out for clinical work? And if so, where did that leave her? The thought of teaching or, worse, becoming just another administrative cog in some government agency left a knot in her stomach. Which left what? Going back to school and starting from scratch?

No, she was definitely not doing that. There was still time to toughen herself up. If Jevet could do it so could she. At least she hoped she could.

THIRTY-FIVE

MALLORY

July 26, 1999

Mallory swore under her breath as she pulled on her warm-ups and simultaneously hunted for her cell phone.

She'd spent the last several nights brainstorming ways Debbie might be able to adapt her IVP program for use at the center. They could offer it as a summer program, a kind of vocational day camp in partnership with local businesses. They could organize it on a rotational basis, offering kids a broad range of career choices. With Estelle's backing there'd be no budgetary constraints to navigate, and the Cavanaugh name would make recruiting partners a snap.

Last night she had finally fleshed the whole thing out on paper, filling the better part of a legal pad with ideas. Unfortunately, at some point, she had dozed off with the pad on her chest, only to awaken with the sun streaming in and just thirty minutes to dress and get to the center for the Monday morning meeting.

It took another several minutes to locate her phone but she finally found it in the tangle of bedcovers. She slid it into her pocket, grabbed her duffel, and headed for the stairs, calling a hasty goodbye as she passed her mother's room.

She was halfway down when she heard the downstairs phone begin to ring. "Hey, can you grab that?" she called up to Helen. "I'm super late."

The ringing had stopped by the time Mallory reached the kitchen. She slowed long enough to grab an apple, then hit the door at a run. She'd have to settle for coffee from the snack bar but if she hit all the lights she could still make it to the center on time.

She had just started down the drive when she suddenly hit the brakes, astonished to see her mother, still in her robe, scrambling down the deck stairs and through the hydrangea hedge dividing Estelle Cavanaugh's property from theirs.

What on earth?

Mallory cut the engine and bolted from the car. Something had to be seriously wrong to send her mother running to Estelle's house.

But the house was unsettlingly quiet as she stepped inside, so quiet she began to wonder if she'd gotten it wrong. Perhaps Helen wasn't here after all. She had just turned back toward the doors when a moan from somewhere upstairs caused her to reverse course.

Dread prickled along the back of her neck as she made her way upstairs. She could hear muffled voices as she reached the landing, and then her mother's words, distinct at last.

"We need to get you into bed. No, not by yourself. Let me help you. Can you sit up?"

Mallory quickened her step, following the sound of her mother's voice, then halted in the open doorway at the end of the hall, where Estelle Cavanaugh lay sprawled unceremoniously on the ivory carpet.

Helen knelt beside her, attempting to help her into a sitting position. "That's it. Now, can you get your feet under you?"

Estelle nodded mutely. For the first time, Mallory saw the dried blood crusting her cheek and chin. It was on the carpet too, a smear of dark russet. Not fresh blood, then.

"What happened?" Mallory blurted.

Helen's head snapped around as she registered her daughter's presence, guilt and surprise warring for control of her expression. "She fell and hit her face on the nightstand. It's not as bad as it looks. Just a split lip, I think. But it's shaken her up. Can you go into the bathroom and bring me a wet washcloth? Warm water, not hot."

Mallory did as asked, setting aside the questions suddenly crowding her mind. By the time she returned, Estelle was sitting on the edge of the bed, the smears of dried blood on her cheeks and chin gruesome against her chalk-white skin. Helen pushed back her hair and went to work with the cloth, tenderly wiping away the encrusted blood.

"There now, that's better. No stitches needed, but it's going to swell, and hurt something fierce for a few days."

It was true. Her lower lip had already begun to swell, and a bluish shadow was forming near her mouth. She'd have a nasty bruise tomorrow. Someone should call for an ambulance. Mallory looked for the phone and finally found it on the floor, where it had apparently been knocked off the nightstand.

"This is who called as I was leaving," Malloy said, aware that her voice held a whiff of accusation.

Helen nodded.

"Why would she call *you*?"

"Aiden isn't here."

"But why *you*? Why not 911?"

Helen threw her an imploring look. "Please, Mallory, this isn't the time. Can you bring me a clean nightgown from the dresser? Top drawer on the right."

Again, Mallory did as her mother asked, but new questions were beginning to bubble. For instance, how did her mother know where Estelle Cavanaugh kept her nightgowns?

Helen accepted the clean gown with a nod of thanks. "Go down to the kitchen. Fill a dish towel with crushed ice and bring it up. The towels are in the drawer next to the sink and there's a meat mallet in the caddy by the stove. We need to get the swelling down on that lip."

"Shouldn't we call for an ambulance?"

"No," Estelle said groggily, speaking for the first time. She looked up at Helen, an unmistakable plea in her eyes. "No ambulance. No hospital."

Helen responded with an almost imperceptible shake of her head, then nodded toward the door, silently urging Mallory to go down and fetch the ice.

In the kitchen, Mallory found the needed items exactly where Helen said she would. But how could that be? As far as she knew, Helen had never set foot in Estelle's kitchen. How would she know where the woman kept her dish towels? Though perhaps even more puzzling was the inexplicable bond she'd glimpsed between the two women. Something strange was going on, and the minute she had her mother alone, she intended to get to the bottom of it.

By the time Mallory returned with the ice, Estelle was freshly gowned and tucked comfortably into the enormous antique four-poster. All traces of blood were gone from her face, though the carpet still bore evidence of the fall. She looked better, but not at all well.

"Thank you, Mallory," Helen said, accepting the makeshift ice pack. She pressed it into Estelle's hand. "Hold it there, but don't press too hard. We don't want it to start bleeding again."

Estelle did as she was told, like a child obeying a parent or nanny. After a moment, she relaxed against the pillows and closed her eyes. Helen released a long sigh.

"I'll call Deb and tell her I won't be able to make it in," Mallory said quietly.

"You don't need to. I've got this."

Mallory glanced pointedly at Estelle's reclined figure. "So it seems. But I think we need to talk about what *this* is, don't you?"

"Yes. All right. I need to stay awhile, but I'll see you at home."

An hour later, Helen returned home looking rather worse for wear. Mallory gave her time to change out of her bloodstained robe but was waiting impatiently in the breakfast room when she reappeared in a gray linen tunic and slacks. She dropped heavily into the chair opposite Mallory, shoulders squared, waiting for the questions she clearly knew were coming.

"What's going on?" Mallory asked abruptly. "What were you doing at Estelle's?"

"She fell and couldn't get up."

"And she called *you*? Not her son. Not 911. You?"

"She didn't need an ambulance. She just bumped her head."

"She bled all over the carpet! But never mind that. I'm asking why she called *you*."

"I was right next door."

Mallory smothered a sigh. Obviously she was going to have to drag it out of her. "How do you know where she keeps her nightgowns?"

Helen's eyes slid away, confirming what Mallory had already begun to suspect.

"She's sick, isn't she."

"She has an inoperable brain tumor."

The words slammed into Mallory, knocking the breath from her chest. "My god . . . how long have you known?"

"Only a few weeks."

"And you never thought to tell me?"

"She doesn't want anyone to know. The only reason *I* know is because I went over to have a word with her about you being back and I noticed that her pupils were uneven. When I guessed the truth, she swore me to secrecy."

Estelle Cavanaugh, dying. Mallory let the news sink in, the fact of it and what it would mean. As if Aiden weren't already dealing with enough, his mother had been diagnosed with an inoperable brain tumor. A thought suddenly occurred. Her head came up slowly. "Wait. Are you saying *Aiden* doesn't know?"

Helen nodded guiltily.

Mallory stood abruptly, pacing the breakfast room as she laid the pieces end to end. Her mother's strange behavior of late. The way she had jumped to Estelle's defense. The nagging suspicion that there was something she wasn't saying. It was *this*—Estelle's tumor. Suddenly she understood why she'd seen Helen stuffing her pockets with herbal teas the other day.

"You've been taking care of her, haven't you? Not just helping her die, but helping her keep the truth from Aiden. That's why she didn't call 911. Because Aiden would find out."

"I've been going over after you leave for work. I bring a few things to help with her symptoms, and we . . . talk."

"How?" The word exploded from Mallory before she could check her tone. "How could you help her keep the truth from Aiden?"

"She begged me, Mallory. She hasn't given up hope that Aiden will come around about his playing and she didn't want to distract him."

"Distract him?" Mallory stared at her, aghast. "She's *dying*. I don't care what else is going on in his life, she doesn't get to keep this from him." She turned away, arms folded, then whirled back to face Helen. "I get Estelle pulling something like this, treating him like he's some fragile piece of porcelain. It's how she's always treated him. But *you*—who love to talk about looking death in the eye—how could *you* be part of it?"

"I didn't want to be," Helen said grimly. "In fact, I've told Estelle everything you just told me, but she's dying, Mallory, and she's afraid. She's also a mother trying to put her broken son back together before the clock runs out. I couldn't let her go through that alone."

"And you think keeping Aiden in the dark is going to help?"

"I don't. But it isn't my secret to tell. I'm bound by confidentiality."

Mallory rolled her eyes. "You're not a doctor. You don't swear an oath to do what you do."

Helen's chin lifted. "I've sworn an oath to myself."

"Well, I haven't. And if Estelle won't tell Aiden the truth, I'm going to."

Helen look horrified. "Mallory, don't. Please. He should hear it from her."

"Yes, he should," Mallory fired back. "But he hasn't, so he's going to hear it from me."

"Please," Helen pleaded again. "Give me a chance to talk to her. Don't blindside her—or Aiden—like that. Neither of them deserves it."

Mallory wasn't sure she bought the whole karma thing, but as far as she was concerned, Estelle deserved whatever fate saw fit to dish out. But Aiden was another matter. If there was a chance that Helen could persuade Estelle to do the right thing, she'd give her a few days. But only that.

"All right," she replied grudgingly. "She's got three days to make this right. If she doesn't, I'm telling him myself."

THIRTY-SIX

MALLORY

July 27, 1999

The next day, Mallory arrived at Estelle's at the prearranged time, entering through the French doors, as Helen had instructed. It was strange walking into the house without knocking, but stranger still to find Estelle in her robe at three in the afternoon, partially reclined on the parlor sofa. She looked pale and startlingly fragile.

"Thank you for coming," Estelle said coolly, nodding toward a nearby chair.

Mallory sat but said nothing. She wasn't sure what the woman hoped to accomplish with this meeting but nothing was going to change her mind about telling Aiden the truth.

"Your mother tells me you're angry that I haven't told my son I'm sick. She says you threatened to tell him yourself."

"Yes," Mallory said flatly. "And you're not sick. Estelle, you're dying. Did you really think you could hide it from him? At the risk of being unkind, you're hardly the picture of health."

Estelle nearly smiled, then caught herself, touching tentative fingers to her split lip. "I can only imagine. I don't look in the mirror much these days. Far too depressing."

Mallory couldn't help feeling a tiny twinge of sympathy. Estelle Cavanaugh had always been a beautiful woman, flawlessly attired and never a hair out of place. Now her expensive robe hung on her thinning frame and her hair was lank and dull. It had to be hard watching her beauty fade—not to mention her health. Still, she was nowhere near ready to let the woman off the hook.

"You didn't answer the question. How long did you think you could keep Aiden in the dark?"

Estelle looked away. "We don't see each other much these days. He's tired of me nagging him about going back to therapy but I can't seem to help myself." Her voice thickened and she suddenly looked up, her eyes swimming with tears. "We argued a few weeks ago. I've hardly seen him since. He goes straight to the guesthouse when he comes home, so I thought . . ."

"You'd lie to him," Mallory supplied.

"Not lie to him . . . *protect* him."

"Like you've always done, you mean. Because you know best."

Estelle inclined her head, not quite agreement, but near enough. "It was only going to be for a few weeks, just until he resumed his therapy. But he hasn't gone back. In fact, he refuses to even discuss it. It breaks my heart to see him give up. He's so . . . changed."

Mallory was silent a moment. However much she disliked Estelle, she couldn't deny that the woman's anguish was genuine. And she wasn't wrong—he had changed—though she wondered if Estelle knew just how much.

"Has he ever told you . . ." She broke off, uncertain about sharing such a confidence, but she had her own concerns. Yesterday morning, in that first panicked moment when she'd spotted her mother scurrying through the hedge, her first thought was that the emergency might involve Aiden, that perhaps he'd done something drastic.

"The other night," Mallory continued evenly, "Aiden and I met for a drink after work. He told me he wonders sometimes if he brought the accident on himself, subconsciously, so he wouldn't have to keep playing."

Estelle swallowed convulsively. "He said that?"

"He did."

"And you . . . you think it's true?"

"No, but I'm worried that *he* might."

Estelle covered her face and began to weep. Mallory reached for a tissue from the box on the coffee table and handed it to her. "I didn't tell you to make you feel bad. I told you because I'm worried about him. You're trying to protect him, but I'm not sure he can live with one more regret. If you wait too long to tell him, until it's too late to make things right between the two of you—" She stopped, unwilling to finish the thought. "I'm not sure he comes back from that."

Estelle dropped her hands and stared at Mallory, horrified. "You think he . . . he could harm himself?"

"I think he's harming himself every day he continues to carry this bitterness around. But I understand it. For the first time in his life, he doesn't know what comes next and he's afraid. He isn't ready to look ahead, he's too busy getting through today. Your illness won't make things any easier, but knowing the truth now, while there's still time, is better than him finding out when things have . . . progressed. Maybe instead of trying to arrange his future, you should think about how you want to spend the time you have left together. He needs that as much as you do."

"You still care for him."

Mallory resisted the urge to look away. "I'll always care for him."

Estelle nodded, dabbing watery eyes. "Can I have a day or two to prepare myself?" She paused, allowing a brief stretch of silence while she fiddled with the large diamond on her left hand. Finally, she looked up. "I know I have no right to ask, but will you be here when I tell him?"

Mallory hadn't seen the request coming but didn't know how to say no. "Yes. If you want me to be."

THIRTY-SEVEN

ESTELLE

July 30, 1999

Estelle squinted at the mantel clock, then at her watch. It hung loose now, spinning annoyingly around her knobby wrist, but there was little point in hiding it now. She turned it until it faced up, then closed one eye. It helped sometimes with the double vision.

She folded her hands in her lap then, feigning a calm she was far from feeling. There was nothing to do now but wait for Aiden to walk through the door. And pray. But then she'd been praying for three days, ever since Mallory delivered her ultimatum. Praying for strength. Praying for words. Praying she wouldn't make a mess of this like she had everything else. And that there would be time to make at least some of it right.

Helen's daughter had essentially blackmailed her into doing the right thing—but it *was* the right thing. She saw that now, albeit grudgingly. It pained her to admit it, but the girl clearly knew more than she did about her son's current mental state. He had confided things to her—unsettling things—that he had never shared with his own mother. Not that that should surprise her. They'd always had that kind of connection, as if tethered to one another by some invisible cord, and the years had apparently done nothing to sever it.

She was relieved that both Mallory and Helen had agreed to be here—for her sake as well as Aiden's. He hadn't seen her since the fall and the sight of her bruised face, despite her carefully applied cosmetics, was bound to be a shock—though certainly not the last of the afternoon.

She had phoned Aiden at the center this morning and asked him to come to the house when he was through for the day, to discuss a bit of family business. He'd been short with her, pressing her to share her news over the phone instead. That's how it was between them now, cool and businesslike.

Eventually, she heard the front door open, the jangle of keys, the scuff of steps on the foyer parquet. Estelle threw Helen an anxious glance and gave her hair one last pat. A moment later, Aiden strode into the room. He halted abruptly, eyes darting from Mallory to Helen, then back to Estelle again.

His gaze narrowed on her face. "What in god's name have you done to yourself?"

"I just took a little spill. It's nothing."

"It doesn't look like nothing. Your lip is split and your jaw is black and blue."

"It's fine, really. Just sit here next to me. I have something to tell you."

Aiden threw Helen and Mallory a wary look as he eased down beside his mother. "What's going on?"

Estelle folded her hands in her lap again, trying to project composure. *Just come out with it,* she told herself. *Calmly and cleanly. Like pulling off a Band-Aid.* "A few months ago, before you came home, I started having headaches and dizzy spells. I went in for tests and was diagnosed with stage four glioblastoma—an aggressive form of brain tumor."

Aiden went still, his face blank. After a moment, he sat up straighter. "Is it . . ."

"It's inoperable," she answered before he could get the rest out. "I've started treatment—they hope it will slow the growth—but they make me so sick I can barely get out of bed. Which is why I'm considering discontinuing them. At this point, the doctors give me somewhere between three and eight months."

"You knew when I came home?"

"Yes."

"And I'm just finding out now?"

"Yes."

Aiden's head snapped in Mallory's direction, blue eyes sharp with accusation. "You knew about this?"

"She didn't," Estelle said before Mallory could respond. "Not until a few days ago. But I thought it might help to have her here when I told you."

He looked lost suddenly, dazed. "Have you seen a specialist? There has to be someone . . . some university where they—"

"Aiden . . . honey." She reached for his hand. His need to deny, to fix, broke her heart. She swallowed a rising tide of tears, fighting to keep her voice even, to be strong for him. "There isn't anyone else. This is what's happening."

He was silent for a long time, head bent, staring at the carpet. Finally, he looked up, his eyes red rimmed and raw. "Why are you just telling me now?"

It was all Estelle could do not to flinch. The steeliness in his tone conveyed his anger more eloquently than his raised voice ever could. "I didn't want to be a distraction."

"A distraction?" he echoed, incredulous. "You're dying!"

"Yes," Estelle said stoically. "I am. But you're not. It's time for you to put your life back together, Aiden. Not for me, and not the way *I* think it should be, but for you. In whatever way makes *you* happy. That's what I want for you. All I want."

Aiden scraped a hand through his hair, his anger simmering in earnest now. "We're not talking about me right now."

"I'm afraid we are," she corrected. "I know you're angry. I kept this from you and I shouldn't have. I've done a lot of things I shouldn't have. Like being so fixated on what *I* wanted that I forgot to ask what *you* wanted. I was selfish. Now, if you'll let me, I'd like to spend whatever time I have left making things right between us. I'll do anything you ask—including stay out of your way, if that's what you want. Just tell me."

Aiden stared at her numbly. "I want you not to be dying."

It was a little boy's answer, impossible and anguish filled, but at that moment, he might as well have been a little boy. He looked so vulnerable, so bereft, the way he looked when she told him his father was dead. She'd give anything to make the pain go away. But this wasn't something she could kiss and make better.

"I know," she said softly, reaching up to push his hair off his forehead. "I want that too, but here we are. I've made such a mess of things—no, I have, we both know it—but I want to do better with the time I have left, to be the kind of mother I should have been."

"I want to talk to your doctors."

She nodded. This was the first stage—denial. Helen had prepared her for that. Helen had prepared her for so much over the last few weeks. "We can do that if you'd like," she told him with a gentle smile. "But it isn't going to change anything. What questions do you have for me?"

Aiden blinked rapidly, and she realized he was fighting tears. "It's okay to be sad, sweetheart. I was sad too when I found out. But talking about it helps."

His Adam's apple bobbed as he briefly looked away, pulling in a deep, shuddering breath. "Are you . . . in a lot of pain?"

"Some. Headaches mostly. The doctor gave me something for them but I don't like taking it. It makes me feel so fuzzy. I might have to take them eventually, but for now, Helen has made me some tonics and teas and has been teaching me breathing and meditation techniques."

Aiden turned to look at Helen, who'd been silent since his entry. There was confusion in the look as he tried to make sense of how she'd gotten involved. But there was gratitude too. She nodded almost imperceptibly, accepting the unspoken thanks. His eyes slid to Mallory's next, shiny with tears of her own, then quickly returned to Estelle's, as if he feared giving too much away. "Should we hire someone . . . a nurse or an aide?"

"Thank you, but Helen has been looking after me and knows what I need. I'd prefer to have her stay on if she's willing. She's going to help me . . . die well."

Aiden's face came close to crumpling. "Mother . . ."

Estelle found his hand, winding her fingers through his. "It helps to say it out loud, sweetheart. To accept the fact of it. These are the kinds of things Helen is helping me with."

"But why would you . . . You told her and not me?"

"I didn't tell her. I wasn't going to tell anyone. But she saw me one day and noticed something wrong with my eyes, and she guessed. It was almost a relief to have someone else know, but I made her swear not to tell anyone—not even Mallory. In her defense, she did push me to tell you. She's been so wonderful. I can't imagine going through this without her."

Aiden turned to Helen, his face ravaged with barely checked emotion. "Can you stay on? Will you?"

"Yes, of course."

Aiden dropped his head and, for the first time, allowed his tears to fall. "Thank you."

Helen caught Mallory's eye with the barest of nods and rose from her chair. "I think we should go now, and leave you two to talk."

Mallory stood too and followed Helen, pausing briefly to lay a hand on Aiden's shoulder. *I'm so sorry,* she mouthed silently.

Estelle looked away, pained by the expression on her son's face, the raw intensity in his eyes when they met Mallory's. How had she not seen what was between them? How much he needed her?

THIRTY-EIGHT

MALLORY

Mallory blew out a long breath as she eased down onto the sill, eyes fixed on the darkened windows of the Cavanaugh guesthouse. She couldn't shake the memory of Aiden's face this afternoon, the naked pain and stunned desolation as the truth slowly penetrated.

Telling him had been the right thing to do, the fair thing, but she ached for him, for what he must be suffering tonight and what he would continue to suffer as Estelle's illness progressed. There would be a lot to deal with in the coming months, arrangements to make, loose ends to tie up, goodbyes to say. But after, when all the doing was over, what happened then? Would he keep the house? Step into Estelle's shoes on the community center board? Or, with no one to anchor him here, would Europe beckon again and take him away from Little Harbor for good?

The thought left her strangely hollow. It shouldn't matter—he'd been out of her life for a decade—but somehow it did. Like the loss of a landmark you've always taken for granted. You don't notice until it's gone, but once you do, you can't quite get your bearings. Aiden was that for her—part of her inner landscape. She couldn't imagine him not being here.

Mallory closed her eyes, willing the thought away. She couldn't afford to be nostalgic. She needed to move forward. *Only* forward. But as she opened her eyes again, she saw the light in the guesthouse window begin to pulse—once, twice, three times.

Aiden was already on the beach when she reached the gate, arms folded, legs planted wide apart, as if afraid the wind might blow him over.

"You came," he said simply. "I didn't think you would. You didn't last time."

"No."

"So this is because of my mother. Because of her . . . news?"

His face looked harsh in the moonlight, all sharp blue-white angles, and for a moment she was tempted to touch his cheek, to share her warmth with him. Instead, she shoved her hands safely into her pockets. "It's about a lot of things."

"Well, beggars can't be choosers, I guess."

She fell in beside him, the sand chilly on the soles of her bare feet as they headed for the jetty. It felt strange walking beside him like this, as if ten years had rolled away. They hadn't, of course. And they couldn't. But she could be here for him now.

When they reached the jetty, Aiden turned and held out a hand. She hesitated briefly before accepting it. She used to know every nook and crevice of these rocks, but she wasn't sure she could make it up on her own now.

The tide was out, the rocks mostly dry. They moved carefully, still hand in hand as they picked their way over the large craggy stones, finally pulling apart when they reached the end. They settled side by side, and for a while, neither spoke, allowing the rhythmic push and pull of the sea to fill the quiet.

The breeze was stiff and chilly off the water, sending fine drops of spray into the air. Mallory zipped her jacket to her throat and pulled her knees to her chest before finally stealing a look at Aiden. With his hair swept off his brow, his profile was sharper than she remembered, faintly granitelike in the moonlight, his jaw shadowed with stubble.

"I'm so sorry," she said, finally breaking the silence. "How's your mom?"

"She's dying."

"I know."

Aiden turned his face away but the tension in his body was palpable. "She should have told me." His voice sounded harsh against the soft thrum of the waves, raw with a tangle of carefully suppressed emotions. "All this time, she's been worrying about me, nagging me to go back to therapy, and she's been sitting on this."

"She meant well," Mallory said, surprised to find herself defending the woman. Aiden's relationship with his mother had always been strained, but one look at his face was enough to see that he was gutted.

He tipped back his head, staring up at the night sky. "She said you gave her an ultimatum—if she didn't tell me, you would." He waited a beat, expecting her to respond. When she didn't he shifted his gaze to her face. "Would you have?"

"Told you?" She shrugged. "I don't know. Maybe."

"Well, the bluff worked. Thank you, by the way."

Mallory nodded, but chose to stay silent. She knew the fastest way to get him to open up was to let the quiet spool out until he felt compelled to fill it. Nature abhorred a vacuum. So did angry people—and Aiden was simmering, doing his best to tamp down his anger because he was afraid of it. Ultimately the need to vent would win out.

"I could strangle her!" he growled after several minutes had ticked by. Mallory nodded. "I know."

"How dare she keep something like that from me! Like it's none of my business. Like I'm a child."

He wanted her to be angry *with* him, to validate what he was feeling, the way she used to when they were kids and Estelle would ride him about practicing. But this was different. Resentment would only get in the way of his making peace with what was coming.

"You're *her* child, Aiden, and always will be. She thought she was protecting you."

"Because she knows best," he shot back. "Even when she doesn't."

"Maybe this is a chance for the two of you to work through some of your issues. It sounds like she's ready to admit her mistakes. For her, that's a huge step."

Aiden dropped his head, shaking it slowly. "I honestly don't know what to think right now. We talked a little after you left, but she was exhausted and I made her go up and lie down." He scrubbed a hand over his face, groaning. "Bloody hell, what a day. I couldn't figure out what you and your mother were doing there when I walked in. And then you wouldn't look at me and I knew it was bad. I was glad you were there, though. It made it . . . easier. And thank god for Helen. You could have knocked me down with a feather when my mother started talking about her making tea and helping her dress. I mean, it would be an incredibly generous thing for *anyone* to do, but given their history . . ."

Mallory couldn't argue with him there. She'd seen that generosity in action the day Estelle fell and split her lip. In fact, once the initial shock wore off, she'd found herself looking at Helen with a new and unexpected sense of admiration. "She's always taken her work very seriously. And I'm glad she was there for your mother."

Suddenly all his pain was there for her to read. "It should have been *me* doing all that stuff for her. But I didn't even realize . . . What kind of crappy son doesn't notice his own mother is sick?"

"You can't blame yourself. She went out of her way to make sure you didn't notice."

"I should have, though. And would have if I hadn't been—"

"Aiden, don't."

"It's true. We had an argument a few weeks ago and I've barely seen her since. And all the time she . . ." His voice fell away and he dropped his chin to his chest. "I'm furious with her—and furious with *myself* for being furious. I feel like I should be able to *fix* it, but I have no idea how. I know that doesn't make sense, that there's no way to fix it, but it's how I feel."

"It does make sense," Mallory said softly. "Especially at this stage. It's only been a few hours. You need to give yourself time to digest, and feel however you feel, even if what you're feeling doesn't make sense. It's a process."

"You're not going to lecture me on the five stages of grief, are you? Because I'm not sure I could bear that."

"No," Mallory said. "Not if you don't want me to."

She was trained in the handling of grief and all its incumbent emotions, but this wasn't one of her clients. This was Aiden. She'd heard the cautionary tales about counseling friends and family, how having a vested interest in a particular outcome could result in a loss of objectivity. One of her professors had referred to it as *having skin in the game.* She got it. She'd need to tread carefully, for both their sakes, and keep a tight rein on her emotions. But right now, she needed to do this, to be here in whatever way he needed her to be.

"I'm just saying give yourself time. Eventually, the anger will lift and you'll be able to deal with what's underneath. In the meantime, the two of you need to just keep talking."

"I know. I just don't know what to say. I tried earlier but we didn't get very far. I wanted to talk about her treatment, about maybe taking her to Boston or New York for a second opinion, but she just kept circling back to me, to *my* future, my happiness. As if any of that matters *now.*"

"But it does matter, Aiden. It matters to *her.* Her whole life has been about making you successful, probably because she thinks success and happiness are the same thing, and now that you've walked away from your music, she's afraid you won't be either. Her mission hasn't changed just because she's dying. She's never going to stop caring about those things."

Aiden stared at her, clearly surprised. "You're taking her side?"

"There *are* no sides, Aiden. Not to this."

"No, I suppose not. Old habits, I guess. Being mad just feels easier right now. Familiar, you know?"

Mallory nodded. She did know. But she'd learned some things since she returned to Little Harbor. "Mothers are complicated. You grow up thinking you know who they are. And then something happens and you realize they have all these layers, pieces of themselves you didn't know were there—because they've been carrying around *stuff* you knew nothing about. But maybe it goes the other way too. Maybe mothers don't always see their children as they really are. I think your mother is starting to figure it out, though. She seems ready to let go a little—to let you be you. I think it might be an opportunity to connect as adults rather than just mother and son."

"Maybe."

Mallory heard the resistance in his tone. He wasn't convinced. "Closure is a good thing, Aiden, even when the ending isn't what we want. Maybe especially then. Because it helps us move on to what's next—even when we don't *know* what's next."

Aiden blew out a long breath but said nothing. Mallory tipped her head back, watching a scrim of clouds slide past the nearly full moon, shredding on the wind and skidding away. Out of nowhere, the word *entropy* popped into her head—the theory that, left unchecked, disorder tended to increase over time. It was true. Nothing stayed the same. Things were always shifting, dissolving and reforming into something else. Sometimes it happened while you weren't looking, other times while you were, but *nothing* stayed the same. Things ended. People left. Sometimes they even died. Estelle's illness was proof of that. And there was Tina, and poor Jacob Ellis—both gone so abruptly, so senselessly.

"When I was little," she said quietly, "I used to think the moon was just the sun with its light switched off, like in the Beatles song. I thought it slept at night like we did, and that's why it got dark at night."

"You told me. What made you think of it now?"

"I don't know." She shook her head, pulling her eyes from the sky. "It's just funny the things we believe when we're kids. We take them as gospel because we don't know any better. Then we grow up and we find out it isn't the way we thought at all—that nothing is. Things are always falling apart, and most of the time there's nothing we can do about any of it."

Aiden was staring at her now, a V-shaped crease between his brows. "Is everything okay? With you, I mean. You seem like you're carrying something around."

Mallory looked away, afraid her face would betray her. "It's just work stuff."

"The thing with your boss?"

"I didn't come out here to talk about me."

"Why *did* you come?"

"I wanted to make sure you were all right."

"Thank you." He managed a smile, then reached up to push a strand of hair off her cheek. "And now I'm checking on you. What's going on, Mal?"

"Nothing. Really."

Aiden continued to study her, clearly not ready to let her off the hook. "We used to tell each other everything."

Yes they had. Back when they were teenagers boiling with angst, right here on this jetty. But they were all grown up now. It seemed impossible—after the way things ended—that they would wind up here again. But they *were* here, and she couldn't deny the pull of those memories, the bond they had shared, the trust.

"A girl died," she said quietly. "A girl under my care. She was murdered."

"Oh god, babe. I'm sorry."

Babe.

It had been a reflex and nothing more, but the word knocked her off balance, and suddenly the rest of the story was tumbling out. Tina's death. Ellis's vindictive media campaign. Her meltdown in the break room. She kept the details to a minimum, but there was no way to sugarcoat the ending. She'd been put on leave because her boss had doubts about her ability to do her job and she was beginning to have them too.

"Anyway," she concluded thickly. "That's why I came back. To hide from the reporters and lick my wounds. Now all I have to do is figure out what to do with the rest of my life."

Aiden reached for her hand, pulling it into the pocket of his jacket along with his own. "I'm so sorry. I know how much you've always wanted to work with kids. You have a gift for caring. It's why I wanted you at the center this summer—and one of the things I love most about you. You'll figure it out, Mal."

"I wish I believed that."

"If it counts for anything, I believe it."

His hand tightened around hers then, warm and sure, and Mallory was struck by how familiar it all felt, how easy. Even now, with everything they were both carrying, it was just the two of them, the way they'd been before everything went south. She had missed this—missed *him*.

"It does count," she said softly. "More than you know. But I shouldn't have dumped my troubles on you. Tonight of all nights."

"You can still tell me anything, Mallory. I know it's hard to believe after . . . well . . . after everything, but I'll always be here for you. Wherever I am. Wherever you are. Always."

Mallory swallowed painfully, the words *thank you* suddenly caught in her throat. His expression was so solemn, etched with yearning for the days when it had been the two of them against the world. But *always* was a dangerous word. It was a promise, easy to make in the moment but ultimately harder to keep. She didn't want there to be any confusion about what they were doing. No illusions or false expectations. Nothing that could be misconstrued as an *always*—because she didn't believe in always.

She slid her hand from his pocket and tucked it between her knees. "Aiden, we really—" She broke off abruptly, realizing with some alarm that he'd been clenching and unclenching the fingers of his injured hand. "Are you okay?"

Aiden dropped his hands self-consciously and pushed them back into his pockets. "I'm fine. It just acts up sometimes when it's cold. When it rains too. Like a mouth full of aching teeth."

"You should go in, then. It's late."

"I don't feel like being alone right now. Unless *you're* cold. God, I'm sorry. I didn't think. I just wanted . . ."

To be with you.

He hadn't said the words out loud—he'd caught himself in time—but she'd heard them just the same. "I'll go with you if you want."

"To the guesthouse?"

Mallory lifted a shoulder in a half-hearted shrug. "I don't feel like being alone either."

Neither of them spoke as they made their way off the jetty and back up the beach, but as they reached the guesthouse courtyard, Mallory began to question the wisdom of returning to a place so rife with memories. But backing out now would look like she didn't trust him—or worse, like she didn't trust herself.

Aiden reached past her and opened the door. She took a deep breath as she stepped inside, braced against the sudden barrage of yesterdays. The day they'd dashed inside out of a freak summer storm, when damp, salty kisses had turned into more. The pelt of rain on the roof and the slow roll of thunder as they made love for the first time.

She stole a look at Aiden, wondering if he was remembering too, but his face was blank, shut up tight against intrusion. He closed the door and unzipped his jacket but made no move to take it off. He simply stood there, facing her in the gloom. Mallory held her breath as the seconds ticked by. Finally, Aiden opened his mouth, then closed it again without speaking. Instead, he reached for her, pulling her to him, until his forehead was pressed to hers.

She could smell the wind in his hair, briny and clean, the way he used to smell. The memory left her faintly dizzy. Her limbs suddenly felt loose and undependable, and when his arms came around her, she didn't resist. His windbreaker felt chilly and slightly damp from the night air, but beneath it was the warmth of him slowly seeping into her bones, the thud of his heart matching hers beat for beat. He was going to kiss her and she was going to let him. It would be a mistake, but then that had been inevitable, hadn't it, the moment she agreed to come here?

His lips were cold and hungry as they closed over hers, unleashing an onslaught of familiar sensations. The way his breath felt against her cheek, the way he tasted, the way their bodies fit, like two halves of the same whole. Her head spun as the kiss deepened and she found herself caught between arousal and panic, reeling, breathless, hungry. And then all at once, his mouth went still and she felt a shudder run through him. He was weeping, she realized. Silently. Gut-wrenchingly. For his mother. For his music. For the glaring question mark his carefully mapped life had suddenly become.

She knew better than to speak. There were no words for such moments, no platitudes, however well meant, that would ease the kind of grief he felt. It simply had to spend itself. And so she remained silent as his tears continued, a lifeline in this unforeseen storm.

Mallory had no idea how long they stood there, clinging to one another, but eventually, she felt the tension begin to ebb from his body. He dropped his arms and backed away, wiping self-consciously at damp cheeks.

"Sorry. I didn't mean to come apart on you like that. I'm just . . . so tired."

Mallory wrapped her arms around her body, compensating for the sudden loss of his warmth. There'd been no mention of the kiss, no acknowledgment that for a moment they'd both let down their barriers. "Don't be sorry. It's normal. Especially in the beginning."

Aiden blinked at her. "Jesus. It *is* just the beginning, isn't it?"

Her eyes had begun to adjust to the darkness and she could make out his face now, hollowed out, all angles and shadows. She'd give anything to be able to contradict him, but the truth was things were going to be hard for a while. "I'm afraid it is, yes."

He shook his head, his eyes bruised with grief and yet unsettlingly empty. "It's like everything I care about, everything I love . . . dies." His voice broke and he looked away. "Sorry. You don't need to stay and listen to this. It's okay."

"I'm staying."

Aiden scrubbed at his eyes with the heels of his hands and blew out a breath. "Thank you. I was hoping you'd say that."

Mallory trailed after him to the living room, then stopped abruptly when she realized the Blüthner baby grand that used to stand at the center of the room—a gift from Estelle on his eighteenth birthday—was gone. Her heart sank. Without it, the room felt all wrong, like its heart had been torn out.

"I donated it to the center," Aiden said, noting the direction of her gaze. "It might as well do someone some good."

Mallory opened her mouth to protest but caught herself in time. He didn't need a lecture right now. Instead, she took his hand and led him to the couch, then reached for the lamp.

"Don't." He caught her arm, pulling her down beside him. "Can we just sit like this? Do you mind?"

"No, I don't mind. Do you want to talk some more?"

"Not really, no."

Mallory pulled her legs under her, angling her body so her shoulder rested against his. Their eyes met briefly and for a moment she thought he would kiss her again. Instead, he wound his fingers through hers and pressed their clasped hands to his chest.

"Thanks," he whispered. "I just want to be with you, to have you close. Is that all right?"

"Yes," Mallory said, laying her head in the familiar crook of his shoulder. "That's all right." For now, while he needed her, she would let it be all right.

THIRTY-NINE

MALLORY

July 31, 1999

Mallory opened her eyes, then quickly closed them again, disoriented by the glare of sunlight cutting into the room. Something was wrong. The sun was on the wrong side, and there was a breeze coming from somewhere, cool and salt scented, whispering against her cheek.

Pushing up onto one elbow, she forced her eyes back open, slowly orienting herself. It took a few moments to reconstruct the events of the previous evening, particularly those that had led her to wake up on Aiden's couch. She remembered laying her head on his shoulder, relaxing into the slow rise and fall of his chest in the darkness, and then . . . nothing. At some point, they must have fallen asleep. She had a vague recollection of stirring during the night and finding him tucked in behind her, an arm about her waist, his breath warm against the side of her neck. But she was alone now.

She followed the smell of coffee to the kitchen, expecting to find him there. He wasn't, but he'd left a mug and spoon on the counter beside the pot. She filled the mug, then padded back to the living room and through the open terrace door.

Aiden stood on the guesthouse's small terrace, his back to her as he looked out over the sea. If possible, he looked even worse than last night. "Morning," he said, turning as she approached. "I see you found the coffee."

"I did." She moaned involuntarily as the first sip went down. Dark roast, brewed strong, the way they both liked it. "Did you sleep?"

"A little. I'm sorry I woke you."

"You didn't."

"I was a little surprised to find you still here when I came to."

Mallory nodded, not meeting his eyes. The conversation was excruciating, a stilted attempt at normalcy, but nothing about them waking up together was normal.

Aiden stared down at his feet, bare and pale on the terrace stones. "You didn't have to stay the night. It was nice, though. Opening my eyes and finding you next to me. It's the first thing that's felt right in a long time."

Mallory took another sip from her mug, an effort to conceal the growing sense of unease at the center of her chest. "Aiden . . ."

"Are you hungry? I could scare us up some breakfast. Eggs and toast. I think there's juice."

"Thanks, I'm good. And I should really get going. I have a meeting with Deb before my first session and I need to get my notes together."

"We could drive in together if you want. Just come back over when you're ready."

The offer took Mallory by surprise. It never occurred to her that he'd be going to the center today. "Aiden, maybe you should take a few days to process. Tell Deb to cancel your classes for a few days and just be with your mom. She'll understand you needing time to deal with everything."

"I'm sure she would, but the first thing my mother did after you left yesterday was swear me to secrecy about all this. She doesn't want anyone to know. And the second thing she did was make me promise not to hover. And to be honest, if I don't have something to keep me busy I'll lose my mind. So as long as I'm going in, I thought we could ride together like we used to."

Like we used to.

Another round of alarm bells sounded. The last thing she wanted was to hurt him but she couldn't let him think last night was about anything other than two people in need of comfort. Yes, there had been a kiss. One she'd let happen, had perhaps even *wanted* to happen. But it hadn't been *that* kind of kiss—the kind that paved the way for reconciliation. It had been born of need, a familiar port in an emotional storm. They couldn't just pick up where they'd left off. For starters, she'd be gone in a few weeks.

"Aiden, last night—"

"If I did anything," he broke in. "Said anything I shouldn't have, I'm sorry. I didn't mean for it to get . . ." He raked a hand through his hair, shrugging awkwardly. "The kiss thing—I didn't plan for that to happen. It was just so good to be with you again, out there, in our place. I'm sorry if I . . . overstepped."

"You didn't," Mallory assured him, relieved that he'd been the one to broach the subject. "And it *was* good. But we've both got a lot going on right now. The last thing either of us needs is another complication."

Aiden flinched visibly. "Is that how you think of me? As a complication?"

Mallory bit her lip, cursing her clumsy delivery. "That's not what I meant. I just think we need to be careful. I have no idea what my life's going to look like going forward, and neither do you. Plus I'm leaving in a few weeks. I think it's important for us to maintain clear boundaries, so things don't get . . . blurry."

"Right," he said, scuffing his knuckles across his stubbled jaw. "You don't belong here anymore—don't belong to *me* anymore. Got it."

Mallory fought the urge to soften the moment. He was in pain, clinging to feelings that weren't real because they felt safe. It was up to her to be the strong one, even if it hurt. "I haven't belonged to you for a long time," she said gently. "Any more than you've belonged to me.

In fact, I sometimes wonder if we *ever* belonged together. Our houses might have been side by side but we've always lived in different worlds. Maybe that's why we fell apart when things got hard. Maybe it was never supposed to be you and me."

Aiden stiffened. "Do you actually believe that?"

Did she? Did it even matter? It was a decade ago, a lifetime. What mattered was here and now, staying focused, moving forward.

"I'm being practical, Aiden. I'm glad we're friends again but we can't go back to the way we were. And you wouldn't want us to. Not really. You're just leaning into something that feels familiar and safe. Right now that's me, but it won't last because it isn't real. Plus I'm going back to Boston soon. That doesn't mean we can't be friends. Like you said last night. Always. Wherever you are. Wherever I am."

"But just friends. And not here."

"I have to go back, Aiden. For now at least. Until I figure things out. Maybe I'll end up staying at New Day. Maybe I'll go back to school and get my PhD. Or I could teach. Jevet has connections at Northwestern."

He blinked at her, startled. "Chicago?"

She shrugged. "Maybe. Teaching isn't where I saw myself ending up—I always thought I was more the hands-on type—but we can't always have what we want."

There was a long beat of silence as their eyes held. Finally, his shoulders slumped. "I guess we really are done, aren't we?"

Mallory blinked against the sudden sting of tears. "Please don't put it like that. I know it isn't what you want to hear right now, but it's what needs to be. For both of us."

"No, you're right," he said, nodding gloomily. "I shouldn't have tried to make any of this about us. It was stupid."

"It wasn't. And I meant what I said about us being friends again. I really am glad."

"Yeah, me too." He surprised her by taking the mug from her hands and nodding toward the terrace steps. "Go on. You're off the hook."

Mallory touched his shoulder, not trusting her voice as she turned away. She should feel relieved that she'd finally managed to affect some kind of closure—it was the goodbye they'd never said, a clear and unambiguous end to what they'd once been to each other. Instead, it felt like a wound had been reopened.

◆ ◆ ◆

It was Mallory's plan to slip into the house and up to her room undetected, but Helen was already downstairs, dressed and standing over the kitchen sink with a bagel and her morning coffee.

"Good morning," she chirped over the rim of her mug, eyeing Mallory's bare feet with the tiniest of smiles. "Up with the sun, I see. Good for you."

Mallory felt her cheeks go hot, as if she'd been caught sneaking in after a date with her shirt on inside out. It was only a matter of time until her mother mentioned the fact that her bed hadn't been slept in.

Helen filled a fresh mug with coffee, stirred in a spoonful of sugar, and handed it to Mallory. "So . . . how was your walk?"

"My what?"

"You look a little windblown. I assumed you'd been out for an early-morning walk?"

"No, I . . ." Mallory paused, running a self-conscious hand through her hair. "I was with Aiden."

Helen took a bite of her bagel, chewing thoughtfully. Mallory waited for her to say something but eventually, the moment grew uncomfortable. "I know what you're thinking, but you're wrong. I met him out on the beach last night and we ended up going out on the jetty to talk. But that's all we did."

"Like old times," Helen said, grinning. "The two of you sneaking out to be together."

Mallory stared at her. "You knew?"

"I can see the jetty from my window the same as you. Did you really think you'd gotten away with sneaking out all those years?"

"I did, actually."

"I saw the light in his window and heard you go out. When you weren't in your room this morning, I just assumed . . ."

Mallory pulled a bagel from the bag on the counter and dropped it into the toaster. "There was nothing to assume. We got cold out on the rocks so we went back to the guesthouse and ended up falling asleep. On his couch," she added pointedly.

"How is he?"

Mallory shook her head. "Angry. Sad. Lost. He's already had so much to deal with and now he finds out his mother's dying. It's a lot."

"I'm glad he has you."

"He doesn't *have* me," Mallory corrected. "We just talked. About Estelle, mostly. I still don't agree with her keeping the truth from him but I tried to make him see her side."

"She really did mean well. She thought she was protecting him."

Mallory made a small snort as she plucked her bagel from the toaster. "People who lie always have some excuse. They claim to be protecting someone else when they're really just protecting themselves. They never bother to think about what will happen when the truth comes out. And of course it does. But by then the damage is done, trust is broken."

Helen set her mug in the sink with a weighty thunk. "We all have secrets, Mallory—and reasons for keeping them. As for wanting to protect yourself while protecting someone else—both things can be true at the same time. Especially for a mother."

Mallory responded with a grudging nod. She wasn't a parent, but on some level she did understand. And for a woman like Estelle, who'd made a career of protecting Aiden, it must be doubly true. "I haven't changed my mind," she said finally. "But I will concede that when it comes to Estelle Cavanaugh I'm not entirely objective. She loves him. I do know that."

"Well, then," Helen said. "That's progress. And now, I have to run." She grabbed her purse and keys from the counter. "Estelle has an appointment this morning—another scan—and she insists on going dressed like a queen. As if that's going to fool the machine."

Mallory abandoned her bagel to follow Helen out to the deck. "How are things? She didn't really talk about it when we spoke."

"Getting harder. She's losing more and more function every day. Her sight is failing and she's become really unsteady on her feet. I'm trying to get her to move to one of the rooms downstairs, but she refuses. She's still not there."

"Not where?"

"Acceptance," Helen said simply. "It's not that she doesn't *believe* it's happening. She understands what's happening to her body. But she's still fighting it, which makes everything harder than it needs to be. She's getting there, though. Little by little."

"And you're *helping* her? With that part, I mean?"

Helen smiled sadly. "I hope so. I'm certainly trying. She isn't always an easy woman to deal with but she isn't quite who I thought she was either. Then I suppose none of us are. We've all got layers no one else sees, but she keeps surprising me. In good ways. Anyway, I've got to get going and so do you. I'll see you tonight."

Mallory watched as her mother disappeared down the deck stairs, off to help a woman who'd made it her mission to blacken her name. She couldn't explain the bond that had sprung up between them but she'd seen it for herself—the silent looks and small, reassuring touches that felt more like friendship than a mere working relationship. She couldn't pretend to understand it, and a month ago she would have railed against such an arrangement, but if it made things easier for Aiden, she was glad. In fact, she was grateful.

FORTY

MALLORY

August 5, 1999

Five days later, Mallory once again returned home to an empty house. She was mostly okay with it, though she was becoming concerned about the growing length of Helen's days. Nearly a week had passed since Estelle's revelation, and her mother had been spending more and more time next door. And as Estelle's illness progressed, her days would only get longer.

The latest scan had shown no improvement. In fact, the tumor appeared to be growing more rapidly than the doctors had predicted, resulting in a downgraded prognosis and cessation of all chemotherapy. Debulking surgery had been mentioned again, as a way of staving off the inevitable, though none of her doctors seemed particularly keen on the idea. And it didn't matter. Once again, Estelle had declined, declaring that she had no intention of ruining whatever time she had left by letting them poke around inside her skull.

Mallory let her gaze wander to the window. She hadn't seen Aiden since the night they'd fallen asleep together on his couch. According to Debbie, they'd found someone to cover his music classes. There'd been no mention of why, only an announcement that effective immediately, a Ms. Lydia Parker would be taking over the music curriculum. Apparently, Estelle's illness was still being kept quiet.

It was a relief in a way, not having to worry about running into him around every corner. She was glad he'd taken her advice about spending more time with his mother. He'd feel better once they'd dealt with her illness head-on, and then they could start working through next steps. It would also give Helen a chance to step away now and then, to paint and practice some much needed self-care.

Upstairs, Mallory traded the day's warm-ups for shorts and a T-shirt as she considered what to do about supper. A big salad, maybe. Or a pot of vegetable soup. There wasn't much she could offer by way of help with Estelle, but she could make sure her mother came home to a proper meal.

She was fishing her cell from the pocket of her duffel, ready to head down to the kitchen, when she bumped the nightstand, sending her father's photograph crashing to the floor. Her heart sank as she bent to retrieve it. Thankfully, the glass was still intact, but there was a large split in the upper right-hand corner of the frame that would need to be repaired.

Where had she just seen glue? Was it the kitchen? No. It was her mother's studio, in a shoebox full of odds and ends. Where she shouldn't have been. She'd just run up and grab it, repair the frame, then put it back. Helen would never know she'd been there.

It took only minutes to locate the glue, but once in the studio the urge to linger was strong. Her last visit had been cut short and she'd nearly been caught trespassing. But Helen wasn't likely to be home for hours. She had time now—though time for *what* she couldn't say.

Suddenly she was remembering the day of Sloane's wedding, when she discovered Helen standing at the desk with a box of some sort. She'd looked so startled, almost guilty, when she realized Mallory was in the doorway. And there was the furtive way she'd nudged the drawer closed. It had seemed peculiar at the time, but there hadn't been time to ask questions. Now, the questions surfaced afresh. What was in the box and why had her mother been so secretive about it?

Curious, she wandered to the desk, pulling back the drawer until the box came into view. It was the size of a small book, made of some satiny-smooth wood, and inlaid with what appeared to be bits of abalone. She lifted it out and set it on the desk, staring at it as she wrestled with her conscience. Did she have the right to look inside? There were so many things her mother never spoke of, careful blanks in her story. Perhaps filling them would bring them closer. At least that's how she justified it when she finally lifted the lid and peered inside.

A set of dog tags on a beaded chain glinted up at her. She lifted them out, running a finger over the stamped letters. WARD, WILLIAM H. There was a series of numbers next—her father's service ID number, presumably—followed by O. POS and CATHOLIC. There was also a religious medallion of some kind. She held it to the light, tilting it back and forth to make out the image. Saint Christopher, the patron saint of travelers and protector against sudden death. If it belonged to her father, it had done him little good.

She closed her fingers around both, moved by the realization that they had been around her father's neck when he died, that someone had physically removed them and taken the trouble to mail them back to her mother. But what were they doing up here, in the same box where Helen found the opal necklace?

A gift from a friend, Helen had explained when asked about its origin. *Not* from her father—from a *friend*. So why keep it with her father's things? Short of asking, she'd never know, and she couldn't ask without giving herself away.

Resigned, she turned her attention back to the box and was surprised to find her father looking up at her. She'd only ever seen his face, but he was standing in this photo, dressed in a dark suit and polished shoes. She wished she could make out his expression but the photo was old and badly worn. On closer inspection she saw that one side had been torn, purposely by the look of it, leaving a not-quite-clean edge. There had been someone else in the photo, she realized, someone whose arm—or at least a part of an arm—was still visible. Her mother or someone else? And where was the rest of her?

Mallory checked the box, hoping the other half might be there. It wasn't. Instead, she found a ring fashioned of hammered silver with a line of gold running around the center. Like the other items, she'd never seen it before, but it was engraved. Closing one eye, she peered at the inscription—TL/OH. Initials apparently, but whose? Not either of her parents'. She stared at the letters, hoping for some flash of recognition, but eventually gave up. Rather than filling in blanks in Helen's past, the box's contents had created a whole new slate of questions.

One at a time, she returned the items to the box, doing her best to arrange them as they'd been when she found them, but when she tried to put the box back where she found it, the drawer refused to budge. On closer inspection, she saw that a book of some sort had become wedged at the back.

She pried it free, attempting to smooth the scuffs from the blue leather cover. It was scarred and shabby, and even closed she could see that the pages were yellowed with age. She fanned through them, assuming it was a ledger of some sort. Instead, she found her mother's familiar script, pages and pages of it, complete with dated headings—a journal.

Her *mother's* journal.

Put it back where you found it. It's none of your business. The words throbbed like a pulse. But there were other words too, louder words. *Just one look. Just to glimpse the dates. Then back in the drawer where you found it.*

Stepping closer to the window, she opened the book to a random page and stared at the lines of crowded script. The page bore no date— apparently, she'd landed in the middle of an entry rather than the beginning of one—but before she could turn the page, she was reading.

When you love someone, you can accept that there might have been someone else—might still be someone else. You know, and you're willing to take them anyway—on any terms—because to live without them is unthinkable.

I wanted you that badly.

Badly enough to forsake my vows—and yours. To live in the shadows with you, if that's what it came to, condemned by the so-called good people. I no longer cared what those people thought. I was willing to do anything, to live any kind of life. Instead, I found myself sentenced to a life I never wanted. Wife to a man I never loved. Mother to a child I never planned on. A life without you, my dearest.

Mallory's hands grew clammy as she stared at her mother's words, disjointed phrases leaping up at her from the page. *Wife to a man I never loved . . . a child I never planned on.* Suddenly it all fell into place. *She* was the unplanned child, her father the unloved man. It also explained why her mother never talked about William. There'd been someone else, someone who'd apparently been unwilling to break his marriage vows, though Helen had clearly been willing to break hers. Spurned by her married lover, she'd been forced to remain with her husband and child—*a life she never wanted.*

She couldn't say how long she'd been staring at the damning lines, trying to decide if she could bear to read on, when the sound of the front door closing suddenly echoed up the stairs. Panicked, she tossed the book into the desk, shoved the drawer closed, and scrambled out into the hall.

"Mallory?" Helen's voice drifted up the stairs, accompanied by the scuff of footsteps. "Sweetheart? Where are you?"

Mallory pulled the door closed behind her, breath held. All she had to do was make it to the second-floor landing before her mother reached the third floor. But it was too late. Helen was already there. She came to an abrupt halt as she reached the landing, pale brows drawn down in a scowl.

"What are you doing up here?"

"I needed some glue," Mallory replied hastily, producing the tube from her pocket as proof. "I knocked Daddy's picture off the nightstand and broke it, and I knew you kept your framing supplies up here, so . . ."

It was odd, feeling defensive after the damning discovery she'd just made, but she wasn't ready to admit to blatantly invading her mother's privacy. She tried to look casual as she stepped past Helen and made for the stairs. "I was about to go down and make some supper. Are you hungry?"

Helen narrowed her eyes, regarding her almost warily, but eventually her shoulders relaxed. "Aiden came home with takeout from Romano's. He was hoping to tempt Estelle but she wouldn't eat, so he sent it home with me. It's in the fridge if you want to heat it up."

"You're not eating?"

Helen shook her head wearily. "I'm dead on my feet. All I want is a shower and my bed. I'll see you in the morning."

Mallory managed a nod, relieved when Helen gave her arm a pat and started back down the stairs. She was nowhere near ready to discuss the journal. She needed time to process it first, to get her arms around her emotions—and if possible, get another look at the journal. Because one thing had become clear—she couldn't trust her mother to tell her the truth.

FORTY-ONE

HELEN

Back in my tower. Back at my desk. I hadn't planned on coming up—I'm so dreadfully tired—but I can't seem to settle. I was uneasy when I saw Mallory coming out of the studio and knew I wouldn't be able to rest until I came up and had a look around, just to reassure myself. She seemed a bit distracted as we said good night, cool and closed off.

It might be that I'm overtired. Or perhaps it's just my conscience. I did promise I wouldn't take on any new charges this summer, and then along comes Estelle—of *all* people. I can't risk repeating the mistakes I made when she was a child, putting work ahead of my daughter. I need to talk to her, to be here for her. First thing in the morning, after I've had some sleep.

I push to my feet, ready to go down and crawl into bed, then go cold when I see that the desk drawer isn't quite closed. I slide it open. The rosewood box has been pushed to one side and as I lift out the journal I see that the cover is folded back on itself, along with several pages, which is certainly not how I left it. A wave of dread washes through me. It was Mallory, of course. Who else could it be?

How much? How much has she read? How much does she know?

A sound like rushing water fills my head as I stare at the badly creased pages, imagining how what's written there might be misconstrued by someone not in possession of all the facts. But how much did she actually read? Enough to know the whole truth? Or only a small slice of it? Either way, it's time to tell her all of it.

◆ ◆ ◆

There's no light under the door as I approach Mallory's room. I turn the knob and tiptoe in, breath held, and come to stand beside her bed. The moon is high and nearly full, spilling through the window and illuminating her face.

The sight of her breaks my heart, the curve of her cheek, the line of her jaw, so familiar in this milky half-light that it makes my chest ache. I hover, recalling the nights, so long ago now, when I would stand over this sleeping child, heart bursting, but terrified too because I knew I was out of my depth, completely unprepared to raise her on my own.

Finally, I touch her cheek. She stirs, then her eyes flutter open. "Is it . . . Estelle?" she asks, her voice thick with sleep.

"No," I say quietly. "I've been upstairs—at my desk."

Her eyes sharpen as she comes fully awake. In the moonlight, I see a brief flicker of guilt, admission of her trespass, followed by a glint of something flatter and colder. "Have you?"

"It's time for us to talk."

She pushes back the covers and sits up, feet already on the floor, but I catch her arm, staying her. I reach for the lamp but decide against it. Confessions are easier in the dark. "You found a journal," I say evenly. "My journal. I don't know how much you read—"

"Did you *ever* love him?" she says, cutting me off. "Or me?"

"Please, Mallory, let me explain."

"You don't need to. I get it. You wanted someone else. Someone you couldn't have. At least I finally know why you never talk about my father. It also explains why you were never around when I was a kid. You never wanted either of us."

Her words are like razors, slicing me open. But they tell me she still doesn't know the truth. She only thinks she does. "Will you let me explain, and listen until I'm finished?"

She doesn't answer. She simply sits there, bristling in the dark.

Suddenly my mouth is dry. Where on earth do I begin? The silence yawns painfully as I grope for some way to soften what's coming. "You know what it's like," I say finally, "to love someone with your whole heart. To find the other half of yourself in another person—the way you felt about Aiden. I loved someone like that once."

"But not my father."

"No," I say evenly. "I never loved William Ward." I feel her stiffen but force myself to keep going. "But I do love his daughter and have from the moment I laid eyes on her. Before I tell you anything else, Mallory, I need you to believe that."

Still she says nothing, but I have her attention now, and after a hard swallow, I plunge ahead. "When I was in school, I met someone. We became inseparable. Friends first, and then later . . . more. I told you there was a scandal, that I had to leave school. Everyone assumed I was innocent in all of it, that I'd been 'touched' against my will. And because I was a coward, I let them think it. I should have spoken up, but I was terrified of what my mother would say. But she knew the truth. I could see it when she looked at me. That's why I was sent away—because she *knew* and she couldn't forgive me. In her eyes, I was damaged. As long as I was at school she wouldn't have to look at me and be reminded of how I'd shamed her."

My hands are shaking now, the memories hauntingly fresh as they unfold in my mind. "It was a relief to be away from my mother but my heart was broken. I had betrayed the only person I ever loved, the only person who ever loved me. I let everyone think . . ."

My voice breaks as the familiar guilt washes over me, a stain I can never wash away. I blink back tears, determined to get through the rest.

"We saw each other years later, but by then it was too late." A pair of tears finally escape, rolling unchecked down my cheeks. "There's never been anyone else."

Mallory turns to look at me, her face washed pale by the moonlight. "But you married my father."

I close my eyes and make myself say it. "No, sweetheart, I didn't. I was never married to your father."

She stiffens as my words register, but she keeps her eyes fixed straight ahead while she adds up the pieces and draws her conclusions. "This man you loved instead of my father," she says finally. "Does he have a name?"

I look away briefly, praying for strength, because we've come to it at last. "It wasn't a man, Mallory. It was a woman—and her name was Poppy."

Her face goes blank. She blinks at me. "A woman?"

"We met when I was fifteen and fell head over heels."

It feels strangely good to say it out loud, as if a boulder has been lifted from my chest. A piece of the secret revealed at last, though not all. Not yet. Mallory is staring at me, and I see that her face has lost some of its hardness.

"So you're saying you're gay? That you love . . . women?"

"I'm saying I loved Poppy. It never occurred to me to care one way or another *what* she was—male *or* female. I only cared *who* she was—and who *I* was when I was with her. There's never been anyone else, before or since."

"Then why be with my father at all?"

"I wasn't," I answer bluntly. "William was Poppy's husband."

"Wait. What?"

"A few months before I was supposed to take my vows, I went to see her. I needed to be sure there was no chance for us. And there wasn't. She was married."

"To William."

"Yes."

"But if William was Poppy's husband . . ."

"Poppy was your mother, Mallory."

She shakes her head as the truth sinks in, eyes wide and empty. "All these years . . ."

"There's more," I say brusquely. There's no going back now. "The following year, I got a call. All she said was *Please come. I need you.* I knew going to her meant I could never return to the order, but I went anyway. She was at a motel across town. The kind that doesn't ask a lot of questions. That's where I met you. You were just a baby, but you looked so much like her. The sight of you broke my heart. Because you were hers—and *his.* I was so jealous. He'd given her something I never could. But he was dead by then, shot down in Vietnam. And she was—" My voice cracks painfully. "She was dying."

I hear Mallory's sharp intake of breath and wait for her to speak. When she doesn't, I steel myself for the worst of it and press on. "I thought she wanted us to finally be together, but that's not why she wanted me to come. She asked me . . ." I swallow again and square my shoulders. "She wanted me to help her die."

Beside me, Mallory goes still. Finally, she turns to me. "But you didn't." There's an urgency in the words, and a look of slow-dawning horror on her face. She pushes to her feet and stands staring at me. "Tell me you told her no."

I don't answer. I can't. Instead, I watch as her jaw goes slack. She already knows, but she asks one more time. "Please. Tell me you said no."

"I'm sorry. I can't."

"My god . . ." She covers her mouth as if afraid she might be sick. The light through the window has bled the color from her face and her eyes are wide, dark pools as she stares back at me. "How . . ." she whispers, the single word full of revulsion.

"She was suffering, Mallory. And so very tired of fighting." A small sob escapes me. I choke it down, the breath shuddering out of me. "She begged me."

"How?" she asks again. "How did you . . . *do* it?"

The question hangs between us, inevitable, unbearable. I close my eyes, letting the tears come at last. "I stirred a handful of crushed pills into some applesauce," I say at last, my voice fraying. "And then I took you."

FORTY-TWO

MALLORY

And then I took you.

The words reverberated through Mallory's chest like a series of small bombs detonating. In the space of twenty minutes, the ground had opened up beneath her feet, plunging her into a newly created abyss.

"Took me where? What are you saying?"

"When I left the hotel that night, I took you with me. There was no court, no lawyer, no adoption papers. I just took you and disappeared."

"As in . . . kidnapped?"

"It wasn't like that."

"You took a child that wasn't yours!"

"It was what she wanted—for me to raise you in her place."

"I suppose she told you that?"

"She did. She told me exactly what she wanted me to do."

"Was that before or after you laced her applesauce?"

Helen stared at her, stricken. "You make it sound like I . . ." She squeezed her eyes tight, breath shuddering. "It was what she wanted, Mallory. You were the most precious thing in her life—her whole world. She needed to know you'd be taken care of when she was gone, loved the way she would have loved you."

Mallory stared at her, unable to wrap her head around what she'd just heard. The woman who had raised her—not her *actual* mother, not even a stepmother—had killed an ex-lover and then stolen her child to raise as her own. It was the stuff of nightmares, the grisly rumors of her childhood, suddenly come to life.

"Say something, Mallory. Please. Say *anything.*"

"You killed a woman and kidnapped a child. What am I supposed to say?"

"Say you understand," Helen said hoarsely. "Say you forgive me."

"How? What you did is unforgivable. As for understanding . . ." She broke off, pressing the heels of both hands to her eyes, desperate to dislodge the images from her brain. "I could have gone the rest of my life without knowing any of this. But I do know it. And now I can never *un*know it. Why on earth would you tell me that ghoulish story? Now, after all these years?"

"Because I promised Poppy I would. She wanted you to know everything. About us. About her. Even about William. Maybe especially about William. And because I knew what you probably thought after finding the journal."

"And this is better?"

"No, but it's what happened. I was always going to tell you but I kept putting it off. In the beginning, you were too young to understand. Then, when you were old enough . . ." Helen closed her eyes, chin quivering. "By then I suppose I loved you too much."

"You loved me so you *lied* to me?"

Helen's shoulders sagged, and for a moment she seemed to grope for words. "I've always known how you felt about me," she said at last. "I was never the mother you wanted. Especially in the beginning, when I was working all the time. And then later, when we came here, we'd already grown so far apart. I was afraid if you knew the truth—that you weren't *really* mine—I'd lose you forever. So I kept putting it off. But tonight, when I realized you'd read the journal and probably gotten the wrong idea, I knew I had to tell you the truth."

Mallory shook her head, slowly, disbelievingly. "All those years, I wondered what was wrong with me, why I always came last with you. And now I know. I wasn't your daughter. I was just some kid you were stuck with."

"That's not true."

"I read it! In your *own* writing. *The child you never planned on . . . the life you never wanted.* You meant *me*."

"I did," Helen said so softly that Mallory nearly missed it. "But not the way you think. I had given my life to the church—or nearly given it. Nuns don't have children. It wasn't that I never wanted you. It was that I never *imagined* you. But when I saw you—the instant I saw you—I was in love in a way I never knew existed. Fiercely. Hopelessly. But I was terrified of you too. I'd only ever known my own mother's brand of parenting. I was afraid I'd be like her, that I'd hurt you the way she hurt me."

Mallory pushed to her feet, suddenly needing to put distance between them. She had no idea how to respond, or where they went from here. She'd let herself believe they were making progress, smoothing over old wounds, building trust. But their entire relationship had been built on a web of unforgivable lies.

"Talk to me," Helen pleaded. "Please. I need to know what you're thinking."

"I'm thinking I don't know where this leaves us, what we are to each other, how we move forward."

Helen flinched as if she'd received a sharp slap. "What we *are* to each other? I'm your mother, Mallory. And you're my daughter. Neither of those things has changed."

"But they *have* changed. Everything's changed."

Helen stood and took a tentative step forward. "I know it's a lot but we can work through it. We just have to keep talking."

"And if I don't *want* to work through it?"

Helen's face was near crumbling now. "Sweetheart . . . please."

"Don't call me that," Mallory snapped. "You don't get to call me that."

She turned away then, pulling her arms around her body, throat aching with the need to scream or weep, or both. The truth was she wasn't sure what she was feeling. Was it rage? Revulsion? Betrayal? Yes, all of that. And something else she didn't have a name for. The disturbing awareness that she'd been set adrift, severed from both her history and herself, and that there was no compass for this, no way to get home.

She'd been such a fool. She'd spent the better part of her childhood denying the rumors about Helen Ward, dodging the nicknames and outrunning the bullies. And all the while she'd been living with a woman capable of . . . what was it? Murder? Manslaughter?

"Tell me something," she said, rounding to face Helen again. "And don't you dare lie to me. All those years, when the kids were calling you those terrible names, is that what you were doing—crushing pills in applesauce?"

Helen appeared genuinely stunned. "You don't believe that. You can't."

"How am I supposed to believe anything else? All those lonely charges putting themselves in your hands. No family. No friends. And all the stuff you've collected over the years. Was it payment for—I don't even know what you call it. Is it mercy killing?"

"Mallory, stop it!" Helen was shaking now, her face chalk white. "I swear to you, it was only Poppy. The others . . . All I did was take care of them, make them comfortable. There was never anything . . . It was only once, Mallory. Only Poppy."

Mallory blew out a long breath. Suddenly she was very tired. "What you did was against the law."

Helen nodded. "Yes."

"And that doesn't *bother* you?"

"Of course it bothers me!" Helen's words rang sharply off the bedroom walls. "It's bothered me for thirty years. But the woman I loved asked me to end her suffering. I couldn't say no." She bowed her head as a sob tore from her throat. After a moment she looked up, her cheeks slick with tears. "It's easy to judge when it isn't you, to think you'd be strong enough to say no, but when it's someone you love, someone you've given your whole heart to, you'll forfeit your soul to ease their pain."

"You killed a woman."

"I helped her die. It's not the same thing. But yes, it was a crime. It may even have been a sin—the church would certainly say so—but when you're forced to watch someone you love being devoured cell by cell, you don't give a damn about sin. Because deep down you know the *real* sin is to let the suffering continue when it's in your power to end it. I spared her a few days of agony, a week at most. If I go to hell for that, so be it."

Her face softened then, and something like a smile touched her mouth. "I wish you could have known her. She was so beautiful. Her hair was just like yours, and she—"

"Stop!" Mallory put her hands over her ears, like a child shutting out bad news. "I don't care what color her hair was. I don't want to hear any more."

Mallory's gaze settled on the framed photograph on her nightstand, the man she'd worshipped since childhood. The newly repaired crack wasn't visible, but she knew it was there, and she couldn't help wondering if this afternoon's mishap had been an omen of things to come.

"What about him?" she asked, pointing to the photo. "Is any of what you told me about my father true? The stuff about him volunteering for a suicide mission to save a bunch of guys who were pinned down in the jungle—was all that made up too?"

"No," Helen said wearily. "I never lied about William. Poppy told me those stories so I could tell them to you. She wanted you to know the kind of man he was. She made me promise to tell you, and I did. Everything I said about him was true."

"Except for the part where he was your husband."

Helen nodded miserably. "Except for that part, yes."

"Well, at least there was that." Mallory went to the dresser, opened both top drawers at once, and began scooping out handfuls of clothing. "I'd like you to go now."

"What are you doing?"

"What does it look like?"

"You're . . . leaving? In the middle of the night?"

"It won't be the first time."

"No, it certainly won't."

Something about the remark pushed Mallory over the edge. Tossing an armload of bras and panties to the bed, she whirled to face Helen. "You do *not* get to judge me. Not now. Not ever again."

"I wasn't judging you. I just want—"

"What?" Mallory demanded. "What is it you *want* from me? My life has just been turned inside out and I don't have a clue how to feel about any of it, but by all means, let's talk about what *you* want!"

"I want you to stop running away!" Helen fired back. "I want you to stay and fight. But it always comes to this—you tossing your things in a suitcase and sprinting for the exit. Just like you did with Aiden. When it gets hard, when it gets scary, you bail. And you're doing it again."

Mallory glared at her, astonished that she felt entitled to offer any kind of advice. "You just confessed to poisoning a woman and kidnapping her baby. Am I supposed to just shrug that off?"

"Of course not. But there was more to it than just that night. There are things I still need to tell you—about who Poppy was and how it all happened. If you'll just let me explain . . ."

"I don't want you to explain. In fact I don't want you to say another word about it. I just want to go back to Boston and forget I was ever here."

"Sweetheart," Helen said before catching herself. "I'm sorry—*Mallory*—you can't keep running away. You have to *deal* with things. You have to deal with *this*."

Mallory nodded crisply toward the open door. "I'd like you to go, please."

Helen mopped at her eyes, attempted to straighten her shoulders, then abandoned the effort. "Yes, all right. But please think about what I said. Not for my sake. For yours. If you leave tonight you'll never come back. We both know it. And you'll lose Aiden for good—the way I lost Poppy."

Mallory blinked at her, thrown off balance by the subtle change of subject. "So this is about *me* now? About *my* happiness? *My* regrets? I haven't begun to process any of this yet, but one thing I know for sure is that dangling Aiden under my nose isn't going to make me stay. In fact, you and I are done talking."

Helen nodded, looking both beaten and numb. "It's late. Will you at least stay the night?"

"I don't know."

Helen walked to the door, but paused before stepping out into the hall. "I love you, Mallory. As much as any mother has ever loved a child. No matter what else you think about me, please believe that."

Mallory turned away, allowing her silence to speak for her. She heard the door close, then moments later, the weary scrape of Helen's footsteps overhead in her studio. Suddenly, the room felt too close, the quiet too fraught with disturbing revelations. She glanced at the clock. If she left now she'd beat the morning rush and be in Boston by dawn.

If you leave tonight you'll never come back . . . And you'll lose Aiden for good.

Well, she'd been right about that, at least. Leaving now—angry and in the middle of the night—meant leaving for good. She'd never come back, never see Helen again. Was that what she wanted? To erase the woman who had raised her?

She'd tried it with Aiden, thinking that with enough time and distance the pain would fade. And for a time it seemed to. But if coming back to Little Harbor had taught her anything, it was that it didn't matter how many years or miles you put between yourself and a thing.

The memories were always there. Because you never *really* left them behind. They traveled *with* you, like shadows, determined to be noticed, to be dealt with.

Wandering to the window, she dropped down onto the sill, willing her disjointed emotions to resolve into something resembling linear thought. Instead, they kept skipping back on themselves, like a phonograph needle stuck in the same maddening groove.

She glanced down at the beach below, the silver sand and the rushing sea, the finger of dark rock glinting wetly in the moonlight. They were a part of her, like her bones and her breath. And now *this* would be part of her too, this awful, unfathomable story. Wherever she went, *whenever* she went, it would go too. A forbidden love. A mercy killing carried out in a cheap motel. A stolen infant. And where did any of it leave her? Did she have *two* mothers now? No mother at all? And in the grand scheme of things, did that part even matter?

Family conflict was supposed to be her area of expertise. So why couldn't she get a handle on what was going on in her own head? In the blink of an eye, the woman she'd called mother for thirty years had become a stranger. But perhaps even more unsettling, she'd become a stranger to herself. Unmoored. Displaced. Alone.

She'd seen the movies. A perfectly well-adjusted adult discovers quite by accident that they were secretly adopted and all at once the sky comes crashing down. They're plunged into a morass of despair and uncertainty, their world completely unraveling. She'd never really bought it as a plot device. But in light of this inexplicable new reality, completely unraveling seemed not only plausible but the only *sane* reaction. Every human on the planet had a story they told themselves, about who they were and where they came from, stories that tethered them to the world. They created a kind of context, a landscape for living. But without those stories, the world became unshaped—and then the storyteller became unshaped.

And what of the grisly new plot twist in her mother's story?

No, *not* her mother now—*Helen.*

She had poisoned a dying woman. Did it matter that the woman had been a lover rather than one of her paying charges? From a moral perspective? Perhaps. But legally? No. In 1969 there were no "death with dignity" laws on the books anywhere. In the eyes of the law, Helen Ward had taken a life. She had committed *murder*.

And yet, Mallory felt a twinge of resistance to the word. Tina Allen had been murdered. Brutally and senselessly. What Helen had done for Poppy was an act of love, of mercy. And though it unsettled her to admit it, she'd been right—taking a life and ending a dying woman's suffering were not the same thing, even if the end result was. Just what that would mean going forward she couldn't say, but in her bones, beneath all the shock and horror, she knew that much was true.

FORTY-THREE

HELEN

August 6, 1999

Mallory is still here, or was when I left to come to Estelle's.

I listened all night for sounds of her leaving, her suitcase bumping down the stairs, her car pulling out of the drive, but the car was still there when the sun came up, though it was gone by the time I came out of the shower. Her bedroom door was closed, and my knock went unanswered, but when I looked in, her things were still there, her bed made, the clothes she'd thrown on the floor last night picked up and put away.

I hope it means she's decided to stay. But if she does go, I want her to have something of Poppy's to take with her. I think of the journal I left on her pillow this morning, my past offered up for her examination. I imagine her turning the pages, combing through the details of my relationship with her mother, and my stomach clenches like a fist.

Mothers aren't supposed to have yesterdays. To our children, we're blank slates, patiently awaiting their appearance so our lives can finally begin. In their minds, we've kept no secrets, dreamed no dreams, committed no sins. But few of us come to motherhood unmarked by life.

We've had pasts and passions—and yes, regrets. I've certainly had my share—and *still* have. And now she'll know them all. So be it.

I would have told her all of it last night, but she wasn't ready. The news was too fresh. But eventually, she'll have questions about the woman who brought her into the world—at least I hope she will—and will perhaps be willing to talk before her anger hardens into something permanent. I pray it hasn't already.

It's unbearable to think of losing her, but I knew there was danger in telling her the truth. For so long, I worried about choosing my moment carefully. Now I see that there was *never* going to be a right moment. All that's left is to live with the fallout and hope that someday she'll forgive me.

I'm almost glad I have Estelle to look after. She's quite pale this morning and today's headache hasn't responded to my tea any better than yesterday's. I offered to give her one of the pills her doctor prescribed, an opiate that's sure to be more effective than my herbal teas, but once again she refused. She's determined to remain sharp as long as possible, but I see the pain beginning to take a toll, steadily wearing her down.

I've spent the morning reading aloud to her. Romance novels, of all things. A whole closetful, as it turns out. And another stack under her bed, hidden from view like contraband. Pirates and cowboys, the occasional prince in disguise. Who would have guessed the chilly woman living beside me all these years had a penchant for such romantic fare? But then so much about these last few weeks with Estelle has come as a surprise.

It's good that Aiden's been spending time with her. They spend hours going through her papers, scribbling notes and discussing plans on how best to carry on with Estelle's beloved center. I'm glad to see it. It's good for them both to stay busy, though I can't help wondering if she's given up hope that he'll eventually return to the piano.

"There," Estelle says curtly, interrupting my thoughts as she holds out her empty mug for inspection. "All gone like a good girl. Is Nanny happy?"

"Nanny is," I reply, taking the mug and setting it on the coffee table beside a splayed copy of *The Flame and the Flower*.

It's a little joke between us, a reference to an argument we had early on when she accused me of treating her like a petulant child. She calls me a bully sometimes too, but only in jest now. I toss out the word *brat* from time to time. Also in jest—mostly. Because she can still be rather bratty when she wants to be. But I suppose that's what comes of always getting your way.

I catch her now and then, when Aiden isn't around, sneaking a cigarette or taking a nip from the small bottle she keeps in her nightstand. I've given up fighting her. If it brings her some pleasure, who am I to say no?

I study her covertly now. The valerian root is slow to take effect today. But that's not so unusual. The woman is positively indefatigable when she sets her mind to it.

"How about a nap?" I suggest, already knowing what her answer will be.

"No. Aiden said he'd come by when he was through with the lawyers and I don't want to be groggy. They're working on transferring control of the center's trust accounts. Poor thing. He's not happy about being in the middle of it."

"I can imagine. But it's good to see the two of you have mended fences."

She sighs and a little frown appears between her brows. "I'm not sure we have. Not entirely. He's still miffed about me keeping all of this a secret, but I can bear his disapproval as long as we're talking again."

She closes her eyes, squeezing them tight. At first, I think it's the headache, but when she opens them again, I see that she's in the throes of a different kind of pain. "Do you believe in atonement, Helen?"

I go still, brought up short by the question. Raised by a zealously Catholic mother, the concept of atonement—the expiation of sin through good works—was part and parcel of my upbringing, not to mention the foundation of my training as an acolyte, but I renounced both years ago. A god who keeps score never seemed quite right to me. Still, old habits die hard. "Yes," I answer evenly. "I do."

"I want to believe in it too. But sometimes I'm afraid it's too late. I've made such an awful mess of my life, Helen. And of other people's lives."

I stay silent, waiting. My work has made me privy to all sorts of confessions over the years, regrets of every color and flavor, but this feels different. Most of my charges begin as strangers, which means I know only what they tell me—*their* side of things. But I have a history with this woman. Some of the wrongs she's done were to me—and to my daughter. She's already asked my forgiveness for those and I've given it. But I'm not sure that in my current state of mind I have the emotional stamina to hear more.

"Aiden's father was going to divorce me," she suddenly blurts without preamble.

I blink at her, stunned. We've talked quite a lot about her late husband. How she fell in love with him at a party and ditched her date to take a drive with him. How proud she was the day she walked down the aisle and took his name, despite his lack of pedigree. How Aiden had worshipped the ground his father walked on. Not once had she hinted that there'd been trouble in paradise.

Her eyes are shiny with tears now. She bats them away, shaking her head. "He told me right before he left for a business trip. We had a horrible fight. And then he got on that plane."

It had been in all the papers and on the radio—a private jet brought down by bad weather. No survivors. The entire town had gone into mourning, but there hadn't been a breath of scandal.

"I didn't know," I reply softly.

"No one did. I made sure of it. And I'd almost convinced myself that he never meant to go through with it. Then one day I was going through his desk, looking for insurance papers, and I . . . found things. Credit card receipts and hotel bills, letters from a lawyer I'd never heard of." She swallows hard, her eyes suddenly clouded with memory. "There was a woman—Anna was her name. I don't know how they met or how I could have missed what was going on, but she was the reason he was leaving."

My thoughts tumble back to the day I learned Poppy was married, the feel of the words as they landed in my gut, a blow I never saw coming. "I'm so sorry," I say inadequately. "Does Aiden know?"

"No. He was eleven at the time and worshipped the ground George walked on. I couldn't break his heart that way. And part of me knew he'd blame me for it, for driving his father away."

"I'm sure that isn't true."

Her eyes flick to mine, raw with anguish. "But it *is* true, Helen. I did drive him away. He'd made up his mind to leave and would have if that plane hadn't crashed." She blinks suddenly, covering her mouth. "I'm so sorry. I'd forgotten that Mallory's father died in a helicopter crash. Please forgive me. I didn't mean to be insensitive. It's just that George has been on my mind lately. I'm starting to realize I did the same thing to Aiden that I did to his father. I was determined to make successes of them both. Instead, I drove them away."

"Estelle, you're tired . . ."

"No, let me say it, Helen. I need to. After Mallory lost the baby . . ." She paused, closing her eyes. "Aiden didn't want to call off the wedding or go to London. Entering the Leeds was my idea. *I* pushed him to go. If I hadn't, he wouldn't have been there the night that window fell and he'd still have his music." Her throat bobs convulsively. "How can I ever atone for that?"

I stare at my hands, folded neatly in my lap, as I search for an appropriate response. I've made the connections myself, at some point might even have said as much out loud, but I can't let her take all the blame.

"Aiden was twenty-two years old when he boarded that plane, Estelle, a grown man with free will. Yes, you pushed him. For all I know, you packed his suitcase. But ultimately, it was his choice. And I know you think you're all powerful, but you didn't make that window fall on his hand. None of us knows why bad things happen, or what good might come out of them when they do. For now, he's home and you're talking. In time, he'll find his path."

A pair of tears slide down her cheeks. "Time isn't something I have a lot of."

"No, but Aiden does, and it's his life. His to live and his to fix."

"I'd give anything to do it all over. Or at least make him understand that every mistake I made I made because I loved him. I don't even need him to forgive me, just to know how sorry I am." She blinks hard, clearly struggling to rein in her emotions. "Will there be time, do you think—to atone?"

I study her from beneath lowered lashes, struggling to find words of reassurance. As it happens, I've been asking myself the same question all morning. "Children can be slow to forgive, Estelle. And it's partly our fault. We let them think we're infallible, that we have all the answers. When it turns out we're human, they don't take it well. But they come around, and so will Aiden. He loves you."

She takes a tissue from the box I hold out and blots her eyes. "Do you really think so?"

I force a smile and think I've pulled it off, but Estelle narrows one eye at me, something she does when she's having trouble focusing. But that isn't what she's doing now. She's studying me.

"Something's wrong," she says, with no hint of a question in her words. "What is it? And don't say nothing. You're not yourself this morning."

"I'm just a little tired."

"You have a terrible poker face, Helen. Tell me what's going on. Is it Mallory?"

I surrender finally and nod.

"I knew it. I could feel the tension between you the other day. It's because you're taking care of me, isn't it?" She smiles sadly. "It's all right. I know how she feels about me. I can find someone if you need to step away. That woman you said you hired. Or I could call an agency. And Aiden is around a lot more now. You've been so wonderful—far more wonderful than I deserve—but I don't want to come between the two of you."

I nearly laugh. How perfectly like her to assume *my* troubles are somehow about *her*. Still, I see what the offer has cost her and I'm grateful. "It wasn't you, Estelle. It was . . . something else."

"Can I help? Or at least offer a shoulder?"

For one mad moment, I consider telling her everything. About Poppy and the applesauce, about my confession to Mallory, about my own daughter thinking I'm a monster. I can't, of course. And so I must leave it vague. "We argued last night, and she's thinking about leaving."

"Leaving? Because of one fight?"

"No, it's been brewing for . . . well, a long time. We've always argued, about everything, but this time is different. This time feels . . . final."

Estelle studies me for a long moment. When she finally speaks her voice is gentle and full of sympathy. "A wise woman once told me children are slow to forgive but they come around."

I nod, realizing she's thrown my words back at me. She means well, but she doesn't know the whole story. If she did, she'd hardly be so sympathetic. "It's been so good having her home. We've always had a rocky relationship, but it felt like we were finally starting to connect. And then last night it all fell apart again." My voice breaks and I look away. "I thought I could use the summer to make things better between us. Instead, I'm going to lose her."

"Oh, Helen," she sighs, reaching for my hand. "Aren't we a pair?"

I nearly smile. The phrase has become a part of so many of our conversations, an ironic jest about the ways our lives have intersected of late. Ways neither of us ever imagined. I push to my feet with a weary smile. "Aren't we just."

Before I can step away, Estelle recaptures my hand. "It'll be all right, Helen. Mallory will come around. She's a good girl." She flashes me the tiniest look of regret. "She must be, or my son wouldn't love her the way he does. Just give it time."

I manage a nod, praying she's right. "I'm going to draw the drapes now, and I want you to close your eyes."

"But I'm not tired. I *told* you. Aiden will be home soon."

"Aiden won't be home for hours yet. You don't have to go upstairs. Just lie back and close your eyes, and let the valerian do its job."

She levels another one-eyed squint at me, as if I'm not entirely trustworthy. "Will you listen for his car, and wake me if you hear it? I don't want him to find me sleeping in the middle of the day like an old woman."

"Yes. I'll listen for his car. But it's not even noon. You have plenty of time."

"All right," she says sullenly. "But I don't think I can." Her eyes close. "Not sleepy."

I sit quietly, waiting for her breathing to deepen. I should go tidy the kitchen. Instead, I stand looking at her, studying the map of tiny blue veins tracing her eyelids, the lavender hollows of her orbits, the sharpness of her cheekbones and the sunken places beneath.

It won't be long, I think. Not as long as the doctors say. The dying keep their own calendars, their own to-do lists. Wrongs to right. Loose ends to tie up. Emotional books to balance. But once they've got all the boxes checked, they tend to make their exits rather quickly.

Estelle has made her list and has already begun checking off boxes. Just what those boxes are, she hasn't said, but I can guess. They're to do with Aiden, with his future and his happiness—and earning forgiveness for the things she got so terribly wrong. Because despite what she says, she *does* want forgiveness. We all do. But will she get it? Will I?

Time will tell, I suppose—for both of us.

FORTY-FOUR

MALLORY

Mallory held her breath as she tiptoed past Helen's closed door. It had been a full day with a morning staff meeting, back-to-back swim sessions, and a CPR class to round out the afternoon. Then she'd stayed late to talk to Deb about adding a lifeguard training program next year. They'd ended up at Romano's for pizza, then stuck around for the Red Sox game, nursing their drafts until the Sox had the game well in hand.

She hadn't been in an especially social mood, but it had given her an excuse not to go home. She wasn't ready to deal with this new reality yet, to have all the grisly details laid end to end for her, which was what Helen would almost certainly want to do. To explain. To justify. But there was no justification. Not for this. And what difference could any of it make now?

Poppy was dead and had been for years, a faceless stranger from her mother's past with whom she happened to share DNA. There were no memories of her, no snatches of softly crooned lullabies or faintly remembered perfume with which to connect her. Not even a photograph. Except the awareness of her was there now—a gaping blank in her history—and it would *always* be there, echoing emptily.

Tired to her marrow, she flipped on her bedroom lamp, kicked off her shoes, and let her duffel slide to the floor, ready to climb straight into bed. As she unzipped her jacket, she caught a glimpse of her reflection in the dresser mirror. Suddenly she was reliving a moment from Sloane's wedding day, when she had studied Helen's reflection beside her own, ticking off all the ways they were alike. Except none of them were real. It was only her imagination *needing* to see those things, wanting to see a connection where there was none.

Legally, Helen was nothing to her—and never had been. Not her mother. Not a foster parent. Not even a legal guardian. She was just the woman who had raised her, ostensibly at Poppy's request, but who knew if that part was true? What, she wondered, would have happened if Helen hadn't agreed to take her? Social services probably, a foster home, then adoption if she was one of the lucky ones. She'd be someone else now, with a different name, a different job, a different past. The idea was both intriguing and unsettling—the road not taken.

It wasn't possible, of course. You lived the life you were given. But what if it *were*? How much of her current history would she be willing to walk away from? Her career? Her mother—or at least the woman she'd always *thought* of as her mother? Aiden? The prospect rattled her more than she cared to admit and she hastily shoved the questions away. She had enough real-world questions to deal with at the moment. She didn't need to invent hypotheticals.

She had just dragged on her Red Sox jersey and was about to run a quick brush through her hair when she spotted the now familiar blue book at the center of her pillow—Helen's journal, presented like a gift. She stared at it as the moment yawned, at the yellowed pages and scuffed leather cover. *Here are all my secrets*, it seemed to say, but in a way that wouldn't require them to sit down face-to-face. Perhaps there was wisdom in that.

She held her breath as she lifted the book from the pillow. It was cool to the touch and heavier than she remembered. Perhaps because she knew more about its contents than she had the last time she'd held it. She fanned through the pages, watching Helen's familiar ink strokes blur past, then stopped when she spotted a note protruding from the pages. Here, too, was Helen's small but careful script.

> *Mallory,*
>
> *You know only the end of the story. The rest is here if you want it. They'll be difficult words to read, I know. But I hope you will read them and come to know Poppy as I did. There's so much more to our story than the way your mother died. I have marked the passages I suspect you'll want to read first, though I hope in time you'll read all of it—and perhaps forgive. I have omitted nothing.*

FORTY-FIVE

HELEN

September 3, 1987

Dearest,

There are so many things about our last days together that I've tried to suppress, unwilling to look too closely at the terrible minutiae of it. But tonight, as I sit here brooding with my pen, I feel the memories tugging me backward, like a tide going out.

How quickly life can change direction. A call answered. A path forsaken. A single moment of choice and everything suddenly becomes irrevocable. I think of that moment now, and how it came for me—while in the kitchen chopping carrots for soup.

Sister Clara appears with her shrewd eyes and perpetual look of knowing. She tells me I'm wanted on the phone—again—and for a moment I have the distinct feeling that she can see right through me, that she has glimpsed my secret and deems me unworthy.

I wipe my hands and go to the hall, where the phone sits on a small oak table. Sister Clara is close on my heels. I wait until she moves away, then pick up the receiver and mumble a tentative hello. There's the brief sound of breathing, then a click and the line goes dead. It's the second time this week. The fifth in a month. Always the same.

I replace the receiver and steal a glance at Sister Clara, who's pretending to tend the plants on the sill, though her head is tilted curiously in my direction. I turn away, preparing to return to my carrots, but before I can take a step the phone rings again. I answer, then hold my breath, waiting for the inevitable hang-up. But there's no click this time. Finally, a voice comes over the line, dry and a little thready, but familiar enough to make my heart slam against my ribs.

"I need you," it says. "I'm at the Colonial Inn on Central Street. Across from the bus station. Room 14."

"Yes," I say thickly. "Thank you for calling."

I'm strangely numb as I hang up the phone. Sister Clara looks up from her plants, pinning me with her gaze. She doesn't ask. No one asks about private things here, mostly because none of us has a private life worthy of curiosity. We're here to renounce the outside world, to renounce ourselves. But I've never been like them. I've always known it. And so have they, I think. This was only ever a place to hide—from the world and from myself.

It's almost a year since you sent me back to Immaculate Heart. A year of prayer and study and quiet duty. I haven't minded the work or even the solitude, but I'm wearied to death of self-reflection. I've prayed so long for a sign, one of those blinding moments of clarity one hears about, and now it has come. Only in a way I never imagined.

I return to the kitchen, then slip up the back stairs, where I swap my apron for a coat and fill a bag with my few personal possessions. I have a little money stashed beneath my mattress. I stuff it into the pocket of my skirt, slide the bag up onto my shoulder, and tiptoe downstairs.

I flip off the burner under my unfinished soup, then duck out the kitchen door and into an ice-cold drizzle, wondering how long it will be before I'm missed and what they'll do about supper. I find the motel, a run-down establishment with a half-burned-out sign and a sloppy parking lot full of puddles and potholes. Room 14 is on the first floor, next to the ice machine and a pay phone with a handwritten out-of-order sign taped over the dial.

I pay the cabbie and make a dash through the rain. By the time I reach the door, my clothes are soaking and I'm chilled to the bone. I raise my hand to knock and realize I'm shaking. Finally, after a second knock, the door pulls back, revealing a small slice of face—one eye and half a nose. They should be familiar, but they're not somehow, and I suddenly wonder if coming was a mistake.

"It's me," I say over the heavy thrum of rain.

The door pulls back and all at once you're standing there, barefoot and wearing a pair of pajamas that clearly don't belong to you. "You came."

You back away slowly, but I linger in the doorway, taking in your surroundings: the stained carpet and the bed with its tangle of dingy sheets, the cheap chest of drawers and scarred bedside table, the sagging chair pushed into one corner.

Eventually, I step inside and you close the door behind me, submerging us in a shabby and airless gloom. You hover in the shadows, your arms at your sides, unnaturally still. Behind the nondescript drapes, rain spatters the large plate-glass window and I hold my breath as the seconds tick past.

"Why are you here?" I ask when I can no longer bear the silence.

"I had to see you."

"Are you alone? Where's—"

"Dead," you answer before I can say his name. "Almost a year now."

Under different circumstances, I might be pleased that you can still finish my sentences, but I'm not pleased. I'm too startled by the news that your husband is dead, too busy processing what it might mean. For you. For us.

"I'm sorry," I manage, but the words feel wooden in my mouth.

"Thank you. And thank you for coming. I wasn't sure you would."

"It was you," I say softly. "Calling and hanging up."

You duck your head awkwardly. "I was trying to get up my nerve. The last time we saw each other . . ."

"You sent me away."

"I had to."

Tears scorch my throat. I choke them back. "But now you're free."

You step out of the shadows to turn on a lamp. "No," you say softly. "I'm not."

My chest goes tight as I glimpse your face for the first time, gaunt and hollow-eyed in the lamp's too-bright glare.

"I'm sick, Helen."

I nod, because some part of me already knew this. Some terrible part. "What . . . is it?"

"A tumor. Tumors, actually. On my liver."

"Is it . . ."

"Yes."

The word lands like a physical blow and for a moment I can't breathe. It can't be true. And yet it is. I can see it plainly now. The parchment-like cast of your skin, the jut of your collarbone, the knobby wrists peeking from the sleeves of your too-large pajamas.

I used to dream of what it would be like to see you again. But it hurts to look at you now, already so frail, a mere husk of the girl I used to know. Still, I can't let it be real. I swallow my panic, my mind racing. "What can we do? There must be something. An operation or chemo."

You meet my eyes, your manner so calm it chills me to my marrow. "It's everywhere, Helen. My lungs. My bones."

I sag onto the nearest thing I can find, too stricken to remain on my feet. I know what it means, how it ends, the grinding pain and slow wasting, and I'm filled with a rage so bitter it feels like poison. What kind of god could punish such a beautiful spirit?

"I need your help," you say quietly. "There's no one else."

I stare at you, horrified. I know what you're asking—to be with you at the end, to watch as you slip away, every day, further and further—and the idea fills me with terror. Suddenly I want to flee, to return to my pile of peeled carrots and pretend none of this ever happened. But I can't. Because this is part of loving. Perhaps the truest part. To hold the hand of one's beloved, not only in their best moments but also in their worst, to take their pain, as far as it's possible, as your own.

I have no idea how long I sit there, too shaken even to weep, but at some point I feel your arms go around me. You rock me like a child, crooning words of comfort against my ear, as if I'm the one dying. But I'm numb, unable to grasp the reality of it.

We've been apart for years now, but I've never truly felt separate from you. Because I knew you were somewhere in the world, walking the earth and breathing in and out, perhaps thinking of me too. It's inconceivable that a day might come when that's no longer true. But it will come and I don't know how I'll ever bear it. I will, though, somehow. I abandoned you once. I won't do it again. This time I must be brave.

"All right," I say quietly. "I'll stay."

Your eyes shine as they hold mine, with gratitude and relief, but the shine quickly gutters and you look away. "There's more I need to tell you, Helen. Things you need to know."

It comes out in disjointed, tearful bursts. William shot down while attempting to rescue several of his brothers-in-arms. His personal effects returned in a plain manila envelope, his dog tags, a Saint Christopher's medal, photographs he took with him when he shipped out.

I don't want to see them but you make me look anyway. There's one of him in uniform, the handsome hero, and so very young. And another of the two of you, arm-in-arm on the day of your wedding. You look so lovely clutching your small posy of flowers, blooming and smiling, as any bride should be, but it hurts me to see it, to know that someone else once occupied the place I thought of as mine.

"I wasn't in love with him," you say softly, as if reading my thoughts. "Not the way it was with us. But I did care for him. He was a good man, kind and . . . patient."

I sit stonily. I don't want to hear about what a wonderful man William Ward was, but I see that you've begun to cry again and I soften. I pull a tissue from the box on the nightstand and press it into your hand. We sit quietly for a time, with only the muffled patter of rain to fill the silence.

"When you came to see me that time," you say finally. "I know I hurt you. I should have explained, told you why . . ."

"None of that matters now."

"But it does." You pull away a little, locking eyes with me. "The why is everything. Because once you know why, you'll understand, and you might forgive me. And I need you to forgive me, Helen."

I stare at you, confused. "Forgive . . . you?"

"I'll never forget the look on your face when I told you I'd married William, like I'd just slapped you. And part of me was glad that I'd hurt you. I shouldn't have been but I was. But I need to explain now—about Billy."

My eyes skitter from yours. The memory of that day still stings, but I mustn't be petty. Not now. "I'm glad you found someone who was good to you. We don't need—"

"Please." You place a hand on my arm, your expression so intense it unsettles me. "I need to explain. And I need you to listen."

I nod, filled with fresh dread. For several minutes you say nothing, just stand there spinning the plain gold band on your ring finger. I haven't noticed it until now and the sight of it fills me with a savage rush of jealousy. I look away.

"He knew about you," you say abruptly. "About . . . us. I told him in the beginning that I was still in love with you, that I'd always be in love with you. I didn't want to lead him on."

"But you married him," I say, unable to keep the sting of accusation from my tone.

"We met at a concert," you say, as if I haven't spoken. "Then went for a drink after. He was just off a bad breakup and sort of a mess. But he was funny and we liked a lot of the same things. We started spending time together—as friends. I'd let him kiss me a few times, but one night, things went further than I meant them to. We were both so lonely. It just . . . happened. That's why I married him—because I had to."

I'm silent for a beat, trying to piece it together. And then it comes at me like a fist in the dark. "You were pregnant."

You nod, but your eyes are wide and glazed, lost somewhere in the past. "He didn't blink when I told him. He just asked when I was free to go for blood tests. Three days later we were married. Three weeks after that, he got his letter. And then he was gone. It was the week you came to see me." She broke off, closing her eyes. "I never saw him again. He never knew he had a daughter."

"A daughter . . ." I echo, letting the word sink in.

"Mallory—after William's late mother."

The obvious question doesn't occur to me immediately, and then it does. "Did she . . ." I break off, swallowing dryly. "What happened to her?"

You push to your feet and take my hand, leading me to a closed door on the opposite side of the room. A slit of sallow light shows beneath the door. You hold a finger to your lips and open it a crack, peering in, then step into what I see is a small, windowless bathroom. A night-light glows softly beside the sink, casting shadows over rippled wallpaper and a scarred linoleum floor. There's an unmistakable scent of bleach and pine-scented cleaner in the air.

You nod toward the tub with its droopy plastic shower curtain, your face unreadable. Surely not, I think. Not the tub. But when I step forward and peer around the curtain, there she is, the most beautiful—the most perfect—thing I've ever seen.

Mallory.

She stares up at me from her makeshift crib with wide, curious eyes, all rosy mouth and wispy copper curls, already the spitting image of you, and I'm filled with wonder and a fierce sense of joy. It feels like a miracle. Your daughter, alive and in the world.

"She's beautiful," I breathe. And quite suddenly I'm in love. Deeply. Hopelessly. Irrevocably.

"Would you like to hold her?"

"No," I answer instantly. I know nothing about babies, save where they come from and how to prevent them. But there's an unfamiliar weight in my chest, a kernel of longing I've never felt before. "How old?" I manage, my throat tight with this strange new emotion.

"Eight months next week."

I try to do the math in my head but can't seem to add it up. "She was born after William died?"

"Yes. I was three months along when he shipped out. Five when I got word that he wouldn't be coming home." You pause, swaying, and grab hold of the doorknob. "He was hoping for a girl. He would have loved her to pieces."

I'm alarmed at your sudden unsteadiness, and by the sheen of perspiration that's begun to gather along your brow. "I think we should sit back down, Poppy." I glance at the tub, where Mallory is now sucking contentedly on her middle two fingers. "Does she . . . need anything?"

"No. She's had her supper and I changed her right before you came."

You allow me to lead you back to the bed and settle you against the pillows. "Is there anything I can get you? Medication or water or anything? Are you in pain?"

"Not too much just now. I'm not taking anything."

"Nothing?"

"The doctor gave me some pills but they make me groggy. I'd rather save them for when things get bad."

I swallow and look away, trying not to imagine what your idea of bad might look like. "How long have you known?"

"That I'm dying?" You meet my eyes, so frank, so unflinching. "It's okay. You can say it. I've made my peace. Or nearly have. Ask me what you want to know."

But there are no words for what I want to know, no way to express the rage I feel. The unfairness and the cruelty are simply beyond words. Instead, I ease down beside you and take your hand, startlingly thin now, and blurt the only thing I can think to say. "I love you, Poppy. That's never stopped."

"Sweet Mouse," you whisper, lifting my hand to your lips. "I love you too. These last few months have been so hard."

"How long have you known? About the cancer, I mean?"

"I found out a few weeks after Billy was killed. But I think I knew something was wrong before that. I'd been having symptoms for a while. Some days I was so sick I couldn't get out of bed, and I was losing weight. My doctor kept telling me it was just morning sickness, but then the pain started. Eventually, they found the mass. They gave me a year—a little longer if I opted for surgery and chemo—but they said I'd lose the baby. If I skipped

treatment there was a chance I could carry to term. There was never a question."

"And she's . . . healthy?"

You smile dreamily. "She is. They had to induce a little early, so she was on the tiny side, but the doctor said she was perfectly healthy. She's a fighter."

"Like her mother," I say softly. "But how have you managed to care for her all by yourself?"

"I didn't. At least not for long. A bunch of the other army wives took turns cooking and cleaning and shopping. They even took shifts so I could sleep. They were wonderful. And so good with Mallory. I don't know what I would have done without them."

"Is there anything . . . Now that you're not pregnant, I mean. Could the chemo still help?"

"No. Not now. And I don't want that kind of ending. All I needed was a few months, to do what I needed to do."

"What did you need to do?"

"Find you."

Your words sear me, reminding me that, once again, I've come too late. And all at once, I'm crying again. We seem to be taking turns. You hand me a tissue and I mop my face, struggling to stem the storm of tears. "I'm here now," I whisper hoarsely. "And I'm staying."

You manage a watery smile, but there's a glimmer of uncertainty in your eyes as they meet mine. "There's something else I need you to do for me, Helen."

I mop my face with my sleeve and smile bravely. "I'll do anything."

"I need you to take her."

I blink at you, baffled. "Take her where?"

"I need you to be her mother, to raise her."

The breath leaves my body in one long exhale. Suddenly, I can't breathe, can't speak. Nothing in my life has prepared me for this. For any of this. But this part least of all. I shake my head firmly, emphatically. "I can't."

I bolt off the bed but you catch my hand. "Helen. Please. I need you to do this. Not because there's no one else, but because I want you to have her—and for her to have you."

"I don't know the first thing about taking care of a baby."

You smile at me with infinite patience. "Neither did I at first, but they teach you."

I've forgotten how easily you were always able to get around me with that smile, though you clearly haven't. Still, it's shocking to realize you've never considered the possibility that I might refuse. "No," I repeat, more firmly this time. "There has to be someone else—someone better."

"Who better to care for my daughter than the person who's always known me best?"

"I can't do what you're asking, Poppy. I'm a single woman with no viable income, which makes my chances of being approved for any sort of adoption nil."

"It won't be like that. I've had time to think it through and it's all taken care of. I've saved a little money and there's an envelope in my suitcase with all the papers you'll need."

The readiness of your answer both unnerves and alarms me. "What kind of papers?"

"The kind that'll help you make a new start—as Mrs. William Ward."

"I don't understand." But part of me does and is horrified. "You can't possibly think . . . What you're *suggesting is against the law. It's fraud or . . . well, it's something."*

"To decide who raises my daughter? I'm her mother, Helen. I know what's best for her. And that's you. So I've fixed it. The papers cost me almost four hundred dollars, but everything needed to match. There's a marriage license, a driver's license for you, and a birth certificate for Mallory. You'd never guess they aren't genuine."

I gape at you. "A forged birth certificate? How on earth . . ."

You grin deviously, and for a moment, I glimpse the girl I fell in love with, the one with the brash smile and laughing eyes—the one who would dare anything. "You'd be surprised at the connections some army wives have. I asked one day as a sort of joke, and later that day, I got a phone call from a guy who knew a guy."

It's ludicrous, like a plot from an old black-and-white melodrama, and yet I see that you're quite serious, as if slipping into someone else's skin—someone else's life— is accomplished every day. I shake my head, slowly but firmly. "I can't."

"Yes, you can, my love. For me, you can." You pull me back down beside you. "Don't you see? She'll be ours. Our girl. Because you'll love her the way I would have, the way no stranger ever could. And it would mean you'd always have a part of me with you. We'd be a sort of family. Maybe not like other families, but then we've never been like other people."

The thought leaves me a little off balance. We would share a name. Share a child. Like any married couple. Suddenly I feel something shift in my chest, a kind of thaw beginning, and it frightens me. "What about William? Wouldn't he want his family to raise his daughter?"

You're silent a moment, clearly searching for the right answer. "Billy was a good man," you say finally. "And he would have been a wonderful father. But he isn't here. And he didn't have any family. That's another reason it has to be you. Someone has to remember him when I'm gone. He deserves that and so does his daughter. Mallory is the most precious thing I have in the world. I need to know she's with someone who'll love her like I do. Billy would want that too."

You wind your fingers through mine then, so thin now, almost translucent, but achingly familiar as I look at them twined with mine. You're asking the impossible, entrusting me with a fragile young life. How can I possibly accept such a responsibility? How can I not?

I'm about to protest again, one last attempt to dissuade you from this disastrous scheme, when a shrill wail shatters the quiet. The sound is foreign and viscerally terrifying. My head jerks in the direction of the bathroom, then back at you. You're smiling.

"Go on," you say softly. "Our girl is calling."

FORTY-SIX

HELEN

September 4, 1987

The next day, I phone Sister Eugenia to tell her I won't be coming back. I say only that I feel led to serve in a different way. Not quite a lie. Still, there's a strange sense of emptiness as I hang up the phone, as if I've just called off my wedding, which in a way, I have. I will not become a bride of Christ. I will become a mother instead.

We spend our first week holed up like newlyweds in our dingy room, the do not disturb sign perpetually on the door. Fresh towels appear on the stoop every few days, the used ones put out to be taken away. Fresh sheets appear on Mondays. Other than that we're left alone.

It's that kind of place, where it's possible to remain anonymous if one chooses, and I suspect many do. There's a woman a few doors down who's been here since I arrived. I rarely see her and don't know her name. But I know she drinks because I've seen her carrying the empty bottles to the trash bin around back. I've also seen a parade of men coming and going after dark. Never the same faces, only the same type. Yesterday, I saw her coming back from the office with a scabbed lip and a deep blue bruise under one eye. We all have our stories, our particular sorrows, though not all of us wish them to be known.

It's a peculiar sort of housekeeping we've set up, making the best of our cramped quarters and makeshift nursery, but it does well enough for the three of us. I've also worked out how to satisfy our day-to-day needs with what's nearby. There's a laundromat on the next block and a Chinese place around the corner where I go for takeout a few times a week. Soup and rice are all you'll take most days. There's also a small market and deli across the street where I buy staples for the small pantry I've set up in one of the dresser drawers, as well as diapers and jarred food for the baby.

The baby.

I've managed to master the basics: diapering, feeding, burping, and bathing. But those day-to-day things were never what terrified me. It's the actual childrearing, the teaching and bonding that's supposed to be instinctive. What if they're not instinctive for me? I live in constant fear of harming her. Not of dropping her or scalding her, but of damaging her in some deep and irreparable way. Because I know firsthand how many ways there are to harm a child, and I know they don't always involve physical scars.

She's a good baby: a good sleeper and a hearty eater. But she's a bit solemn. Sometimes I catch her looking at me with those wide copper eyes of hers—eyes so disturbingly like yours, dearest—and I can't help wondering if she senses my uneasiness, and knows you've made a terrible mistake. You, however, appear to have no such misgivings. But then you've always given me more credit than I deserved.

Part of my education is to learn about William— Billy, as you call him. To memorize all the details of his life and yours, like a catechism, so I can regurgitate them one day when Mallory is old enough. I do my best to conceal my jealousy. I'm not proud of resenting a dead man—but I do. Perhaps it's the contrast between myself and a decorated war hero that I find so uncomfortable. William Ward died trying to save his brothers-in-arms. I betrayed you to save myself.

I've tried more than once to talk to you about that day in the principal's office, but you cut me off every time, reminding me that our time together is too precious to waste on tears. Instead, we must savor the hours and minutes we have left. But how can I?

It's excruciating to watch you suffer, to know each day will be worse than the last, that every day I'll have less of you. And there's nothing I can do—nothing anyone can do. You still refuse to take anything. You do your best to be stoic, but I see you trying to cover the pain.

This morning, I suggested—for the third time—that we go to the hospital, where they'd be able to make you more comfortable, but you refused. You don't want to spend your final days attached to bags and tubes, surrounded by strangers and hospital smells. You're determined to ride it out in our tiny room—with me close by to hold your hand. And so begins my vigil.

I already know what lies ahead. Night after night, lying beside you in the dark, listening to you breathe, ter- rified that you'll suddenly stop, that you'll slip away while I sleep. If only it could be that easy, dearest.

If only.

◆ ◆ ◆

Our days are spent quietly, cocooned in the musty gloom of our motel room. We watch game shows and old movies, then I read aloud until you doze off. You thought to bring books. The old classics we used to read when we were first together and used to take turns reading to one another, sprawled out on a blanket under the big oak tree in your mother's backyard. Austen, Gaskell, the Brontës.

Of course, it's Wuthering Heights you ask for first. The parallels are inescapable. A dying heroine, a love realized too late, the heart-wrenching prospect of a world without you in it. How keenly I feel Heathcliff's tortured plea as I read it, begging to be haunted rather than left alone.

Time is the enemy now, the too-rapid slipping of days through my fingers. The jaundice has become more pronounced, your skin a sickly yellow that mimics a suntan but isn't. And there's the pain, endlessly gnawing. Still, you insist on reading to Mallory every day, silly stories about rabbits and bears and hungry caterpillars. The sight of you with her tears my heart, and I find myself wondering how much longer you can hold on. And then one afternoon I have my answer.

I've just put Mallory down for a nap and am settled beside you on the bed, the copy of Wuthering Heights open on my lap. I pick up the book, but you stop me, looking at me in a way that makes my throat go dry.

"It's time for us to talk again."

I tell myself to be strong. It won't do either of us any good to fall apart now. "All right."

"Sweet Mouse." Your chin quivers as you attempt a smile. "You've been so good to me—to us. I know what it cost you to come here—what you gave up—and there are no words to say how grateful I am to you for that."

"I gave up nothing," I say softly, fighting the catch in my throat. "Nothing."

"Please, dearest. Let me get through it." You wince and press your lips together, silent a moment before continuing. "I'm tired. And so are you."

Dread pools in my belly. There's something new in your voice, a weariness I haven't heard until now. It's all I can do not to rush in to fill the silence, to stop whatever's coming.

"I need you to do something for me, Helen. I need you to get the pills out of the nightstand."

"Is the pain worse today?"

"It's worse every day."

I nod and go to the nightstand, relieved that you're finally willing to take something for the pain. But when I attempt to open the bottle, you reach for my arm, stopping me.

"I wasn't asking for one. I want to talk to you about them. There are nineteen pills left. I know because I've been saving them—for when things got bad."

"Saving them?" I stare at you, too incredulous to hide my annoyance. You've said it before but it feels different now. "For god's sake, Poppy, it's been bad for days, for weeks!"

"I'm asking you to help me die, Helen."

You say it so quietly that for a moment I think I've misheard. "You're . . . what?"

"Please, dearest. I need your help. It's a lot of pills. I don't think I can get them down on my own."

I need to stand up, to move away from you, but I can't seem to make my legs work. I'm frozen in place, paralyzed by the images suddenly filling my head. "Are you out of your mind?"

"For thinking that how and when I leave this world is my choice?"

"But you can't! Not like that!" I finally manage to stand and step away from the bed, but it doesn't help. Your request fills every corner of the room. "It's wrong, Poppy. It's a sin."

"I don't believe that, dearest. I never have."

"But I'm the one you're asking to do it, and I do believe it."

You study me, weighing my level of resolve. "Do you really? Or is it just what you've been taught to believe? Does it make sense to you—a god who demands we suffer?"

The question brings me up short. Do I believe it? I have no idea. It's simply a given in the Catholic Church, like transubstantiation or purgation. You don't question it. It's simply a fact.

"It's also a crime," I add quietly.

"It is. But it shouldn't be."

Tears blur my vision. I struggle briefly to check them, then give up and let them spill down my cheeks. Of all the ways I imagined our story might end, never once have I imagined this. "We don't get to decide, Poppy."

"Why?" Your eyes flash with surprising heat. "When we know what happens next. And we do. We both know. So why not . . . expedite things? I've done what I needed to do. I've seen Mallory safely to you and we've said our goodbyes—or will. There's nothing left but the dying. Why shouldn't I do it on my terms? And it isn't only about me. You have a daughter to think of now. You can't just sit around waiting for me to go. You're exhausted. And it isn't good for Mallory to be here. It's time for the two

of you to start your new life and you can't do that until I'm gone."

I stare at the floor, unable to look at you. Everything you're saying makes sense, and yet the idea horrifies me. "Please, please, Poppy. Don't ask me to do this."

"Who else can I ask? There is no one else."

It occurs to me that we've had a similar conversation, when you asked me to take Mallory. I said no then too, in the beginning, before you wore me down. But this is different. This is impossible. And yet I see now that this has been the plan from the beginning.

"You always meant to do this," I say, my tone faintly accusing. "When you called me and asked me to come. You already knew you were going to ask me to do this."

"Yes."

"And you haven't said a word until now."

Your eyes slide from mine. "I was afraid you'd say no."

"You were right," I tell her flatly. "My answer is no."

"Helen . . ."

I'm shaking now, furious that I've allowed myself to be maneuvered so skillfully. "I left a convent to come here. An actual convent! And now you want me—" I stop myself, as a question suddenly fills my head. "Would you have asked William to do it?"

"Billy?" You shake your head. "No, you're the only one I could ever ask to do this—the only one who loves me enough."

Anger suddenly gives way to anguish as I look at you, so fragile now, propped against your pillows. "Poppy. Please. You're not being fair. I've done everything you asked, walked away from my life, agreed to take Mallory, but I can't do this. My god, Poppy, I can't . . . kill you."

"You won't be killing me, dearest. You'll be freeing me. And you can do that. You can free me."

◆ ◆ ◆

You ask every day, and every day I refuse. But the cloak of death continues to tighten around the three of us, the inevitability of it, lurking in the dim, tiny room. I tell myself that if I just keep saying no, I can run out the clock, that nature will do for you what I cannot. But the body is a stubborn thing, even in its last throes, and yours stubbornly refuses to surrender.

Every day brings fresh agony, watching the slow but steady wasting of your body, the unendurable pain etched into the planes and hollows of your face, knowing all the while that I have the means to ease your suffering—to end it. And then one day you're asleep, a rare respite for us both. Mallory is on a blanket at my feet, drowsing with a bottle. I'm in a chair beside the bed, watching the steady rise and fall of your chest, and I realize it's the first time in weeks that you've looked truly at peace. The tension is gone from your face and your breathing is deep and slow. You look almost young. Almost . . . free. Then I remind myself that you'll wake up at some point and the pain will start again, each breath bringing fresh, grinding agony. And tomorrow will be the same—only worse.

I'm startled when I suddenly realize your eyes are open and on me, searching, pleading.

"All right," I say softly.

I ask for a few days, to resign myself to the act itself, and to prepare for what will happen after. I begin gathering the things I'll take when I leave for the last time—diapers, formula, the remaining jars of strained peas and carrots, the envelope containing the money and doctored certificates, your copy of Wuthering Heights—and stow them in a large canvas duffel.

You make sure I have the small wooden box containing William's personal effects and the slender black case that holds the Purple Heart the army bestowed on him after his death.

When the agreed-upon day comes, I wake with a stone in my stomach—and a hole in my heart where I'll soon carry your memory. I walk to the market on the corner to buy what I need. Applesauce has been decided upon, with honey stirred in to help cover the bitterness.

We wait until Mallory is asleep, and then one by one I begin to crush the tablets and stir them into the applesauce. I force myself to keep my hand steady, to not cry while I work, to not fling the bowl across the room and splatter its tainted contents all over the walls. It's only the memory of your words that keep me on task—You can do that, dearest. You can free me.

And so I will.

I put Mallory down for a nap, help you into a clean nightgown and brush your hair in long, soothing strokes, the way I used to when we were newly in love. We say our goodbyes then, with looks mostly. We've already said every-thing that needs saying, and if I speak now, I'm afraid of what might come out. The imploring, the backpedaling— the plea that this cup might be allowed to pass from me. But there's no going back now. The thing must be done.

I do as you ask and remove the opal necklace you've worn as long as I've known you, a gift from your mother.

"For Mallory," you say thickly. "When she's older."

I slip it into my pocket, then reach for your hand. The hammered silver band slips easily from your thumb, a gift from me on your seventeenth birthday. My vision smears as I look at the inscription—TL/OH—short for Two Lives, One Heart. I saved up for months to buy the ring, but when it came time to have it engraved I didn't have the money to pay for all the words and had to settle for the letters instead.

William's ring I leave on your hand. Right or wrong, I begrudge every moment William Ward spent with you, every touch, every word. But without him, there would be no Mallory. For her sake then, I'll take all the rest, but not that. Not the ring that made you his. I prefer to remember you as mine alone.

I carry the mug of applesauce to the bed and sit down beside you, asking with my eyes if it's still what you want. You place your hand on mine and I have my answer. I nod, the bargain sealed. There will be no pleading on my part—and no change of heart on yours. It will be an act of love, I tell myself. An act of mercy.

There's only the light from the bathroom bleeding into the room now—the only way I can carry it out, with both our faces in shadow. It takes nearly an hour to spoon the applesauce into you. You struggle to swallow and retch with almost every mouthful, but eventually, the job is done and there's nothing to do but wait.

You're already groggy by the time I set aside the empty mug, your breathing growing slower, more peaceful. Or perhaps it's only what I want to believe. Perhaps it has nothing to do with peace. And suddenly the panic is there, the certainty that this is a mistake, a sin. There's still time to get to the market, to purchase a bottle of peroxide and pour it down your throat, to make you bring it all up. Yes. I'll go. I can get there and be back in ten minutes. I'll stop it. I'll save you. And then, as if sensing my panic, you reach for my hand. This is right, your touch says. This is what we decided.

I want you to go peacefully, without fear or regret. And yet every cell in my body cries out. Stay with me! Don't leave me! But this quiet death is what I promised, a final act of devotion for the woman I've loved since I knew what the word meant.

Yes. God help me. This is what we decided.

Without thinking, I pull my rosary from my pocket and begin counting off the beads, my lips moving silently. What I'm praying for, I cannot say. For forgiveness, I suppose. For the care of your sweet soul. And for the baby girl who will soon find herself at the mercy of a woman who has no idea how to raise her.

Eventually, my prayers run dry and I let the rosary slip from my fingers. Hollowed out, I simply sit with you in the darkness, every nerve in my body attuned and raw as I listen to your breathing, pleading for it to be over, terrified that it soon will be. And then suddenly, a missed breath, followed by . . . nothing.

The emptiness is so abrupt, so complete, that for a moment I'm unable to breathe myself. Tears flood up into my throat, the pressure in my chest like a dam ready to break. But there isn't time for tears now. I have plans to carry out, an exit to make.

I retrieve my rosary and push to my feet, then lean over to press a final kiss to your lips. You look so peaceful, almost otherworldly with your copper hair fanned out around you on the pillow, your face no longer lined with pain. I should be relieved for you, for both of us. Your suffering is over at last. But I find I'm strangely numb as I stand beside the bed, emptied after the three-week ordeal.

Eventually, my brain reengages and I begin running through next steps. We've been over it all at least a dozen times. Not just the pills and the applesauce, but what comes after. The part where I take your name and your child, and disappear into the night. Now, all that remains is to see it through.

I've spent the better part of the last two days stripping the closet, the bureau drawers, the bathroom vanity, even under the bed, removing every hint of my presence. When I finally slip from the room, there will be no sign of what actually happened here, the pill vials swept from the nightstand, the mug used for the applesauce carefully washed, dried, and returned to its paper coaster beside the grungy hotplate.

Nearly finished now.

I lift the phone from its cradle and let it drop to the floor as if it tumbled from your hand before you could hang it up. I'm staging a crime scene, I realize with something bordering on horror, tampering with evidence. But is what I've done truly a crime? I haven't time to examine the question just now, though I suspect I will later—likely for years to come.

I check the duffel once more, then shrug into my coat, checking the pockets for your car keys and the dime I'll need in a few minutes. Not even that has been left to chance.

In the bathroom, I pluck Mallory from her make-shift crib. She whimpers briefly, then settles against my chest, asleep again. I slide the duffel up onto my shoulder and head for the door, denying myself a backward glance. You're not here anymore, I remind myself. You're gone. Not only from the room but from the world.

The reality hits like a fist as I pull back the door and step out into the cold night air. Of all the agonies I've endured these past weeks, leaving you this way, alone in the dark in a cheap motel, is the hardest of all. But this was the plan. There's no going back now.

Be with me always, I plead, silently echoing Heathcliff's anguish as I close the door behind me. Take any form—drive me mad!—only do not leave me in this abyss, where I cannot find you!

I drive to the pay phone on the corner and leave the engine running while I call for an ambulance. I give a passable performance, gulping through the tears I finally allow myself to shed. I tell them I'm sick. I tell them I'm dying, that I'm afraid of dying alone. Then I lay the phone down and walk back to the car. My hands begin to shake as I take hold of the wheel and the reality of what I've just done hits me squarely. It's over.

And it's just beginning.

FORTY-SEVEN

MALLORY

August 7, 1999

By three o'clock, Mallory's day had slipped into slow motion, lack of sleep beginning to take its toll as she hauled out the mannequins for her afternoon CPR class. She'd read late into the night, turning pages until her eyes were gritty and her head swam with disturbing images.

She wasn't sure what she was expecting when she opened the journal, but even knowing the outcome hadn't prepared her for what had unfolded in that dingy motel room. There was still so much to digest that she hardly knew where to begin. Helen's love for Poppy had been the first surprise. Not that she'd loved a woman, but that she'd been so *completely* in love—enough to do the seemingly unthinkable.

Poppy had presented Helen with an impossible choice—one that went against everything her faith had taught her—but somehow she'd found the strength to carry it out. There was almost something admirable about that part. But the actual doing of it, the steeliness required to see it through to the last spoonful, still left her faintly queasy. Those images were indelible now, not only part of Helen's story but part of her own as well, and sharing them had been an act of faith on Helen's part—disturbing and terrible, but brave too.

I have omitted nothing, her note had promised, and she'd kept that promise. But it was the way she'd recorded it all, the tender entries addressed to *Dearest*—as if penning letters to a ghost—that resonated with Mallory this afternoon.

But what of the other ghost in Helen's story? What of William? Had her father truly loved Poppy, or had he married her only because she was pregnant? That part hadn't been made clear. Perhaps Helen didn't know, though she suspected the omission had been intentional. Helen made no secret of the fact that she'd never made peace with Poppy's marriage. Nor had she considered marriage for herself, choosing to remain alone instead, raising another woman's child. It was a tragic tale, but beautiful too, in a way. It also explained why Helen had chosen the work she did. Though perhaps she hadn't chosen the work; perhaps the work had chosen her.

It was an oddly comforting thought, the idea that they were all part of some well-oiled cosmic plan, with soulmates and soul-work simply waiting to be discovered, that in ways we couldn't see or imagine, it all made sense. She'd always scoffed at her mother's New Age views, dismissing them as nonsense. Now she wondered if there might be some truth in it. Or maybe she was just looking for a way to forgive Helen.

Eventually, they'd have to talk, but not yet. First, she needed to get through the rest of the journal entries, to know the rest of the story. It wouldn't be an easy conversation, but it was one they needed to have, to address this new reality and decide how to live with it going forward—if they *were* going to go forward. Until then she'd do her best to steer clear of Helen. Maybe she'd stay late and work on the new session schedules.

Debbie suddenly appeared in the doorway, looking distinctly anxious. She waved Mallory over, miming something that appeared to involve a phone call. Mallory instructed the class to partner up in groups of four, then stepped away.

"Hey. What's up?"

"You have a call. A woman. She says it's urgent."

Mallory's pulse notched up at the word *urgent*. "Did she give you her name?"

"No. She just said she needed you. She was talking so fast I could barely understand her, sort of panicky, so I just put her on hold and came looking for you. I'll hang out here and get them started. You can take the call in my office."

Mallory's heart dropped to her ankles. It could only be Helen. She mumbled her thanks as she brushed past Deb, then set off down the hall at a clip. Had Estelle taken a turn for the worse? Where was Aiden? By the time she reached the office and picked up the phone, she had imagined a half dozen scenarios, none of them good.

"Mother? What's wrong?"

"It isn't Helen. It's Estelle. I need you to come. I need help."

Mallory's emotions waffled between relief and confusion. "What kind of help? Where's my mother?"

"She's fine," Estelle managed, her voice a little breathless. "But she's gone to the market and Aiden's in Providence, meeting with the lawyers. I'm alone and I've fallen again. I can't seem to get myself up. Please come."

The temporary rush of relief was quickly replaced by visions of Estelle sprawled out on her bedroom floor. "Are you hurt?"

"I don't know. Just come. Please."

"I think I should call 911."

"No," Estelle shot back before softening her tone. "Please. I don't want all that fuss. I promised your mother I wouldn't move until she got back. She'll skin me alive if she finds out I've taken another spill. Just come help me back into bed. You're only ten minutes away."

"All right. I'm on my way. Don't try to move. Just stay put."

By the time Mallory pulled into the Cavanaugh driveway, she had added several new scenarios to her list, one of which included a tumble down the stairs and several broken bones. She'd forgotten to ask where in the house Estelle had fallen, but she'd mentioned getting her back to bed. Presumably, she was upstairs in her room.

The front door was unlocked. She let herself in, calling out from the foyer. "Estelle? Where are you?"

"In here," Estelle called. "In the parlor."

Mallory stopped short as she entered the room. She'd been prepared for a helpless and possibly bloody Estelle. Instead, the woman was stretched out on the sofa, wrapped in a robe of pink silk, with barely a hair out of place.

"There you are," Estelle said coolly, pausing to peer up at the mantel clock. "I thought you'd gotten lost."

Mallory stared at her, flabbergasted. "You said you fell."

"I needed to talk to you without Aiden or your mother here. I didn't think you'd come unless something was wrong."

"I was in the middle of a CPR class!"

Estelle stared back at her, unfazed. "Will you sit?"

"I'm going back to the center."

"Please. I think we should talk, don't you?"

Mallory stared at her, seething. No. She absolutely did *not* think they should talk, and was preparing to say so when she registered the startling changes in Estelle's appearance. For want of a better word, she was . . . *diminished*, all sharp edges and sunken places, with an alarming air of fragility. How was it possible that she'd deteriorated so dramatically in the space of a few weeks?

"All right," Mallory agreed, dropping into a nearby chair. She was still annoyed about being summoned under false pretenses, but part of her wanted to know what this was all about. "What are we talking about?"

"I wanted to thank you for forcing my hand with Aiden. I was wrong and you were right. Things are better between us now. Not fixed, but better."

"I'm glad. But you could have said that over the phone."

Estelle sighed, as if realizing this was going to be harder than antic-ipated. "I also wanted to thank you for sharing your mother with me. She's been such a . . ." She paused, frowning. "I was going to say *help*, but *friend* is a better word."

"I'm glad she's been helping you. For Aiden's sake."

"I'm going to be hiring a nurse," Estelle said rather abruptly. "Though I suspect it would take an army of nurses to fill your mother's shoes. I'll miss her nagging, but things are going to get . . . *messy* soon. More than she'll be able to handle on her own."

Mallory blinked at her, taken aback. "You're firing her?"

"Don't be silly. You can't *fire* a friend. And I doubt your mother would go if I turned the hose on her. But she should be spending time with you, not waiting on me every minute. Aiden's talking about mov-ing back into the house, and he's promised to help me hire someone. I've resisted until now but it's time. For her sake as much as mine. That's the other reason I wanted to talk to you."

"I'm not sure what this has to do with me."

Estelle leveled startlingly keen eyes at Mallory. "Your mother is starting to fray around the edges, Mallory. Part of that is to do with me, but not all. She says the two of you are going through a bit of a rough patch, that you've quarreled. She wouldn't say about what, but whatever it is, she's afraid she's going to lose you."

Mallory felt a sharp pang of annoyance. Her relationship with Helen was none of Estelle's business. "I'm not really comfortable talking about this with you. We're working through some things right now, complicated things, but they're between us."

She nodded. "I understand. But I need to say this and I hope you'll listen. Over the last few weeks, I've discovered that your mother and I have much more in common than I would have thought possible. We're both mothers who love our children so much that, without meaning to, we've ended up hurting them. And we'd both give anything to go back and do it all over again, to do it right this time, but it doesn't work that way. This is the one we get. All we can hope for now is enough time to atone for our mistakes. I don't know what's happened between the two of you or who's to blame—your mother seems to think she is—but whatever it is, don't let it fester. None of us knows how many summers we have left."

She paused, studying the large diamond on her left hand, spinning it slowly on her bone-thin finger. Finally, she looked up. "Forgive her. For whatever mistakes she's made. For whatever ways she's failed you. Remember how much she loves you and forgive her."

Mallory was surprised to find herself on the brink of tears. It was strange to hear this woman, of all people, advocating for Helen's forgiveness, but she had no doubt that the sentiment was genuine. "I'm sorry," she said quietly. "For snapping just now. I'm glad you and my mother are finally friends. I'm just sorry it had to happen like this."

"Don't be," Estelle said, waving a hand. "I felt awfully sorry for myself in the beginning. There was still so much to do yet, for Aiden. I was going to fix it—fix *him*. I thought there'd be time." She paused, shaking her head. "I didn't realize dying was a full-time job. But in a way, it's been good. I'm seeing things clearly for the first time in my life. Ironic, isn't it? Figuring it all out just as I'm getting ready to make my exit."

Mallory had no idea how to respond to such frankness. She ran her eyes around the room, settling on the end table crowded with sickroom items: a tissue box, a water glass, a paperback splayed open face down. She couldn't make out the title but there was no missing the bare-chested pirate on the cover.

Estelle grinned, noting the direction of her gaze. "Your mother's been reading to me. She actually blushes at the juicy parts." She paused, chuckling. "I'll bet you never imagined me as the romantic type."

Mallory nearly smiled. "Not really, no."

Estelle caught and held her gaze, her eyes the same disconcerting blue as her son's. "I was wrong about you," she said abruptly, as if she'd only just made up her mind. "About you and Aiden, I mean. You would have been good for him."

Once again, Mallory found herself at a loss for words. She sat mutely with her hands in her lap, keenly aware of the slow, heavy tick of the mantel clock.

"I've made a lot of mistakes," Estelle went on. "But my biggest was splitting the two of you up. I'm not saying this because I want your forgiveness. Although I do. Everyone wants forgiveness. Even people who *aren't* sorry. But I *am*. I'm very sorry. I'm not asking to be let off the hook. Some things are beyond forgiveness. But I know now how wrong I was. How . . . cruel. You'd just lost the baby, my *grandchild*, and all I felt—"

She broke off, swallowing a sob, then remained silent for a time, eyes closed, as if waiting for a physical pain to pass. At length, her eyes opened again, shiny with tears. "And all I felt was . . . relief," she finished. "Aiden was free again to pursue his music, to be what *I* wanted him to be. So I arranged to get him as far away as possible. I thought he'd forget. I didn't realize how much my son loved you—or how much *you* loved him. I was so proud of myself for arranging it all. Now, when I think about where he'd be, the life he'd be living if I hadn't interfered, I'm heartbroken and ashamed."

She was weeping now, quietly but unchecked. Mallory reached for a tissue and handed it to her. It couldn't be good for her to upset herself this way. And there was really no point. "None of it matters now, Estelle."

"But it does," Estelle said desperately. "He'd be happy now, with a wife and a family who love him. I took that from him, from both of you. And now, when I'm gone, he'll be alone."

"He won't," Mallory said evenly. "I'll always be his friend."

"But just his friend?"

"Yes."

"Is there no way? Nothing I can say?"

So this was why she'd been summoned. In true Estelle fashion, the woman thought she could simply broker a reconciliation. "I know you mean well, Estelle, but you're doing it again. You think you can just put us back together, because it's how *you* think things should be. But it isn't like it is in books, all sunsets and violins. We had our ending, just not a happy one."

"You were children then, in an impossible situation. But you're not children now. You could make it work. I know you could."

"It was ten years ago, Estelle. We're different people, in different places."

"He tells me you're going back to Boston in a few weeks."

"My leave is up at the end of August."

Estelle went quiet, staring once again at the diamond on her left hand. Finally, her head came up and she met Mallory's gaze squarely. "I need you to stay, Mallory. To be here after I'm gone."

Mallory forced herself not to blink. Illness may have blunted Estelle Cavanaugh's brittle edges but the imperiousness was still there, glinting behind that unsettling blue gaze. "I have a job, Estelle. I can't ask for more time off."

"I'm not asking you to take more time off. I'm asking you to stay. Permanently. Not just for his sake, but for yours—to make things right again."

Mallory clenched her fists in her lap and silently counted to ten. "Is that how you think it works? You just sweep up the pieces of someone's heart, glue them back together, and everything's forgotten?"

"Not forgotten, no. But mended. In time."

"Some things break forever, Estelle."

Estelle closed her eyes, sending a fresh trail of tears down her cheeks. "Hate me forever—I've certainly earned it—but please don't punish Aiden for *my* sins."

Mallory sat still, absorbing every word. They'd been long in coming, a decade in fact, and while she appreciated Estelle's willingness to take the blame, it didn't change the fact that it was Aiden who'd broken their engagement, Aiden who'd chosen London over her. He'd made his choice. Now it was her turn to choose, and she chose safety over the prospect of another heartbreak.

"I can't do what you're asking, Estelle. I'm sorry. I'll be his friend. We'll always be friends. But that's all it can be."

"He needs you, Mallory. Now more than ever."

"No, he doesn't. I'm just a distraction from things he'd rather not deal with right now, but sooner or later he's going to realize it isn't real and he won't need me anymore. It'll be better for everyone if we skip that part and go our separate ways now."

"Is there someone in your life? Someone back in Boston who means something to you?"

Estelle's eyes were narrowed on her now and it was all Mallory could do not to squirm. "This isn't about—"

"Are you still in love with my son?"

The question came so quickly that for a moment Mallory couldn't make her mouth move. She was still trying to form an answer when a small blur of movement caught her eye. She turned, expecting to find her mother. Instead, Aiden hovered in the doorway, clearly waiting for an answer to his mother's question.

"Darling," Estelle cooed, suddenly all smiles. "I wasn't expecting you back so soon. Mallory and I have been having the loveliest chat."

Aiden nodded curtly, shifting his attention to Mallory. "How are you?"

"I'm fine," Mallory said, pushing to her feet. "I was just leaving. My mother should be back from the market any minute."

Estelle frowned, the corners of her mouth turning down. "And we were having such a nice talk. Why not stay for dinner? Aiden promised to cook."

"No, I . . . No, thank you." She turned stiffly, avoiding Aiden's gaze as she stepped past him. "Have a good night."

To her dismay, Aiden followed her to the foyer. He touched her hand as she reached for the knob, the barest brush of his fingers. "It's just dinner, Mallory. Stay."

She could feel the pull of him, the current so powerful it was like an ache in her chest. All their yesterdays seemed to flicker in his eyes, a yearning for all they'd once been and had together. But those things could never be again. Not even if he believed it was what he wanted.

"I can't, Aiden."

"Because some things break forever?"

Mallory looked away. She hated that he'd heard her say it, but that didn't make it any less true. "I'm sorry."

FORTY-EIGHT

MALLORY

Mallory stood at the deck railing, her forgotten glass of chardonnay creating a circle of sweat on the weathered wood. She was still reeling from her meeting with Estelle. Still annoyed. Still confused. Still mortified at the awkward way it had ended.

She had no way of knowing how long Aiden had been hovering in the doorway. She only knew it had been long enough to overhear things she wished he hadn't. Had Estelle's timing been a coincidence or had she heard him come in and seized the chance to force a declaration? After all her claims of regret, was she *still* scheming? Mallory hated to think so, but after being lured to the house with a lie, it was hard to give the woman the benefit of the doubt.

And yet, part of her understood Estelle's need to put them back together. She was trying to clean up the mess she'd made a decade ago. Not for her sake, but for her son's. She couldn't buy herself more time, but in this small way, she hoped to turn back the clock for Aiden, to give him back the years he'd lost with the woman he loved—as if it were that simple.

But Aiden hadn't been Estelle's only topic of conversation. It had been strange to hear her take up for Helen. Once upon a time, she'd been Helen Ward's most vicious detractor, happily greasing Little

Harbor's rumor mill with lurid stories about her strange new neighbor. Now, suddenly, she'd become Helen's champion, urging forgiveness without knowing any of the particulars.

Forgiveness.

The word seemed to be woven through everything these days. Through mother and daughter, and mother and son, through lost loves and bitter neighbors. Repeated, again and again. Was that what this summer was about, then? A lesson in forgiveness? About reciprocity and grace and turning the other cheek? The topic certainly came up often enough during her counseling sessions. But was it all just lip service? Was it actually possible to let go of old wounds, to simply slough one's scars like molted skin?

Beside her on the railing, her cell phone went off. Jevet's number lit up the screen. "Hey, Jevet."

"Hey, stranger," Jevet said warmly. "It's been a while."

Mallory reached for her wineglass and took a quick swallow. It *had* been a while, three weeks in fact. "Sorry. There's a lot going on here."

"Well, there's a lot going on here too. I have news."

"What kind of news?"

"The committee finished their review into Tina's death and they're satisfied that all protocols were followed. You did everything you were supposed to."

Mallory's vision blurred as tears pooled in her eyes. "Oh, thank God."

"CPS has closed their investigation as well, which means you can finally let yourself off the hook. And there's more. I pitched your program to the board this morning and they're ready to green-light the funding."

"Wait." Mallory put down her glass and grabbed hold of the railing, not sure what to react to first. "I didn't think it was ready to present."

"I put together a PowerPoint with the numbers you gave me and filled in the blanks with my own estimates. They loved the idea of partnering with local businesses and keeping it close to home. They think the community will really get behind it."

"You know, I've actually been thinking about ways something similar might work here, at the center. Maybe a summer program. It could be on a rotational basis, three weeks each, and the kids could sign up for the fields they're interested in."

"Sounds like you've given this some real thought."

"Just brainstorming. But I think it could work."

"Do you want to know the rest of my news?"

"There's more?"

"They asked me who I had in mind to head it up. I'm going to give them your name."

"Mine?"

"Who else would I recommend? It's always been your baby. It's only right that you be the one to run with it. And the timing couldn't be better. It's the perfect solution."

Jevet's use of the word *solution* felt vaguely unsettling, as if she were a problem that needed solving. "You mean it's a perfect way to move me out of my current position," she said quietly. "Because even with the committee's findings, you don't think I'm cut out to be a counselor."

"Mallory . . ."

"No, I get it. The IVP program is my lifeboat."

"It's an opportunity, honey. You know you've struggled with parts of the job. This would allow you to still do what you love without the angst. It's also a chance to use your leadership skills. And they want to get it off the ground next quarter, which means you're going to need to get back here ASAP and start lining up partners."

Mallory took another gulp from her wineglass. Everything Jevet said was true. It *was* a solution—a win-win. So why wasn't she relieved?

"Mal?"

"Yeah. Yeah, I'm here."

"I thought you'd be doing cartwheels, but you're pretty quiet. Maybe this isn't what you want anymore?"

"No, I want it. It's just . . ."

"Say it, honey. This is me."

"It's Aiden."

"I thought it might be."

"No, not like that. He's just struggling right now, with a *lot* of things, and he's expecting me to be here through the end of the month. Plus there's my job at the center. Leaving now . . ."

"Honey, you don't need to justify it. If your heart's telling you to stay—"

"It's not. I just need a few more weeks."

"Are you sure? Because it sounds like you're starting to realize you want something else. Something that isn't here. Maybe you're just afraid to admit it. But if there's a chance . . . all I'm saying is make sure whatever you decide—whether it's here or there—is based on what you *want* and not what you're *afraid* of."

Mallory knew better than to leave that kind of remark unanswered for too long. "I'm not afraid, Jevet. And there's nothing to decide. My life is in Boston."

"No, honey. Your *apartment* is in Boston. Your *job* is in Boston. But I'm guessing your heart is still in Little Harbor. And if there's even a chance that that's true, you need to stay there and figure out how to make it work."

"You just told me you were recommending me for the IVP program. Now you're telling me not to come back?"

"I don't want you to take this position because it's safe, Mallory. I want you to take it because you *want* it. I don't know what's going on there, but it's obviously something. So maybe it's time to decide what you want the rest of your life to look like. Not just what's *next*, but what you *want*."

"What I want is to head up the IVP program," Mallory replied evenly. "I just need a couple weeks to tie things up here. I'll get to work on a list of potential partners as soon as I hang up. That way I can start making calls the minute I get back."

"Or . . . you could just do it there."

"Make the calls, you mean?"

"Set up the program there. *Do* it there. At the center. With *him*."

"With . . ." It took a moment but finally Mallory understood. "No."

"You just said you thought it would work."

"I meant the *idea* would work. I didn't mean with me running it."

"Lord, give me strength," Jevet muttered under her breath. "Okay, I'm about to shift out of boss mode now because you need to hear this from a friend. It sounds like everything you want, everything you've *ever* wanted, is right there in Little Harbor. All you have to do is get out of your own way. Is he still in love with you?"

"What?"

"Is Aiden still in love with you?"

Mallory blew out a long breath. "I think he *thinks* he is. But it isn't real, Jevet."

"Do you want it to be?"

"No."

"Are you sure about that?"

"It's just . . . nostalgia. It feels comfortable between us. Familiar, you know? But that's all it is."

"Mallory? Honey?"

Mallory groaned. She knew that tone of voice. "Why do I feel a lecture coming on?"

"Because there's a lecture coming on," Jevet shot back. "You may be too stubborn to see it, but life is giving you a great big do-over. Are you really going to throw it away? Because I sure wouldn't." She broke off with an abrupt little snort. "You know what? I'm just going to leave it there. Just remember—second chances don't grow on trees. Think long and hard before you walk away from this one. And now, I've got to run. I have a meeting in fifteen. Just think about what I said. I'd hate like hell to lose you, but I'd hate it even more if you came back for the wrong reasons."

Mallory couldn't let the call end this way, with the question unanswered. Jevet was right about one thing. Second chances didn't grow on trees. Maybe the IVP program was hers. She and Aiden had had their time, but that was over now. It was time to close that door and move forward.

"I have thought about it, Jevet. I'll wrap up here and see you next week."

◆ ◆ ◆

It was after eight when Mallory finally heard Helen come in. She closed the journal almost guiltily and slid it beneath her pillow. There was something unseemly about reading another person's private thoughts, even if it *was* by invitation.

She'd spent the last hour and a half filling in the blank places in Helen and Poppy's story, going back to the very beginning. It was all there, painstakingly recorded in Helen's tidy script. How they'd met in the library, how they'd become inseparable, until Helen's mother had separated them. So much grief and loss. And yet they'd found their way back to one another in the end.

It reminded her of a Bible verse she'd heard once, about love bearing all things. Prejudice. Betrayal. Separation. Even death. Helen had borne them all, yet her love for Poppy lived on, not just on the page but in her heart. The thought made her strangely happy, but a little sad too. She had stopped believing in that kind of love, the kind that bore all things. She was glad Helen hadn't.

Helen was coming up the stairs now, her feet heavy on the treads, reminding Mallory of Estelle's words. *Your mother is starting to fray around the edges.*

It was true, she realized with an uncomfortable shock when Helen appeared in her doorway. Her eyes were heavily shadowed, her shoulders rounded with fatigue—and perhaps grief. For the first time, it struck her that Helen wasn't just caring for a dying charge, she was losing a friend. And in that moment, Mallory saw the woman who had lived through those last terrible days with Poppy, the unendurable pain, the grinding, helpless inevitability.

"Have you eaten?" she asked Helen. "There's still some of that pasta from the other night in the fridge. I could heat it up."

Helen blinked at her, clearly startled by the unexpected olive branch. "I'm okay, but . . . thank you. Aiden made tomato soup and grilled cheese sandwiches. He's moved his things back into the house, so naturally Estelle made a big fuss about me staying for supper. She wanted me to invite you but I didn't think you'd come."

She was right, Mallory thought. She wouldn't have come, but not for the reasons Helen thought, though she was glad to hear that Aiden had moved back into the house. It would make things easier for everyone—except perhaps Aiden. But right now there were other things to discuss.

"Are you up to talking? If not, it can wait until morning."

Helen brightened. "Of course we can talk."

Mallory waited until Helen had eased down onto the foot of the bed, then retrieved the journal and placed it in her lap. "I'm sorry I've been avoiding you since the other night. It wasn't about punishing you. I knew you wanted to talk, to tell me more about Poppy, but I wasn't ready. It was just . . . so much. But I've been reading and I'm ready now. I want to know everything."

Helen cleared her throat, then looked down at the floor, shaking her head. "I promised myself I wouldn't push you to talk until you were ready, and now that you are, I don't know where to begin. I was wrong to keep the truth from you, to lie to you all these years, but I was so afraid of losing you . . . I don't think I could have borne it."

For whatever mistakes she's made . . . For whatever ways she's failed you . . . Remember how much she loves you and forgive her.

"The other night," Mallory said in a voice gone suddenly wobbly, "I said things. Terrible things I knew weren't true. I'm sorry."

Helen sighed. "I didn't pick my moment very well, waking you out of a sound sleep to tell you what I did, but when I realized you'd found the journal, I panicked. I had no idea how much you'd read, but I knew I had to tell you everything. I'm not making excuses—there aren't any—but I am sorry. So very sorry."

"It's okay," Mallory said quietly, because somehow it was. Or would be. They had taken the first step. The rest would come. "Tell me about her. About Poppy."

FORTY-NINE

HELEN

Mallory sits quietly, hugging the journal to her chest as I go back to the beginning. The telling is disjointed, a scattershot of memories spilling out in fits and starts. How I fell in love with Poppy the moment I saw her—before I even knew what love was. Her crooked smile, her penchant for dark, brooding heroes, her insatiable love of peaches. How kind she was, and how bravely she died.

Mallory is silent when my words run out, and I hold my breath, waiting. Eventually, she sets the journal aside. Her eyes are shiny with tears. She brushes them away and blinks up at me. "Would you do it again?" she asks quietly.

I look down at my hands. Hands that crushed a handful of pills and stirred them into applesauce. Hands that counted off prayers, bead by bead, as the woman I loved lay dying. Hands that picked up a child who wasn't mine and fled into the night. I force myself to meet Mallory's eyes, eyes so like Poppy's they still steal my breath. "I've asked myself that question every day for thirty years, and I don't think I knew the answer until now."

"So . . . would you?"

"God help me, I would." My throat goes tight and I look away. "Does that make me unforgivable?"

Mallory considers the question, then shakes her head. "No. Once I might have said yes, but not anymore. Somehow, knowing you'd do it again tells me you made the only decision you could have made. I'd be lying if I said I wasn't shocked by all of this. It's not the kind of thing that happens in real life. Except it did. It happened to you."

She pushes her hair out of her eyes, suddenly reluctant to meet my gaze. "I hated your work when I was little. It freaked me out. Plus, I never got why you preferred to spend time with a bunch of sick people rather than your own . . . than with *me*. But I understand now. It was because of Poppy. You couldn't walk away from her, and now you can't walk away from anyone else who's in that place, dying alone."

I struggle to swallow past the knot in my throat. To hear those words from her, that she understands, is more than I ever hoped for. "For your sake, and mine too, I suppose, I sometimes wished I had chosen another path, something *normal*, but when it's your work—and you *know* it's your work—you *do* it."

She touches my hand and gives me a shaky smile. "I see how much you care, how much of yourself you give every day. I didn't until now—until Estelle—and I'm sorry for that. Sorry I never . . . *valued* you and what you do. And then on top of everything else, you were saddled with a child you never wanted, a reminder of everything you'd lost. You raised me as your own and all you got for your trouble was resentment. I'm sorry for that too."

My eyes sting and her face blurs, a watery kaleidoscope. "You were a gift, Mallory. One I could never have dreamed of. You were what made it all bearable."

Mallory drops her head and her hair falls back into her face. When she looks up again, her cheeks are streaked with tears. I touch her hand and push to my feet. "Will you come upstairs with me? There's something I want to show you."

She follows me to the studio, but seems reluctant to enter when I open the door. I wave her in and cross to my desk to turn on the lamp. I withdraw the rosewood box from the drawer and hand it to her. "These things belong to you. They were your father's. It isn't much, but Poppy wanted you to have them."

She nods but doesn't open the box. I suspect she's already seen what's inside. I leave her briefly, negotiating the maze of detritus I've accumulated over the years, and eventually return with a canvas shrouded in a heavy white sheet. She eyes me with a mix of wariness and curiosity, then her breath catches as I lift away the cloth, revealing the portrait beneath.

"This is Poppy," I say softly. "This is your mother."

My heart squeezes at the sight of her face on the canvas, arrestingly pale amid a sea of copper waves, and for an instant I imagine I can smell her perfume, earthy and green over the studio's mingled scents of paint and linseed oil. Eyes of warm amber look out from beneath a fringe of dark lashes, their depths lit with bright flecks of gold. Her lips are slightly parted. Not a smile, not quite, but there's the hint of a secret there, of something kept carefully close. But the focal point of the piece is the butterfly resting in her open palm, its velvety black-and-blue wings half-spread.

Mallory reaches out, nearly touching the canvas, but stops herself. "She's beautiful." Her voice is barely a whisper, her tone almost reverent. "How old was she here?"

"No age, really. I painted it from memory after we moved here. She'd been gone nearly fifteen years by then. It took years to finish and I actually abandoned it several times. I was convinced no brush could ever do her justice—certainly not mine—but once I'd begun it, I had to finish. I couldn't bear to think of her abandoned and incomplete. And I wanted you to see her one day."

"The butterfly," Mallory says, finally allowing herself to touch the canvas. "It's like the ones hanging above your nightstand." She turns to me, brow furrowed thoughtfully. "Is it . . . is there some connection?"

I can't help but smile. "They used to land on her all the time. On her hand or shoulder, as if they were stopping by to say hello. They'd stay a few minutes, then flutter away. I was amazed the first time I saw it happen. She never thought much about it, but for me it was like magic."

"Poppy . . ." she says softly. "The Butterfly Girl." She pulls her eyes from the canvas. "This is why you spent so much time up here. And why I was never allowed. Because *she* was here."

"I was afraid you'd find it and ask questions I wasn't ready to answer. But it's yours now. I'll frame it if you like."

"No, you should keep it. But no more hiding her under a sheet. Hang her where you'll see her every day—and where she can see you."

For a moment I'm too choked up to speak. I look at the painting, imagine it hanging in my room where the sun will touch it every morning, but I've kept her to myself for too long. It's time to make things right. "She's your mother," I say softly.

I'm surprised when Mallory takes hold of my hand. "Yes, she is. But so are you. Because that's what Poppy wanted—for me to have *you*. And now I want you to have *her*."

Hearing those words from her feels like the sun coming out from behind the clouds, an assurance that the world will keep on turning. I reach up and touch her cheek, marveling at how like her mother she is. Not only in her looks, but in her heart, in her goodness and her ability to forgive. "She would be so proud of you, Mallory. Of the woman you've become and the work you do."

"I think she'd be proud of you too." Her eyes drift back to the portrait and she appears to remember something. "Can I ask you a question? All the things you've been given over the years, the silver, the crystal." She pauses, rolling her eyes for effect. "The not-at-*all*-creepy doll collection in the room down the hall. They're because of her too, somehow, aren't they?"

"They're because of you," I say warmly. "You were the most important thing in Poppy's life, so tiny and impossibly fragile. She needed to know you'd be cherished the way *she* would have cherished you. So she gave you to me. I don't know how it started with the other things. It was Janice Randall's crystal bells, I think. They'd been passed down for generations and all of a sudden there was no one to leave them to. So I promised I'd look after them. After that, it just kept happening and I couldn't say no. Because they were all like Poppy—they had no one." She pulls me into her arms then, murmuring against my cheek. "I love you. Not because you're my mother and I have to, but because you're an amazing woman with a wonderful heart. I'm sorry I didn't realize it until now—sorry about a lot of things."

"Don't be sorry," I tell her, seeing as I step back that my tears have left a damp place on her shoulder. "I'm just glad it's out now. And so grateful to you for staying. There's still so much to tell. Good things."

There's an almost imperceptible change in her posture as her gaze shifts from mine. "I had a call from Jevet this afternoon. The board green-lighted my IVP program, and she wants me to head it up. I have to go back to Boston next week."

"Oh." The news briefly knocks the wind out of me. I was hoping to use our remaining weeks to shore up this tender new truce, but I summon a smile. There will be other visits, I tell myself, other summers. For now, I must be content with that. "That's wonderful news. And it solves the job question nicely. But why the long face? Aren't you happy?"

"I think I need to sleep. It's been a long day."

I nod, swallowing the questions that crowd into my head. There's something else going on. I can see it. But she's right. It *has* been a long day. Perhaps we both need a little space to process. I press a kiss to my fingertips, then touch them to her cheek, the way I used to when she was little. "We'll talk in the morning. Go down now, and get some rest."

"Aren't you coming?"

My eyes flick to Poppy's portrait. "I think I'll stay up here for a while."

Mallory nods with the tiniest of smiles. "All right, then. See you in the morning."

She takes the rosewood box from the desk, clutching it to her chest as she heads for the door. I feel a sharp pang of relief as I watch her go, almost a lightness. I'm no longer custodian of William Ward's things. They belong to his daughter now. I turn to meet Poppy's amber eyes on the canvas and, for the first time, feel no guilt. There's only love between us now, memories clear and sweet, undimmed by broken promises.

FIFTY

MALLORY

Two hours after leaving Helen in her studio, Mallory was still awake, staring up into the milky darkness of her room. So much had been resolved. With Jevet, with her mother, to an extent even with Estelle. She should have been pleased, eager to embark on a brand-new future. Instead, she was restless. Because there was still one bit of business she hadn't dealt with.

Kicking off the covers, she padded to the window. Beyond the shore the sky was a velvety blue-black, pocked with stars and a fat three-quarter moon. She lifted the sash and the night air rushed in, crisp and clean, chilly for early August. The night had that inevitable end-of-summer feel, the breeze ripe with the first wisps of fall.

Her gaze wandered past the hydrangea hedge. The windows in the guesthouse were dark. He was back in the house now, back in his old room presumably, in order to be close to Estelle. Was he asleep, she wondered? Or was he awake too, brooding about the things she'd said this afternoon—and the things she hadn't. He deserved better.

Before Mallory could change her mind, she reached for the lamp, flicking the switch once, twice, three times. She held her breath, waiting as the seconds ticked by, then let it out again when she realized he wouldn't answer. Did she really think he was sitting over there staring at her window on the off chance that she was up? But just as she was about to turn away, she saw his light flick on, once, twice, three times.

Aiden was waiting when she reached the beach, his windbreaker zipped to his chin, hands shoved deep into his pockets. He nodded toward the jetty and she fell into step beside him, turning wordlessly into the chilly breeze. When they reached the rocks, he offered his hand. She took it long enough to climb up, then followed him out to the end. Eventually, they settled side by side, knees hugged close to their chests.

"Cold," Aiden said, finally breaking the silence.

Mallory nodded, pushing the hair off her face. "It is. And it's only August."

"I'm not ready for summer to be over."

His voice was thick and flat, leeched of emotion. Mallory turned, studying him openly in the moonlight. His face already showed signs of strain, foreshadowing the grief and loss to come, and she knew it wasn't just the end of the season he was dreading.

"It's not over," Mallory said softly. "There's time yet." She wasn't sure what she meant. Time with Estelle, she supposed. Time to make things right between them. Time to say goodbye.

Aiden said nothing for several moments. The wind was stiff off the water, whipping his hair into dark little peaks at the crown. He attempted to rake it down but soon gave up. "I moved some of my stuff back into the house tonight. It was time."

"Your mother told me you were thinking about it."

He cocked his head to look at her, a crease between his brows. "What was that about, by the way? How'd you end up at my mother's house in the middle of the day?"

Mallory briefly considered telling him the truth, that his mother had faked a fall to lure her to the house, but nothing would be served by ratting Estelle out. "I needed to tell my mother something," she fibbed. "But she'd gone to the market. I was just leaving when you came home."

"My mother told me what you two talked about, what she asked you to do. I'm sorry she put you on the spot like that. Apparently, she's still determined to have her way."

"No, it wasn't about her this time. She's afraid, Aiden. She feels responsible for you not having the life you wanted, for pushing you to leave, for pulling us apart. She wants to fix things—to put them back the way they were."

"She can't, though, can she? No one can. I spent my life working for something I never wanted and now that it's gone, I can't see anything else." He laughed, the sound dark and abrupt. "I wanted to be John Lennon when I grew up, to write my own stuff, maybe even record. Instead, I was dragged from recital to recital in a tiny tuxedo, regurgitating Tchaikovsky and Mozart. All I wanted to do was make music—*my* music."

"Then do it, Aiden. Do it now. Be John Lennon."

He held up his damaged hand, his eyes hard as they met with hers. It looked pale and bleached in the moonlight, the scars on the backs of his fingers standing out angrily. "Bit late for that now, don't you think?"

"No," Mallory said flatly. "And neither should you. Because you don't *know*, Aiden. Once things settle, you'll get focused again and you'll get it back. I know you."

"No," he countered coolly. "You *knew* me." He shoved his damaged hand back into the pocket of his windbreaker and sat staring out over the water. "I'm not the guy I was back then," he said when the silence began to stretch. "I haven't been for a long time. I'm just . . . done."

Mallory studied him, unsettled by the bleakness of his tone. "I've never seen this side of you. The side that won't fight for what you want."

"It's the only side I have left."

"You're not allowed to quit until you try, Aiden."

He shrugged. "Sorry. You didn't come out here to listen to me feeling sorry for myself." He paused, cocking an eye at her. "Why *did* you come out?"

"I felt like you deserved an explanation about today. I don't know how long you were standing there or how much you heard, but I know you heard Estelle ask . . . what she asked."

"If you were still in love with me."

"Yes," she said, looking away. "She caught me completely off guard, and then I saw you in the doorway and I just . . . froze. I know what you wanted me to say, but it would have been a mistake—for *both* of us. We can't look back just because it feels familiar."

"Is there someone else? Back in Boston, I mean? Someone you left back there? I never thought to ask." He paused for a beat. "No, that's not true. I chose not to ask. But is that it?"

"No, there's no one in Boston. But my job is there, which means my future is there."

Neither spoke for a time. Mallory watched the steady push of the waves creeping ever higher along the jetty. The tide was coming in. They'd need to climb down soon, but she wasn't ready to go back. It was probably the last time they'd sit together like this and she didn't want it to be over yet.

"Stay," he whispered hoarsely. "Not forever. And not the way we used to be. I know that isn't what you want. But for a while. Until we both figure things out."

"Aiden . . ."

"I know I said my mother had no right to ask, but this is *me* asking. I don't think I can get through this without you. I don't know what comes next. I'm not sure I even want to."

His face was just inches from hers, close enough to feel the warmth of his breath against her cheek. His nearness, coupled with the intensity of his gaze, was like a drug. Perhaps the most dangerous drug of all. Because she knew what his mouth felt like on hers, how he tasted and how they fit. But she also knew where it would lead—and how it would end.

In the ten years that they'd been apart, he hadn't picked up the phone once. Not even after the accident. Now, suddenly, he needed her. Or thought he did. She didn't blame him. He was a drowning man, desperate for something, anything, to keep him afloat. But the first thing they taught you in water rescue class was the danger of being dragged under during a rescue.

She'd gone under once, and had nearly hit bottom. She couldn't risk it again.

"I'm leaving next week," she told him softly.

He stared at her, clearly startled. "I thought you were here through the end of the month."

"I was, but before I left, I pitched an idea for a jobs program matching local kids with different businesses, and I just found out it's moving forward. It's mine to head if I want it."

"And you do."

"I've been working on the project for almost a year. It's my baby. So, yes, I do want it. But I'll always be here for you. Even when I'm back in Boston. I'll only ever be a phone call away."

"Right." He dropped his head to his chest, shaking it slowly. "Sorry. I shouldn't have put you on the spot like that. It's not like you haven't said all this before. I just couldn't let you go without . . . you know. Anyway . . ." He pushed to his feet then, and held out a hand. "Time to go in."

Mallory blinked up at him. "We don't have to. We can stay and talk."

"The tide's coming in and your lips are turning blue."

They made their way off the jetty and back up the beach, careful and quiet. Aiden halted when they reached the gate. "I guess this is where I leave you."

There was a finality to the words, a sense of resignation that plucked at Mallory's already raw conscience. "We'll see each other before I go."

Aiden nodded, then looked down at his bare feet. "Yeah. Sure. But if we don't . . . congratulations."

"Aiden—"

"It's okay. Really. I'm okay."

It felt wrong to walk away and leave him standing in the dark. But they'd said everything there was to say—except the actual word *good-bye*, which was what this was. She'd done what she'd come to do. Their unfinished business was finally finished, the door to their yesterdays firmly closed. Adding anything now would only risk that.

Instead, she pressed a kiss to his cheek, savoring the faint rasp of stubble against her lower lip, the trace of salt clinging to his skin. Something to take back with her to Boston.

She pulled away, briefly laying a hand on his arm before stepping through the gate and heading up the path. He was still there when she reached the deck, his face bathed white by the moonlight. She lifted a hand as she ducked into the house, but lingered in the doorway, throat aching as she watched him turn and move back down the beach.

Things would be hard for a while, but in time he'd put his life back together. They both would. Until then, all either of them could do was put one foot in front of the other and keep moving forward.

FIFTY-ONE

MALLORY

August 8, 1999

Mallory dropped a spoonful of sugar into her second cup of coffee, mindlessly stirring as she stared out the kitchen window. With the breakfast dishes dried and put away, Sunday morning stretched before her with zero plans.

Helen would be gone most of the day, off to Newport with Estelle, who'd taken to reminiscing about all the places she and Aiden's father had gone while dating, in particular an old dairy bar in Middletown reported to make the best banana split in three states.

It was something Helen encouraged her charges to do, to reconnect with their happy memories and relive them if possible. These were the things Mallory had never bothered to know about her mother's work, the small kindnesses woven into her daily care, simple gestures meant to honor the lives they had lived. And collectively, those kindnesses represented Helen's legacy. Her work. Her calling.

And now, at long last, it would seem she had found her own calling. She'd still be with New Day but in a new capacity, doing the kind of work she'd always envisioned. And tomorrow she'd have to break the news to Deb that she would be leaving earlier than expected.

It would mean missing the last week of summer session, but it couldn't be helped and Deb was already interviewing candidates to fill her position. Hopefully, one of them would be available to start right away. Still, she dreaded the conversation, and not just because she hated letting Deb down. She'd come to enjoy her time at the center and would miss it when she was back in Boston.

I'm guessing your heart is still in Little Harbor.

Jevet's words seemed to follow her as she wandered out onto the deck. Scanning the beach, scraped clean now by the outgoing tide, it was hard to believe she'd ever hated it here. She had, though. She'd been painfully out of her element in the beginning, a proverbial fish out of water among Little Harbor's yacht and tennis club kids. But gradually, the brine-soaked breezes and endlessly rolling waves had crept beneath her skin, winding themselves inextricably through the strands of her DNA. And they would always be there now.

Closing her eyes, she leaned against the railing, savoring the steady thrum of the sea, the way its pulse seemed to beat in time with her own. Soon it would be replaced with honking horns and the grind of fume-belching buses, but for now she would soak it in, storing it up for times when life got too fast or too noisy.

But the sea wasn't all she would remember from this summer. She and Aiden had finally made their peace and said their goodbyes. They would part friends. And stay friends, she thought. Because they'd finally said what needed saying. Or at least he had. He had helped her understand his side of things. The panic when his future had suddenly been upended, the confusion he felt when she shut him out, the desperate need to move forward.

He'd given her the gift of closure, an end to the questions and the bitterness. But it occurred to her now, quite suddenly, that she hadn't done the same for him. She had assigned him all of the blame back then, accepting none herself, but she'd had a share in what happened too—perhaps the larger share. And she'd never acknowledged any of it. Instead, she'd punished him with her silence, leaving him baffled and adrift. All these years, she'd been blaming him for the way things ended, but she'd been equally culpable.

They'd been so young, and made such a mess of everything. Her mother had been right about that. And given the chance to do it over again now, she'd like to think she'd be wiser, but that wasn't how it worked. You couldn't go back and live those choices over. All you could do was live with what might have been.

As the thought formed, another snippet from yesterday's conversation with Jevet came floating back. *Life is giving you a great big do-over. Are you really going to throw it away?* Was she right? After all these years, could there still be a chance for them? Not as they'd been, but as they *could* be—now? Older, wiser, equipped for whatever life had in store, because they would face it together.

The thought set off a swirl of tiny wings in Mallory's belly. Maybe Jevet was right. Maybe it *was* time to decide what she wanted the rest of her life to look like. Not in Boston . . . but here in Little Harbor—with Aiden.

She stood with the thought a moment, feeling the weight of it, the truth of it. And then she heard it—notes scattered on the breeze. She cocked her head, trying to locate the sound, but heard only the white noise of wind and waves. Her mind—her *heart*—was playing tricks on her.

But as she stepped away from the railing, she heard it again, a series of broken notes, like raindrops carried on the wind. She pivoted slowly, breath held, but she already knew the source of those uneven notes, because she'd lived this moment before, fifteen summers ago—the day she met Aiden.

Her pulse skittered dizzily as she clamored down the steps and plunged through the hedge, following the music as she had that first day, across the lawn and back up onto the terrace, where the French doors had been thrown open.

She stood frozen, eyes closed as the music spilled out, the opening phrase of Beethoven's "Moonlight Sonata," clumsily repeating, once, twice, then stopping abruptly halfway through a third. There was a brief beat of emptiness, and then something new began, a series of chords that felt vaguely familiar, even to her untrained ear. It took a moment to recognize it as the song Aiden had written for Sloane and Kenny's wedding.

Breath held, she stepped to the open doors. The sudden wave of déjà vu when she glimpsed him seated before the black Bechstein grand made her throat go tight. His back ramrod straight, head bent over the keys. She'd heard him play hundreds of times, thousands. Hour upon hour of exhaustive repetition as he strove to master an intricate counter-melody or a tricky series of jumps. Forever chasing perfection. But this wasn't perfection. It was messy and uncertain, wholly inelegant. And it was the most glorious thing she'd ever heard.

She wasn't sure how long she hovered there, watching as he stopped and started, stopped and started, but eventually she noted a fresh tension in his shoulders, a slight change in the angle of his head. He'd sensed her presence, she realized. He knew she was here.

Still, he went on playing, his features set with determination, even when she crossed the room and slid onto the bench beside him. He didn't look up or acknowledge her in any visible way, but there was an almost imperceptible squaring of his shoulders as he pushed through each note, the scars across the knuckles of his left hand stretching and contracting.

She was used to seeing him in command, imposing and assured at the bench, the keys a seeming extension of his body, but there was nothing assured about his playing now. It was tentative and clumsy, every movement executed with agonizing, almost ruthless intensity as he pushed through the song's final phrase.

He sat silently for a time when the song ended, hands resting on his thighs, breathing slow and heavy, his brow lightly sheened with perspiration. Finally, he turned to look at her, his expression startlingly vulnerable. "Hello."

The moment was so rife with memory that for an instant Mallory struggled to find words. "I was on the deck," she said simply. "I thought I was hearing things at first. But I knew it had to be you. I recognized the second song, the one you wrote for Kenny and Sloane's wedding."

Aiden closed his eyes, breathing long and slow as the exertion of playing caught up to him. "I didn't write it for Kenny and Sloane. I wrote it for us. For *our* wedding."

"Aiden . . ."

"No. Let me get it out first. When Kenny asked me to write a song for the wedding, I didn't know how to say no. We've been friends forever. But every time I sat down to write the thing, I came up empty. There was nothing there—nothing left. So I gave him *our* song. I'm sorry. I never would have done it if I knew you'd be there to hear it." He looked away, throat bobbing convulsively. "Anyway, I wanted you to know before you left. In case I didn't see you again."

There were so many emotions to process all at once that Mallory struggled to find a response. His face had gone blurry, smeared behind a sudden rush of tears. "Please don't say you're sorry, Aiden. It's a beautiful song and I'm glad you shared it with them. But why on earth didn't you tell me you've been playing?"

"Because I haven't. This was the first time. And I'm not sure you should call it playing."

He'd been wincing as he spoke, reflexively curling and uncurling the fingers of his left hand. Mallory laid a hand on his arm. "Does it hurt?"

He nodded, dropping his hand back to his lap. "Like hell, actually. I've lost so much strength in three and four, and my wrists are on fire. Even my shoulders hurt. I had no idea you could lose it so quickly."

"You haven't lost it, Aiden. You were just *playing*. But why now? What changed?"

"It was what you said last night—that I'm not allowed to quit until I try. It made me take a long, hard look in the mirror, and when I did I saw a quitter looking back."

"I shouldn't have said that. I was—"

"No. Don't take it back. You were right. I did quit."

"Does that mean . . ." She paused, not sure how far to press him. "Are you thinking about resuming your therapy?"

He responded with a half shrug. "I don't know what it means yet. But I can't go on like this, hating the world, blaming everyone else for how things turned out. I've made a hash of so many things, Mallory. But it all started with me getting on that plane. I should never have left for London the way I did. I should have waited and talked to you about what you wanted. It never occurred to me that you wouldn't be here when I got back." He looked away, shaking his head. "There will never be enough ways to say I'm sorry, but I am. So very sorry." He dropped his chin, cleared his throat. "That was the other thing I wanted you to know before you left. That I was the one. It was me. My fault."

"It wasn't *just* you, Aiden. It was me too. For years—" She broke off, placing a hand on his chest when she saw he was about to interrupt. "No, it's my turn. For years I've made you the bad guy in all of this, but I was wrong. When I told you I was pregnant, you didn't bat an eye. You just withdrew from the Leeds so we could get married. Problem solved—for *me*. I was marrying the boy next door with a ready-made family waiting in the wings. But I never stopped to consider what you were giving up. Not really. I just let you withdraw. And then after, when we knew there wasn't going to be a baby, it made sense to postpone the wedding so you could compete as planned. It was your year, Aiden. And instead of supporting you, I shut you out. Last night, I said you weren't allowed to quit without trying. But that's exactly what I did. I quit on *us*. If I hadn't, everything might have been different."

Aiden closed his hand over hers, pressing until she could feel the hard, heavy beat of his heart against her palm. "That day in the bookstore, when I saw you standing there, for a split second it felt like everything was all right again. I haven't been happy in a very long time, and all of a sudden, there you were. It felt like a second chance, like there might be a way . . ."

He dropped his hand abruptly. "Sorry. I promised myself I wouldn't do that. But I'm happy we got the chance to clear the air. And I'm glad about the new job. I hate that you're leaving, but I want you to be happy, Mallory. If that means Boston, then that's what I want too."

His words were so sincere they brought a lump to her throat. But Boston *wasn't* what she wanted. She knew that now, with sudden and irrevocable clarity. Jevet was right. Everything she wanted *was* right here. All she had to do was get out of her own way.

"Well, then," she said with the tiniest of smiles. "I'm afraid I'm about to disappoint you because I'm not going back to Boston."

Aiden's face went blank. "What?"

"I haven't gotten up the nerve yet, but as soon as I do, I plan to ask your mother for a job."

"But I thought . . . What about Boston and the new program? You said it was your baby."

"It is. I just want to do it here."

Aiden's expression ran the gamut from surprise to confusion. "So you're staying? Permanently?"

"Yes. And I'm going to need a job—and a sizable chunk of money to get the new program off the ground. I can have it up and running by next summer—I've been brainstorming for weeks on how to do it—but I'm going to need Estelle's approval. Which means I'll need you to lobby on my behalf."

He said nothing for a moment, brow furrowed as he attempted to digest all of this. "And . . . us?" he asked finally. "Where does that leave us?"

"I don't know," Mallory said, dropping her gaze for a moment. "But I want to find out." She reached for his hand then and turned it palm up, tracing a finger over the pattern of shiny pink scars. Once upon a time, she had known every line and crease of his hand, like roads on a map. They looked different now, rerouted by life and time, but there would be time to learn them again. She folded his fingers closed, but kept hold of his hand. "I've missed you, Aiden. I don't think I realized how much until I came back. But I'd be lying if I said I'm not just a little bit scared. Ten years is a long time."

Aiden stared down at her hand folded over his, then shifted on the bench, squaring his shoulders with hers. "Yesterday, you told my mother I only *thought* I was in love with you, and that when I realized I wasn't, I wouldn't need you anymore. And then, when she asked point-blank if you were still in love with me, you didn't answer. If you're not I guess I'll have to live with it. But if you are still in love with me—even a little bit—you need to know that I'll *always* need you, Mallory. And that I will never *not* be in love with you. Not tomorrow. Not ten years from now. Not ever. And I'll do whatever I have to do to prove it, and *keep* proving it to you until you know it for sure."

Mallory closed her eyes, processing Aiden's declaration. Now, in this moment, he meant every word—every promise. But could it really be that simple, when they'd hurt each other so deeply? He had made promises before—they both had—and at the first real test, those promises had fallen apart. Was she really prepared to risk everything on a love she'd already lost once? And then it occurred to her that that was precisely what Helen and Poppy had done.

They'd each broken their share of promises over the years, hurt each other in seemingly unforgivable ways, but in the end, none of it mattered. They'd chosen to forgive, to make peace with their yesterdays in order to savor a few precious tomorrows. Because when life gave you a second chance at that kind of love—the kind that filled all the empty places in your soul—you took it.

"Let's not make it about that," Mallory said softly. "About proving anything. We both made mistakes, but we aren't those people now. We've both been shaped by the things we've lived through, and we can never go back. But maybe we can start over from where we are now—as *who* we are now."

"No more apologies," Aiden murmured. "No looking back."

"No looking back," Mallory agreed, then pulled away, plying him with a coy smile. "Does that mean you'll put in a good word for me about the program?"

"I might," Aiden replied huskily. "*If* . . . you ask me nicely."

"Why, sir, are you suggesting a bribe?"

"I am, indeed."

This time when he kissed her, it felt like coming home. Because in spite of everything, all that had happened and all the years apart, he had *always* been her home—the one who knew her best.

FIFTY-TWO

ESTELLE

October 18, 1999

Estelle looked at the clock through one narrowed eye. If she was reading the thing right, Helen and Mallory should be along any minute. She'd asked Aiden to phone this morning and invite them over for a little talk.

Poor Aiden. Having Mallory to lean on had been a help, but watching helplessly as his mother was reduced to childlike dependency had clearly been hard on him. She had two full-time caregivers now, though Helen still insisted on spending several hours with her each day. She hadn't quite reached *last days*—as Helen called them—but they weren't far off now. The periods of brain fog were becoming longer and more frequent, and at times she struggled with speech as well. It was simply a matter of time at this point. But there were things she wanted to say while she could still say them, and she'd decided to say them today.

She'd had to abandon her bedroom and move into one of the first-floor rooms. It was equipped with a hospital bed but Aiden had moved most of her things down, to make it feel less like a sickroom. She was propped up against her pillows now, wearing her favorite pink robe. She didn't bother with makeup anymore—there wasn't much point—but it seemed impolite to frighten one's guests, so she'd at least taken some pains with her hair, pinning it into a messy chignon.

Two o'clock was the agreed-upon time, and it was nearly that when she heard hushed voices outside her door. Moments later, Aiden stuck his head in, looking grim. "They're here."

Estelle pasted on a smile and gave her hair one last pat.

A short time later, Aiden reappeared with Mallory in tow. Helen followed, looking dour and a little pale. Poor woman. She wasn't used to grieving relatives and deathbed goodbyes. Her charges were typically alone in the world, without friends or family to attend their final hours. No tears or angst. No broken hearts. Just a quiet, solitary passing. But this would be different. This time there would be mourners—and Helen would be one of them. For that, she was sorry. But it couldn't be helped. They were friends now, and friends mourned one another.

"Such somber faces," she scolded as they all filed in. "Has someone died?"

Aiden scowled but let the remark pass. He'd made it clear that he didn't appreciate her gallows humor, but it helped sometimes to laugh at it all. Perpetual sorrow was so exhausting.

"All right," Estelle said with a sulky sigh. "It appears a future in stand-up comedy is out. Please, everyone, sit down." She gestured toward the chairs she'd had brought in and arranged near the bed, waiting until everyone was settled, before flashing a wide smile. "There now. Isn't this cozy?"

No one seemed to know what to say, and for an awkward moment, silence filled the room. Aiden stared at the floor. Mallory's eyes were fixed on her hands, tightly entwined with Aiden's. Helen simply looked at Estelle, waiting for whatever was coming.

"I have some things to say," Estelle announced finally. "And since I don't know how long I'll be able to say them, I've decided to go ahead and get them out now."

Her speech was slow and slushy today, the combined effect of her tumor and the opiates she'd grudgingly begun to take. She'd taken only a half this morning, though, so she'd be sharp. She reached for Aiden's hand, folding her fingers over his. "My darling boy. Can I still call you that? My *boy*? How I wish . . ." She paused, swallowing thickly. "I wish your father could see the man you've become. He'd be so proud. As for myself . . . you're all a mother could ever want in a son. You have so many gifts, and music is just one of them. I should have seen that sooner. I should have trusted you more and steered you less. I cost you so much."

"Mother, please—"

"No. Let me say it once more and then I promise I won't say it again. I was wrong about so many things. If I could take them back, do them over again, I would. I can't, though. All I can do is ask for your forgiveness and pray you know how much I love you. I don't know what life holds for you. That's for you to decide. All I want for you now is your happiness, and you've found that."

Her gaze slid to Mallory next, sitting beside Aiden with red-rimmed eyes, her lower lip caught between her teeth in an effort to stem her tears. "Please don't cry, my dear. There's no need. But there's something I need from you. I asked you once and you didn't answer, so I'm going to ask again—do you love my son?"

Mallory dropped her gaze, blinking hard. A fat pair of tears squeezed from between her lids. She wiped them away, nodding. "Yes. I do."

"Well, then," Estelle replied firmly. "That's settled." She looked at her left hand, at the ring George Cavanaugh had placed there thirty-seven years ago. It had fit snugly then but slid effortlessly from her finger now. She handed it to Aiden. "I'd like her to have the ring your father gave me—if that's all right with you, Mallory."

Mallory shot an uncomfortable look at Aiden. "But we're not . . . We haven't—"

"Not yet," Estelle said, waving the now bare hand to cut her off. "But you will. And soon, I hope. Please don't think you have to hide your happiness on my account, or wait to make your plans. I've kept the two of you apart long enough. It's time to get on with it."

Aiden stared at the ring, his throat bobbing convulsively. "I don't know what to say."

Estelle grinned, attempting a sly wink. "Oh, I think you do—only don't say it now. Wait until you have her alone and do it properly."

It was Helen's turn next and for a moment Estelle found herself unable to speak. Words were getting harder and harder to chase these days, especially when she was emotional or tired. And she was both at the moment. But there were things to say.

"And to you, my dear friend," she managed, laying a hand on Helen's knee. "How can I convey what you've come to mean to me in these few short months? When I think of all the time we missed, I'm sadder than I can say. But for the time we did have, I'm so very grateful. For the undeserved gift of your friendship, for all your care and your wisdom. I've never believed in the notion of sainthood, but I think I do now."

She paused, closing her eyes. Getting tired now. So very tired. But she was determined to get through the last part—the hardest part. She opened her eyes again, blinking away a hot film of tears. "I'm not afraid now. I was. I was afraid of leaving such a mess behind, so many broken hearts and . . . interrupted lives. But I'm at peace now, and happy if all of this has served some purpose. And it has. I see that it has. So I'm ready for whatever comes next. My lawyers have seen to the financial business—the who gets what and how—but the things I hold most precious can't be bestowed with paper and ink. I can only give those with my heart, which is why I've asked you here."

She licked her lips, her mouth gone cottony. Helen was there instantly, helping her manage the water glass from the nightstand. When she finished, she relinquished the glass, sloshing a bit onto the sheets. She'd become frightfully clumsy in the last few weeks, like a marionette whose strings weren't properly attached.

"Aiden. I've entrusted you with my center to oversee in whatever way you see fit. Other than bringing you into the world, it's the only truly good thing I've ever done and there's no one I trust more than you to ensure that that good continues."

Aiden nodded, mopping his eyes with his sleeve. "I will. I promise."

"Helen. I am entrusting you with my grandchildren. I don't know when they'll come or how many there will be, but they will come. Now and then, talk to them about their Mimi Estelle. Tell them how much I love them, though we'll never meet. And most importantly, tell them how grateful I was to have had their Nana Helen as my friend."

Helen made a small hiccup of sound as she reached for a tissue and blotted her eyes. Her mouth worked soundlessly for a moment, but eventually she abandoned her effort to reply and quietly blew her nose.

"Sweet Helen," Estelle said, dabbing at her own eyes. "I'm touched that you think me worthy of your tears, but do stop blubbering. You're bringing down the room."

Helen managed a watery smile. Estelle returned it. "Yes. That's better."

She pulled in a breath. Almost finished now. Just this last bit to go—the hardest bit—and then she could rest.

She reached for Mallory's hand, clutching the girl's fingers with a ferocity that surprised even her. "And you, darling girl, I saved for last because it is to you that I entrust the most precious thing I have in this world—my son. He was a rare boy growing up and he's grown into a rare man. It's only right that he should find a rare woman with whom to spend his life, and he has. We've had our battles, you and I, all of them my fault, but we're past that now, I hope. Aiden has a lot of work ahead of him, decisions to make and responsibilities to shoulder, but my heart is easy knowing he'll have you to love him through it."

"Yes, he will," Mallory said softly, squeezing Estelle's hand with equal ferocity. "Always."

◆　◆　◆

Afternoon was sliding toward evening, long shadows stretching across the floor as the light through the windows shifted direction. Estelle gathered the rumpled tissues littering the bed and stuffed them into the pockets of her robe, to be quietly flushed the next time she was taken to the bathroom. She'd sent everyone away after saying her piece, asking to be left alone. She'd needed time to cry her own tears and preferred not to have company when she did. But those tears hadn't been the result of regret or self-pity; they'd been tears of relief—of peace.

Once she might have railed against her fate, declaring it unfair that her life should be snuffed out so early, but not now. Not when her heart was finally full. Everyone was given their portion in life and she'd had hers. Some of it—perhaps most of it—she had selfishly squandered. But in these last few months and weeks, she'd finally come to understand why each soul was sent out into the world. It was to love—and to leave the mark of that love on the world when the time came to leave it. This, at long last, she had done.

FIFTY-THREE

HELEN

March 28, 2000

Dearest,

How strange it seems to be writing this sitting out on the deck in plain sight rather than in secret up in my tower, but the weather has turned mild and it's simply impossible to remain indoors when the breeze is so warm and the sun is shining off the water.

I've purchased a new journal, one with a bright-yellow cover. It feels like a time for new beginnings. Life has been so full of late. So many changes. Estelle transitioned just after Christmas. She went peacefully, with all of us nearby, and was buried beside her husband. There was a memorial at the center the following week to celebrate her life. She would have been pleased. The whole town turned out. Aiden gave a beautiful tribute, focusing on her love for the center and her vision for it going forward, and then he handed the mic over to me.

There was quite a murmur as I stood up. Given our embattled history, I hardly seemed a likely candidate to memorialize the woman. Few knew the real Estelle: the betrayed wife; the mother painfully aware of her shortcomings; the flawed woman desperate to atone. Those secrets are ours alone. Instead, I spoke about the woman I came to know in the last days and weeks of her life. Of a friend who, at the end, taught me more about dying with grace than anyone I've ever known—save you, of course, my darling.

I am grateful to her for that. And to all my charges, but I've decided that Estelle will be the last. With her transition I feel a sense of completion, of closure. If I ever had anything to atone for, I believe I've done it. If not, I'll answer for it when the time comes. For now, I've accepted a position teaching art classes at the community center, and am helping Mallory finalize plans for the new vocational program.

The center has been renamed for both George and Estelle, and a new director has been named—Mallory Ward, who I'm pleased to announce will become Mallory Ward Cavanaugh in July. More than a decade later than planned, but love has a way of making things right.

Aiden will remain on the board in his mother's place but is too busy with his musical endeavors to play a role in the day-to-day operations. He's playing a little and singing at one of the jazz clubs downtown. And apparently, there's a new wedding song in the works, though he refuses to let anyone hear it. We shall have to wait until the big day.

So much has come right, dearest. At long last, our girl is happy. But she'll be gone soon. She'll only be next door, but I'm missing her already. At least I have your portrait now, hanging above my bureau, but sometimes I think it makes the missing harder, a reminder that you're really gone, that all this time I've only been imagining the faint whiffs of your perfume, the feathery touch of your hand on my cheek as I come awake in the morning. It's silly, I suppose, to think you might be out there waiting for me, but the nights are so long and quiet.

The breeze has picked up, the salty air rustling my pages. I lay my hand flat to hold them down, then go still as a pair of black-and-blue wings flits into view. The thing hovers a moment, then alights on the back of my hand, wings beating slowly, softly, a bright and fragile miracle. My breath catches at the sight of it. Could it be . . . And then I smile. Yes. Of course it is.

Hello, dearest.

EPILOGUE

POPPY

Yes, it's me. It's always been me.

Every whiff of patchouli, every unseen caress. I've never been far away. Nor have you ever been alone. I've heard every word, felt every sob, been beside you through every heart-wrenching dream. But it's different for me. There is no suffering here, no longing, no loneliness. Only pure love and a sense of inevitability. The waiting is not hard on this side, because our reunion is merely a matter of time—and time here is nothing. The blink of an eye, the beat of a heart, the release of a breath, and it's done.

Until then, sweet Helen, be happy. Cook. Paint. Laugh. Maybe even dance a little. There's a wedding coming soon, and perhaps little ones to follow. You've given so much of your life to others. But that work is finished now. It's time to have a life of your own, to spread your wings in new directions and see where the wind takes you. I promise to cheer you every step of the way and hold you in my heart until we're together again.

Give our girl a kiss from me, and look for me now and again.

I'll always be here.

ACKNOWLEDGMENTS

At the end of every book comes a time of reflection, a looking back at how the thing actually came into being, from that first nebulous concept to the final printed copy, including the personal journey I took along the way. This was especially true with *Every Precious and Fragile Thing*, which I happened to be writing when my husband, Tom, received a cancer diagnosis that rocked our world. Suddenly, several of the book's central themes seemed to be at play in my own life, making the work particularly difficult as I navigated my husband's surgeries, treatments, and prognosis. For someone who likes every single scene to be plotted out in advance, and operates on the premise that we should all always write our own endings, the uncertainty was excruciating, at times even debilitating.

Thank God for friends. Thank God for family. Thank God for a million tiny kindnesses that weren't tiny at all. Tom is now cancer-free and is on the long road to recovery. So many people helped pull me through this grueling year, and I hope with all my heart that I remember to thank them all here.

To my fellow authors at Blue Sky Book Chat—Thelma Adams, Paulette Kennedy, Joy Jordan Lake, Christine Nolfi, Marilyn Simon Rothstein, Patricia Sands, and Susan Walter—thank you for your kind words, your prayers, your comfort gifts, and your support. I'm privileged to call each of you friend.

To admin, friend, and confidant Kerry Schaffer, who always makes it okay for me to slow down and take a breath—and who knew what was going on in my world before *anyone* else—your check-ins and gentle wisdom have been such a salve to my weary soul. You made juggling all the balls so much easier.

To author Grace Sammons, who has walked a mile in my shoes, shared invaluable advice, and regularly checked in to make sure I was taking care of myself as well as Tom, you've been such a rock for me. More than you'll ever know.

To Linda Rosen, Terry Lynn Thomas, Mo Cordeiro, Linda McKenna, Sheila Choromanski, who each performed periodic wellness checks, offering wisdom, food, and most importantly, a much-appreciated shoulder, your kindness will never be forgotten.

To brothers and sisters David, Todd, Gina, Scott, Nanette, John, Donna, Betty, Joe, and Bob, knowing you were there for absolutely anything made everything easier.

To my amazing agent, Nalini Akolekar of Spencerhill Literary Associates, you've had my back from the beginning and have never failed me. Thank you for always being in my corner, and for always making it about me first, and *then* the books. Here's to even bigger adventures ahead! And to the rest of the Spencerhill Team, you guys simply rock.

To Danielle Marshall at Lake Union Publishing, thank you for giving me the time and the space I needed to take care of a loved one, and for reminding me in your own wonderful way that *"It's not world hunger—it's just books."* And to the entire Lake Union / APub team, who make this crazy author-life a little easier by being such wonderful cheerleaders and consummate professionals, many, many thanks.

To my irreplaceable developmental editor, Charlotte Herscher, who always pushes me to reach a little higher and dig a little deeper, you're the reason my writing continues to evolve, and I'm so very grateful. We may only work together once the book is turned in, but I write every word with you on my shoulder.

To my husband, Tom, who despite his own trials and tribulations, never stopped showering me with his love and support. You've always been my hero, but the pedestal is even higher now. As always, my darling . . . it's you and me against the world.

And finally, to you, my wonderful readers, who have sent avalanches of prayers and kindnesses in response to Tom's illness. I adore you all, and am so grateful for you. There are truly no better friends than book friends.

PS—If I forgot anyone, feel free to call me out, and I'll come cook you dinner. Seriously. Dinner.

DISCUSSION QUESTIONS

1. How well do you feel the title—*Every Precious and Fragile Thing*—ties in to the various aspects of the story?

2. Helen Ward is a death doula by trade and has spent her life caring for terminally ill patients who have no friends or family. Before reading the book, had you ever heard of a death doula? Do you now have an understanding of what they do, and do you feel the profession has value?

3. The concept of "death with dignity" features heavily in the book. End-of-life choice has long been a controversial topic, often for religious reasons, though not always. Before reading, did you have a strong belief one way or another on the subject? Do you think your feelings have changed at all after reading Poppy and Helen's story?

4. At one point, Helen observes that children rarely expect their mothers to have pasts, and that parents' lives are seen as blank slates until their children come along. Have you personally encountered this kind of thinking in your own life? If so, from which angle (i.e., as parent or child)?

5. The concept of vocation or "right work" appears as part of the story arc for several of the book's main characters. In what ways is right work key to the plot, and how does the search for right work move the story forward for each character?

6. How did your opinion of Estelle Cavanaugh change over the course of the novel, and why? By the end of the book, did you feel she had redeemed herself? Why or why not?

7. At different points in the book, Helen and Mallory make references to so-called silver linings occurring in the wake of tragedy. Can you think of examples in the book where good came from tragic circumstances? Have you ever experienced these kinds of silver linings yourself after a seeming tragedy?

8. Early on in the book, Mallory views the myriad keepsakes her mother has amassed over the years as creepy and perhaps even suspect, but by the end of the book, she has come to see them quite differently. What do you feel brought about her change of heart? Did it ring true for you?

9. In what ways do you feel Mallory was shaped by Helen's work over the years? How did her opinion of her mother's work change over the course of the book? What do you feel led to these new realizations?

10. What role, if any, do you feel prejudice and/or social pressures played in Helen's and Mallory's early character development? What lasting effects do we see for each as their stories unfold throughout the book?

11. How surprised were you when you learned the true identity of "Dearest"? Why do you think your reaction was what it was? Did it affect how you felt about their relationship, and if so, why?

12. In your opinion, is there one central theme that kept repeating through the book, that seemed to touch each of the characters in some way?

ABOUT THE AUTHOR

Photo © 2015 Lisa Aube

Barbara Davis is the Amazon Charts bestselling author of nine novels, including *The Echo of Old Books*, *The Keeper of Happy Endings*, and *The Last of the Moon Girls*. She spent more than a decade as an executive in the jewelry business before leaving the corporate world to pursue her lifelong passion for writing. A Jersey girl raised in the south, Barbara now lives in Poinciana, Florida, with her husband, Tom. She's currently working on her tenth book. Visit her at www.barbaradavis-author.com.